PORTIAD

YORNKEY

LESTOCH

WYSTAN

LINAOC

XESTA

VODAEARD

CROWNS OF BLOOD AND SALT

Published by Inimitable Books, LLC
www.inimitablebooksllc.com

CROWNS OF BLOOD AND SALT. Copyright © 2025 by Kay Adams.
Map copyright © 2023 by Grayson Wilde.
Athena font © 2019 medialoot on creativemarket.com.
All rights reserved. Printed in Canada.

Library of Congress Cataloguing-in-Publication Data is available.

No part of this book may be reproduced in any form or by any electronic or mechanical means, including information storage and retrieval systems, without written permission from the author, except for the use of brief quotations in a book review.

NO AI TRAINING: Without in any way limiting the author's exclusive rights under copyright, any use of this publication to "train" generative artificial intelligence (AI) technologies to generate text is expressly prohibited. The author reserves all rights to license uses of this work for generative AI training and development of machine learning language models.

First edition, 2025
Cover design by Keylin Rivers

ISBN 978-1-958607-50-3 (hardcover)
10 9 8 7 6 5 4 3 2 1

CROWNS OF BLOOD AND SALT

KAY ADAMS

INIMITABLE
BOOKS
UNFORGETTABLE STORIES

To those who feel so deeply, emotions are carved into their bones.

I sat with my anger long enough until she told me her real name was grief.

-C. S. Lewis

TRIGGER WARNING

In general, this book is bloodier than the first, and there are several descriptions of body horror related to bones that are crucial to the respective character. With that in mind, please be aware of the following content warnings while reading: graphic depictions of fantasy violence, attempted filicide (killing one's daughter), patricide (killing one's father), grief pertaining to death, mention of severed body parts, description of drowning victim, vomiting, depictions and implications of torture.

ONE

Kalei Maristela was dying.

She stood in the shadow of the shrouded portrait of my parents outside the throne room, small shoulders hunched under a wool shawl. Everything in the cliff-side castle was cold—from the freezing stone walls soaking up the salt-spray chill to the low-guttering torches casting meagre pools of wan light against the carpets—but none as cold as her frail frame. Shivers wracked her body despite the layers of clothes, visible even as I approached from the connecting corridor, though she tried to hide them by shifting beneath the thick shawl as my feet shuffled over the carpet towards her.

Her neck was craned back to take in the full height of the portrait, its edge skimming the high ceiling, but she dropped her haunted eyes to me as a corner of the shroud flitted in the stale air. A shudder tapped my spine at the movement, bringing to mind the image of ghosts and death.

Silently, she slipped her freezing fingers into mine, and we stood like that for a long moment. My skin burned with feverish intensity, while hers seemed to crack like ice beneath my touch. I rubbed a hand along her arm, desperate to ease some semblance of warmth, of life, back into her veins, but nothing I did seemed to work. She had lost more than just her power that day three months ago on the beach—she lost her family, her connection to the moon, and nearly lost her life as well—and every day I feared she wouldn't wake, succumbing to the monster that chased her.

The sirens had told me she would always be dying—that was the price for exchanging one life with another—but I had hoped she was strong enough to survive. She took up space wherever she went, commanded it as grandly as one commands armies, planting roots to sprout like weeds in her absence. Always leaving an earthy scent in her wake, as if she were made from clod and rain-soaked graves. Cold things. Dead things. A tickle on my tongue that reminded me of the change in seasons. A constant.

Now, she didn't know how to exist in this world. She was haunted and hollow, frail and feeble, about to crack with the slightest sea breeze. I didn't know how to fix it, and it terrified me to think she might not see the new year in a few weeks. It was supposed to be a celebration of new beginnings, of life, but Kalei was losing hers.

"How are you feeling today?" I asked, the latest note from her father burning in my pocket. A sizable stack of them was hidden in a drawer in my room, each of them with their own demands that I had spent the last three months fulfilling, unable to refuse out of the fear that he would hurt my brother. I swallowed hard, conflicting thoughts of Alekey swimming through my mind, and turned my full attention to the girl next to me.

Bone-dusted hair brushed her shoulders as she shrugged. The strands were dull and dry, not longer gleaming white like freshly fallen snow. She didn't seem to mind the embedded chips of bone in her hair and hands anymore. There had been a time when they moved and writhed, especially during our times in the catacombs beneath Xesta. A jewel of a city brought low by her frightening power. Magic that no longer thrummed in her veins, no longer made her the Princess of Death. She didn't hold sway over the dead anymore, and the beads of bone in her hair didn't rattle anymore.

"Cold," she answered, pulling her hand free to curl it beneath the folds of her shawl. That was her usual answer these days. Some days, she felt *sick* or *tired*, but most days, she was cold and unable to get warm. Still, I wrapped my arms around her neck, ignoring the way her shoulder dug into my throat, skin pulled taut over the sharp bones, and turned my head away from the pieces of bone in her hair that tickled my cheek. She stiffened for a moment, then leaned against my chest with a shuddering breath, eyelashes stark against her cheekbones as they fluttered shut.

In the silence that followed, my heart beating a steady rhythm against her back, I gazed up at the portrait of my parents. Kalei had offered once to bring them back from the depths, but I had refused to allow life to be planted in their mangled bodies. Chests carved open. Heads bashed in. Limbs twisted at odd angles, like spiders, reaching for me in the blood-stained throne room. Their screams echoed even now, carried on phantom breezes that cut through the chilly corridors, their ghosts hovering at the peripheries of my si dght. All fluttering death shrouds, skeletal fingers, hollow eyes. I closed mine with an uneasy sigh, but that didn't stop their ghosts from finding me in the confines of my mind. Painted across the black in angry strokes of red and blue. Blood and water. Even if she had caught their souls and brought them back, they'd look like that forever.

Not how they were painted. Happy and proud, and so very alive.

I wanted to remember them as they were. Before war. Before death. But too much had happened in the last few months that any memories associated with them had been tainted with blood and salt. It was too hard to think of any happier memory, so I had stopped trying. The people in this portrait weren't my parents, because my parents were dead. At the hands of Kalei's father.

My muscles tightened, an involuntary reaction at the memory of that vile man. He had stolen the vibrant life from Kalei's veins, had ruined countless others, all in pursuit of a legend that turned out to be true. Immortality.

The amount of pain and suffering he could continue to do with that power caused my stomach to sour.

Kalei twisted to face me, sunken eyes half-lidded. "Ev?" she whispered, concern creeping into her voice.

I heard her as if from a distance, painful memories crashing into the front of my mind to drown out everything else. The painting, the hall, the girl beside me all vanished into the rioting turmoil. A wash of dark waters, frigid and filled with death, loomed over my head, bearing down like the waves that took my life.

Cold arms wrapped around my middle. The shawl slipped, revealing Kalei's ashen skin as she held tight. Bones brushed my cheek, the sensation rippling through me. I drew in a shuddering breath and blinked away the tidal wave until the hall came back into focus. My mother and father looked down at me from the portrait, their painted eyes shining with love and understanding. They had always wanted me to be happy, but they had also wanted me to be a ruler. To follow in their footsteps and lead our people. Sit on a throne that was designed for a much greater person. With this fear closing my throat and stealing my breath, I couldn't be that person.

Cheeks burning with shame, I glanced away. Kalei's head was nestled in the crook of my neck, and I gave her a lingering kiss on the top of her head between chips of bone in her hair. The quiet moment gave me time to breathe, to calm my racing heart.

She had done something similar once, long ago, on a mountainside, when I thought the world was crumbling around me. Anxiety had eaten away my rationality, created monsters of snow and shadow and smoke in that cave, and Kalei had healed my fear the same way she had healed my shoulder, her magic wrapping around me until I felt safe again. She didn't have her magic now, but I felt her power all the same, strong and solid.

Kalei craned her neck back to gaze up at me. There was a glimmer in her eyes, a haunted glaze that shone in the torchlight. It reminded me of the things I saw on that cold, dark beach after the waters pulled me to their depths. Black sands shimmering with lost souls. Creatures of shadow and smoke swooping out of the grey sky. It reminded me of the siren's baleful gazes, hate and rage in slitted pupils, beings not of this world.

She was losing herself, and it terrified me every time I looked at her. The shine in her eyes faded with a slow, tired blink.

"Where did you go this time?" she asked, her question a breathy whisper in the cold corridor.

When I answered, my voice shook. "You know where."

Icy water, the kiss of death, the abrupt loss of air in my straining lungs. A knife between my ribs. A wave crashing over my head, a constant struggle to break the surface, water filling, filling, filling my lungs until all I knew was cold. Those waters swept through my sleep at night. I moved as if through a nightmare, unable to scream out, unable to run away, unable to do anything to stop the torment that scraped at my bones. I had spent three months gasping for air, expected to hold my head high even though I felt like I was drowning, and no one was there to keep me above the crashing waves of agony. My brother was gone, Kalei was dying, and the kingdom needed a queen who was as strong and solid as its foundation. I tried to be that queen for them, to keep them safe, but I was running short on time, and they needed someone who wasn't trapped in a single moment in the past.

"You don't sleep anymore," Kalei observed. She tugged the shawl back onto her shoulders, frail frame disappearing beneath the cloth.

"Neither do you," I pointed out. I'd heard her screams almost every night since that blood-red day beneath a blood-red moon. There was nothing I could do to stop the screams but hold her until she fell asleep, exhausted and torn. It was a nightly routine, and it kept my own nightmares at bay because I was forced to keep watch over her. To make sure she survived the night. To monitor each laboured breath until morning arrived, and she was still alive, though a little closer to death, a little more like a ghost.

"You're alive, Ev," she replied, the same refrain she'd been saying since my nightmares started. It wasn't bitter or angry, but it cut me all the same. I couldn't be happy with my life while she was losing hers. I owed her mine, and I would do whatever it took to give hers back. Even if it meant obeying the demands of an immortal tyrant across the sea.

I pressed another kiss to the top of her head in an attempt to hide the shame burning my cheeks. "So are you," I said with more conviction than I felt. I was going to find a cure, if such a thing could be cured. I was going to find a way to save her, as she had saved me.

"Your Majesty," a voice interrupted at the end of the hall.

I turned to see Talen, my trusted advisor and first mate, striding past the lit sconces. The plush carpet muffled his heavy footfalls until he came to a stop before us, eyes skimming over Kalei to land on mine. He appeared taller, muscles stretching over his shoulders to ripple down his arms in thick cords beneath a light-coloured tunic. A belt fitted with a regal sword wrapped around his slim waist. The jewel in his ear glittered faintly, visible now that he had shorn his hair. With the crest of Vodaeard emblazoned on his clothes, he looked more like a prince than a pirate, though he was neither. Talen had been my father's advisor, and now he aided me.

The corners of my mouth lifted briefly in a smile, until I saw the creases between Talen's brows.

I disentangled myself from Kalei, hand slipping into my pocket. The note from her father grazed my fingertips.

"Your ship is ready," Talen announced without looking down at Kalei. He had never liked the princess, seeing her as an extension of her father's cruelty, someone to blame for the chief's sins. And after that moment in the dungeons, a time that seemed so long ago and yet so recent, he had closed himself off from her completely. He didn't trust the girl-turned-wraith in the palace, in the kingdom, in my life. The way his eyes skimmed over her like she was already a ghost made my skin prickle with unease, but he was unerringly loyal to me, and I needed someone I could trust. Talen was that person, so I could tolerate his distrust of the princess.

Kalei didn't even seem to notice. And if she did, she didn't care.

She did, however, look up at me with a slight furrow of her brow. "Your...ship," she echoed, flat as the glassy surface of a calm sea.

My stomach lurched.

CROWNS OF BLOOD AND SALT

There was pain deep in her chest, the barest tremor in her voice only I could notice. Whatever was passing through her mind, she was scared of it, and trying not to show it.

I withdrew my hand from my pocket. A bone-coloured piece of parchment hung between my fingertips, as though the letters scrawled on its surface were poisonous vipers waiting to strike.

Her sapphire eyes darted to the broken seal, the full moon and crossbones insignia that had waved over her father's army when they invaded my home. A hand flew to her chest, where the ugly scar of the moonstone spread over her heart. When she had woken up on the rocks, she had torn pieces of that necklace out of skin and bone, and it was still a source of constant pain for her. Fingers curled into the fabric of her shirt, face twisting.

"He...sent a message?" she whispered, tearing her eyes away from the note to look at me. Fear shone in their depths, and I ached for the girl she had been before that man stole the life from her veins and replaced it with this decaying husk. She had been brave and determined to stop him, and now the mere sight of his sigil filled her with horror.

Guilt swept through me. It didn't seem fair. How scared she was of the man I felt nothing but burning hatred for. The fact that I had complied with his demands for months only stoked the anger in my soul. I couldn't let fear dictate my life anymore, and I wouldn't let it dictate Kalei's either.

"I know where my brother is," I told her. There was more to the note, but I tucked it back into my pocket before Kalei could look closer. A trade, the chief had written—Alekey for me, in the land of assassins across the sea. I wasn't meant to come back, and I couldn't bring myself to add that grief to Kalei's shoulders right now.

Her mouth twitched at the mention of Alekey, fear twisting into disgust. She had never forgiven him for the decisions that led to that fateful moment on the beach. Even though Talen and Icana had both advocated for him, had reiterated that his choices were to protect them, Kalei had let her heart grow cold against my brother.

I didn't give her a chance to protest. "I'm taking an army to find my brother and bring him home." Half of that was a lie, but I had been practicing how to tell her all day, and my voice didn't shake.

I wasn't going to bring him home. My makeshift army would. Without me.

They weren't a real army. Centuries ago, invaders from Wystan to the north had nearly pushed us into the sea, and the treaty that let us keep our land had abolished our military. Any form of dissent was seen as an act of rebellion, so this army had to be discreet. We'd plucked men and women plucked from the streets and handed them weapons they didn't know how to wield. They weren't soldiers any more than I was a queen. I didn't know how to kill an immortal man, but I did know that reckless impulsivity was in my nature as much as the sea was in my blood. Some plans were meant to be made up as they unfolded.

But I had already planned to stay. No one else knew, not even Talen. The army was a lie, a show of force. I didn't have any fight left in me.

I could only hope Chief Mikala kept his word and let them leave with Alekey.

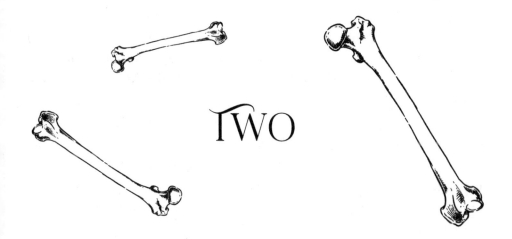

Two

Evhen Lockes was drowning.

She looked at me like she was sinking, trapped, unable to reach the surface. She'd been looking like that for months now, half-gasping with every breath as if she couldn't quite fill her lungs—or like something else was in the way. The sunset mosaic in her eyes remained firmly locked on me, but it was like looking at her under the surface of a wide-dark sea. A blurry, rippling reflection of the girl I once knew. Some part of her lost across the Dunes of Forever. There was desperation in her eyes and hope in her voice, and if I looked at her any longer, I was going to drown alongside her.

The note from my father disappeared into her pocket. I tried to understand. I really did. She'd been grieving for months, losing herself to the expectations of her kingdom and the duties of being the queen they needed. I stood by and watched her drown and tried to be the rock she clung to while the waters swept her away. Whenever she looked scared or frozen, I would wrap my arms around her and remind her of the time when I could have healed her fear. When she thought no one was looking and let her mask slip, I was there to see through it and help her fit it back into place before she walked these ghostly halls.

She told me everything, but she hadn't told me about this. I didn't understand this.

"Your coronation," I whispered around the tight band of fear in my throat. I hadn't been able to sleep, knowing my father was still out there in the world, abusing a life he had stolen from me. He had taken my power and used the lives I brought back to make himself immortal. I didn't want to talk about him. I didn't want to think about him. But Evhen held a note from him. Who was to say how many more she had gotten over the months?

And now, with her coronation so close, she was leaving. There were more immediate matters to tend to here. Ones that didn't take her so very far away from me. Ones that didn't threaten the very life I had brought back from the depths.

A weight pulled on her shoulders, heavier than the crown they wanted to put on her head, because it was the weight of a dying kingdom. Vodaeard was going to be swept into the sea if she left, scratched off the map. And it was the only thing I could think to do to make her stay.

She straightened to ease that weight, the one of an uncertain future, off her back. "I will not accept a crown while my kingdom is still in danger. Not until my brother is back."

Her eyes met mine, pain lancing across her features and in her voice when she spoke again. "How else will I know I'm worthy of it?"

She had always been worthy of it. I told her as much every night when the halls were silent, and we couldn't sleep unless we were in each other's arms. But she seemed suddenly, irrationally determined. The same kind of determination that had spurred her from her kingdom last time, drove her across the sea to my shores, my tower, my life. The kind of determination that made her act recklessly.

"How does leaving prove that?" There was nothing for her out on the sea except more pain. Her brother had made that clear with his decision to betray us. If he was the kind of person who would betray his own family, then he wasn't the kind of person who could lead a kingdom. Evhen didn't seem to understand that. She wanted him back so he could rule and we could live together for as long as I had life in me. But he had made his choice, and I had made mine—to rebuild these walls with a queen, not a coward.

"I made my decision, Kalei," she said, bringing a hand up to rest on my arm. It felt heavy beneath the shawl, and for the first time in months, I pulled back.

Hurt flared in her eyes, brief and bright, before she sealed it away behind her stony walls. She turned away, and with a final, resolute nod at Talen, marched down the hall, boots clicking hard enough through the carpet to echo on the stone beneath. A shiver rattled through me in her absence. I never felt warmth anymore, except when she was near, and then it was like the bursting sun after a storm. I reached for her, grasping at air as Talen stepped in front of me to block my view of the retreating queen, a protest, an apology, dying on my tongue at the scowl he lowered at me.

"I told you once," he growled, "if you hurt Evhen's heart, I will hurt all of you." The vibrations pulsed through my bones, a warning laced in his words.

"I don't want to hurt her," I told him, fighting the spark of anger in my chest. It was refreshing to feel something sharp for once, instead of cold, hollow, and empty. Anger filled the cracks, but rising to his bait would only satisfy him and his need for a reason to blame me for something I didn't do. I knew how he felt about me, his distrust plain. I understood Talen. I just didn't care for his attitude.

"Your very presence here is hurting her," he said, voice low and taut. "If you can't see that by now, then you're not worthy of her."

I glanced around him, but the hall was empty. Evhen had disappeared, which emboldened Talen. I doubted he would hurt me, but his words were bordering on threats, and I opened my mouth to call for help. Surely, Evhen was still close enough to hear me if I shouted.

Talen spoke before I could make a sound. "If you actually cared about the queen, you'd leave."

My blood ran cold, all the anger leeching from my body at the look in his eyes. I'd seen that look before. Manic, ruthless, dark. It was the same way my father looked at me when he drained the life from my veins. It was the look of someone who didn't care how many people he hurt to get what he wanted.

When he first threatened to hurt me months ago in a glittering ballroom, I almost didn't believe him. I was so caught up in the flurry of emotion I felt for the queen, that anything he might have felt for her was pale in comparison. I had allowed myself to believe that Evhen wouldn't let him hurt me. But he didn't care now. He would go against his queen's wishes if it meant making me suffer. And I couldn't protect myself anymore. I didn't have the power of the moon on my side, and I barely had the strength to stand straight, much less the strength to fight against his bulk.

"Leave me alone, Talen," I said, trying to emulate the queen's commanding tone. "You don't know what she needs. You're not the one who holds her when the nightmares come."

I brushed past him, but his hand lashed out, fingers wrapping around my arm. They touched on either side like a band and still left space for me to wiggle. But when he didn't let go, I tipped my chin back to glare up at him, hoping some of the anger I still felt wasn't lost to the icy grip of fear thrumming in my veins.

"You're the reason she has nightmares," he growled. "You're the reason the prince is missing."

I shook my arm, a feeble attempt to loosen his hold. "Don't talk to me about the prince," I snapped. "Don't mention that coward to me."

His other hand came up, quick as a whip, and connected with my cheek. The slap echoed in my ears as he shoved me away, and the force of his hit knocked me to the ground, dazed. Cheek stinging, the taste of salt in my mouth, I stared up at his looming form with narrowed eyes. My heart slammed against my rib cage, painfully reminding me that it still beat, still hurt.

He crouched in front of me, pale eyes dark, and pinched a hand around my throat to pull my face close to his. I barely felt the pressure, but instinct had me scrabbling at his skin.

"You'll be on that ship tomorrow morning," he said, "and when Evhen finds her brother, you're going to disappear. Go back to your father, drown in your beloved depths—I don't care. Just don't come back."

With what little strength I had, I surged forward, snarling in his face. "Will you even be there?" I said hotly. "You haven't been there for Evhen so far."

Rage twisted his features. I had never seen him look so monstrous. "Evhen trusts me to stay behind, to protect the kingdom, which is exactly what I'm doing by telling you to leave. If you come back here, I'm going to make you wish you had died next to your mother."

He released me hard enough to leave a scorching sensation on my neck. I didn't move, tears pricking my eyes, but I wasn't going to cry in front of him.

Instead, I curled my lip and said through the sting of salt, "I'm already dying. There's nothing you can do to me that my father hasn't."

He straightened, wiping his hands as though clearing away some unwanted dirt. "I saw what he did to the king and queen. I can do worse."

His heavy footfalls faded down the corridor.

When he was gone, I whimpered into the carpet, allowing the cold stone beneath to seep into my bones. The heavy stares of Evhen's parents fell on my shoulders. I had never seen them alive, but the portrait above me captured a remarkable likeness that I had seen reflected in both of their children. Evhen shared her unruly red hair—the colour of flames and sunsets and garnets—with her father. The harsh angle of her jaw was mirrored in his, beneath the shadow of a black and red peppered beard. Next to him, the queen stood tall and proud, her glossy raven hair the same deep shade as her son's. Evhen shared her mother's eyes, and her brother's were closer to his father's, but they were incredibly similar—it was almost like looking at older versions of them. Versions that smiled, versions that could have been happy. Before my parents destroyed their lives.

The light of the torches died around me before I found the courage to get up again. My arms shook, a tremble that had little to do with the cold and a lot to do with the renewed fear pulsing hot and cold through my body. My father, a man I once loved unconditionally, a man who had killed and stolen and tortured, had made contact with Evhen after so many months of silence. Evhen said she knew where her brother was, but I knew the queen's small expressions. When she thought no one else was looking, I had learned how to read her. I knew when she was lying. There was more to that note, and I needed to know what it said. I needed to know why she was leaving days before her coronation.

And why she hadn't asked me to go with her.

Was it because she knew I hated her brother? Didn't want him to come home? Didn't want him to be king? Evhen's coronation was purely ceremonial. She didn't want to be queen, but there was pressure from her council to accept the crown as a show of strength. Of resilience. But if she left now, Vodaeard would be vulnerable. *She* would be vulnerable, running headlong into another fight. I had saved her once, but I didn't have the power to save her again.

Maybe Talen was right. The heart that barely beat in my chest beneath the moonstone's mark ached to think so, but maybe it would be easier if I left. Once I was gone, Evhen would have the chance to heal. Vodaeard could heal. I'd heard their whispers—I was a stain on this kingdom, a reminder of the bloodshed. The least I could do was stop it from returning to these shores.

First, I had to see what that note said. Gritting my teeth against the lingering pain in my jaw, I went to find it.

THREE

My parents died in the summer.

I had been gone a month after their deaths, the mild weather giving way to cool autumn upon my return. But now a wintery wind blew off the ocean and icy rain pelted the landscape.

Vodaeard had never experienced seasons the same way the rest of the continent did. It jutted into the southern seas, salt-encrusted rock drenched with summer storms and winter blizzards. It was cold on its best days and unbearable on the rest, and I loved it. Over the years, I'd learned to withstand the frigid air. More recently, I had survived the icy waters. I was used to the cold.

But I wasn't used to the coldness that blew off Kalei's body when she pulled away from me in the hallway. We had spent months rebuilding what her parents tried to ruin, holding each other when the night brought its terrors, memories of that blood-drenched day tugging us both beneath the surface. She screamed herself hoarse, and I froze under the weight of worry. We promised each other that these long, dark nights were going to pass.

But then she pulled away from me in what felt like an act of defiance. It stung much more than I cared to admit, ripped open a part of my heart that I had sewn shut long ago. I hadn't asked for her support in this decision, but I thought she knew me better than that. I thought she knew it was what I needed. And to have her pull away from me spoke louder than her screams in the night.

For the first time in months, we weren't on the same page.

KAY ADAMS

I paced my chambers. Wind lashed through the room from the open window, flinging the curtains wide and blowing snow and sleet across the floor. The fire in the hearth shivered, but continued to roar in defiance of the pressing cold. A heap of letters sat on my desk, weighed down by a rock that looked remarkably like the moonstone. Jagged and dark, its sharp edges glinting in the firelight. I paused in front of the desk, breath clouding as it escaped my lips, and picked up the paperweight. The letters fluttered, but I held them down with my free hand before they could fly away.

My chest ached, looking at both the pile of letters and the piece of rock. I hadn't considered the stone's similarity to that seas-damned necklace before. It had come from the same mountain, a relic from a warm summer up north years ago, one of the first times my father had taken me into the range. A child's habit, collecting stones and shells and seeds. They had littered my windowsill until, inevitably, I grew out of the habit. This rock had survived the purging, but now I wrapped my fist around it until my skin opened beneath its sharp edges, and then I flung it out the window.

The letters I couldn't throw away. I couldn't burn them or tear them or lose them to the wind or sea. They were a reminder of what I had sacrificed for my kingdom. What I was willing to sacrifice.

What I still had to do.

And I couldn't part with them yet, not until my brother and my kingdom were safe from the very man who had written them.

Another note sat unfinished on my desk beside the chief's pile. Addressed to Talen, it explained my decision to leave, what I hoped to accomplish by trading myself for my brother, and what I needed him to do in my absence to prepare my brother for the crown. It was an apology and a confession and a goodbye. And it was the hardest thing I'd ever had to write.

I shoved the chief's letters into the drawer and slumped into the chair. Talen would inevitably find this note. I could imagine him, in a fit of rage, barging down my bedroom door in search of an answer for why I didn't come home. He'd find it here, the quill and inkpot still waiting for the final words I couldn't find.

I picked up the quill, inked the tip, and froze with my hand hovering over the parchment. What could I possibly say that would make any of this right? *I'm sorry? I had to? Forgive me?*

None of it was right. Nothing felt right, not while I was still here and my brother was so far away and Kalei...

My heart snagged on thoughts of the princess. What would she say when I didn't return? Would it be the thing that broke her soul or set her free? How could I possibly leave without saying anything to her?

A wet spot appeared on the dark text before me, and I was surprised to feel more slip down my cheeks. I swiped at them in anger, and then stopped, hand hovering uncertainly near the corner of my eyes. Once, I would have cursed the tears, blamed the salty spray of the sea for the wetness on my face, and refused to let myself cry— whether in sadness or anger or both. Talen was right—I hadn't let myself grieve. And I was falling back into that dangerous habit, wiping away any emotion before I allowed it to consume me. Emotions were a weakness I couldn't afford, but now, in the privacy of my chambers, I could. I could allow myself to feel everything. I could cry and lie to myself and tell myself it would be okay.

I didn't do any of that. The letter sat unfinished as I pushed myself up from the chair, snatched a cloak from its hook beside the door, and swept out of the room to go somewhere where my thoughts could be free and unrestrained.

Frothy waves slammed into the jagged rocks beneath the cliff where I had regained my life all those months ago. Black stones jutted out from the sea, cracked, broken, dangerous, water-logged, and slippery. Algae covered their surfaces, and with the sunlight fading beyond the blurry edges of the storm, I almost lost my footing once or twice, climbing down from the slope to the shore. It wasn't so much a shore here as an abrupt line where the rocks ended and the ocean started, its depth deceivingly shallow. One missed step, one twisted ankle, and I could crack my head on a shard of black stone.

But I was more sure of my footing than most things. Despite the closing darkness and slanting rain, I made my way to the edge of the water and stopped to stare out at the world. A sliver of white caught my eye between a break in the storm clouds heaving across the sky, and I frowned at the pale curve of the crescent moon. All my life, it had been a point of light in the night, a guiding beacon during long journeys on the ocean. Until I met the princess, it didn't hold much weight aside from that. But her devotion to it had stirred something in me. A kind of belief I had gone so long refusing to acknowledge, that there was something else out there in the world, something tugging and pulling at all of us. Something greater than our small lives.

But I had seen it die. In those days leading up to the Blood Moon, I had started to feel its power. Combined with Kalei's, I could almost believe in something bigger than myself. Until it turned crimson and painted the beach in swaths of blood red. Its light had gone dim. Now, it seemed distant and dead where it hung in the sky, and I reviled it.

The clouds surged forth to cover it again, and I exhaled a breath that shook with anger. Then I screamed, the sound snatched away by a rumbling roll of thunder.

My throat ached, raw and shredded, when the scream tapered into silence. The world didn't bend or shudder at my rage. The rain didn't so much as let up. It continued to pelt my face, wind slipping beneath the folds of my cloak to burrow deep into my bones. The cold reached a part of me that burned hot and bright, nearly extinguishing the flames that had been my driving force for so long. Surrounded by wind and waters that didn't care if they dashed me against the rocks or not, I felt breathlessly free. As if I could finally let go. Drown my anger and hate beneath the waves. Let it carry me to the depth.

Icy water lapped against the toes of my boots when I finally looked down. An eerie face peered up at me from the oily surface, two sets of eyelids blinking at me.

Crowns of Blood and Salt

The siren's sudden appearance didn't scare me, not this time. They seemed to show themselves when emotions were high, when vulnerabilities were on display. When they chose. When they had something to gain.

It used scaly arms to pull itself partially out of the waves, causing me to take a few steps back to allow it room on the rocks. As soon as my boots were free of the water, I felt a tether snap through my body, as though something had been drawing me closer and closer to the water, and it finally went slack. A shiver trailed up my spine. Had I come here to set my emotions free or set myself free?

I didn't know, but the siren seemed to. It gazed up at me, neither male nor female, but its own distinct features that gave it an otherworldly quality. These things transcended our world, had magic of their own that didn't rely on the push and pull of the moon. Every time we encountered one, it seemed to demand an exchange. A heart for a life. My cutlass for my princess.

What did this one want now?

"You want peace," the creature said, tongue sliding between sharp teeth. Its eyes shimmered like sunlight on water.

My heart strained at the simplicity of its words. Peace. Was that what I searched for? Was that what I yearned for? Could I find that below the waves or beyond the storm? It didn't seem possible, not while my brother was somewhere across the sea. Until he was safe, until my kingdom could thrive, I wouldn't know peace.

"How do I find it?" I asked, voice cracked from the force of my anger and sorrow. The sea salt tasted strong on my tongue and, briefly, it tasted like freedom. I just didn't know whether that freedom could be found below the waves or on top of them.

Sinking or sailing.

"Bring us a death." The siren pushed back, slipping beneath the surface for a moment before reappearing a few feet from the shore. Two more faces bobbed next to it, eyes shining with their own light, the colour of their skin and scales melting into the darkness.

Wind howled against the cliff behind me. I caught my balance on the rocks, heart lurching into my throat as the reality of danger set in. These rocks didn't care if I lived or died. And I was almost certain it wasn't my death the sirens were looking for.

""Whose?" I called as they swam backwards, away, down. "Whose death do you want?" Their tails flashed, and they disappeared. "Wait!"

My hand reached for them as if I could stop them, prevent them from leaving. But they could not be tied to the demands of mortals.

Huffing, I turned away. The world tipped sideways for a dangerous second, and I gasped as the sensation of falling overcame me. My arms flailed, though I knew deep down I wasn't actually falling. It was a memory, a moment from months ago when I had fallen, thrown from the top of this very cliff. Chains around my ankles and wrists, pulling me below the surface. It was a wonder the water hadn't broken me on the rocks. Otherwise, there might not have been a body to come back to.

When the world righted itself, I found myself half-sprawled on the rocks, a pale arm wrapped around my middle. Something metallic scraped the rocks, and I followed the arm to a shoulder, then to Icana's face, twisted with the effort of holding me up.

"You're fortunate I follow you everywhere," she grunted, and then her arm slipped. Her serpent-headed cane clattered to the ground, and we both collapsed onto a relatively flat portion of stone.

I sorted myself out before she did, shaking water out of my eyes and reaching for her cane where it had lodged in a crack. She rubbed her side, annoyance plain on her face as she wrapped scarred fingers around the cane. Her body hadn't healed properly from the chief's torture, and now the silver cane had become part of her usual attire. She didn't complain about it, but I knew she felt limited.

That didn't stop her from indeed following me without me ever knowing it.

"Thank you," I mumbled, rising to my feet on the slick rocks. Icana ignored the hand I offered, using her cane to push herself up. Even with the aid, she was steadier on the rocks than I was. She had been bred in a worse environment than this, and even though she had been living in Vodaeard for the past five years, some things were hard to carve from her muscle memory.

We started up the steep slope back to the castle. Wind tugged at our cloaks. The ocean roared behind us. It sounded like a monster denied its prey, and I shivered again.

"Do I want to know why you were all the way down here?" Icana asked when the slope leveled out, and we were no longer focused on the wet rocks, gaze sliding sideways to me. Lights flickered behind the shuttered windows of the palace, like glowing eyes in the darkness, winking and blinking and beckoning.

"Probably not," I answered.

As we approached the doors, barred against the storm, Icana turned to face me. Her hair had grown longer, her face paler, her eyes sharper. She searched my face for the answer she wanted, and didn't seem to find it.

Her cane thudded on the floor as she crossed the threshold. The mosaic chips sounded different from the courtyard stone beneath the metal. She glanced at me again, framed by warm golden light, eyes darker than the storm at my back.

"Don't throw away what she gave her life for," she said, and I knew exactly who she was talking about.

FOUR

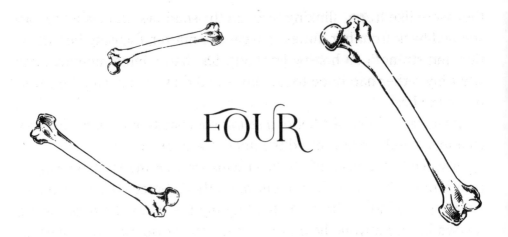

The castle moaned. Eerie creaks and hollow groans echoed through the hallways, filling the palace with the sounds of dying things. A summer gone to rest. The laments of a changing season. The cries of those who had given their lives on the beach just a few short months ago. Every scream, every wail felt trapped within these walls. I heard them in the dead of night, a time when I was used to feeling rejuvenated and revived. A time when the moon's glow would wake my bones, and I would feel so very *alive*.

Now I felt as though the dark depths of Death's domain were pulling me under, waiting for the moment my heart finally gave up to wash over me. I struggled to keep my head above those black waters, to cling to the remaining speck of life in my veins. Every day, the screams of the dead got louder, and every night, I tried to block them out with my own.

Vodaeard hadn't seen a storm like this in all the time I'd been here. Evhen had said the winters were tough, but this seemed unbearable. The very foundation shook as blasts of winter wind struck the castle. Wooden shutters creaked, more likely than not to break from their hinges. A howl raised bumps on my arm, and it took me a moment to realize it was coming from Evhen's room.

No one roamed the halls this close to the queen's chambers. She didn't have a personal guard, or if she did, I hadn't seen them. Maybe they were like Icana, slinking through the shadows. But even she had stepped back from her duties as weapons master, focusing her attention and strength on honing her body. She had limited mobility after what my father had done to her, but she didn't let that stop her from being the best.

As it was, I didn't see her or a retinue of guards outside the queen's chambers, and when I tested the door, it was unlocked.

A voice in the back of my head whispered at me to step away, to turn around. To ask Evhen about my father's letter instead of this—sneaking around in the dark, holding my breath as the door swung inward in case anyone heard the sound. Any noise was swallowed up by the howling wind outside, anyway.

The curtains flapped erratically over the open window on the other side of the room. Papers littered the floor, and an inkpot had spilled over the desk. A fire beat against the grate opposite the window. I frowned at the empty room, so dull without the queen to fill it with her fiery presence.

With a quick glance both ways down the hall, I carefully shut the door behind me and locked it. I hadn't been in here without Evhen sprawled in the bed before, or slumped at her desk, or perched on the windowsill. Even at night, she was always in constant motion, tossing and turning while I lay next to her. Night terrors seized her in those moments, and she always woke with a kick and a gasp, limbs flailing as if she fought an invisible foe. I was always there to soothe her back to sleep, because sleep never came to me anymore.

The room felt at once too large and too small without her. A twinge of guilt festered in my gut. In a lot of ways, it was wrong to be in here without her. Sneaking around and snooping through her things. But she was keeping something from me, and that wasn't right.

I pushed down the guilt and pushed against the gale to force her window shut. The glass panes rattled. Icy rain pinged off them, a melody that reminded me of the chiming bone shards in my hair. I twisted away with a sour expression before those memories could swell.

The bones didn't move anymore. They hadn't since the moon turned pale in the sky. Since I had given my life beneath its glow. That wasn't something I wanted to relive right now, so I tucked those thoughts away into the deep recesses of my mind, where only the nightmares could pry at them, and turned to Evhen's desk.

The inkpot had fallen over, spilling its contents across the glossy surface of her desk, staining a piece of parchment that looked to be written in her tight script. I leaned closer, trying to read the words beneath the stain, but it had spread too far. It was addressed to Talen—that much was clear at the top—but the rest had bled together into one giant blot. I passed over it, Talen's most recent threat to me ringing in my mind. The marks he left on my throat pulsed. Whatever Evhen had been writing to him wasn't worth my time. In my opinion, he didn't deserve whatever she'd been attempting to say. He had shown himself to be a jealous, violent man, and I was starting to think Evhen needed to distance herself from him. For her own sake.

My fingers snagged the edge of the parchment, and before I really thought about it, I carried it over to the hearth and tossed it into the flames. They ate away at the letter in earnest, swallowing it in a flash of embers. Smiling to myself, I turned to examine the rest of the room.

Bits of Evhen were evident. Clothes spilling out of the drawers. Weapons leaning in the corner. The permeating scent of ocean air. It was a modest room, with an unmade bed and wardrobe large enough to walk into and a bathing chamber attached to the main section, but it didn't feel like a room for a queen. It was dark, with heavy drapery, and nothing regal to show that Evhen was, in fact, the queen of Vodaeard. I had never asked why she didn't move into a larger room—I knew why. The only room larger than this one had been her parents. Those chambers were going to stay empty for a long time.

With the window closed, the papers on the floor had gone still, gathered in a spiral at the centre of the room as though they had been caught in the eye of a hurricane. My gaze snagged on one close to my foot, face-down, prominently showing the seal on its back. And though I had prepared myself for this, my heart still gave an uncomfortable lurch at the sight of my father's seal.

I toed another letter, lifting the edge slightly to confirm what I already knew—all of these letters, at least a dozen of them, were from my father. Each seal was a different colour, waxy symbols of the full moon and crossbones. My father's familiar handwriting slanted across each page. I wanted to be sick. I wanted to be angry.

Instead, all I felt was a hollow unbecoming. As though every part of me had been untethered and left to rot, pieces of my heart strewn across the floor like these letters. I loved my father. I couldn't deny that I still loved him. But he had ruined so many lives. His quest for immortality, something only I could grant him, had turned him into a monster—someone to hate. And I had hoped, perhaps foolishly, that when he escaped the beach that day, he was out of my life for good.

But he had never left. Not really. These letters proved as much. He'd been in contact with the queen this whole time. Three letters a month, nearly once a week, since he escaped with her brother as his captive. My stomach flipped and twisted into knots as I bent to pick up a letter.

Little pirate, it started. The title grated against my nerves, belittling and demeaning at the same time. When I first met Evhen, she had called herself a pirate, a captain. She had concealed her identity as a princess, heir to the throne of Vodaeard. Soon her secret had unravelled, but that didn't stop me from loving her all the same. Pirate was how my father saw her, not as a princess or a queen or even a captain. In his mind, she was a lowly thing, but she was so much grander than that.

My fingers tightened over the parchment, and the corners dented, but I continued reading.

Allow me the honour of reminding you of your vulnerable position. With your brother's life and your kingdom's future, in my hands, you will carry out these requests. And you will do so without complaint and in secret. After all, what would your co-conspirators think if they knew their so-called queen was a traitor?

Tears welled in my eyes at the words. The emotions collided like exploding stars in my mind, each one more violent than the last, and I couldn't tell whether my tears were from anger or sorrow or disbelief.

Swiping them away, I bent to pick up another letter. It started the same way—*Little pirate*—and I could almost hear my father's voice, the way he had spoken to and about Evhen on the mountain when he found us. A drawl like she was a misbehaving child, and he was the chiding father figure she needed. After all, he had killed hers, and had attempted to take her throne by force. Maybe he saw himself as the leader her kingdom needed, and it bothered me how easily I could hear that voice in his writing. How quickly his kind tone had turned cruel in my mind.

Your continued cooperation is appreciated...

I crumpled the paper in my fist as I glanced at another.

Little pirate...

Little pirate...

Little pirate...

A hurt that felt shockingly similar to the prince's betrayal sparked along my veins, but it wasn't aimed at Evhen, not directly. I suddenly understood, and even though I didn't think her brother was worth any of this, I couldn't fault Evhen for holding out hope. My father, wherever he was, was threatening her, her brother, and her kingdom, and she was the only thing standing between him and total oblivion. That burden was too heavy for her shoulders, and it wasn't fair.

What I didn't understand was why she had kept it a secret from *me*. We had foiled my parents once—she had killed my mother right in front of me—so it stood to reason that we could destroy the threat together. The threat being my father. But she was clearly worried about what he would do to her brother, and the hurt racing through my body in waves was from her apparent lack of trust in me. In *us*.

None of the letters were dated, so there was no timeline to my father's threats and demands, but one letter in particular caught my eye through the curtain of tears.

Evhen.

My heart skipped a beat, tapping against my ribs in an unsteady rhythm, one that felt like fingers crawling along my bones. I lifted the letter to the light.

Evhen, Your information has proved accurate and useful. There is one final thing I ask of you. In exchange for your brothers life, give up your own to me. Come to Geirvar within the fortnight. I will be waiting in the palace of the monarch of assassins.

The letter fluttered from my grasp to land amongst the others. Rain battered the windows. My heart battered my ribs. This couldn't be real. I could excuse every other demand—information about Vodaeard's allies, secrets only monarchs would know, funds—but I could not grapple with the idea that my father wanted to kill Evhen in exchange for her brother.

And she was going to sail right into his hands.

Whether she planned to die or not, I wasn't going to let her go alone. I had promised to save her, and even if I wasn't going to live much longer, my job wasn't done yet. Maybe this was how I saved her. Maybe this was how I stopped the bloodshed from returning to these shores.

Resolution took root in my heart, shoving aside the guilt and fear and replacing them with an anger that burned hot and bright. It was an anger that outshone the moon, the kind of rage I had felt that fateful day on the beach when I lost my power. I could be terrifying again. I could make my father regret everything he had ever done.

If Talen wanted me to stay away, then he would get his wish. I would leave, and I would make sure Evhen knew *why* I was leaving. Because she deserved a chance to live. She deserved to make something out of the life I had given her.

I was going to die soon, anyway. Suddenly, I didn't mind dying in the place of someone I loved.

FIVE

It was a bad day for sailing.

The storm from last night had covered the shore in a thick layer of slush and icy spikes that scraped against the hull of my waiting ship. Thick clouds hung in the distance, promising more rain and snow. Frosty air prickled my nose beneath a scarf as I shuffled down the pier, hands deep in my pockets, fingertips brushing the final letter from the chief.

I had found it on the floor after returning from the cliff last night. My room had been in disarray, and I'd remembered leaving the window open in my haste to expel my emotions, though it had been closed upon my return. The letters had flown across the ground, and at least two had made it into the fireplace, along with the letter I'd been writing to Talen.

I had considered writing a new one, but decided it didn't matter either way. There was nothing I could say that would make it better. I was going to be gone, and Talen could be angry at me forever, but he would know what to do. He would know how to prepare Alekey for the role I wasn't brave enough to take.

The figure at the end of the pier startled me, her presence out of place among the bustling crew. Kalei stood at the edge of the dock, facing the horizon, where a sheet of grey rain blurred the line between sea and sky. Beside her, a ship laden with cannons bobbed up and down on the swelling waves, hull creaking with the weight of its cargo. It was a massive vessel in comparison to the *Grey Bard*, requiring a much larger crew, and people moved across the deck preparing it for departure.

Midnight Saint was written across the bow in vivid crimson paint that looked like splashes of blood. I shifted my gaze away before a memory could stir and looked at Kalei instead.

She was wearing woollen pants and layers of shirts beneath a thick brocade coat. The shards of bone in her hair rustled in the whipping wind like the chimes that hung from the mainmast to ward off bad seas. Like she was her own kind of charm against bad omens. Leather boots hugged her legs. Everything was very Vodaeard, greys and blacks to match the cliffs, designed to withstand the sea. We were fishers above everything else—salt was in our blood, and it was permanently crusted on our clothes.

For the first time in months, she wasn't wearing a shawl resembling a mourning shroud. I'd never been happier to see her in our clothes.

But she wasn't supposed to be here. Dawn flecked the sky in misty greys and muted blues, and I thought she wouldn't wake until we had long set sail. I had spent the night convincing myself that it was easier to leave without a goodbye, but here she stood as if expecting one.

Rain dripped from her eyelashes. Beneath the pewter clouds rolling in from the sea, her eyes were the shade of the ocean at midnight, so deep they were nearly black. There was colour in her cheeks, but I suspected it was from the wind tugging at our sails. I opened my mouth to say something, but she spoke first.

"I'm coming." As she turned her head to face me, a flash of something dark rolled across her eyes, gone in a blink. Her lips pressed into a thin line, as if she was preparing for an argument. A refusal.

"Wh-what?" I stammered. A howling wind whipped over the surface of the sea, slamming into my ship and knocking me back a step. At least, I thought it was the wind.

It could have been my instinct to run, to hide.

The colours of the ocean blended in her eyes, until they settled on storm blue, like the dark sky ahead of us. I had seen every shade of blue that her eyes were capable of, but this stormy colour was a riot of emotions that I had never seen before. Anger and pain rolled into one brilliant shade that shone with resolution. One that left no room for argument.

"I'm coming with you," she said again, slow and precise. For once, she didn't cower into the collar of her coat or shiver beneath a shawl. She stood a little straighter, head held a little higher. Pride swelled in my chest at the slight change in her demeanour.

I hadn't seen this side of Kalei since that night the *Grey Bard* exploded, when she promised to do whatever it took to stop her father. It had been a promise made in anger, but the words had been said with sincerity.

"You'll need my help if you encounter my father," she continued, her words flat at the end. Yesterday, the mention of him had filled her with fear, but now she seemed to have purged herself of any emotion associated with the man. Or she was very good at hiding her true feelings. I couldn't read anything in the glassy sheen of her gaze.

"But…" The arguments tapered off my tongue, each one more pathetic than the rest. Anything I said now would be a disservice to her bravery and strength. *He might hurt you. I don't want you to see me die.* Anything I said now would be a disservice to her bravery and strength.

"I made my decision, Evhen," she said, throwing my words back at me. "I'm not letting you go alone."

"I'm not," I muttered, tilting my face up to watch the crew moving across the deck. When I had set sail on the *Grey Bard*, it was just me, Talen, and Icana. We were nobodies. We were anonymous. We were all we needed.

Now, above the din of a bustling crew and approaching storm, I could hear my weapons master yelling at someone on deck. A smile tugged at my lips, but it wasn't a happy one.

"Icana will be with me." She would understand better than anyone why I was choosing to stay. It wasn't fair to her, to carry that burden home, but she would make her own peace with it.

Kalei gave me a knowing look, and I hated what I read there. Icana had been tortured, and while we all carried emotional scars, she carried more physical scars than we did. Her body hadn't healed, rattling like her bones would never fit back into the right places. Her cane was a reminder. That while Icana had proved to be an excellent weapons master, she had failed to protect me, almost losing her life in her effort to do so. She didn't stand a chance in another battle, and we all knew it.

Kalei had more grace than to say it out loud. "If you get hurt," Kalei pressed, her voice taking on a desperate quality, almost as if she were pleading with me to see reason, "if something happens, I couldn't bear the thought of not being there to help you. Please let me do this, Evhen. I need this to end."

I didn't know what she meant by *this*, and I was too scared to ask. If she meant her father's life, I would let her have it, gladly. But if there were some other meaning, some other motive for her to sail so far away from home, I couldn't think of one that didn't worry me. Anything else was too painful to contemplate.

With a steadying breath, I nodded. "All right." What else could I say? Turning, I placed a foot on the ramp that would take me up to the deck and away from these shores. I was leaving—again—and it wasn't any easier this time. The agony that permeated the air here was suffocating. Maybe I'd be able to breathe easier out on the ocean. Except I didn't think I'd be able to breathe at all until my brother was safe again.

As we climbed aboard, a flag with the Vodaeard crest came into view above the deck, snapping in the frigid wind. A mountain peak rising out of the water. Stone and sea. Hard and unforgiving. That was us. That was Vodaeard. My heart lifted at the sight of it over the mainmast. It was a solid enough reminder that whatever we suffered, we would bring down tenfold on those who made us suffer.

The call of the sea prickled at my fingertips. This is where I was meant to be. This is what I was meant to be doing. My future couldn't be determined behind the walls of my castle, cloistered among stuffy stones and haunted halls and concerned councillors. It couldn't be decided beneath the weight of my father's crown. It was out here, gulls crying in the fresh air, wind tousling my curls, and salt spraying my face.

Kalei wandered to the railing beside a mess of rigging and leaned on the banister. Glowing white flashed in my mind at the sight of her, a moment so long ago when she had stood on another ship and commanded the dead of the deep to rise out of the water. Her hair had shone with moonlight then, streaked with luminescence, her power flowing through her veins and sparking the air. I was scared and mesmerized in the same breath. She'd been an omen, a creature not of this world like the dead sirens she had pulled from the sea.

Now, with the power purged from her veins, her hair a dull grey like the rocky shore surrounding Vodaeard, she simply looked human. Tragically mortal. If I couldn't give her back her life, I could at least give her this true taste of freedom. Show her why I was drawn to the sea. Maybe, at the end of all this, we'd find each other in the Endless Seas.

With that thought, I climbed up to the helm. A ship this size required a larger crew than I was used to, and I felt overlooked. Here, I wasn't a queen or even a captain. I was just somebody with a plan.

Deckhands rushed by, pausing long enough to bow, and those in what passed for a uniform saluted on their way below deck. Most of them had the wide-eyed terror of people facing death for the first time. As sailors, they all understood what needed to be done to set sail and assigned duties amongst themselves without needing to be told. As soldiers, they wouldn't know what to do without someone to lead them. I felt unmoored with that knowledge—they didn't need me to be a captain, but I wasn't sure I could be a commander either. I didn't know what I was anymore.

Icana was perched on the railing in front of the wheel, glaring at the young helmsman, who was dutifully ignoring her to call out directions to the crew below. Her hair was tucked beneath a wide-brimmed hat, which she held down with one hand as the wind threatened to send it spiralling into the sea.

The cane rested against the post next to her, the top curling into the shape of a sea serpent, green gems for eyes watching the water. She was just as deadly with the cane as she was with a crossbow.

"Your Majesty," the helmsman said, dipping his chin. I'd seen him before, years ago when he was a deckhand running underfoot on my father's ship, an orphan swept in from the sea with dark skin, hair, and eyes.

He wouldn't have been spotted on the piece of driftwood he clung to if it hadn't been for the white scrap of cloth in his frozen fingers. My father had pulled him out of the water, close to death and weak as he was, and gave him a home on the fishing vessels. He was a few years older than me, closer to Talen's age, *Eiramis* written across the front of his uniform in gold thread.

"Your weapons master was just informing me I must be doing something wrong." His deep voice rumbled against my skin with the distant roll of thunder.

"Icana," I warned, glancing askew at her.

"He is!" she exclaimed. "He's much too fresh to manage a ship this size." She wrinkled her nose at his neatly pressed uniform, the sharp lines of his collar, the gleaming cuffs and shining buttons, and the glistening cutlass at his hip. Clothes and weapons that hadn't seen battle. That hadn't known war.

Eiramis leaned over the wheel to pin her with a sharp stare that glinted in the lantern light. "What do you know about ships, my lady? You are a sell-sword, not a sailor."

"I am a weapons master." Icana's well-known rage flared in her sharp tone, hiding a wound that hadn't healed. "A ship is just another kind of weapon."

"You can call a ship a weapon," Eiramis quipped, "but that doesn't make you her master."

Icana narrowed her eyes, pinpricks of light beneath her hat. "Tell me, Helmsman Eiramis, what makes you more qualified than me? You and I both have lone names."

Eiramis bristled. Tension corded between them, thick enough to cut with his sword, but I didn't dare say anything lest it snapped back in my face. Eiramis had been too young to remember his family name when my father rescued him, but Icana refused to give hers.

She had left Geirvar, the very place we were trying to reach now, five years ago, had stowed away on my father's ship, and he only found her after she had sneaked into the castle kitchens for food. She had tried to fight her way out, but he made her a promise—become my weapons trainer, and she would never want for food again. Icana never spoke about Geirvar and her life there, had vowed never to return, and fought every day to prove she was worthy of the title. Some people just proved themselves faster and rose higher.

"Icana," I sighed, an ache blooming behind my eyes. "Please let Eiramis do his job. You should be managing the weapons inventory."

She stuck her nose in the air and sniffed. Something on the deck below caught her attention, and she narrowed her eyes. "You're right. Some of us have better things to do." She slid off the railing and scooped up her cane.

"We have a long journey ahead of us, Icana," I called after her as she descended to the deck. "Please don't make too many enemies on board."

Eiramis's deep gaze met mine over the spokes of the wheel. "You haven't said where we're going."

I lifted my gaze past the ship, past the cliffs, towards the horizon that seemed so far off. Rain slanted into the ocean in the distance, blurring the line between sky and sea, making it appear as though the world never ended. Somewhere out there, Chief Mikala had my brother. I felt the tug beneath my sternum, an ache that pulled me towards the open ocean. I wanted to be out there, sailing forever, but not like this. Not under these circumstances.

I pulled the chief's letter from my pocket and handed it to him.

He scanned it in silence, then said, "Oh."

Nothing more, nothing less, just a simple *oh* that made me wonder if I'd given him the wrong parchment. But no, there was the black script, the grey seal, the damning drop of blood over Alekey's name. It might not have been blood. It could have been wine, a squashed berry, or any number of red things that might have spilled. Eiramis ran his finger over it, and then carefully folded the paper into a square before handing it back.

"I won't make promises I can't keep, Your Majesty," he said quietly, the wind catching his words. "But I'm sure we'll see Alekey again."

An unsteady sigh shuddered through me. "I know we will," I whispered. Dead or alive, I would bring my brother home.

"Is this why your weapons master is so…prickly?" Eiramis stared down at Icana, who stood in the middle of the deck and yelled at unsuspecting deckhands.

More than a few gave her a wide berth as they moved chests and crates of weapons to the cargo hold. Eiramis's brows pulled in the centre of his forehead, as if she were a puzzle he was trying to piece together. Unsuccessfully, because no one could understand Icana, but I had to admire his attempt.

I shook my head. "She doesn't know."

Everyone knew where Icana came from. It was obvious in her skin tone, her hair colour, her overall appearance, but no one, not even I, knew why she had run away. It was a past she didn't want to talk about, and we all knew better than to pry.

If she knew where we were going, we would never make it beyond the shore in one piece. She was less likely to burn down a ship she was already trapped on.

Below, a young deckhand slipped on the wet boards and crashed to the deck with his load. The chest popped open, spilling cutlasses and rapiers, the sound of falling steel ringing through the air.

I winced.

"Sweet seas help the soul that has to tell her," Eiramis muttered when she started yelling even louder, looming over the fumbling boy as he scrambled to stuff the fallen weapons back in the chest.

She purposefully kicked one out of his reach, and he burst into tears. "Get me someone who can take care of these properly, or I'll stuff you in that crate." Icana's threat wove through the shroud of mist, up the mainmast, curled around the tattered flag, and floated back to us at the helm.

The seas, unfortunately, had never been sweet to me.

SIX

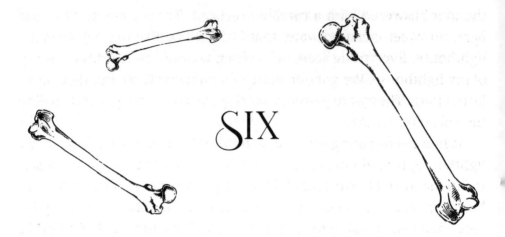

The sea roiled around us, bubbling and slapping against the hull. A storm drenched the upper decks—I heard rain lashing against the sails and wind howling through the portholes—but it was stuffy and dry in my cabin.

It was a modest cabin. Nothing adorned the walls, no framed pictures or maps. There was a bed bolted into the wall and tightly tucked quilts, a deck bolted to the floor, and tightly locked drawers. Nothing could fall or roll around on the high swells of the sea.

My fingers pulled at a thread in the quilt. This cabin was much larger than the one on the *Grey Bard*, but even that one had glimpses of Evhen. The bed sheets that hadn't been slept in. The letters strewn across the desk, smudged ink where something had spilled onto the parchment. The cutlass she always kept close at hand.

This ship felt too new to hold on to the memory of her, but I could feel it in other places. The chime of beads hanging from the mainmast. The current of the sea beneath us. The air twisting through the boards. She was everywhere all at once, even if this wasn't her cabin.

I shoved myself up from the bed and paced to the small circular window above the desk.

Waves rose and crashed against the hull, spraying up foam. Storm clouds pressed close, forming a grey slate over the sky, turning the sea a deep sapphire. Lightning forked the sky in the distance, and thunder answered with a rumble overhead. There were no birds out here, no sweet-incensed water that I used to be able to smell from my lighthouse. Everything seemed brighter, warmer, clearer from the top of my lighthouse. We got our share of summer storms, but they never lasted long. They were gentle, watering the coconut trees and cooling the volcano mouths.

It had been raining the day I left. The day Evhen found me in my lighthouse, brought me to my knees for the first time, and threatened to kill me to end a war I didn't know anything about. She had been so hurt by it, and I had been so scared to realize she was exactly the princess I had been looking for. It had been raining when she locked me in the cargo hold of the *Grey Bard*, and sunny when I saw the sky again.

I couldn't remember a clear day since. The changing seasons had slammed into Vodaeard without warning. First, perpetual drizzles and salt spray from the sea, wet rock and stone, rivers running through the courtyards. Then, winter storms like the one we sailed through now. But, at least on land, there were birds. Gulls crying over the fishing vessels. Eagles building nests in the foothills. Out here, it was only water and thunder.

My stomach twisted in knots. We had set sail not too long ago, but the storm had only gotten worse, as if we were sailing directly into its heart. I knew from stories that most storms had a calm centre, a place where even the sun was visible in the sky, but such places only hid a bigger terror on the other side. I hoped we were already through the worst of it—I didn't have much left in my stomach to empty.

A knock sounded at my door as I considered reaching for the bucket again. Swallowing thickly, I followed the tip and dip of the ship to the door, stumbling as I pulled it open.

Evhen, a red flush colouring her cheeks, stood in the narrow hall. The glow from the fire illuminated her curls, limning her in a warm rust shade.

A young deckhand stood next to her, bowed under the weight of a trunk.

"Hi," she said, breathless, as if the storm had snatched away her voice. She gestured to the boy and the trunk decorated with scrolling filigree. "I didn't know if you had brought your own clothes." She said this awkwardly, as if she had needed an excuse to come visit me.

My mouth twitched at the corners. "You didn't know I was coming," I pointed out. "Whose are those?"

"Mine."

The boy lumbered past me ungracefully and deposited the trunk in the middle of my cabin, landing with a thump. Then he shuffled back out into the hall, wiping his hands on his pants.

I clutched the door to keep myself steady and eyed the trunk, my heart aching with the simple kindness of the act. When I looked back at Evhen, she was alone, fiddling with the large signet ring on her third finger.

It glinted in the firelight, and I caught the insignia in the centre of the oval—a key surrounded by a bursting sun. *Lockes*. It didn't quite fit her finger, made for a larger hand. This was my first time seeing it.

"Why haven't you worn that before?" I asked, nodding to the ring.

She glanced down, as if seeing it for the first time herself, and tucked her hands behind her back to hide their fidgeting. "It was my father's," she answered. Her golden eyes unfocused for a moment, then she came back to the present. "I wanted something of him with me." There seemed to be more she wanted to say, but her words trailed into silence.

The contents of my father's note surged to the front of my mind. "You haven't said where we're going," I pressed.

Her brows pulled together, a small crease appearing as she pursed her lips, considering what to say. "Your—" She hesitated, and started again. "Chief Mikala has taken Alekey to Geirvar, a country in the Eyrland Sea. It's one of the most hostile places in the world. Chief Mikala's army doesn't compare to the kinds of murderers and assassins Geirvar produces. They are known for ending monarchies."

A chill creaked down my spine.

She spoke with the kind of voice that suggested she'd had experiences with them in the past, and they weren't something she wanted to relive now. My father's war had spread far enough on this side of the world, but did it even touch nations across the ocean? Why did he take the prince to such a place?

"It's a week and a half journey there," she continued. "I didn't know if you had packed enough for the round trip, so..." She gestured at the trunk again.

My stomach flopped. I hadn't. I didn't know how long we would be traveling, and I certainly hadn't considered the return, because I had already decided I wasn't rejoining the ship.

We were sailing towards one of the most hostile places, into a trap, and she still didn't trust me with the truth. That she hadn't packed enough for the voyage back to Vodaeard, either.

A swell of anger rose inside me like a tide. She must have had a reason for keeping the truth from me, but none of them could be considered good enough. She had been surprised to see me on the dock because she wanted to escape without a farewell. I wasn't going to let her leave so easily. I wasn't going to let her hurt me like that, not after everything we'd been through.

"Did you pack enough for the return?" I blurted, accusation shrill in my voice. I hadn't meant to shout it, or even say it. I wanted to give her the benefit of the doubt, to tell me when she was ready. But I couldn't stand knowing the truth of that letter, and letting her go through with it.

She took a step back, eyes widening in surprise, and then in suspicion. "Of course..." she intoned.

"I saw the note, Ev," I said, lowering my voice again. "What my father asked of you. You were going to leave, weren't you?" Grief crackled through my voice, and tears threatened to fall. I thought I could be strong like her, unbreakable like my lighthouse, but this hollow emptiness inside of me was overflowing with sorrow at the idea of losing her again.

She moved forward like a tidal wave, wrapping her arms around me. Curly red hair fell against my cheeks as she pressed a kiss to the top of my head.

I buried my face in the crook of her neck, inhaling her—salt and steel and cinnamon.

"I should have known you were the one in my room last night," she whispered. There was a tightness in her embrace, and I stiffened under it, unable to relax. It felt too much like a goodbye, and I didn't want to face it. I didn't want it to end.

"Is it true?" I asked, voice muffled against the collar of her shirt.

"I have to save Alekey," she answered.

I shoved away from her, allowing that spark of anger to bring enough force to the movement that she stumbled. My arms hadn't been strong enough to do much lately, and the exertion immediately weakened me. My chest heaved, trying to catch my breath amid the flood of emotions. "When were you going to tell me? *Why* didn't you tell me?" The words spewed out of my mouth. "I don't care that he has your brother. I won't let you die for him!"

Her eyes softened, and I hated the pity that shone in them. "You can hate me all you want, Kal. This is the only option that saves both Alekey and Vodaeard."

"I don't hate you, Ev! I love you!"

I hadn't said it before, and now the words hung heavy in the air between us. After that day on the beach, I'd been too scared to say it, afraid that the truth of it would be lost amid the fact that I was dying. Now, my heart slammed against my ribs with the lurching of the ship, and I couldn't take them back.

"I love you, Ev," I continued, "and you were going to leave without saying goodbye." Energy spent on emotions, I felt hollow again, chiselled out.

She was quiet for a moment, surprised by my outburst. The redness in her cheeks was fading. "Is that why you came?" she whispered finally. "Because I didn't say goodbye?"

"I came to stop you. To ensure you returned home." I wanted to reach for her, to feel her arms around me, as I had so many nights recently. When I was with her, I was safe—the war beyond our shores barely touched my mind. If I closed my eyes hard enough, I could pretend it wasn't happening. But now she was chasing it again, slipping through my fingers like the seaweed-like souls I brought back from the depths. There was no pretending now. We were sailing very far away from the one place that could be considered safe, and Death would find one or both of us either way.

Her gaze fell to the ring she twirled absently around her finger, and I noticed something else I hadn't spotted before. There was discolouration from old scars, but no new wounds around her nails. She used to bite her fingers and lips so often they would bleed. Already, she was turning that attention to the ring, a new distraction to keep her hands occupied. Her chest heaved with a sigh.

"I'm not going back home, Kal," she replied. When she looked up at me again, her eyes were brimming with tears. They reflected the glow of the fire behind me, like twin flames caught in her gaze. She was the sun to my moon, and though my light had gone dark, hers shone brighter than ever. "I'm going to give the chief what he wants, and he's going to leave my kingdom alone. You can't save me from this one."

A burning tear marked a path down my cheek. I let it shine in the firelight. "I can damn well try."

"I won't let you!" Her voice slammed against me, all the force of a gale, knocking me back a step. The room tilted around me. "I hate this, Kal. Believe me, I do. But I don't have a choice." The crack in her voice knifed through me. She looked at me, hurt and hate glazing over her eyes, and shook her head. "It would have been easier if you'd stayed behind."

Pain lanced up my ribs at her words. "Leaving would have been easier?" I echoed. She didn't mean it. She couldn't mean it. When she didn't answer, it felt like a door slamming closed between us. I balled my hands into fists. "Remember what I said in Xesta? *Let's not die together*—I still believe that, Evhen, even if you don't."

Her lip trembled, but she raised her chin a fraction. "You shouldn't."

SEVEN

"Your Majesty?" The concerned voice of my councillor pierced through my thoughts.

My father's ring slipped from my finger as I jerked my head up.

The three councillors gathered around the table in front of me watched as the band of gold bounced across a map of ocean routes and charted islands and fell off the edge of the world, skittering to a stop against the closed doors with a tinny clang.

Night was falling outside the portholes, casting the churning waves in crimson where the sun dazzled the horizon beyond the storm clouds. Rain pattered softly against the windows, but it was still dark in every direction. It was going to be a long night.

The conversation with Kalei replayed through my head, echoing in my mind like a stone chamber. No other thoughts had been able to form since I left her cabin, all quashed by those damning words. The ones that came from my own mouth.

I still believe that. You shouldn't.

Somewhere along the way, my heart had betrayed me. I had fallen in love with the princess who could raise the dead, but when she brought me back, she left something behind. Pieces of me shattered on the shores of a dark beach, tatters lost in a blood-drenched throne room with the remains of my parents' chests.

I had tried, these last few months, to be strong and brave and alive for Kalei. But the Evhen who had fallen in love with the girl who raised an army of bones in Xesta was dead, and this Evhen was tired of pretending to be her. Because whoever I had been before, the darkness of the depths had been left there.

Taking a breath—it was all I could do not to cry—I rounded the table and bent to scoop up my father's signet ring. It didn't fit. It wouldn't fit, designed for a much larger hand. A much more powerful hand.

I took my place on the other side of the table again, curling my fingers on the wood to hide their trembling. "Repeat yourself, Breva."

Three of my five councillors had agreed to come with me. The others stayed back with Talen, to manage the kingdom in my absence and prepare for my eventual coronation. It was supposed to be today. The thought was sobering, reminding me that I had left my kingdom vulnerable once again. Only this time, I hadn't run away from the dead. I was running towards it, fleeing the responsibility that a crown gave me so I wouldn't feel as guilty. Vodaeard needed a monarch that didn't run, and I couldn't do anything but.

Kalei's words from yesterday pounded against my head. *How does leaving prove that?*

She didn't understand. It had never been about proving myself worthy of the crown. I didn't want it. That was just an excuse to leave before it was forced on my head.

The thought of her cut deep. Once, she had weeded herself into the hole left by my parents, and festered there like sweet-smelling rot. She had become like air, so deeply entrenched in my bones that I couldn't breathe without her close by. Now, I had carved her from my skin and bones.

I almost wanted her to hate me, in my sick, self-destructive way. It would be easier if she did.

Breva cleared her throat. She was an older woman, hair grey and back bent from years of knifing fish. In truth, most of my councillors looked like that, old and weather-worn. But they had been part of Vodaeard's foundation long enough that my father had trusted them to help make decisions that were beneficial for the kingdom. I wasn't so sure yet.

"You haven't said where we're sailing," she said in her kind, grandmotherly voice.

My nails chipped the wood. Anger blossomed in my chest, quick as fire in a hearth.

At least that part of me hadn't been lost to the seas.

The kindling anger in my veins made my decisions easier, if rasher. "Do you not trust me to get you there in one piece?" I snapped.

"Breva is right, Your Highness," Haret added.

My teeth gritted at his tone. He looked like a hawk, eyes shrewd and narrowed whenever they landed on me across the table. As if he was regretting his decision to come, to watch over me like I was still a child in need of a parent.

I bit my tongue when I frowned at him.

"Your enemy will hold the advantage if we cannot provide you with a strategy based on our destination."

Your enemy. Not *our enemy*. Not *our war*. They had advised me against this journey. They wanted to trap me in a broken kingdom with a blood-stained crown on my head. According to tradition, I wasn't old enough to rule without a regent. Any decisions I made had to be approved by the council, even after my coronation, at least for the next year. No one in the kingdom thought I was fit to rule, and they wanted to use their power over me for as long as they had power to use. They'd have me cower. They'd have me ignore the threat that was Kalei's father. When he took Alekey, when I begged him to take me instead, he said this would keep me compliant.

I was done with it. Done letting someone else dictate my decisions for me. A council of old people couldn't tell me how to save my brother. This decision was my own, and I intended to see it through. The chief would get what he wanted, once and for all, and that would be the end of his tyranny against Vodaeard. Against my home. Against my family. Against me.

"If you don't have anything useful to tell me, then get out."

"Your Majesty?" Breva said, thin white eyebrows drawn together.

"You've seen the map." I waved a hand at the intricate parchment spread in front of us. The dark lines of islands and borders. The wide expanse of the ocean. The known world.

The map had been commissioned by my father years ago, before war touched our lands and tarnished our lives. Vodaeard sat proudly in the western waters, labelled with the same insignia on our flag. Far below Vodaeard, Marama's crescent-shaped island filled the southern seas. Beyond that, sirens bobbed out of the deep blue and sea beasts curled through the waves between the mainland and the rest of the world. It was a map of legends come true.

And there, far to the east, Geirvar nestled between two long strips of land, a chain of deadly nations in the Eyrland Sea, all of them marked with crossed swords. Assassins. Mercenaries. Saboteurs. Deadly criminals for hire. Those countries seemed to beckon me, pull me towards them with a strong gravity I couldn't escape. And not a single one of my councillors could determine our destination.

They nodded, shifting in place. Nervous energy and the sound of rustling clothes scratched against the inside of my head. I was used to doing things on my own, and now they flocked around me like chirping birds, crowding the silence with their words and fidgeting. They constantly moved around me like I was a fragile thing, something made of glass, easily broken. And not so easily repaired. As if they were never sure what to say, what would anger me or pacify me.

I eyed the room, holding their gazes long enough to let the silence stretch. For a long moment, the only sound was the crackle of flame from a lantern hanging on a beam above us. I hadn't noticed how dark the room was now, storm clouds spreading across the night sky outside the window. The lantern swayed with the rock of the ship, and the light spun around the map, casting half the world in darkness. Shadows filled the spaces between my councillors and edged into the corners of the cabin. Everything would be dark soon.

"If war meets us at sea," I said, staring at the large expanse of water, "I expect my council to be prepared. If war meets us on land,

I expect my council to be prepared. You should be able to offer me strategy, no matter where we are, at any time. Unless I've chosen the wrong people for my council."

My eyes flicked up to Breva before sliding to Haret, almost daring them to challenge me again. We weren't in Vodaeard anymore. I didn't have the demand to adhere to protocol and etiquette anymore. We were on the seas, and the seas were in my blood.

This was my domain.

This was my strength, not the weakness they assumed.

They were the ones who had become complacent on land. They were the ones who cowered when I had set my sights on Marama's navy.

"Of course not, Your Majesty," Akev spoke up, dipping his head in my direction. He was the youngest member of the council, Talen's age, the only one I had chosen specifically. Everyone else had been assigned or continued the role after my parents' deaths. Akev was the only one I liked.

"We're honoured you've elected us," he added. "And we will not disappoint you."

I planted both hands on the table, leaning over the map to stare at our current location. Not what we left behind. Not what we sought ahead. Just the empty ocean and black seas that I hoped were sweet. The light swung around me. Shadows climbed up the walls, into my heart. I wasn't afraid of my council disappointing me.

I was afraid of disappointing my entire kingdom.

"Perhaps we should retire," Breva suggested. "It is late. We'll reconvene in the morning."

"We'll reconvene when I say we do," I snapped, and immediately regretted my words. Tension tightened my shoulders. It was still hard to accept the help they were offering. All I wanted to do was snap and lash out and break every rule. That was how I had always done things. Court life bored me. Small talk bored me.

Alekey was much better at charming politicians and attending meetings. He was the perfect prince. I was the dour daughter. But that wasn't my role anymore, and I was still learning to hold my tongue. I was still learning to accept that I didn't have all the answers.

"Leave me," I muttered to the table. An ache bloomed in my clenched jaw as I fought to stem tears of frustration. How could I be expected to let go of my pride when that was the only thing keeping my head above tumultuous waters? How could I save my brother and make peace with this decision when I was already at war with everyone else around me?

Black seas, I needed Talen here.

As the room emptied, my fingers dug grooves into the table. Talen's absence was a disturbingly familiar hole in the space next to me. It was the shape of him, the feel of him, the strength of him that I craved, because he had been there through *everything*. He had dragged me from the throne room while my parents strangled out their final breaths. He had wrapped strong arms around me when I finally broke down in my grief. But Talen needed to stay back—he was the only one I trusted to keep Vodaeard safe when I was gone. If he had come, if he had learned what I was going to do, he never would have let me.

I had planned to die there, I told him after we had stolen Kalei away from her island. I didn't want to live in a world void of my parents, where the responsibility of their crowns was forced on my head. He had said it was selfish to leave Alekey alone in this world. But Alekey wouldn't be alone. He would have Talen, and Icana, and a whole slew of councillors who would listen to him, and he, in turn, would listen to them.

A presence moved to fill the spot next to me, warm and sturdy and here. I glanced sideways at Akev as he leaned against the edge of the table, hands braced behind him, the mantle of councillor falling from his shoulders between one breath and the next.

Looking at him like this, dark hair falling in curls over his eyes, half his face cast in shadow from the lantern above, he reminded me of Alekey. Same calm demeanour. Same smug tilt to his chin. But when he looked at me with that unbearable softness in his grey eyes, I felt like the younger sibling.

"You carry too much, Captain," he said. He reached across the space and folded his hand over mine. "Let us lessen the burden."

A shaky breath escaped me. Most of my councillors had been by my father's side during his reign. Akev was the only one who was still studying at the university in Wystan when I approached him weeks ago. He was young enough to understand how the world was changing, and how dangerous it was to remain stagnant. It was something the older councillors hadn't yet realized. They wanted to advise me the way they advised my father.

But my father was dead, and so were their views. Akev was practical. The rest were pragmatic. I valued his thoughts above anyone else's, but this closeness was something I didn't allow with anyone.

Pulling my hand free, I paced to the locked window behind the desk. The swaying lantern light formed a misty halo around my reflection in the wet glass. A line of fire rimmed the dark clouds on the horizon, fading into the ashy blackness of the storm and sea. Water frothed up the side of the ship. We were mere hours away from Vodaeard and days away from Geirvar, sailing directly into a storm. Who knew what would emerge on the other side?

I turned from my haggard reflection. Sleep hadn't come easy after my parents' death, and it was likely to continue evading me until we landed on the other side of the world. Until my brother was safe. Exhaustion was a constant worry dragging at my bones, filling the spaces left empty by those I loved, but I wasn't ready to show anyone just how tired I was.

Not even Akev.

""I appreciate your concern, Councillor," I said. Guilt shot through my stomach at the way his gaze wavered, the softness shuttering behind an uncertain distance. The mantle fitted back into place in splinters, as if he wasn't quite sure which role he was supposed to play anymore. "This 'burden' everyone keeps mentioning is my birthright.

It's mine to bear, mine to wear. My other councillors don't think it will fit. They want to use my age to their advantage. What do you want?"

His brows pulled together, taken aback. Hesitation flickered across his face before he replied, "Captain?"

I should have been more bothered by the way he called me *Captain* in private, but I was too tired to summon the energy to remind him of my title. It was a relief to escape the addresses of *Your Highness*, *Your Majesty*, and *My Queen* that the other councillors were so fond of overusing. *Captain* was the one title that had always felt right. That felt like me. *Captain* was cut into my very bones. But Akev used it with the tenderness of someone who knew me. Someone who was familiar with me.

Only Kalei had ever truly known me like that.

"I don't trust my other councillors to make decisions that benefit my kingdom," I said in a low voice, acutely aware of the thin walls.

Sound travelled with ease through the bowels of ships, up through floorboards, and down through hallways. The last thing I needed was for those very councillors to hear my misgivings about them.

"They want to act as parliament, regent, and king until I come of age. I will not tolerate any kind of behaviour that undermines my authority, especially when that behaviour threatens the prosperity of my kingdom. I asked you to join my council because our views are closely aligned. So what do you want, Akev? Do you want the council to rule in my stead and cower in the face of war?"

His jaw hardened. Akev was smart. At least, his professors seemed to think he was. There were only so many ways someone like him could charm someone like me before he ran out of bluffs.

"I think the council is old," he said. "I think the council needs to be reformed. But I also think they're scared."

"Scared of what?" I scoffed.

"You."

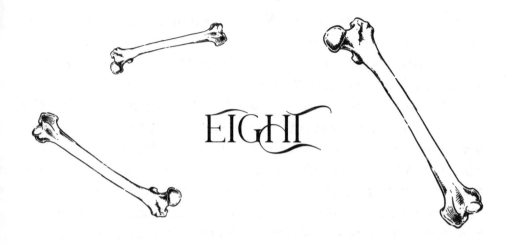

EIGHT

Cross-legged and bare-footed, I sat amid a tangled thicket of rope at the bow, idly counting the bone shards in my hands. The boards were wet from last night's storm, the rope soggy where it bent around me, and a handful of deckhands moved about with buckets and mops. From my vantage point, it was easy to watch the crew without getting in the way. And based on the wide berths and hostile glances they gave me, they didn't want anything to do with me either.

In the months since the Blood Moon, unable to sleep, I'd spent hours poring over Vodaeard's history in the grand library.

Grand might be a generous word for the stony space, just as *grand* might be generous for the entrance or the ballroom or the throne room. Nothing about Evhen's home was grand, except for the way it had survived time and time again, enough that most of the tomes in the library were dedicated to Vodaeard's victories in countless squabbles with its northern neighbours. There were no books on poetry, no great fictional works, nothing fantastical like the fairytales I had lost all those months ago.

Instead, all I had encountered was pain. Each tome that described the treaty that separated Vodaeard from Wystan in the north contained loss and lessons. Half their land had been taken, their military abolished, and now their monarchs served simply as figureheads. Wystan essentially controlled Vodaeard, from their trade deals to their vague land borders. The country had been a great kingdom once, as vast and sprawling as Xesta.

The comparison made me shudder every time I came across it. It was in every book—"vast and sprawling as the greatest kingdom in the south." Xesta was not great. Xesta was loathsome. It was a beauty built on bones. I had encountered those bones firsthand in the crypts beneath the city, raised them to raze the city. Those bones now protruded from my skin and clung to the short clumps of hair that brushed my neck.

I had counted them numerous times—six in each hand, a shard cutting into my jaw, an extra rib around my heart, a second femur next to my own. And then a dozen pieces in what remained of my hair, rattling like beads in the salty breeze that blew off the ocean. The sound had almost become a comfort since I cut my hair, a new kind of familiarity. It was the one thing I could be sure of when everything else was so uncertain.

It amazed me how a city like Vodaeard could withstand so much—the constant battering of the ocean, the invasion from the north, my father—and yet they looked at me with venomous vitriol as if I was one misstep away from toppling their foundation into the sea. As if I had been the cause of all their pain and loss in the centuries since they became a nation. How they couldn't look past the Princess of Death, the monster who raised the dead to build her father's army, to see the battered and beaten girl beneath who had lost everything on a blood-drenched beach. The bones sticking out of my skin turned me into the grotesque figure they all wanted me to be.

So I was content to sit away from them and watch, to wonder how it might have been different had myth not become truth. Had legend not become my worst fear. The fairytales I'd cherished as a child had hidden dark revelations that had torn my family apart. And I wasn't sure I knew how to reconcile what I'd known about my father before his quest for the legends in those fairytales with what I knew about him now.

CROWNS OF BLOOD AND SALT

All I knew was what I had to do for Evhen, for Vodaeard, and that meant becoming a ghost once we landed. Talen was right. With everyone staring at me like I was still the enemy, it was the best and only choice to fix what I had broken. I didn't have the energy to convince them otherwise. If they wanted to see me as a monster, bone-studded and black-hearted, then so be it.

Evhen was the only one who managed to look at me with anything other than hate in her gold-gilded gaze. But after last night, I wasn't so sure anymore. Maybe I had truly lost her to the depths. Maybe the girl I loved had died the same day my mother did.

She had come up from her quarters not too long ago, but she moved across the deck as though she was lost. Unsure of her place if it wasn't at the helm. She dressed differently now—gone were the outfits of pirates, replaced with the heavy fabrics of queens, the detailing designed to show her rank in sweeping strokes of gold and red. Vodaeard's colours, like the sea at sunset. The clothes suited her, but there was a visible discomfort in the tense line of her shoulders, as though she wasn't used to the stiffness of her position. The inability to move and act as she might have, had she still been captain of the *Grey Bard*. The title of Captain was now merely for show—someone else gave the orders on this ship, and she didn't know where she fit in anymore.

I watched while she turned to the side, as if to make a comment to someone, and saw the space beside her was empty. Shoulders slumping, she turned back and joined the helmsman at his post. Wind caught her hair, pulling strands loose from its bun, but she didn't move to pin them back in place. Everything around her was a whirlwind of movement, and she was the calm centre of the storm, but that didn't suit the Evhen I had known. That Evhen would have dived right into the fray and flurry. She wouldn't have stopped moving. She wouldn't have given up. But this Evhen was just as lost as I was until we landed. There was nothing for her to do here, and it was clear she was bored.

For the first time since she had climbed my lighthouse, my path was clear. Determined. Save her, even if she was so intent on destroying herself in the process. I loved her too much to let that happen.

Maybe when I was gone, maybe after she'd had time to forgive and forget me, her path would become clear. Until then, darkness swirled around her, tinged with magic from the depths, the same kind of shadows I'd seen in the mountain cave that clouded her mind. I couldn't take away that anxiety, not like I'd done then. I could only leave. I could only let her heal.

Movement across the deck dragged my attention away from Evhen. On a ship this size, everyone was moving. Everyone was doing something. It was easy to get distracted, and hard to focus on a single thing, so my brows pulled down in the centre when I noticed someone heading straight for me. Trying to ignore the way my heart sped up, aggravating the extra rib in my chest, I waited until his shadow fell over me before I lifted my head.

He was older, with grey hair flopping about his head in stringy lines. Deep trenches marred his face, pulled by the scowl that graced his hard mouth. He looked like every other Vodaeard citizen, roughened by the sea and burned by the sun. A sword hung from his hip, marking him as a soldier and not a sailor—but I had seen enough soldiers in my life to know he was only pretending. Real soldiers knew how to hold their weapons.

Squinting across the deck, I glanced around him towards Evhen. But she was too deep in her own mind to notice. The man leaned forward. The way he gripped his sword's hilt was worrying. Tight. Knuckles white. Unyielding as the sun beating down on us.

"Do you recognize my face?" he asked, a hiss in his voice.

I shook my head. Though it was winter, it was warm today, the sun blisteringly hot where it landed on the boards. But a shiver crawled down my spine, regardless.

"I was there." He angled his body, blocking my sight of Evhen. "On the beach. I saw you looking at the bodies. My son was one of them."

Chest tight, I fought for breath as the clang of battle echoed in my ears—the ring of swords and wails of pain that filled the air. I tried to force myself to forget that night, but I remembered. Night terrors had plagued me for months. I made them believe I had forgotten, because I didn't want to talk about it. Not now. Not ever. There were some horrors in the past that were meant to stay there, not be dragged into the light like this man was doing now.

"Do you remember my face now?" he snarled. I was so focused on trying not to see him, even as I stared directly at him, that I didn't notice him draw the blade until its tip sparkled in the sunlight. "Why should you get to live while he's dead?"

We were gaining an audience now, but it was clear no one was going to step in. They had all been hurt by what my parents did. More than likely, they had all lost someone that day on the beach. But I had lost, too. The problem was, they thought I deserved it.

I struggled to squeeze the words out. "I'm sorry about your son—"

"'Sorry'?" he spat back in my face, making me flinch. "'Sorry' won't bring my son back."

His blade arced through the air, faster than I expected, given his age and frame, and I threw myself backwards, coming up short against the side of the ship. The tip of his sword, when it stopped swinging, shone with a dark-coloured liquid. And then I felt the pain. A sharp, white heat across my cheek, easing a startled cry from my lips. I slapped a hand over the cut to stifle the spill of blood, grimacing as the bones in my knuckles writhed beneath my skin.

Power unfurled.

It started as a flare of light behind my eyes, warmth spreading through my veins for the first time in months. The tension in my body eased. All at once, I felt awake and angry and *alive*.

And it terrified me.

The trickle of blood staining my fingers wasn't enough. Invigorated by the pain he'd caused me, the man lumbered forward, gripping his sword with both hands.

The anger in his eyes told me plenty—he wanted me dead. Justice for his son's death. Yet I didn't have anywhere to go, pressed up against the bow of the ship, tangled in the coils of rope around my legs. And though warmth rushed through my body, quick as lightning and just as hot, I wasn't sure I had the strength to fight back, even if I wanted to.

It was strangely quiet on deck, as though no one wanted to bring attention to what was happening. Because they wanted it to happen. They wanted my blood to spill for all that I had helped to spill.

I wasn't scared anymore. There had been a time when I'd been afraid of what came after, unsure of what waited on the other side of the Dunes of Forever. I had always been meant to save souls from seeing that side, but after the Blood Moon, after I'd become part of Death's dark shores, I wasn't scared to face it anymore. Deep down, I was sure I deserved it.

Light flashed as his sword came down again. Before it landed, a figure slipped in front of me, catching the man's wrist with a grunt. Startled, the older man strained, teeth gritted, but the younger man was stronger. From what I could see in the brief seconds it took him to disarm the older man, he didn't carry a weapon. Which meant he wasn't a soldier. He simply pinched the fragile bones in the other man's wrist and let the sword clatter to the deck boards.

"Councillor." The man growled the title like it was a curse.

I watched them, trying to place the young man's face among Evhen's councillors, but I was sure I hadn't seen him before.

"Princess Kalei is our guest," he told the older man, a threat lacing every word. My stomach turned at the honorific—*Princess of Death*, he seemed to be saying instead. That's what I heard whenever someone still called me *Princess*. I wanted to put that part of myself as far in the past as possible. And I couldn't do that with them reminding me at every turn.

"None of the men here would agree with that," the older man said, shooting me a glare. "She's an abomination."

The same word so many others had used to describe me.

"Is that right?" The councillor looked around at the gathered audience. "Her Majesty allowed Princess Kalei to come aboard. Do you also disagree with her?"

The crowd shuffled uncomfortably, silent. I wanted to scoff at the fear that clung to them like fog.

"That's what I thought," the councillor mumbled, frowning at the group. "If anyone else raises a hand or a sword against the princess, I will personally escort them off the plank. As for you," he added, turning to face the older man once more, "the brig will be your new home until we reach our destination."

The man blanched, fumbling for an excuse or an argument, even as the councillor called for a security officer to bring him below deck. The commotion finally caught Evhen's attention on the other side of the deck, and I felt the heat of her gaze even at a distance. When I raised my head to her, fury sparked off her like leaping embers.

The crowd dispersed at a snapped word from the councillor. As Evhen slowly made her way across the deck, frowning so hard I thought she would crack like stone, the young man offered a hand and helped me up.

I kept my palm pressed firmly against my cheek, afraid that if I let the blood flow freely, the bones in my skin would react in a way I wouldn't be able to control. That brief flare of magic, of power, of something *new* scared me.

I wasn't supposed to have magic anymore. But I wanted it. I couldn't deny that, even as I shoved down the power. They may see me as a monster, but I didn't want to hurt anyone else.

The young councillor had soft grey eyes that reminded me of the sea just before a storm. Cloudy, but still calm. He seemed almost too young to be a council member, maybe a year or two older than Evhen, and I suspected she had chosen him personally.

"Do you want the physician to look at that?" he asked, nodding to my cheek. My hand trembled, not from the shock of the cut or the cold that had replaced its heat, but from the reaction of the bones as blood slicked my skin.

"No," I croaked, turning away before Evhen got too close.

If she touched me, if she asked me how I was, I didn't know what would happen. My emotions were in turmoil after what she'd said yesterday. She wanted to push me away, to make her decision easier. And if I couldn't control this magic any more than I could control my emotions, I could hurt her as well.

"Thank you," I added, trailing off when I realized I didn't know his name. My heart thudded with tangled worry.

"Akev," he provided with a crooked grin that reminded me suddenly of another young boy with dark hair and kind eyes. My stomach flipped as I lurched away from him. I needed to get away.

Evhen reached for my arm as I passed on my way off the deck, but I spun out of her grip, shouldering through disgruntled crew members to the passageway.

The door to my room shut with a rattling click, and I pressed my back against the frame, drawing my hand down from my face. Black blood smeared across my palm. Fresh air bit into the cut on my cheek. Pain blossomed in my chest, and I pinched my eyes shut, unable to hold in my scream. It filled the cramped chamber and seeped up through the floorboards above.

When I opened my eyes, a strange sight greeted me across the small space. Embedded into the wall around the porthole were a dozen shards of bone. And as I watched, they wiggled out of the wood and shot back into my skin.

The pain I expected didn't follow.

Instead, it felt like a relief.

It felt right.

NINE

Kalei hadn't wanted me to see, but as she'd passed, I'd caught a glimpse of black blood oozing between her fingers. The sight had frightened me more than the enraged scream that tore through the ship mere moments later. My feet remained firmly planted in the middle of the deck, heart thudding a painful drumbeat. I barely noticed Akev calling my name until he was standing right in front of me.

I blinked rapidly to bring my focus back to him.

"What was that?" I asked. My voice didn't sound like my own. It sounded like it belonged to a scared child, the same child who had seen a monster cut out her parents' hearts. The same child who had fled such frightening situations, only to find herself deeply entrenched in a new kind of horror. In the form of a frail girl with black blood and angry eyes.

"Some of the crew seem to think it was a bad idea to bring Princess Kalei aboard," he said, hands folded behind his back. He narrowed his eyes at some of the men I'd seen gathered around Kalei. "I've reminded them that the princess is our guest, and any action against her is a direct action against you."

Nerves fluttered in my stomach. We were barely a day out from Vodaeard, and already the crew was acting mutinous.

Against Kalei, no less.

I shouldn't have expected any different. The hostility of my people was everywhere—why did I think this ship would be better?

"Is she all right?" I asked, throat tight.

Akev pinned me with a heavy stare. There was no judgement in his eyes, which I was thankful for, but it seemed as though he was resting yet another crown of responsibility atop my head. If I couldn't figure out how to control this crew, I'd collapse under its weight.

"She didn't sound okay," he answered.

There was no denying the scream had been hers, and I was already familiar enough with the sound to know. My only concern was that it didn't sound like she was in pain.

This was anger, ripped from a deep well of rage that wouldn't be empty until the entire world burned. I knew that rage. I'd once felt the same—I could have decimated nations with my fury when my only goal was revenge on her father. But somewhere along the way, she had shown me that anger wasn't the motivation I'd thought it was to save the world. Anger wouldn't bring my parents back. Anger wouldn't bring my brother back.

But anger had brought her power. It had shown her what she was truly capable of. She had raised an army of bones to bring down the greatest city on the continent, all because she was angry. She had almost lost herself to her rage then, a chokehold of power she couldn't claw herself out of. That was the first time Kalei had truly frightened me.

And now I worried she was slipping back into that all-too-familiar emotion. I had made peace with my own anger, but did Kalei understand its consequences? Would she be able to stop herself?

"What should I do about them?" I asked before remembering Akev wasn't Talen. Here, he was a member of my war council. Back home, the council that guided me through this uncertain transition into queendom. He wasn't my advisor when it came to personal matters, but if I made rash decisions here, it would affect everyone. I needed someone to tell me what was right and what wasn't, because nothing had felt right in months.

"Your other council members would probably advise you against a display of power," he murmured, casting a cursory glance around the deck. At the helm, Eiramis's watchful gaze was tacked to my back.

I wondered what he would suggest—if his views on these political games were as closely aligned with mine as Akev's were. But Eiramis was a sailor, not a politician. It wouldn't be appropriate to ask someone who hadn't grown up in court. Which, maybe, was why the other councillors didn't like Akev's position among them.

"But," he added, "I think that's exactly what this crew needs to see. They're angry. They want justice."

I scoffed. Revenge wasn't justice, and Kalei didn't deserve it.

Akev went on, "And most of them won't stop until you do something about it. Show them you are a queen not to be crossed."

I had said something similar to Kalei less than a day after meeting her when I threatened to throw her moonstone overboard if she angered me. Back then, I had kept her in line with fear. Not respect. Was it wrong to use that again now? To lead through fear?

But his words reminded me of what today was. Coronation day. They had already been planning it when Chief Mikala's letter arrived. Maybe I didn't have to strike fear into this crew. Maybe I just had to put a crown on my head at last.

I met his gaze. "Do you know what the requirements are to make a coronation official?" There were rules to follow. Certain people had to be present. I'd left all that planning for my council. All I knew was that I had to stand there and say some words.

"No, but I can find out," he replied, brows drawn together. "You want to go through with it here?"

It wasn't ideal. But if we had the right people, the right arrangements, it could work. The title of *Captain* didn't mean anything anymore. I had to accept the one my parents had left for me.

I had to become the queen they needed me to be.

As Akev went to convene the council, I went down to the brig. Anger thrummed in my fingertips, a steady pulse that beat in time with my heart. It was comfortable, familiar. Down here, I didn't have to worry about wearing a mask and playing a role. Until that crown sat on my head, I was still just Evhen, and Evhen let her anger guide her.

I had asked Icana for a knife. She'd been sitting at the helm with Eiramis, keen gaze watching him for any small mistake. She didn't question me when I slipped the thin blade into my sleeve, though Eirmais had opened his mouth to make a comment when Icana shot him a dark glare. Something strange glinted in his eyes then. Admiration. Towards my weapons master. I'd left them as quickly as I had approached, made uncomfortable by the stirring emotion.

Now, in the fuse-scented gloom, I let the knife fall into my hand. It fit my palm perfectly. The thin tip gleamed wickedly in the swaying lantern light.

The brig wasn't a comfortable place. It was cramped, with narrow cells huddled in the middle of the room and iron bars bolted into the ceiling and floor. The locks rattled with each rise and fall of the ship. Shadows leapt up the walls, the corners melting into the darkness behind crates and chests. To anyone else, it might have looked like a proper holding space, but I knew the cells were new. I had asked for them to be installed specifically for a situation like this. And since only one of them was occupied, it was easy to tell who the instigator was.

The man looked up when he heard my boots on the boards. Fear flashed in his eyes for a brief moment before he lumbered to his feet and offered a short bow.

"Your Highness," he grumbled. His voice was hoarse from years of toiling on ships, calling out to deckhands and dock workers. Sun-roughened skin stretched over his otherwise feeble frame, but I suspected there was muscle hiding beneath. Sailors like him had to be strong, but the years had whittled him down. Maybe that was where the anger in his eyes came from. Knowing he was that much closer to retirement—to death—than to the prosperity of his youth.

"It's 'Your Majesty', actually," I reminded him.

He didn't say anything, coughing into the crook of his elbow. There was a rattle in his chest that I'd heard in many of the fishermen. They all suffered from the same disease that plagued their lungs due to the constant rain and salt. My parents had done all they could to lengthen their lives, had given them the medicines they needed to survive the harsh climate. But now my parents were dead, and that responsibility fell to me. Vodaeard relied on our fisheries and our fishermen. This was just another reminder of all the things I'd unexpectedly inherited when my parents died.

But in this moment, I didn't care what he suffered from. His actions against Kalei would not be tolerated.

"Princess Kalei is under my protection," I told him, holding his watery gaze until it wavered. "I assume Councillor Akev warned you about the implications of hurting her?"

His throat bobbed as he swallowed.

"Any action against her is an action against me," I continued. "Any disagreement with her is a disagreement with me."

"She killed my son," he argued, voice rising despite the eerie quietness around us. Only the rush of lantern flames could be heard over the slap of waves against the hull. Men like him thought they needed to shout to be heard, but I had learned long ago that lowering my voice was even more effective.

"We all lost someone that day." I tipped my chin down so my face fell into shadows. "Your pain is not any worse than mine. But that doesn't give you the right to attack anyone."

Red crawled up his neck in furious splotches. "She doesn't belong here. She doesn't belong anywhere."

Sadness pulled at my stomach, seeping through my veins from a place of anguish that had followed me for weeks. A few months ago, I had said the same thing. Kalei's power didn't belong in this world, but that didn't mean she had to be denied a place, too. Now that I had let her into my life, I was hearing the same declarations over and over again. No one understood her.

No one wanted to.

This man was no different.

Quick as lightning, I reached through the bars and fisted a hand in his collar, pulling his face flush against the iron with a dull thud. He yelped when I pressed the thin knife to his cheek, eyes wide in terror.

"Wh-what are you doing?" he exclaimed, writhing weakly.

In one swift motion, before I could rethink, I sliced a line in his face from ear to mouth.

The sound that came out of him was deliciously satisfying, igniting a spark in me that hadn't known retribution in a long time.

I stepped back before his blood could stain my sleeve

"Reminding you what happens when you hurt my princess," I replied with a low hiss. "I am your queen, and anything you do to her, I will have done to you. A cut for a cut." I grinned, all teeth. "You're welcome, by the way."

"For what?" he croaked, poking the skin around the cut. It was a clean line. He'd have a scar, but no permanent damage. Icana had taught me well enough.

My lip curled, and he paled visibly beneath the stream of blood. Fear had quickly replaced his false bravado.

"For not throwing you overboard to swim with the sirens," I said. My heel dug a groove into the wood as I spun around to leave.

The gloom of the brig was almost behind me when his voice slithered through the shadows.

"You bear their faces and wear their clothes, but you will never be like them."

The hallway ahead of me tunnelled as my vision blurred. An emotion I knew all too well tightened like a band over my chest, but with every strangled breath, it felt like I was drowning all over again. How dare he mention my parents?

My fingers clenched the blade's hilt so tight I felt the cold press of it in my palm. My other hand braced against the door frame as the ship rocked. I grounded myself in the sensations on my skin, the leather and steel and wood beneath my callouses, because if I let myself rise to his bait, I wouldn't leave this room as a queen.

CROWNS OF BLOOD AND SALT

I'd leave as a murderer.

"You'll never be my queen," his insidious voice brushed against my ears, carrying with it all the whispers of doubt that had followed me since I was old enough to understand a future with a crown.

My eyes slid shut. Red burned behind my eyelids—red for my rage, red for his blood, red for the flames I wanted to set against this ship and everyone on it. I was already turning before I realized it, but movement down the hallway caught my attention, and I froze as Breva appeared on the stairs, illuminated by the early winter sun.

Her eyes glistened in the swaying torchlight. She climbed down the stairs with slightly more hesitation than a moment ago, eyeing first my face, then the blade still held firm in my grasp.

"Your Majesty?" It was a question wrapped in a pretty package, uncertainty in the title. She peered around me into the brig.

All the tension bunched in my shoulders bled out of me. I slipped the thin knife into my sleeve before her gaze could find it again. Before she looked too closely and saw the thin line of red on the steel.

"What is it?" I asked, pressing a knuckle into the space between my brows. My father's signet ring bumped against my forehead, its weight as heavy as any crown, but a solid reminder that I had come too far to let one man's doubts make me a monster.

Those doubts were always going to follow me. If I was going to become a monster, it was because another man wanted my family dead, and I wanted retribution. I wanted safety. I wanted freedom. Those things would only come when I took them.

Breva folded her hands in front of her. "The council is ready for you," she said. "They've agreed to your request."

It took me a moment to realize what she meant, and then the breath stuck in my throat as understanding crashed on top of me. The coronation. They were going to go through with it. I had asked for this after avoiding it for so long, but now it came with a whole slew of new things to learn. A queen would know when to rein in her anger. A queen wouldn't do what I'd just done to that man.

KAY ADAMS

But maybe that was exactly the queen I wanted to be. One who wasn't afraid to get her hands bloody.

I didn't need to earn my crown.

I needed to take it.

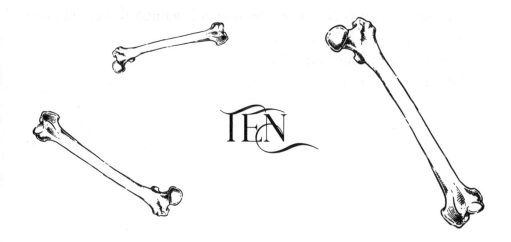

TEN

A hesitant knock came at my door as the sky outside my window turned grey with dusk. They'd been standing in the hallway long enough for me to sense their hesitation, the pale shadow of feet visible beneath the door, but I had chosen to ignore them until they decided to knock. When they did, I finally sat up and crossed the room. The bones had changed positions, and now pieces bit into the blackened skin of my right palm. They brushed painfully against the wood as I pulled the door open to reveal the young councillor whose name I had already forgotten. When he'd said it, all I could hear was a trilling buzz like a swarm of bees in my head, blood rushing to answer a new kind of magic.

Magic that terrified me.

Magic that thrilled me.

"Councillor," I said, blinking in surprise before slipping my features into a calm mask. My hands fidgeted, unsure of the proper etiquette for greeting a council member, so I gave him a short bow that felt disingenuous and awkward.

"Akev is fine," he said, looking just as awkward at receiving my bow as I'd been giving it. "That's really not necessary. If anything, I should be bowing to you, Princess."

"Please don't." My voice was strained, the thought of him bowing sinking uncomfortably in the pit of my stomach. "Just…call me Kalei."

I must have looked desperate enough—broken enough—because his gaze softened, and he nodded. An inexplicable sense of relief shot through me, and I felt myself relax. Evhen had always been deserving of her kingdom, but when I'd learned the truth about my parents' war, I didn't believe I was worthy of their throne, and the title of Princess carried too much pain with it. The Princess of Death had died that day on the beach, and I didn't know who I was supposed to be in the aftermath.

"Okay," he said quietly, testing my name in silence. Something about his demeanour, about his soft eyes and kind smile, made me want to trust him. Or at least befriend him. He seemed like the sort of person whose opinions Evhen valued, and I desperately needed someone on this ship who didn't want to murder me. There was no darkness surrounding Akev, no tumultuous thoughts that threatened to sweep me away to the dark depths, only a gentleness that he shared with everyone around him.

He grinned, seeming to remember why he'd come, his previous awkwardness forgotten. Had he been nervous to talk to me? Or had he been scared? No doubt they had heard my scream, but had any of them come close enough to hear my cries? Hopefully, he was enough like Evhen to look past the shards of bone to the blood beneath.

"Her Majesty requests your presence on deck," he said. Firelight from the hearth behind me sparked in his eyes, illuminating an emotion I almost didn't recognize—pride. Ever since that day on the beach, people had been walking around Evhen as if on eggshells. Or hot coals. Likely to be burned if they said or did the wrong thing. They were hesitant and uncertain around her.

So what could she have possibly done to earn Akev's pride?

"What for?" I asked, brows pinched.

A private grin tugged at the corner of his mouth. "A...celebration," he said cryptically. Evasively.

Chills snaked over my skin despite the heat of the fire at my back, aggravating the displaced bones. I had almost gotten used to their previous positions, moving deliberately so I wouldn't upset them, but their new spots in my skin were sore. They twitched with every new sensation that hit my body, including the icy dread that crept up from a hollow well inside me. What kind of celebration could Evhen possibly be planning, here of all places?

And why now?

Akev didn't seem to notice my discomfort. "She says there are dresses in your trunk," he added, jutting his chin towards the heavy chest in the centre of my room. I hadn't moved it, hadn't opened it, since the deckhand dropped it off yesterday.

Now I eyed it with trepidation. Why hadn't Evhen come down to deliver this message herself? What was she celebrating?

"She wants to start in thirty minutes," Akev said before departing, leaving me to shut myself in with a chest full of clothes someone else had packed.

Enough for the return journey. Because I hadn't planned on coming back, and neither did she, so she had given me what she didn't need anymore.

In a fit of rage, I tore apart every dress in that damned-to-the-depths chest.

When I was done, I sank to the floor, gasping for breath. A stitch formed in my side, sharply pulsing against the extra bone in my rib cage. I had been strong once—running barefoot across the golden beaches back home, climbing trees to knock down the coconuts for my morning coffee, racing up and down my lighthouse with fresh air filling my lungs. Now, every small movement seemed to steal my breath.

Minutes later, I clothed myself in the closest thing to mourning attire I could find—a billowing black shirt with a lacy collar tucked into snug black pants. There were no embellishments, no embroidery, nothing to denote that these clothes were designed for royalty.

Before leaving, I pulled my shawl from its hiding place beneath my pillow, slipped it over my shoulders, and then climbed out of the bowels of the ship.

Dusk had embraced the sky with swaths of indigo and navy when I emerged onto the crowded deck. Every sailor, soldier, and steward was crammed between the bow and the aft, chatting animatedly with one other. An infectious excitement ran through them like forked lightning, but I had become immune to any kind of joy. This wasn't the place for it. This wasn't the time for it.

I slipped through the packed bodies without being noticed, weaving under jabbing elbows and bulging arms towards the direction everyone was facing, and then suddenly I was at the front of the crowd and silence fell as I beheld Evhen on the quarterdeck, surrounded by her council members.

One of them held a crown.

All the air rushed out of me in a hiss that was drowned out by the sound of the ship cutting through the waves. Sails snapped in the breeze overhead, each flap like the wail of lost souls in my mind. This felt just as wrong as seeing her in the depths, but I couldn't push her out now. Akev had been proud, which meant Evhen had made this decision herself. I frowned, ill-boding rolling through my stomach..

She had just told me, not two days ago, that she wouldn't take her crown until her brother was back home.

What had changed?

When her gaze landed on me, it burned. Once, I had seen her across a vast ballroom, and time had slowed to a stillness until there was only us. I had thought there was no one else's stare I craved more. She had been the first person to see me, really see me, and even when the truth had tumbled out, I knew she had changed her mind about killing me.

But now, her gaze bore into me with the intensity of a volcano.

Her brows pulled together in the middle as she took in my outfit, lips parting slightly as if she wanted to ask a question. I had made myself a stain in her life, on her celebration, while she glowed like the rising sun over an endless ocean. A velvet dress dyed crimson—like blood, like rage—fell from her shoulders to the deck. Gold embroidery swirled up the skirt in the shape of leaping flames, adding to the illusion that she was a fiery sunset on the sea.

Her hair was longer than I'd ever seen it, tumbling in waves down her back. Gems sparkled in the wild strands. A pendant hung from her neck, a circular disc resting against her collarbone—even from below, I could see her family's crest engraved in the metal. A key haloed by a sunburst. It matched the scar on her shoulder from when I had shot her with a crossbow bolt. She looked like the kind of person who could command the very sea to her will.

Her sharp gaze, hot as molten gold, snapped to the cut on my cheek. I had cleaned it as best I could, but I wasn't going to hide it behind a bandage. There was fury on her face as she shut her jaw, and I realized with sickening dread why she was doing this. Someone on her crew had attacked me, undermining her authority. She was doing what she had to in order to take back control.

My heart ached for the girl I had lost in the depths, because this Evhen wasn't her. This Evhen had lied for months and had followed my father's orders. The Evhen I had known wouldn't give herself up without trying *everything* to win. She wasn't even going to try to fight my father.

She was going to give herself up as a martyr. A noble sacrifice. The ultimate display of dedication to her kingdom.

She was going to die as a queen.

Her gaze raked over my body, noting the bones that had changed positions in my skin. The black veins that crawled over my right hand into the centre of my chest, where a hole that had once housed my heart now sat empty. I tried to fill my lungs with a proper breath, mouth falling open.

One of her councillors stepped forward to address the crowd, and all I could do was stare at her. The councillor's words droned on, something about traditions and treaties and threats, but I didn't hear him over the blood rushing in my ears. Every ragged breath felt like a dagger shredding my throat. Evhen had always been deserving of her kingdom—she didn't need me to tell her that—but this didn't feel like a celebration. It felt like a funeral.

I was back in the depths, plodding towards the Dune of Forever, unable to stop walking to a death I couldn't bring myself back from. It was like a door shutting on a crypt, locking me in with the bones and bodies. With all the memories I had tried so hard to escape. A finality.

The crowd around me erupted into applause, shaking me from my thoughts and fading back into silence just as quickly, and then suddenly, I was the only person left standing. A spiky crown sat atop Evhen's head, rods of gold mimicking the sun's rays, but she didn't look at the crowd bowing to her. She looked at me, searching my face in silent wonder, holding her breath as she had that day in Xesta. As if by moving, she would break whatever spell we were under.

The calm sea turned into a storm inside of me. Vicious waves crashed against my lighthouse walls. Stone crumbled. So I did the only thing I could think of doing. I turned around and walked away.

If they had thought ill of me before, this surely made it worse. The crowd rose out of their bows as I passed, a murmur like a wave following me to the darkness of the ship's interior. I heard their vile whispers and veiled protests, but a sense of unease chased every forked word against me. The implications were clear enough—Evhen was queen now, and she would throw this whole crew into the brig if anyone threatened me again.

I stumbled into the gloom, escaping sunlight and stares and silence. My thoughts wouldn't organize, tumbling together in a frantic flurry. Everything was tinged red—Evhen's hair, Evhen's dress—and everything was wrong, so wrong, but looking at her had been right. I wanted to save her—my heart still believed that, but she had sealed her fate with that crown.

I closed my eyes in the dark, leaning my head back against a cool wood beam. The sway of the ship calmed me, made me think of the depths, the tunnel of swirling waters leading to Death's domain. If I thought hard enough, I could almost imagine it—the sprawl of black beach, the gentle hush of black water lapping the shore, the glowing souls like seaweed along the banks. And there, a crucial part of Evhen that had been left behind.

Her anger.

I tucked it inside of me and opened my eyes, delving into the belly of the ship. The anger pulled me like a thread towards a dark room, alive with shadows and the scent of despair. It was a tangy sort of smell that prickled my nose, woven through with the bitter contents of explosives. My eyes adjusted slowly. Iron bars came into view, bolted into the floor and ceiling.

"I hope you're not here for an apology," a man's voice slithered out of the darkness.

I stepped towards the cell in the middle of the room. The man who'd attacked me glowered at me from within, hostility gleaming in his beady gaze. He appeared taller than he had on the deck, but the small cell made him look more like a caged animal than a man. A scowl danced across his lips, drawing my attention to the cut on his cheek that mirrored my own.

"Did Evhen do that?" I asked, tilting my head. A calmness settled over me, knowing he couldn't hurt me from in there—knowing I had a dangerous kind of magic that I desperately wanted to reveal. How satisfying it would be to see the terror in his face, to become the monster he wanted me to be. But for now, I allowed myself to feel my anger. To accept its icy grip around my heart. Anything Evhen did to him, I'd do worse.

He didn't answer, which was answer enough. So, that was the kind of queen Evhen was going to be. A thrill jolted through me at the realization. Maybe she still had use for her anger after all.

"I'm not looking for an apology," I told him. I gauged the distance between us, how quickly he could reach through the bars and grab me before I could react, but he seemed to be doing the same. He stayed firmly planted in the centre of the cell, watching me like a bird of prey. Because a deep part of him knew I was the predator.

"Good," he snarled. "I'm not sorry for what I did. Only sorry I didn't do worse. You're an abomination." He spat at me, but there wasn't enough force behind the action.

"And you're a coward." Once, I had spared men like him. I hadn't wanted any more blood to be shed on my account. On my behalf. Now, I wanted to choose whose blood to spill and when. Starting with his. "Do you know what happens when you attack a princess?"

He scoffed, the sound grating. "You have no power here."

He had no idea just how wrong he was. Let him underestimate me. Men with more sway than him had learned the hard way just how powerful I could be.

"But Evhen does," I reminded him.

He muttered a curse. "She's not queen yet."

"Oh, isn't she? The crown she just put on her head certainly suggests otherwise."

The man paled, visibly shaken by the announcement. Whatever he had said to Evhen earlier seemed to be running through his mind once more, and—perhaps cruelly—I hoped he was coming to the conclusion that he had crossed the wrong girls.

"You're lying," he finally said, as though the word of a monster didn't count as truth. As fact.

And I knew from experience it rarely did.

Still, I narrowed my eyes at his accusation. My finger brushed the bars. A hollow *tap tap tap* filled the air as a shard of bone in my fingertip hit each piece of iron like a methodical clock.

The sound made him wince and flinch back when he realized what was causing it.

"Why would I lie about something like that to a nobody like you?" I mused. "You wouldn't believe a word I say. But I don't even have to hurt you. You'll rot down here. Perhaps you'll die before we reach land, and you can meet your son in the depths."

"You bitch!" He lunged for the bars, swiping at me, but the moment I'd thought the words, I'd anticipated his reaction. What I'd said was cruel, but I was tired of holding my tongue when the world deserved its lashing.

I stepped out of the way of his reaching fingers. He pulled back and moved to the corner of the cage to try again, but it gave me enough time to draw my blade from my boot. Icana had given me the small knife just this morning when I had asked her for a weapon, and though she hadn't wondered why, I figured she knew it was for my own safety in the days to come. When the man grasped for me, I caught his wrist and slammed the blade upward through his forearm, past muscle and bone.

He howled, writhing, curses flying from his mouth like spittle. Hot blood poured from the wound down the hilt of my weapon, and I didn't pull back when it coated my hand. The warmth spread over my hand, over the bones embedded in my skin, and I expected the flare of power, like light, behind my eyes. When it didn't come, when the bones remained firmly set, I let a chilling smile spread across my face.

"Careful," I whispered. He stopped squirming at the warning laced in that one word. "A little to the side, and I slice something vital, and then you won't live to see just how powerful I am."

"Kal?"

A voice like honey wafted through the darkness.

ELEVEN

I hadn't been able to focus on Haret's words during my coronation. When Kalei stepped to the front of the crowd, everything narrowed to that single point. Seeing her in that black outfit reminded me of another time, when she appeared at the top of a gilded staircase donned in a dress like the night sky. I had lost my breath then, and I'd lost it again

There was so much I wanted to say to her in that moment, but then Breva placed the crown on my head, and I said the words they recited, and it was over. Kalei had stared at me the entire time like I was a wild animal on display in a glass cage. Trapped. A victim to tradition. An uncomfortable sense of dread had fallen into the pit of my stomach and grown roots out of my feet into the deck, but I didn't regret the weight that sat on my head. I'd spent too long running away from it to turn back now.

When Kalei had fled—like she couldn't get out of there fast enough—I'd forced a smile to my lips and announced myself as their new queen. Their rightful queen. My parents' legacy was heavier than the moulded piece of metal tangled in my hair, but I was going to make it work.

I had to. The fate of my kingdom depended on it.

It hadn't been easy to follow her, and without Talen to help me navigate all the politeness of this newfound position, I'd felt lost as I weaved through the crowd. Everyone wanted to greet and congratulate me, tell me how excited they were to have me as their queen, but it all rang as disingenuous. For most of my life, I'd heard the same thing—no one wanted me to be queen. It was a hard thing to hear as a child, that no one wanted me, but back then, it had felt like a needless worry. Now, it was reality, and their false niceness stung when I turned my back. Because that was when they whispered. That was when they said all the vile things they'd never say to my face. I'd seen it in Xesta.

So I wasn't surprised it was happening on my own ship.

Akev had followed me into the belly of the ship—I had already declared him as my new chief advisor, and the council couldn't do a damned thing about it—when I heard Kalei's voice, low and smooth, floating out of the darkness in the direction of the brig. I followed it like it was a line cast into a raging sea until I stood in the doorway to the brig and watched Kalei stab the man through his arm.

Akev made a small noise in the back of his throat.

Fear ricocheted through me—fear that she'd kill the man, fear that I'd finally, truly lost her—but when I called her name, she froze. I would be forever drawn to her, my bones calling out to her like a thing to be worshipped, but my course was set, and I wasn't bringing her along. I wasn't going to let her destroy herself to save me this time. Even though she seemed determined to.

Breathing evenly through the panic clawing at my chest, I stepped into the room until I could see her eyes, my hands outstretched like she was a startled animal.

She didn't take her gaze off the man in front of her, though his attention slid to me, noting the crown on my head.

"Call for the physician," I said to Akev, and he hurried down the hallway. I turned to Kalei again, angling my body in a way that wasn't threatening, but I knew she had already taken stock of the ceremonial sword at my hip. "Kalei, let go of him."

"Traitors," she hissed the word, earning a grimace from the man whose life was one wrong twitch away from ending, "like him should be hanged, not imprisoned."

"Then hang *me*!" I exclaimed, an ache blossoming in my chest. Grief was familiar. Anger was familiar. Heartache wasn't. I didn't know how else to navigate this new emotion.

She turned her head to look at me. Confusion flitted across her face in fractured bursts.

"You saw the letters," I reminded her, guilt gnawing at my ribs. "You know what I did to keep my kingdom safe from *your* father. Don't be like him now."

Please don't be like him.

Her eyes jumped to the tip of the blade protruding from the man's arm, as if seeing it for the first time. Blood pulsed from the underside, running down her arm in rivulets. The mourning shawl soaked up most of it, but there was a steadily spreading pool at her feet. It was a long, thin blade like the one Icana had given me, easily tucked away in boots or sleeves, not likely to cause much damage. But Kalei was smart when it came to the body. I didn't doubt that she knew exactly where to slice to sever something vital. A death on the ship so soon after my coronation would not be a good look.

I hadn't been afraid to kill him earlier, but I knew what kind of person I was. Kalei wasn't the sort to kill out of anger. She had given her people a choice on the beach—to lay down their swords and live—but she had cried with every new death when they refused. The Kalei in front of me was frightening because if I stared too long, I saw myself.

And I didn't like that. I didn't want her to become that.

"Kal," I said again, desperation leeching into my voice.

Her fingers clenched around the man's wrist, but the hand on her blade was steady. "Stop saying my name like that!"

"Like what?" I heard the childish hurt in my voice, but it was like I was watching this unfold from far outside of my body. I was thrown back to a time that seemed so long ago when I had mockingly called her *Princess* with loathing in every breath, hate for her carved into my very being. When she had told me her name, crossing some invisible line I hadn't realized I'd drawn, I'd thought it was the most beautiful sound. I couldn't stop saying it.

"Like you know me."

"I *do* know you." Carefully, I took a step forward. When she didn't move, I took another. "I know you like coconut in your coffee. I know you like poison berries and guitar and reading—*seas*, you love to read. I know you love your island fiercely, and I know you find joy in the small things—beating Icana at card games, dipping your toes in the ocean, watching the sunrise from the tallest window, counting how many different birds you can hear, collecting seashells along the beach because you want it to be a place of happiness again. I know you don't want to hurt people. I know that you're a good person."

A tear slipped down her cheek, bright in the torchlight, though her face contorted in anger.

"Maybe I don't want to be a good person anymore," she said, teeth gritted. "Maybe they deserve to feel my pain."

"Maybe they do," I said quietly. Her gaze flickered to me, and she didn't pull back when I wrapped my fingers over her arm. "But not like this. I can't protect you if you murder him."

An unnerving smile cracked over her lips. I wanted to recoil from it, to shrink away from the darkness it revealed, but I remained where I was.

"I have my own protection," she said.

I didn't have a chance to ask her what she meant. At that moment, Akev returned with the physician, and Kalei let go of both her blade and the man's arm and moved aside to let them attend him. She locked eyes with me, blue like the hottest flames, and seemed to say, *There, I spared him.*

"You two are perfect for each other," the man snarled, obscured by the physician. "You're both horrible people."

I sighed, long and hard. "Your death can still look like an accident."

Akev snorted—I was glad he didn't admonish me as the rest of my council would have—and the physician dutifully ignored me.

The prisoner didn't say another word, and I followed Kalei out of the brig.

She moved quickly through the hall as if she couldn't escape me fast enough, and even with the distance growing, I felt like the space was suddenly too cramped. Her shawl flitted behind her, a shadow, a ghost, and it was the only tether I could follow. I caught up to her at the door to her cabin, where she whirled to face me, blue eyes blazing.

"I won't apologize for it," she spat, the force of her words bringing me to an abrupt halt.

"I don't want an apology," I replied. Rimmed by the darkness of her cabin, she looked almost like the creature I'd seen the day I died. If only the shadows coalesced into wings behind her.

"Then what do you want?" The way she said it sounded more like, *Why are you here?*

Why are you chasing me?

What are you running away from?

And the truth was I didn't know anymore. I had been chasing Kalei, and now I pushed her away. I had been running away from my crown, and now I wore it. Pieces of me had been lost to the sea, and I couldn't scavenge them together to make a picture of the Evhen I used to be. My heart would never stop loving her—my soul would search for hers in the Endless Seas or her dark depths or wherever we all went when we died—but I had done unforgivable things. She was right to hate me. I just needed to know how to make *her* stop chasing *me*.

At my silence, she sank onto the bed and looked up at me with a broken stare. Like waves on a rocky shore, a mix of emotions crashed behind her eyes. Love, hate, anger, remorse. All combined to create a fractured picture of agony on her face.

"What do you want, Ev?" she repeated, voice flat. "Because clearly you don't want me to save you."

"How were you going to save me, Kal?" I asked, nails biting into my palm to keep my frustration down. I was tired of being treated like someone who needed saving. "You don't have magic anymore."

"I do!" she cried, spreading her hands open on her lap. The chips of bone stood out against her darker skin. "It's new and scary, but it's something. I can help! We can fight. You don't have to surrender. You don't have to give up."

I shook my head, not wanting to hear her pleas. "You weren't supposed to be here, Kal. You were never supposed to know."

"Then you should have kept better care of your secrets," she spat, and I saw the flash of anger in her stormy eyes. "Better yet, you should have trusted me. Or does *all of you* mean nothing when you've already made up your mind about dying?"

The words I had spoken to her on the beach. Her bones, her darkness, her borrowed time. Everything that she was. But even this new magic might not be powerful enough to stop her immortal father, and I didn't want to see her try on my account.

So I clamped my teeth together. She was angry. Good. It was easier that way.

I straightened my back, turning for the door again. This was ending one way or another.

"If you wanted a goodbye, this is it."

She exhaled shakily. The sound brought my head up and drew me back to her like a thread pulled too tight. Her eyes lifted to me once more. For the first time tonight, they were clear. Like a mirror into my own pain. And it scared me, because I knew how to handle my pain, but I didn't know how to handle Kalei's.

"I don't want a goodbye," she said softly. "I want you, Evhen. And I'm going to do whatever it takes to keep you alive."

My heart stuttered. It was a promise and a threat. And I finally understood the princess.

My pain was self-destructive.

Hers was world-ending.

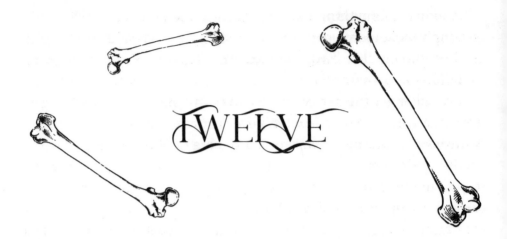

TWELVE

On the fourth day of sailing, there was a change in the air. Two days passed by without incident. For the most part, the crew ignored me, though I wasn't sure if that was Evhen's doing or my own. And just as well—there was a living, electrifying energy running through my veins that demanded release, and I wouldn't be able to contain it if anyone tried to approach me.

The bones needed to move again, and I felt sick trying to hold them back. Until the wind turned cold and the waves turned choppy. Then I simply felt sick.

Fingers clenched around the railing at the bow, I inhaled deeply to ease the current of bile threatening to fill my throat. Frigid air pricked my lungs, signalling an early change in the seasons—or a change in our geography.

There were no maps for me to pore over here, except for the one Evhen kept in her quarters, so I had to rely on what little I understood about directions to figure out we were headed much more north than anticipated, where snow and ice and darkness lurked.

This kind of cold was unfamiliar, stabbing through skin and bone, but I barely felt it. I was so used to the cold at this point that it didn't affect me. If anything, it eased the need for release coursing through my veins.

It chilled the hot rage that had settled in my heart.

It didn't do anything to calm the way my stomach lurched with the ship's movements over the crashing waves. Icy bits of sea spray needled into my face, and I choked, clamping my teeth tight together.

I didn't know what Evhen found so appealing about the sea.

I couldn't get the image of her out of my head. The look she gave me when I held that traitor's life in my hand. As if I had somehow betrayed her. Maybe I had crossed a line, but I would never betray her like that. She just didn't know what to do with her newfound responsibility, that damned crown on her head. She didn't know how to ask for help. With me, she'd never had to. I had been there when the darkness came. I had pushed her out of the darkness, and I would continue to do it until my dying breath.

Sighing, I dropped my head to the railing and closed my eyes. Behind me, the sounds of sparring filled the air. The soldiers had found that the easiest way to pass the time was to train, and the crew cheered them on, placing bets for every new match. As the clang of swords and grunts of pain drifted across the deck, my thoughts wandered to strategy. To a time when I'd felt so young and naive. When I didn't understand anything about the world beyond my lighthouse. When I'd held a blade in defence for the first time in my life and used every technique I'd only read about to fend off my attackers. It hadn't been strategic. It'd been desperation. But I knew different things now. I knew how to look for someone's weaknesses, their tells before they struck.

A weapon clattered across the deck boards in my direction. I cracked open one eye to see a spear resting against the wall a few feet away. When I straightened, the clamour of the crowd fell silent. They waited, breath held, to see what I would do.

Sunlight sparked off the weapon. It would be so easy to pick it up and hurl it through the closest person. Or to ask them to let me spar with it. Or to toss it overboard. So many options presented themselves, but none of them felt right. Not a single soldier among them would give me a chance to even get close to it before they put their own weapons through me.

I didn't need a spear or a sword to bring them to their knees. I just needed a drop of blood. And then my bones would find their marks.

Someone moved into my periphery, and it was enough of a distraction for the soldier to dart across the deck and retrieve his fallen weapon. Feigning disinterest in their sparring match, I turned to see one of Evhen's councillors hovering at my elbow. The man who had officiated her coronation. He had a balding head and a rather distrustful air about him.

"Princess," he said blandly, dipping his chin in the slightest approximation of a bow.

I didn't say anything, having learned from Akev that a reciprocal bow was not necessary for a councillor. My lack of a greeting seemed to frustrate him, though, and he cleared his throat to hide the disgruntled downturn of his mouth.

"Are you well?" the man asked, tilting his head to study me.

I wasn't sure if he meant my stomach or my heart, neither of which were *well*. "The sea doesn't agree with me," I finally replied.

"Nor I," he said. "I am much more suited to earth under my feet." A dark gaze pinned me beneath heavy brows. "And you are much more suited to your island, are you not?"

My teeth clicked together. Instead of a sense of alarm, though, annoyance flitted through me. This man was one of Evhen's councillors, and this sounded very much like a disagreement with her decision to let me stay on board. She had made it clear that no one was to harm me, though to what end, I didn't know anymore. Not after the words she'd spoken in my cabin. *If you want a goodbye, this is it.*

"Why do you think that?" I asked. I didn't have any connections to my island anymore. No matter if her councillor thought I should be there instead of here.

He smiled. There was no malice behind the action, but it wasn't pleasant either. "You are a solitary creature, Princess. That much is evident. Her Highness needs people around her who are not actively trying to contain her in a solitary life. She has much larger concerns than being able to give you a life in Vodaeard. Especially when you'd rather live out your days alone."

A tightness spread through my stomach, all sickness forgotten with his speech. He wasn't wrong, but something he'd said worried me much more than the subtle threat woven through his words.

"Her Majesty," I corrected, the word breaking over my lips. Everyone knew that. He had been the one to make that official.

"Of course," he said pleasantly. "Forgive my blunder. It's all so new still. But surely you can see my meaning. As queen, she has a whole kingdom to take care of. She can't waste time on someone who doesn't want it."

I sighed inwardly. Oh, how I wanted to let the bone shards fly into his skull. He wasn't frightening me the way he'd intended, which made this conversation more annoying than anything. Because I had already thought the exact same things. I had already made the decision to leave. What did he expect me to do, jump ship and swim back to Vodaeard? Hope the sirens would come to my rescue?

I nearly laughed at the idea.

Narrowing my eyes, I let a smirk curl my lips. Men like him said things like that because they were scared. He wasn't in power anymore. He had forfeited that when he crowned Evhen. So he wanted to cause discord. He wanted to plant seeds of doubt.

So I was going to scare him even more.

I leaned close to whisper in his ear. "What do you think Her Majesty would do when she heard one of her councillors was telling me to leave? Because that sounds a lot like you are disagreeing with her." He shivered as a piece of bone-studded hair brushed his cheek. "You don't scare me, Councillor. But you should watch your tongue."

When I straightened, I caught a brief glimpse of terror on his face before he masked it. He cleared his throat again and adjusted his sleeves. Sweat beaded on his forehead.

"Think about her future, Princess," he said in a low voice, turning to leave.

"I am," I growled at his back. He stiffened for a moment and then strode out of sight.

As soon as he was gone, I slammed my hands down on the railing. The bones in my palms dug grooves into the wood and tore my flesh, easing a sharp *fuck* from me. Evhen was fond of the word, and I found that I liked the feel of it on my tongue.

Pain spread across my skin as blood oozed around the bones. My vision blurred where I stared out at the icy sea. I kept my hands firmly locked around the railing, afraid that if I moved them, I'd lose control of the other bones. They writhed like maggots beneath my skin, tugging at my hair, clamouring to be free. Teeth gritted, I bent against the pain, like many needles sliding in and out, though I knew if I just let them free, I'd feel relief. The pain would lessen.

"Kal!" a raspy voice shouted from the other side of the deck, tearing my thoughts away from the pain.

I jerked away from the railing, breathing heavily, hands trembling as blood dripped in slow drops to the deck. Shards of bone protruded from the wood, stained black. A low groan built in my throat as I turned to see Icana waving at me from the passageway. Her pale eyes narrowed at the sight of blood, but before she could take a step towards me, the bones shot out of the wood and back into my skin, causing me to stumble forward. I swore again. For a moment, the ship and its surroundings went black, and then light filtered back in fragmented strokes. Icy air bit into the cuts on my palms.

I was right. It was a relief. The pain did lessen. But it was immediately followed by a wave of weakness. As though the energy it took to release the bones bled me of any strength I had left in my limbs.

Shaking, I joined Icana in the passageway, aware of the blood splattering in my wake like a path to the depths.

Before the Blood Moon, my spilled blood was a ruby path to guide me out of the depths during every Resurrection. This black blood seemed to do the opposite, showing me the way into the depths, but not a way out.

As I approached her, Icana raised a slim eyebrow. "That's new," she quipped. The rasp in her voice, the way she leaned on the serpent's head cane, was hard to ignore, and a twinge of guilt tapped against the base of my spine. I knew Icana didn't blame me for what my parents did to her in the dungeons, but it was another reminder of the hurt I had caused all the same. I nodded, flexing my fingers. The small wounds were already starting to crust over, the blood thickening before it fell. Each bit of torn flesh would soon be another scar added to my collection.

"You don't look well, Kal," Icana murmured, eyes like a sun-bleached sky scanning my face. "Your cycle?"

I shook my head, remembering how she'd helped me through that pain the last time. A clump of hair fell into my face with the movement, but I refrained from brushing it aside. I didn't want to smear blood onto the bones still nestled in the strands. "I don't get it anymore," I answered, and didn't explain anymore. It had stopped the same time the moon died. "I think it's just the sea."

"I don't think it's *just* the sea," she said wryly, twisting her mouth. Without saying anything more on the topic, she jutted her chin to the short hallway leading to Evhen's quarters. "Captain wants a word."

It was, surprisingly, such a relief to hear her say *Captain* instead of all the other titles everyone else was fond of throwing around. That was the only one that ever seemed to suit her.

I squeezed past Icana in the narrow archway and listened to the thud of her cane against the deck as she walked away. Before I could summon the courage to seek Evhen, I turned back and called out to the weapons master.

She twisted her head around, brow still quirked.

A lump formed in my throat. I swallowed thickly. "Next time I ask for a weapon," I said, warmth spreading into my cheeks, "don't give me one."

The corner of her mouth twitched up, eyes sparkling with mischief. "What did you do, Kal?" she teased.

"Nothing you wouldn't have done."

Her laughter followed me down the hall to Evhen's quarters. Whispered voices drifted out of the cracked door. A warm light seeped out.

I raised a hand to knock, but Evhen called out to me first. "Come in, Kalei."

Worry settled in my veins as I pushed the door open. Evhen sounded…exhausted wasn't the right word. Defeated, I realized, when my gaze landed on her on the other side of a massive table in the middle of the room. Deep hollows blackened her eyes. Normally, they shone with their own special light, a mosaic of sunlight caught in the facets of clear-cut gems, but now there was no light. There was no spark.

Akev stood next to her, biting a nail. A frown made his face look more like a theatre mask than that of a councillor. The ship's doctor stood at the edge of the table.

"What—" My eyes finally fell to the table, to the map spread there—and someone's severed arm. Cut at the elbow, blood still fresh. A cloth had stopped it from staining the map.

My stomach flopped. "Who—" But I already knew. A bandage, newly wrapped, covered the wound I'd given him. The man from the brig.

My eyes flew to Evhen's. "I didn't do this," I whispered. As much as I wanted to. As much as I thought he deserved it.

Evhen shook her head, silencing my protests. Strands of wild hair, curling in the heat from the fire behind her, slipped free of the crown atop her head. "I know you didn't," she said tonelessly.

Her gaze lifted from the appendage to my face, something cracking in the mask she had carefully placed over her features. "He's dead, if that wasn't obvious."

A strange sensation tugged at my core. Seeing the arm, knowing he was dead—I almost thought it was the call of the depths pulling me to seek out his soul. But that wasn't it at all. His wasn't a soul I wanted to retrieve even if I could. Instead, it was a disquieting sense of grim satisfaction. Knowing he had deserved it. Silently wishing I'd been the one to deliver.

But Evhen didn't look at me like I was the murderer. She looked at me like she was lost, like she was drowning, and I was the only person who could cast a line to save her. I'd told her as much. Maybe now she'd let me.

As a newly crowned queen, a murder on her ship—under her command—wouldn't go unnoticed. She had wanted to protect me from the backlash of that choice if I'd made it, but ultimately, the responsibility fell on her shoulders to make sure no harm came to anyone under her protection. Even the prisoners.

"Leave us," I ordered the physician.

His eyebrows shot up in surprise, and his mouth flapped open to argue, but one look at Evhen told him enough. He bowed rigidly and hurried out, shutting the door behind him.

THIRTEEN

I was glad Kalei told the doctor to leave because I didn't have the energy to give the order myself

As soon as he was gone, a sob burst out of me. I doubled over, clutching my stomach as if that could stop the well of agony from overflowing. Kalei slipped around the table and guided me to the chair behind the desk beneath the window. Her hands were slick on my clammy skin, a slimy sensation that gave me something to focus on instead of the thoughts of failure swarming like bees in my head. She knelt next to me, running a thumb over the back of my hand, smearing that curious black blood, but she didn't seem to notice, eyes rising to Akev.

"Akev," she said, drawing his attention from the severed arm. "Tea?"

How could she be so calm? But that was Kalei—a stone against the sea. Calm amid chaos. She had always been the one to silence my frantic thoughts when they got too loud.

When she wasn't looking, I stared at her. The motion of her thumb reminded me of the things I loved—the swell of the sea, the thrill of her touch. Her cheeks had lost their youthful roundness, sunken to hollows beneath icy eyes. Her mouth still quirked up in the middle, and I longed to press mine to it more than anything else.

But I couldn't. What I told her needed to be the truth.

My limbs betrayed me. I lifted a hand to cup her cheek. She jumped at the touch, startled eyes flying to me, but the moment she looked at me, I lost all coherent thought. Even when she had been fighting for her life in the lighthouse, her eyes had been the most stunning thing I'd ever seen.

But there were cracks, too. Broken bits of the girl she'd been not too long ago. Her cropped hair had turned ashen in the short weeks since the Blood Moon, more grey than white now. A small scar appeared in the corner of her mouth, presumably from when Talen had punched her aboard the *Grey Bard*. The memory twisted my stomach.

And then there were the marks swirling up her arm. Black stained her fingertips as if she had dipped her hands in permanent ink. An indentation in the shape of the moonstone ruined her palm. Those events had only happened a month ago, but they looked old, as though she had fought in some long-ago battle. Half-moon scars circled both wrists, and I knew the stories for each of them.

Her lips parted. She gazed up at me like she had that day in the cave, when we made so many new promises to each other, when I said *All of you*, and now I wanted to close that distance again. My heart ached at the thought of any distance between us, stretching, stretching, stretching.

I wanted to know what she tasted like, if it was everything I'd been imagining since that day. But I didn't.

"You're bleeding," I said instead. Bits of my heart shattered with the words, and all the hope vanished from her face, locked away behind stone.

She curled her fingers into fists. "Don't worry about me right now," she murmured.

Her tone brushed against the parts of me that were always suspicious, always wary. What had she done?

"Do we have any suspects?" she continued.

"What?" I blinked, barely remembering why we were here in the first place.

Akev hovered into view, sliding a teacup across the desk. "Not yet," he said in response to Kalei.

I picked up the fragile porcelain—hardly feeling the scalding temperature due to the callouses on my fingers—and took a sip. The fragrant tea burned my throat and cleared my head. It brought the room back into focus in sharp clarity, and I stared at the arm on the table, frowning as if it would give me the answers I sought.

"The doctor went down to reapply the bandages and found him dead," I explained, recounting what the physician had told me only minutes ago. "The arm was already gone, and when he came up to tell me, he found it outside my door."

I shuddered for the second time since learning the murderer had stood outside my doors, mere feet away from me, to plant the severed limb there. Not many people passed through this hallway—someone might have seen something.

But these were people of Vodaeard. Why would any of them murder one of their own?

I took another burning gulp before my thoughts could spiral like a leaf in a gale.

"So, the physician," Kalei said, rising to her feet. She shuffled through an assortment of papers on the desk before finding a blank piece of parchment. After filling the quill with ink, she made a mark on the paper. *The doctor*, I read, leaning closer.

"You think the doctor did it?" I asked, cringing at the disbelief in my own voice.

Kalei shrugged. "I don't think he did, but he's a suspect."

"How?" I peered at her, trying to parse how her thoughts had gone straight to him.

"He was the first and only person to see the body," Akev said, slowly puzzling it out. "Maybe he did it and only *claimed* to have found the arm outside your door."

A frown pulled at my lips. "You're saying he brought the evidence that incriminates himself to me so that I'd...not suspect him?"

Kalei tapped the feathered end of the quill against her chin. "I'm not saying it makes sense, but we need a list. Oh," she added, and scrawled another mark onto the paper, this one longer than the first. Her script was precise, perfect.

I tilted my head to read it. *Councillor who officiated your*—"Haret?" I blurted, jumping to my feet. I motioned for the quill, scratched out the description, and added *Haret* in my own messy hand next to hers. The slash through the *t* felt like a knife through my ribs. "I really don't think any of my councillors are responsible."

There were dangerous consequences to implicating a member of my council, but she wasn't entirely wrong either. Haret had always been outspoken in meetings. But was he capable of killing someone to aid his case against me? He had agreed to my coronation.

Hadn't he?

"He spoke with me," Kalei said softly, ponderously, then her face shifted into disgust. "He said you'd be better off if I left." Her gaze lifted to mine, bright and angry. My stomach twisted. "I don't like him."

Pushing down the panic that swelled at her words, I exhaled unevenly. The quill came to rest on the table with my hand over it. "You can't suspect everyone you don't like. Or everyone who doesn't like you, for that matter."

A coy smile touched her lips, much like the one I'd seen in the brig. "Oh, that'd be a very long list," she said, nearly inaudible. A strange light gleamed in her eyes, and I wondered—not for the first time—if she truly hadn't done it.

I didn't want to doubt her. I didn't want to believe she was capable of such a heinous act. But I'd seen her in Xesta. I'd seen her when power claimed control. She was capable of it, but was she so far gone that she wouldn't even regret it? That she'd lie about it?

"Who else?" she said. As she stared down at the two damning names on the parchment, the light left her eyes. For a moment, something dark replaced it, but then she looked how I felt.

Tired. Distressed.

This was not how I saw the first part of our journey unfolding. My sights had been set on Chief Mikala for so long, so singularly focused, that I hadn't even considered something dangerous could be much closer. He was a whole world away. An entire ocean, with all its monsters, separated me from the man who broke my family. And yet, danger had found me here. When I was most vulnerable. If there was a murderer on this ship, anyone could be next. We were trapped together for at least another week.

How many more people could die in that time?

I rubbed the tender spot between my eyebrows. "Everyone can be a victim."

"Everyone can be a suspect," Kalei replied. Her eyes were on me again, but I refused to look up. I refused to acknowledge what I knew deep down. There was a mirror in her gaze into my own soul, and I didn't want to see what lurked there. It was the kind of distrust we'd both caged in our hearts when we first met.

"That's the problem," Akev said. "This kind of situation can make everyone suspicious of everyone else. There's no way for us to narrow down a list of suspects, but we can be certain that everyone may be a target. How do you propose we keep panic levels low?"

Akev's eyes bored into the top of my head, as heavy as the crown there, but Kalei glanced away, likely remembering the last time someone had asked me what to do. But this time, I didn't have anywhere to run. I couldn't jump overboard and swim back home and escape this responsibility. I had to stop running.

But how was I supposed to handle their panic when I couldn't even handle my own?

"I don't know," I answered truthfully. My whole life, I had been expected to have all the answers, because I had been expected to eventually make all the decisions. If I didn't have an answer, I sought it out. My parents offered as much of their knowledge and wisdom as they could in seventeen short years, but deep down, I knew my lack of discipline was disappointing to them. Even as a child, I refused to accept help when it was offered because I had learned early on that I needed to be self-sufficient if I was going to rule one day.

So I pretended. I masqueraded as someone who knew all the answers. But now, people were beginning to see through that mask, and it terrified me.

It hurt to admit I didn't have an answer. It felt like a failure. It felt like I was purposefully spitting on my parents' legacy by not retaining anything they taught me.

I wanted to honour them. I wanted the people to remember them through me. That was the reason this crown now sat on my head. Their legacy wasn't something to run away from—it was something to grasp firmly. To cultivate. I was just one person, but I had a whole slew of people whose sole purpose was to help me.

I couldn't do everything on my own.

"Akev." I lifted my gaze to him. "Convene the council. They need to know."

He bowed his head. "Your Majesty." A glance at the princess. "Kalei." With that, he departed.

I sank back into the desk chair, rubbing my temples. Kalei paced to the other side of the table.

"Kal," I whispered, my voice breaking on her name. She pinned me with a stare from across the expanse, head cocked to the side, waiting.

The things I wanted to say stuck in my throat and turned to ash in my mouth. She was the moon pulling my tide. She was the shore shaping my ocean. She was the path to my Endless Seas.

When I didn't say any of them, she straightened, brow furrowed. "Is there something you want to tell me, Evhen?"

I shook my head, shame twinging in my chest. I kept telling myself it was easier this way, but nothing about this felt easy

The crackle of the fire filled the silence that stretched between us. Wind howled outside the porthole. The weather was already turning cold. Winter came early to this part of the world, and we were sailing straight into unforgiving climates. Danger beckoned us into the unknown ahead.

She huffed. "Why won't you let me help you?" she demanded.

Because I love you too much to let you die for me. Because I couldn't bear the thought of you getting hurt again. Because I am a coward.

I sank further into the chair. "You can help me by finding who killed that man." I propped my chin on my fist, peering over the table and at the lump of dismembered flesh at Kalei. She bent over the map, eyes scanning the detailed drawing, eyes widening with each pass over the countries and continents. Heedless of the arm that covered our current location in the middle of the ocean. "Why did you stab him?"

"The world is big," she murmured, awed at the scope of the map. Crimson light danced in the hollows of her face, setting her hair aflame, turning her into a creature of smoke and shadows. Her hand hovered over a spot on the map before she smacked her palm down. I flinched at the sound—a bomb exploding, a door shutting, a book closing.

When I thought she wouldn't answer my question, she shot back, "Why did you cut him?" Her eyes flicked up, alive with leaping flames, narrowed beneath sharp brows that reminded me of daggers.

My teeth clicked when I snapped my jaw shut. There wasn't a reason. Not a good one, anyway. I'd been angry, and I'd acted on it. Irresponsibly and irrationally.

"Because he hurt you," I answered. It was as close to the truth as I could get.

Her gaze darkened, the light from the fire disappearing into the sapphire depths of her eyes. It was like an ocean I wanted to explore. An ocean I was too terrified to explore. "Would you have killed him for me?"

My breath stuck in my throat, clogged behind all the distressing things I'd done for her. All the things I would do for her. But the reason I'd almost turned back was because he had insulted my parents. If he had held his tongue, I wouldn't have even considered the notion of ending his life. There was only one person I would kill for her.

"No," I answered with a shake of my head. "Not him."

She sucked her lip between her teeth. "Good. I told you I didn't want anyone else getting hurt because of me."

The reminder pricked at my ribs. Too many people had gotten hurt because of her. Because of the things she'd done with the belief that she was helping. The world needed healing from all the pain her parents had wrought on it, and of course, we couldn't do that if we were focusing on the ignorant and inconsequential.

"But you would have killed him," I said, trying to keep the accusation from my tone.

Her gaze fell to the table, the map, the arm. She seemed a shell, hollow and empty, existing like a husk. Something else had taken up residency in her bones, and she was struggling to understand how to live with it. What it meant. Ever since that moment on the beach, I'd been living with two different versions of Kalei. They warred within her at any given moment. One of them was stronger, and that was the one that rose to the surface when she finally answered.

"Yes."

FOURTEEN

When Evhen's councillors filed into the room, I slipped out, heart constricting with every step lengthening the distance between me and the queen. Part of me wanted to stay, to prove my innocence, but I wasn't a councillor. I was hardly even a princess anymore. There was no place for me among the nobility here, and Evhen already believed I was innocent. That was enough for me, but would it be enough for her other councillors? Her eyes drilled into my back, like lashes of a whip, until I was out of sight down the passageway.

Blazing sunlight washed the deck in gold. Unclouded sky stretched from horizon to horizon, creating the illusion that the sea never ended. Icy air filled my lungs, but every breath felt tainted with a sweet poison, a sense of dread that expanded to fill every crevice. The world was so big. Much bigger than I ever realized. My island was such a small part, and even though my parents' war had tarnished the mainland, there were so many other continents and countries. So many other places where maybe war hadn't reached them yet.

Maybe Evhen was right. Maybe the whole world didn't hate me. But that thought wasn't the comfort it could have been. Instead, looking out at a never-ending ocean, not a soul in sight, I felt like there was no corner where I could hide. The world was big, and I was small, but death followed me wherever I went. It would find me, follow me, to any land, to any continent. I couldn't escape it.

The severed arm flashed in my mind as I wandered over to the railing. Death had even followed me to this cage of a ship. If Death found me here, Evhen would have no choice but to continue on. She couldn't save me from the depths. She wouldn't have to search the world and ruin herself trying to save me. I'd be gone, and she'd know peace at last.

And if I died in her place, nothing could reverse that.

Maybe I would let it happen. Maybe I should let it happen. There was a murderer on this ship, and who knew how many more people they would try to kill before we reached land? But what was their goal? What were they trying to accomplish by doing this?

All the answers eluded me.

Wind tugged at the bones in my hair. They clattered together, a hollow sound around my ears.

If there was one thing I could do for Evhen, it was this. I could find the murderer. Then go in her place. She couldn't stop me, not with this new power crawling through my veins, waiting to be unleashed. Controlled. Mastered. I was the Princess of Death, and I would seek it out on my terms.

The soldiers were still training. From what I could tell, they were practicing different techniques with one person on defense against two attackers. As I watched, a third person jumped in from the circle of onlookers, earning a cheer when they smacked the flat edge of their blade against the legs of the single person. Instead of falling, however, the one on defense maintained their balance and swung to push the third attacker back out of the cleared space. The other two used the distraction to advance, closing the distance. A grunt as one of their blades landed on the padded armour, and then the single man was on his knees. He chuckled, accepting defeat in good spirits, and then stepped out of the circle to let someone else take his place.

A woman's voice called out from the other side of the deck, and the gathered soldiers turned, weapons falling to rest at their sides. The woman stepped forward, authority written in every line of her body. Black hair dropped straight down her back in a tightly woven braid, not a strand out of place except for a streak of silver at her forehead. She wore training gear—padded armour that wouldn't hinder her movements but mimicked the weight of actual armour—but there was something about the way she carried herself, the way everyone watched her, that made me think she wasn't an ordinary soldier.

Her gaze found mine past the crowd, and my spine crackled with a shiver. A whole multitude of weapons garnished her waist and chest, and I had the crawling feeling she was imagining every different way she could use them against me. Her sharp eyes narrowed when I stared back without a flicker of the fear I felt.

Finally, she turned her gaze back to the crowd and began addressing them like she was in charge. Like she was a commander.

Icana's blonde hair caught my sight on the railing of the quarterdeck above me, where I had seen her perch almost every day since we departed Vodaeard. I had gotten used to seeing her at the helm of the *Grey Bard*, so it was strange seeing someone else in her spot, but she sat there with an air of authority. As though she was still the one guiding the ship through the waves.

I climbed the stairs to join her, tripping into the railing as a particularly choppy wave slapped the side of the ship. Her hair was free of its wide-brimmed hat today, pin-straight strands flying in the freezing breeze as she turned her head to me.

"How do I still have better balance than you?" she mused, mouth quirking. The cane rested against her crossed legs, as still as she was, even though the ship listed side to side. The helmsman fought to keep the wheel steady, though he looked unbothered by the waves.

"I was never allowed to board a ship before," I told her. The simple truth sent a pang through my heart, but it wasn't said with longing or remorse for a past I could mourn. Instead, anger burned deep down, embers igniting, each one a lost opportunity at a normal life. I'd been deprived of so much, of so many experiences, and there wasn't enough time left to have them all now.

A strange look crossed her face, softening her harsh features. Pity, I realized with a cringe of discomfort. The look didn't suit her, but she had changed in the dungeons. "The first time you were on a ship was when we kidnapped you?"

Under any other circumstance, the statement might have made me laugh. We'd come a long way since that night. We'd grown close and fallen apart. It was ridiculous to think they'd kidnapped me when, in truth, they had set me free. But I couldn't find the humour to laugh.

"One that wasn't docked, yes," I answered, rubbing the spot on my chest where the moonstone had burned through flesh and heart. "I'm not used to the waves."

"It's probably only going to get worse," the helmsman stated. "But nothing I can't handle."

Icana's narrowed gaze slid to him, sharp as her twin blades. She tapped a finger against the serpent's head of her cane, the small movement surprisingly threatening. But the helmsman didn't notice. And if he did, he purposely chose to ignore her.

"Where are we going anyway, Helmsman Eiramis?" she asked.

His dark eyes flicked to her for a second, something cracking on the surface before sliding up to the waves ahead again. A muscle leapt in his jaw. Unease coiled in my belly at the dark look she sent him. Icana didn't know. The helmsman knew, but he must have been ordered not to tell anyone.

Why would Evhen keep our destination a secret from the crew? From Icana?

"It is Her Majesty's prerogative to tell you or not," the helmsman—Eiramis—said evasively. "Not mine."

Icana's lip curled. "And it'll be my prerogative to rip out your eyes and feed them to a seagull. You can't sail us anywhere if you continue to be useless."

The corner of Eiramis's mouth twitched up. Sunlight caught the mirth in his eyes, turning their dark shade to a warm hue. "Please do continue threatening me, Master Icana. I rather enjoy it."

Icana's cheeks actually turned red. Her body, however, tensed as though she was about to leap across the short distance and dig her fingers into his eyes. Instead of entertaining her hostility, which frightened me more than it frightened the helmsman, I glanced down at the soldiers training below.

"Who's that?" I asked, abruptly pulling Icana's attention away from Eiramis.

The tension disappeared between one breath and the next as Icana turned, shoulders relaxing, to peer down. The weapons master had always been hard to read—she was deadly and dangerous, but she had her moments that made me wonder if it was all just an act. It didn't happen often, only in fractured bursts, where she cast off her threatening persona for someone so disinterested in everything, but she did it now, and her sudden lack of attention for the helmsman felt intentional. Felt like it was designed to hurt.

"Evhen's aunt," she answered when she spotted who I was inquiring after. My surprise must have been clear on my face because she gave a short laugh, void of mirth, eyes tracking the woman's movements like a snake about to strike. "Caz. Cazendra."

The woman's black braid swung as she leapt into the circle. I held my breath as she disarmed three men in quick succession.

"You don't like her?"

Icana made a noise between a growl and a hiss. "Evhen's mother's family is from the northern kingdom."

"Wystan?" Surprise coloured my voice as I looked down again. The resemblance was easier to see now that I knew what to look for. Dark hair, soft features, hard eyes.

Icana quirked a brow at me. "You know the history?"

I shrugged. "I read a lot." I didn't want to tell her that there had been nothing else for me to do in the last few months other than peruse the library until the torches guttered out.

Vodaeard's treaty with Wystan was what kept the smaller kingdom from toppling into the sea. Centuries ago, Wystan had invaded and won a war that spanned many years. The peace treaty that came from so much bloodshed meant that Wystan controlled most of Vodaeard's trade, but the monarchy could set its own laws. The two countries did not get along in any of the texts I'd read. I never would have guessed Evhen's mother's family originated there.

Maybe she had fled. Maybe the marriage had been designed to strengthen both lands. I couldn't ask Evhen about it now.

The woman below glanced up after she had dispatched two more men, who lay sprawled on the floor at her feet, moaning. She raised her curved blade to point it at Icana, as if challenging her to join the match. Evhen's weapons master shook her head, tapping the top of her cane.

"Aunt Caz doesn't like me because she thinks *she* should have been the one to lead Evhen's weapons training," she said with a tight smile. "Even though she doesn't live in Vodaeard, and I'm the closest thing to a friend Evhen has ever had. Besides," she added with a crooked grin at me, "her father threatened to send me back where I came from if I refused. It's been a rather good deal. Caz is jealous, that's all."

Cazendra's glare needled into me next. The hostility rolling off her like tongues of fire suddenly made sense. My father killed her sister. It seemed only right that she looked at me the same way everyone else did—like I was responsible.

"Then why is she here?"

The tip of the blade jerked sideways, and I felt the challenge like a knife to my heart.

"Family," Icana murmured, and then twisted to me, grabbing my wrist before I'd even made the conscious decision to move. Her fingers brushed bone, and we both shuddered—her with disgust, me with impatience. "Don't. She will beat you, she will hurt you, and she will smile while doing it."

I held Cazendra's glare for a beat too long. She mouthed something that set my blood on fire—*You're not worthy*—and I yanked my arm out of Icana's grasp.

Icana heaved a sigh and reached over to flip a hidden compartment in her cane. A needle-thin blade popped free from the serpent's head. She shrugged as she placed it in my hand.

"You didn't ask for it," she said, eyes gleaming with wicked pleasure. Despite her warning, she wanted to witness this. Maybe she had been waiting a long time for someone to accept Cazendra's challenge.

And I wasn't worried about accepting that challenge. Icana's blade was feather-light in my grip, but I had a different weapon that neither of them would be prepared for.

I met Cazendra on the deck, lifting the dagger between us. She was pretty, in the same way foxglove was pretty. Nice to look at from afar, but deadly to touch. Her eyes—up close, I could see the pale flecks of honey amid a deep shade of brown that marked her as related to Evhen—raked over me, as gently as a serrated knife. They lingered on my hair and then fell to the small dagger. Without a word, she unbuckled her belt and bandolier, depositing the assortment of weapons onto the deck. She kicked it aside, never taking her eyes off of me. All that remained was a dagger like mine, the thick blade giving the impression that it was designed for hacking.

"How does this work?" I asked, letting the blade slide through my fingers in a spiral pattern, just like Icana had taught me. It was fancy, deft work that trained my hands to anticipate the shifts in weight. Cazendra did not seem impressed.

"First blood," she said, adjusting her grip.

I motioned for her to start, curling the fingers of my free hand. If she wanted to make me bleed, I'd make her regret it.

Nostrils flaring, she lunged to the excited cheers of the crowd. Sunlight flashed on her blade as it arced down. I slipped under her swing, feet moving like we were caught in a dance, but I extended my arm before rising from my crouch. Her elbows pulled back, only to the point that her blade wouldn't completely sever my arm, but the tip snagged on my sleeve. When I straightened, she drew her blade back into a defensive position, ripping through the rest of the fabric.

The tattered sleeve flapped in the cutting breeze, revealing a straight line of black blood from elbow to wrist.

Cazendra stepped out of her stance, blade at her side. Her braid was still swinging. Barely ten seconds had elapsed, but I didn't plan on this fight taking too long. Thick blood stained my shirt, too dark to see on the black satin, and dripped in heavy drops from my fingertips. Movement wiggled beneath my skin, a clamouring.

"First blood," Cazendra announced. "I don't think I've ever won so fast before." Her mocking tone reached me as if through tar, muddled among the clanging inside my skull as the shards of bone awoke.

I inhaled deeply. As I exhaled, various pieces of bone shot out of my skin and hair. Vision tinted black and red—blood and this strange new magic—I grinned as the tension seeped out of my body and leeched away with the release of the extra bones. Ice replaced the hot fire in my veins, and my head spun, my energy spent.

Cazendra grunted. When my vision cleared, I saw where the bones had pierced. A dozen shards in a cluster at the centre of her chest. Her heart protected by the training padding.

I was learning how to control them.

One shard, though, had nicked her jaw. As the fragments flew back at me, one by one, each nestling into a different part of my flesh like puzzle pieces slotting into place, Cazendra touched the small cut on her face.

Her eyes blazed. Without warning, she lunged forward again, dagger gripped in both hands. I scrambled back, recognizing the fury on her face—it was the same fury Evhen displayed in the lighthouse when she wanted to kill me for something I hadn't done. Revenge. She wouldn't stop until more of my blood spilled.

My knees buckled, and I crashed to the deck, a tangle of limbs as thin as rope.

Before Cazendra could plunge her blade into my heart, a voice rang out through the eerie silence on board.

"Aunt Caz!"

FIFTEEN

The soldiers gathered around Kalei, and Aunt Caz fell out of the circle to face me, some of them bowing their heads. I didn't have eyes for any of them. All I could do was stare at Aunt Caz in horror. Rage twitched through my bloodstream, but I pushed it aside for impatience. Annoyance

"Explain," I ordered. Aunt Caz was family, but that didn't mean I had to treat her as such. Not when her dagger was poised to hurt Kalei. To kill her.

Aunt Caz's chest heaved. The dagger came to rest at her side, the edge glazed in a thick coat of black blood. My eyes slid to Kalei. Worry made my pulse spike higher when I saw the tattered sleeve, the straight cut, the embedded bones.

"Are you okay?" I whispered.

"Fine," she answered, a bit too cheerfully despite the heaving of her chest. "Cazendra and I were having a sparring match." Her gaze, when it landed on Aunt Caz, was as cold as the deepest part of the ocean.

"To first blood," Aunt Caz snapped. "You dishonoured the rules."

Kalei scoffed.

Kalei scoffed. I'd never heard such a sound from her before, like it was a curse against the entire world.

"I'm the Princess of Death," she replied. "The rules don't apply to me."

"Aunt Caz," I said quickly, stepping between her and Kalei when it looked like she was going to strike again. "If you want a challenge, spar with me."

I felt, rather than saw, Kalei roll her eyes. "I can handle my own battles, Ev."

"I know," I growled. "That's the problem." Kalei handling her own battles was causing more problems than I could handle. I'd seen the bones in her skin change position. It stood to reason that she'd let Aunt Caz cut her in order to use the bones against her. It was dangerous. It was reckless. It was terrifying. If Kalei continued to use this power, unchecked, there was no telling how many people she would hurt. Including herself.

"Alright then," Aunt Caz said. "Let's see if your weapons master taught you well."

My fingertips buzzed with restless energy. I hadn't sparred in months—since before my parents died. There hadn't been time with everything going on to train, and it pained me to think if I had the time, I would have been fast enough to save Alekey.

To stop the chief's army. To stop him from leaving.

It was pointless to think about that now, though. Alekey was gone, and this would give me a chance to hone my skills for when I met the chief again. He wouldn't win this time. I'd be ready.

Besides, Aunt Caz was prideful. My father had chosen Icana to be my weapons master, and Aunt Caz was jealous. Jealousy had no place on my ship. Someone had to teach her that.

"Clear the deck!" I shouted. Obediently, the soldiers scurried off the deck, rushing to fill the quarterdeck above and cram themselves against the bow and sides. Kalei pushed herself up off the gleaming deck, limbs shaking. A flush coloured her cheeks, but the rest of her looked sallow. She watched me with a puzzled stare, but maybe I was the confused one. Why had she agreed to a fight with Aunt Caz? Why had Aunt Caz issued the challenge in the first place?

There were only so many things I could guess at.

Breathing evenly to calm my racing heart, I carefully disentangled the crown from my head and handed it to Kalei. She looked disgusted as she took it, as if the molten gold burned her. Maybe it had, in places I couldn't see. She had lost so much of her glow that I couldn't see past the surface anymore. I didn't know what was going on inside.

"Why are you doing this?" Kalei asked as Aunt Caz selected a weapon from her array. The crown dangled from the princess's fingers, as if she didn't want it to touch any more flesh than was necessary, and an unwarranted image flashed through my mind. Kalei, snapping the thin rods of gold in her rage, scattering the pieces to the ocean of her hate. I wiped away that image with a hand across my sweating brow.

"She wants a fight," I said with a shrug. "I'll give her one that's worthy of her."

Aside from Icana, I was the only one trained in combat. The surrounding soldiers were doing their best when it came to sparring, but Aunt Caz wanted a fight that would last more than a few seconds. No one else could give her that.

Except maybe Kalei, but she had already shown that she'd ignore the rules to win. No matter what.

Kalei narrowed her eyes at Aunt Caz. I wondered what was going on inside her head. What she was trying to understand about Aunt Caz. Whether she was imagining what a proper fight between them would be like. Or if she was simply thinking about all the ways her bones could hurt. Perhaps it was for the best that I didn't know what was going through her mind. I'd only find something that hurt me. I'd only find ghosts, echoes of the girl I fell in love with.

"Be careful," Kalei said hesitantly, as if the words tasted wrong in her mouth. "I think I pissed her off."

She flashed a vicious grin—there it was, that version of Kalei I didn't know at all—and retreated up the steps to join Icana on the railing. Eiramis was too far back to see from where I stood, so I only hoped he was paying more attention to the waves than the deck.

Don't fight fair, Icana mouthed before I turned towards my aunt.

"Pick." Aunt Caz gestured to her assortment of weapons—swords and daggers, long and short, all perfectly crafted to fit someone else's hand. Her hand. She would have the advantage of using her own weapons. I wasn't so lucky. The ceremonial cutlass was just that—ceremonial. I didn't have my own weapon.

Nothing here fit my hand properly.

But Icana *had* taught me well. She taught me to adapt and to use what I had. There were more weapons on this deck than just the blades Aunt Caz carried.

I pointed to one I was familiar with—a rapier, long and thin. Aunt Caz chuckled, kicking the sword towards me. It bumped against my foot, and when I bent to pick it up, Aunt Caz lunged.

Golden sun glinted off her twin blades—I frowned at her choice, wondering if she was mocking Icana by using my weapons master's favourite weapons—and I ducked under her swings, rolling into a crouch before she could spin around. My rapier came up in front of my face as both of her blades came down, metal sparking. Breath stuttering, I clenched my teeth and pushed her back. When I rose out of my crouch, her foot connected with my chest and sent me sprawling backwards to an astonished gasp from the crowd.

"Fuck," I groaned, pressing a hand against my chest. Something was bruised, but nothing had broken. I glared across the deck as Aunt Caz stalked towards me.

If she wanted to fight dirty, I'd show her dirty. Getting my feet under me, I shifted my stance so the railing was behind me.

"What are you so pissed about, Aunt Caz?" I asked, taking one step back for every one of hers forward. "If there's something you want to talk about, there are better ways to get my attention."

She advanced, narrowing her eyes at me. The railing got closer behind me. "You don't listen. That's always been your problem. Have you ever once considered how it looks to be so close to the girl whose father killed your parents—my sister?"

The painful reminder rippled through me, bringing me to a stop. An ache spread over my jaw. The deck was silent, so I knew Kalei heard every word, but I didn't lift my gaze from Aunt Caz.

My voice was gravel when I spoke. "I know exactly how it looks."

"Do you?" she countered. "Because it doesn't seem like you do. She's too dangerous to have on board. You saw what she just did. And that was only sparring. How many people could she hurt if she actually wanted to?"

Despite the chill in the air, sweat beaded on my brow. Sunlight blazed down my back. These were the same arguments I'd had with my councillors in the months since the Blood Moon. The same concerns. The same doubts. Everyone said the same things over and over, and I'd tried to protect Kalei from them, even when she had been trying to avoid me. But now Aunt Caz was voicing them here, on purpose, and there was nothing I could do to stop Kalei from hearing them now.

Fighting every instinct that yelled at me to keep my eyes on Aunt Caz, I glanced up. Icana was wrapping a bandage around Kalei's arm, but the princess's eyes were locked on me. There was a darkness in their depths, sparking with a mixture of pain and rage. Even from where I stood, I could see she was holding her breath. In the brief moment I looked up, something shifted in her hair, and then her eyes widened slightly. I looked back in time to see a flash of steel and Aunt Caz's blades arcing through the air. I jumped for the railing, grabbing the rigging to haul myself over the side. Aunt Caz's momentum pulled her forward, and I kicked my foot up into her jaw when she couldn't stop in time. She staggered back and swallowed, but when a grin split her face, there was no blood on her teeth.

The rigging gave me the advantage I needed. Aunt Caz was tall—Alekey got his height from our mother's side of the family—so now she had to crane her neck back to look up at me, directly into the sun. It blinded her briefly, and from where I hung onto the ropes. I saw the confusion on her face before she twisted to the side and swung at the rigging with her eyes closed. Her blade narrowly missed my free hand, but the brazen attack startled me enough that I slipped. Bits of rope snagged around my ankle as I fell. My stomach plummeted for one terrifying second when the only thing I saw beneath me was the ocean. Then I listed sideways with a swell and caught the edge of the rigging, muscles straining to pull myself back over the deck.

Aunt Caz watched my flailing, an amused expression on her face, waiting until I righted myself and landed hard on the deck before striking again. Sparks jumped into the air, landing hot on my face, when our blades connected. Her second blade swiped at my exposed side. I twisted my elbow, forcing her first blade away, and stepped into her space. My shoulder slammed into her chest, and I turned with the momentum, jerking my elbow back into her forearm. A surprised grunt wheezed out of her, the hits causing her to relent a step. When I spun back around to face her, she had gathered herself, blades poised to attack. Sunlight streaked along the deadly edges. Glinting with promise.

With every step, something twinged in my side as we circled each other. Aunt Caz moved like a wraith, a living shadow, a black stain against the clear sky. Every movement, every step, was deliberate, exact. Calculated. Her dark eyes watched me, looking for the same tells I was looking for in her. But she was unreadable. She was definitive in the choices she made—when to strike, where to strike, how to strike. I hadn't seen Aunt Caz in years, but in the few minutes we'd been sparring, I understood how she had earned her position in Wystan's army. She was a snake—quick, precise. As deadly as her weapons. Maybe if she had been my weapons teacher, I'd know how to defeat her. Icana was good—if she hadn't been injured, this fight would have been very different—but she had a unique set of skills that didn't exactly work to her advantage in a sparring match. She aimed to kill every time. She didn't know when to pull back.

That was all I knew. And I didn't exactly want to kill Aunt Caz. But I didn't know how to disarm her in a way that didn't hurt her. There were no obvious weaknesses that I could see, nothing to tell me where to strike. Breath whistled through my teeth. Each lungful of air pulled at a stitch in my side. If I bothered to look, I was sure there would be a bruise flowering along my ribs.

I pressed a hand against my other side, hoping Aunt Caz would fall for the bluff. A beat passed before I realized she wasn't mirroring my moves anymore, and my next step brought me too close. She swung in quick succession—the first strike came from my injured side, and when I tried to block, her other fist smashed into my unguarded side. My knee scraped against the deck, a choked sound lodging in my throat.

"Black seas," I groaned, vision swimming. I tilted my head back as her shadow loomed over me.

"Both sides hurt now, don't they?" she asked. "You can't trick me, Evhen. Get up."

"Finish this," I spat, wincing from the force of my words.

Aunt Caz planted her foot against my chest and shoved me backwards, but not nearly as forcefully. "Get up!"

I rolled onto my stomach and jumped up. Sweat coated my skin and slicked my palms. I adjusted my grip on the rapier as I turned, scampering across the deck to put distance between us. Distance she was rapidly shortening.

"What are you trying to prove?" Anger made my voice shake.

"What are *you* trying to prove?" she shot back.

Hair fell into my face, sticking to my forehead. "Nothing! You wanted a fight, but for sea's sake, Aunt Caz, you're a commander in an army! I'm a seventeen-year-old girl. Of course, you're going to be better. So why didn't you finish it?"

"Because you're smart, Evhen," she said, stopping when I reached the mainmast, "but you're making stupid decisions."

Both hands wrapped around the rapier's hilt. "I told you, letting Kal into my life was not—"

"I'm not talking about your fucking girlfriend," Aunt Caz growled. The term did something inexplicable to my stomach, but she wasn't done. She pointed a blade at the side of the ship. "You jumped onto the rigging with no way down. What were you going to do? Dive over my head?" Her swords arced—*slash, slash*—as if an imaginary body were soaring over her. "Right through the ankles."

Creases nestled in my brow as I played it out in my head.

"Unfortunately, she's right," Icana called from the upper deck.

I glared up at her. "Whose side are you on?" I grumbled.

My weapons master didn't answer other than the silent laughter dancing across her face as she blocked the sun from her eyes. Beside her, Kalei sat as still as a statue, as dark as the figure I saw that day on the cliff. Her mother. Unmoving. Unbreachable.

Chest constricting, I redirected my attention back to Aunt Caz with a frown. "So this has been—what? A lesson?"

"You're queen," she said, the title needling into my chest. It hurt as much as the stitch in my side. "Everything you do is a lesson."

I had never been good at listening. Most things I did my own way, just to prove they could be done differently. This was just another situation with rules that could be bent. Broken. Anything to win, anything to get to first blood.

"Then *teach* me, Aunt Caz," I said through my teeth, sarcasm lacing every word. "Stop pulling back."

Her lip curled, but she lowered her blades. Shoulders straight, the tension uncoiled from her lithe body. "No. You clearly can't be taught. Bring me someone who will listen to my direction."

"*You* are not my weapons master or my fighting instructor," I reminded her. "I don't need to listen to your fucking orders!"

Aunt Caz's gaze snapped to Icana. One blade angled up, as if she had guessed my movements before I knew them, to keep me from attacking while she was distracted. "Some teacher you are," she said to my weapons master.

Kalei bristled, hands curled into fists. But Icana simply flipped her middle finger at Aunt Caz and then swung her legs over the railing. The thud of her cane against the deck was like a hammer to my chest.

I darted forward and slid across the deck on my knees until I was close enough to use the rapier to knock aside Aunt Caz's blade. She relinquished her hold on it, only to wrap her other arm around my neck and slam me down onto the deck. Hard. Shadows swished across my vision like black curtains. It was a moment before I was able to gasp in air, and when my vision cleared, Aunt Caz's face loomed close.

"We're done here," she said. One hand was braced next to my head, her knees blocking me from getting up. Her remaining blade kissed my neck, the steel ice against the fire in my jumping pulse.

Wood splinters brushed against my fingertips as I scrambled for my fallen sword. "You said *first blood*," I said, choking through the pain in my lungs.

Metal met my fingers, but before I could fold my hand over the hilt, before I could even suck in my next desperate breath, Aunt Caz swiped the tip of her blade across my chest. She stood, immediately wiping her sword clean, face set into a vicious scowl.

"We're done here," she repeated, walking away without a backwards glance.

Air fought its way into my lungs again. Sunlight dazzled my burning eyes, setting my skin on fire. Blue sky stretched above me in an unbroken dome.

I touched the small cut on my chest and confirmed the blood on my fingertips was mine before dropping my arm back to the deck.

"Fuck."

SIXTEEN

It was the first time I'd seen Evhen injured since losing my power. She lay on the deck as if she had been nailed to the boards, arms outstretched to greet her defeat, eyes closed as the sun beat down on her. If I hadn't been looking so closely, if I hadn't noticed the telltale shudder of a sob in the rise of her chest, I'd say she might have been sleeping.

As the deck cleared, her face twisted into a look I was beginning to associate with masks. Charades and facades and lighthouse walls. It didn't quite fit, pulled into place a little too crookedly, unable to fully cover the cracks beneath. She was embarrassed. She was frustrated. And she was trying to hide all those useless emotions. I'd become used to seeing rage act as a mask for her, something to sink into when her insecurities rose to the surface, so this blank slate was unsettling.

She did it on purpose, too. She was so careful with her acts and masks, so good at showing the world exactly what it wanted to see. But I had seen the true version of Evhen. I'd known her when she shed those masks and let down her guard. I knew what she was hiding beneath.

At the bottom of the stairs, Cazendra appeared briefly in the passageway, coming from the direction of Evhen's quarters. She didn't move past me, lurking in the shadows, eyes hidden in the darkness. A chill caressed my spine, feeling strangely like fingers against the base of my skull. She hadn't removed her training gear, wearing the puncture marks where my bones had pierced the padding like a medal. Like a reminder. She frowned at me, and I moved away before the urge to do worse could tickle my fingertips. Evhen might have been able to stop herself from hurting her aunt, but I wasn't so sure I had the same restraint.

Evhen sat up at my approach, arm over a crooked knee, fingers caught in her torch-like hair. She was touched by the sun, its glow painting her cheeks in crimson, each strand of flyaway hair a thread of red around her face. Liquid gold and melted honey mingled in her eyes as she looked up at me. Creases appeared between her brows, lines that I wanted to smooth with a gentle touch.

I hadn't been gentle with her in so long. I didn't know how anymore.

"Well, that went horribly," she quipped, peering behind me to where Cazendra still hovered in the hallway. I didn't need to turn to know she was glaring at us, her hatred as hot as any furnace. Her vitriol was as violent as a whip. That kind of anger fell around me like a cloak, perfectly fitted to my shoulders. Like it was mine to bear. Like I could use it as a shield to protect those it would otherwise hurt.

Such as Evhen. She didn't deserve her aunt's attitude. I didn't deserve her anger either, but I was used to it by now. The mainland was full of people who hated me because of who my father was. Because of what he'd done. When I followed Evhen across the continent, I had made myself an easy target.

Because if they couldn't hurt my father, at least they could hurt me. So I took Cazendra's disdain like a dagger to the back.

"Maybe you need to train with the others," I suggested, only partially in jest, holding out Evhen's crown to her.

She made a face at the band of metal as she pushed herself up. "Icana can still teach," she said, as if the idea of training with commoners disgusted her so thoroughly.

From the passageway came Cazendra's scoff, a sound that served as a flint to my own anger. Evhen's gaze bored into me, straight into the part of me that wanted to act, telling me to think instead. Consequences be damned. They all already saw me as a monster. It wouldn't come as any surprise to act, to turn around and shoot my bones at her. This time, I wouldn't hit her padding.

Evhen set a hand on my injured arm. Her fingers brushed the broken skin. The sensation—the slight hesitation that reminded me of a time when our lips almost touched for the first time—sent all thoughts tumbling from my mind.

There was suddenly only Evhen—her skin on mine, her eyes on mine, her mouth…

"I'm not having this argument with you, Aunt Caz," Evhen's mouth was saying. "I asked you to come because you have military experience, but you have no rank here. Icana has more authority than you do, and I will not tolerate you belittling her because your fucking pride can't handle it."

Cazendra stepped into the light. She had undone her hair, letting it fall like oil straight down her back. A purpling bruise covered her jaw. "Well, maybe if your weapons master had accepted my challenge, I wouldn't feel the need to think so little of her. I've yet to see her so-called authority."

Evhen bristled, her fingers briefly tightening on my arm before she let go. "You challenged Icana?" Her voice was dangerously low—the kind of low that meant she was angered well beyond the point of yelling. "She was fucking tortured. She nearly died. The fact that she can still walk shows a strength I can only dream of. So next time you want a challenge, take one of your swords and shove it up your ass."

"She was tortured because of her!" Cazendra pointed a finger at me, each word another sword in her arsenal. "My sister *died* because of her!"

Evhen grabbed the crown from my hands and smashed it on top of her curls. "My mother died because she was defending the people she loved." Her gaze hardened, openly daring Cazendra to defy her again. "I will do the same. That includes Kalei."

Shame coursed through my veins. My fingers stung where I'd held the crown, but I realized it served as a cloak for Evhen. A shield against the world. In the same way I bore their anger to protect her, she wore her crown to protect me from their hatred. We were so used to letting the world chip away pieces of ourselves so the other wouldn't get hurt, without realizing we were only harming ourselves in the process. One of us had to break so the other could be whole.

"I don't want to see the rest of my family get hurt because of her," Cazendra said, almost softly, but her eyes were hard when they flicked to me with the promise of pain.

"She hasn't hurt anyone," Evhen replied, voice quiet in a way that indicated she was tired. Tired of the same old arguments—tired of the same old complaints.

Tired of defending me.

"Not yet," Cazendra murmured before stalking away to collect the rest of her weapons.

When I looked back at Evhen after glaring at Cazendra off the deck, the queen's face was tilted to the sky, eyes pinched shut as if the sun's warmth could burn away her emotions. She had always been made of hard lines—angled jaw and sharp cheekbones and severe brow—but now she looked soft beneath the late afternoon glow in a way that made her appear both younger and weaker.

The crown nestled in her curls wasn't the piece of armour she thought it was. It was a vulnerability. But I realized, as I watched her bring her gaze back to the deck, she wore it like a piece of jewellery. A statement. An accent. It was the easiest way to stress to everyone around us who she was when they all seemed so determined to forget and cast her aside. Too young. Too brash. Too inexperienced.

She had chosen it. She didn't wear it because she *had* to—she wore it because she *wanted* to. It was something she could take off whenever she wanted to, but she put it on to serve as a notice. A declaration. Stating the obvious without saying a word. Because if everyone else was so quick to dismiss her, she'd be quick to remind them.

Her eyes met mine across what felt like an unspannable distance. The boat fell away. The crew fell away. The world fell away. Until there was only us staring at each other across a chasm neither of us had the strength to cross. Something twisted in my stomach, but when I blinked, the sky came back in dazzling clarity, and Evhen sighed.

"Can you send the physician to my quarters?" she asked, hand pressed against her side.

I opened my mouth to say something I'd regret, her own words—*I'm not a seas-damned servant*—souring on my tongue, but I simply nodded. If she had broken something, there was no telling how long it would take to heal. And even though I didn't exactly trust the physician, I also didn't have my power to heal her. "I'll be along in a moment," I said, gaze drifting across the deck.

Evhen's eyes followed mine. A frown creased her forehead. "Kal," she said, the word strained and full of pain.

I inwardly flinched at the way it sounded on her lips, like it was a fragile thing breaking.

"Please don't go after my aunt.."

I scrunched my face into a scowl. "You can't stop me, Evhen," I said, both a reminder and threat, and spun away from her. Her sharp inhale was as loud as an explosion on the quiet deck, but she didn't call out to me, didn't try to stop me. She'd seen what I could do with these bones.

I found Cazendra exactly where I thought she would be—in the armoury, polishing her blades. She glanced up when I shut the door behind me and then resumed her work without a flicker of fear on her face. Her motions, though, became sharper, more deliberate.

"Does Evhen know you're here?" she asked. Hair spilled over one shoulder, a curtain drawn over her face. Muscles bunched in her shoulders. She might have looked calm, but she was expecting me to do something.

"Yes," I said, following the wall of the small room until I was across from her.

Chests and crates of weapons filled the room, and more hung from pegs on the wall. A table in the corner was covered in other supplies, names and purposes that I didn't have.

Cazendra slowly set down the cloth she was using and looked up at me. The knife she'd used in our match lay across her knees, gleaming in the light of the lantern that swung from the ceiling. "What do you want?"

I noticed she had discarded her training gear. It hung over the back of her chair, each piece folded with care. Her eyes narrowed on the bandage covering my forearm. Thick blood-stained the cloth.

"I wanted to tell you that you're right," I said. The weapons at my back were so close, but Cazendra's reflexes were faster. She'd have that knife in my chest before I could pull one blade from the wall. Before I could dip my fingers in my own blood.

Suspicion sparked in her narrowed gaze. She leaned back, folding her arms over her chest as if the pose was meant to be disarming. Calming. It only made her more terrifying. "How so?"

"Evhen is going to get hurt, but I'm not the one who's going to hurt her." I moved away from the wall of weapons. Knives didn't do me any good when I had my own weapons embedded in my skin. "She plans to trade herself for her brother in Geirvar." The name eased a sharp gasp from Cazendra, and I wondered, again, why Evhen hadn't told anyone. "My father won't settle for a mere trade. He wants to kill Evhen. And I can't let that happen."

The harsh angle of Cazendra's brow softened. "Why are you telling me this?"

"So you can stop her." I pinned her with a dark stare, watching with a twisted sense of pleasure as a shiver rolled through her. "So that when the time comes, and I give myself in her place, you'll make sure she leaves."

Cazendra stood, taking a moment to examine her knife in the lantern light before returning it to her belt. "I assume you haven't told her any of this."

I shook my head. "She's so determined to sacrifice herself, but I'm more determined to save her."

"Why?"

Before, the sharp tone might have caused me to flinch, to cower away from the anger and suspicion and hate. Now, I lifted my chin. "Because I love her too much to let her hurt herself. Because I think she deserves to rule her kingdom. But she can only do that if I'm gone. Will you help me with that or not?"

"Gladly." She stood, crossed to the door, and yanked it open. Light from the hall spilled into the room like a river of gold. The collection of weapons on her belt clinked together. "Now leave."

After I crossed the threshold, her voice wound through the darkness of my thoughts towards me. "She really loves you, you know? Are you sure this won't hurt her more?"

I swallowed thickly before I answered. "It might. But she deserves a chance to live in a world that wants her."

Because it didn't want me.

SEVENTEEN

The doctor prodded my ribs while Kalei paced the room, from table to window, becoming more and more agitated with every step. The bones in her skin were still in the same position I'd last seen them, after her match with Aunt Caz, but it gave me no small comfort to think she'd gone to speak to my aunt.

"Black seas," I hissed, twitching away from the physician's jabbing fingers. He frowned at me, and I wondered if it was because he thought a queen shouldn't curse, or a girl shouldn't. I scowled in response and tugged my shirt back into place. Every limb felt sore, every bone bruised. Aunt Caz knew exactly where to strike to cause the most amount of pain without any actual damage.

She was lucky nothing was broken.

I was lucky nothing was broken.

The doctor straightened from his crouch. "The swelling will go down in a few days," he said, adjusting his spectacles. "Try not to do anything—" *Reckless*, I thought he was going to say. "Extraneous."

I made no promises in that regard.

He bowed before departing, to both me and Kalei—she wasn't looking at him, but her shoulders tensed, indicating she had noticed—and stepped around Icana as she entered, cane thudding against the floor until it met the rug in the centre of my quarters.

"Seas, you look awful," Icana muttered. She leaned back against the table with the map spread across its surface and crossed her ankles, keen eyes darting from me to Kalei and back again. "You know, before we left, Talen asked me to make sure you didn't get hurt on this voyage. What lie am I going to tell him about this?"

A tired laugh touched my lips, soundless and weary. There was something so familiar about Icana lying for me that it sent a wave of longing coursing through me. For the way it had been, years ago, when we were twelve and sixteen, and Icana had been the closest thing to a friend even though she was a bit older and wiser and faster and wilder. After she learned that my parents didn't really care if she lied for me—as long as I wasn't hurt or in danger—my parents didn't really care what we did. As long as there was a reason.

So she became very good at lying. She was skilled with both weapons and words. Talented with swords and secrets. A force with lances and lies. All the things that made her an excellent weapons master made her an even better friend.

But this kind of lie was one we'd promised not to tell. I *was* hurt. Because of my own reckless foolishness, and Icana would see through that lie like water. This kind of lie was useless. And longing for a past that was stained in blood and death was just as useless.

Kalei whirled away from the window, the stripe of sea visible beyond tainted gold by the now-setting sun, and crossed to the desk beside me. Only a few hours had passed since we created the list of murder suspects. Now she snatched it up, flattened it with movements sharp enough to tear the parchment if she wanted to, and plucked the quill from its spot next to the inkwell. Her fingers gripped the stem tight, as if she meant to snap it in half, the tip hovering just over the yellowed paper. When her eyes flicked to my face, I flinched at the hot blue flames in her gaze.

"How do you spell *Cazendra*?"

I jumped to my feet, hissing as the bruises pulled and stretched over my stomach. "You are *not* adding my aunt's name to that list."

No matter how angry I was at Aunt Caz, no matter how frustrated or embarrassed, her name did not belong on that list. It seemed almost treasonous to think otherwise. It seemed like a betrayal against my parents' memories to even have the inkling of the idea that my mother's sister could have killed someone on this ship.

"She's very capable," Kalei said, tongue like a whip against her teeth.

I couldn't argue to the contrary, because Aunt Caz was, in fact, very capable. That was why I had asked her to come. But it seemed too improbable for her to commit such an act.

There is no reason for her to murder anyone," I said, assuming the kind of authoritative voice Aunt Caz spoke with. That one that made her heard among ranks of soldiers in an army. That one that left no room for argument, even if it was from Kalei, who could be very persuasive herself. Who was the only person I didn't want to argue with—about anything. There was something in my chest that pulled and strained with the very idea of going back to those two versions of ourselves from the first day we met, when all we did was fight. I had been weak then, unable to land the killing blow, but I was even weaker now.

"She has *every* reason," Kalei muttered, denting the parchment with the quill's sharp tip without making a mark in ink. Her gaze flicked up, red in the candlelight. "You heard her, Ev. She's angry. Maybe this is her way of avenging her sister's death."

"By murdering Vodaeardeans?" My voice rose to a pitch. "Listen to yourself, Kal. It doesn't make sense. Aunt Caz wouldn't murder my citizens because she's angry."

"And why not?" Kalei shot back. "She's from Wystan, isn't she? Doesn't that make her an enemy?"

"Stop!" I cried. My heart lurched to a halt. There was a moment between breaths when it didn't beat at all, and then it started again, quick as a downpour, thudding hard enough to bruise from the inside. It ached as I stared at Kalei. "Black seas, Kal. My entire council thinks you're the one who did it, and this sounds *exactly* like you're trying to blame someone else. Stop talking, stop..." The words died in my throat, the sudden heat of anger leeching from my chest at the expression on her face. "Just stop, *please*."

If someone had asked me, I wouldn't have been able to pick out one emotion on her face. It was a myriad, a mosaic, a mottled painting where each new feeling was a broad stroke over the last. First, surprise at my outburst, replaced quickly by—anger? Annoyance?—at the revelation of what my council thought.

She seemed equal parts betrayed and resigned, as if she had guessed they would reach that conclusion soon enough, but it still stung. Fury, chased by meddling suspicion, crossed her face briefly before the kind of hurt that came from heartache settled over her features. The flame in her blue eyes died to smouldering embers that hinted at tears, but not quite, and she dropped the quill. It rolled over the parchment and clattered to the ground, forgotten as she crossed the room, tilting with the rise of the ship over a swell, and disappeared through the open door.

I watched the threshold, breath stuttering in and out, waiting for her to reappear. Waiting for my own tears to fall. But nothing happened. She didn't come back, and my tears didn't spill over, and Icana was looking at me with a questioning quirk to her brows.

"I think I missed something important," she said. "Who's murdering Vodaeardeans?"

I pressed the pad of my thumb into the space between my eyes, rubbing away the ache that seemed perpetually caught at the forefront of my head. I'd forgotten I hadn't told Icana what had happened—even though she had been the one to fetch Kalei, I hadn't let her see the arm. Only my council knew. And the doctor.

And Kalei.

Soon, the entire ship would know. It wasn't something I could keep a secret for too long, not when we feared who might be next. The crew deserved to know. They deserved to be aware and prepared.

"The man who attacked Kalei a few days ago? He was found dead this morning." Found dead? Or murdered by the doctor? By Haret? My aunt? For what reason? Kalei hadn't done it—I believed her in that regard, even if the council didn't. Even if all the signs of guilt pointed to her. She had seemed almost frightened when she saw the man's arm, which was safely stored away now. As if that was exactly what she knew everyone else would think. Was someone trying to make it look as though she'd done it? Why?

There were so many questions, and not nearly enough answers. I was drowning in them.

Icana nodded to herself. "Kalei is…?"

"Innocent," I said. To anyone else, my answer might have seemed too quick. Too practiced. Too certain. But until I had proof, I refused to believe Kalei was responsible.

"But the council…?"

"Doesn't agree," I huffed, dropping back into my chair. The wood creaked beneath me. A soft curse feathered over my lips, more to fill the silence than to satisfy my need to swear at the world that twisted everything I cared about into ugly voids.

Icana hobbled over to the seat beneath the window and tucked herself into the crevice. "So someone wants to make Kalei look guilty."

"Or to make me look weak." I shoved a hand through my hair, fingers catching in the rods of metal adorning my crown. It was so light, I'd forgotten I was wearing it. "I don't know why anyone would do this. What their aim is. But I'm…" What was I? Scared? Lost? There were so many things I was, so many things a queen shouldn't be, and I couldn't put a word to any of them. I couldn't breathe life into any of my insecurities.

Because that made them real.

Icana hummed, a sound she often made to indicate she'd heard me but didn't necessitate words. It meant she was listening to what I wasn't saying. What I couldn't say. It meant she understood.

We sat in silence while the sky and sea beyond the window darkened to a plum, navy pitch. Thoughts, each one more destructive than the last, swirled through my mind in a maelstrom of worry, tossed up like leaves in a gale against the barren landscape of my skull. Not so much stinging as sticking, heavy and rotten, dead foliage littering a forest floor after a storm. I felt like weeds. Like everything left to sink into a forgotten realm beneath the canopy of things so much older and wiser.

I couldn't breathe beneath the weight of it, and then Icana spoke up, shattering the buzzing silence.

"Why won't you tell me where we're going?"

Half of her face was cast in shadow when I glanced up, though her reflection in the pane of glass was clear, the bronze lantern light turning her blonde hair into a burning russet. Her pale gaze was a weight of its own, like twin shackles.

"Because you won't like it."

Her jaw tightened, and I had the sneaking suspicion that she already knew. She was smart. She could have guessed based on our position. But she didn't say anything to confirm whether or not she knew, simply nodded. "I trust you," she said quietly.

She shouldn't. After what happened after Xesta, Icana had no reason to trust me. No reason to keep any amount of faith in me. I was why she couldn't walk properly. I was why there was a rattle in her chest every time she spoke.

Icana was family, and I had failed my family time and time again since the moment I saw Kalei in that lighthouse and couldn't kill her. And though I didn't regret saving Kalei, everything went wrong in that moment. My family had broken apart. Icana had no reason to keep following me when there was still so much more to lose. Not across the world. Not to the one place she'd sworn never to return.

I could only hope her trust wouldn't shatter when she learned the truth. After everything we'd been through, hopefully, this wasn't the thing that broke that bond.

Several minutes passed in ponderous silence, the only sound coming from the roar of the waves outside the windows. Icana wasn't one to fill the quiet, but I needed noise. I needed something to drown out the thoughts in my head. If left too long to think, to reminisce, to pine after something I couldn't have, I'd do something I would regret. My mind was a dangerous place to be all alone.

The chair scraped across the floor as I lurched to my feet and paced to the window. Outside, the colours of the world were changing—where once I had only known the blacks of Vodaeard's cliffs, the whites of the mountains in the distance, the greys of a dreary sky perpetually obscured by rain clouds, out here there was blue sky and blue waves. Everything was so bright, deceptively so, as the weather became frigid, but that made it all the more beautiful. Sunlight caught in the breaking waves turned them gold, gems sparkling with each crash against the hull. As the sun sank towards the horizon, one side of the world was already dark, yellows and pinks and oranges stretched like shadows through the blue on the other. The world was clear, untouched out here.

Untarnished.

This was what I wanted to see every morning and every night. This was where I wanted to spend the rest of my life.

My finger tapped the glass, drawing patterns in the colours, memorizing the details of a world I would never know.

"Am I making a mistake?" I asked.

Icana's eyes flicked to me, a question in the crease of her brow.

"With Kal," I clarified. I dropped my hand from the pane and turned to her. Shadows crept up in the corners of the room as the last rays of sunlight vanished from the sky.

"What do you mean?" she pressed.

My next inhale was shaky. These were the thoughts I didn't want to acknowledge alone, but they needed to be voiced. They needed to get out of my head, be heard by someone else, someone I trusted.

"Should I let her go?" My throat tightened around the words, making them croak on the way out.

Grunting, Icana unfolded herself from the window seat and faced me, gripping my hands in a rare display of emotion. The skin on her knuckles was scarred, red and pink, and I tried not to think about how she had received those marks. I knew they didn't come from training exercises in Vodaeard.

"Evhen," she said, and there was a shakiness to her voice that had nothing to do with her injuries. "I'm not sure what's going on between the both of you, but you're making it sound like you're going to do something reckless that will result in losing her."

I shifted uncomfortably beneath her gaze.

She was right. Of course, she was.

It didn't make this moment any easier.

She narrowed her pale eyes at me. "You don't have to tell me," she continued, "but I know you, Ev. Why else would you think you need to let her go if you weren't going to do something stupid once we land?"

My breath wobbled. "It's her father," I whispered. "He's in my head. He took everyone from me, and I'm scared he'll take Kalei, too."

Icana brushed a thumb under my eye, and I realized I was crying. "You wouldn't let that happen."

I nodded, because I didn't have the energy to say anything. My world, the only life I had ever known, had been filled with doubts since I was a child. I'd thought putting this crown on my head would silence at least some of those doubts, the loudest ones I'd been hearing for years.

But it only brought new ones to the surface. Because what if it wasn't enough?

What if I couldn't save everyone?

EIGHTEEN

The next day, someone fell overboard.

By the time the woman was reported missing and spotted in the waters, she was dead. I stood at the railing, away from the crew, as they hastily cast lines into the sea and dragged up her bloated body. The waves were calm today, but a heavy air settled over the ship, palpable tension that made my skin itch.

Evhen stood by the mainmast, posture rigid, nibbling on a fingernail. Stress emanated from her, sharp eyes dancing across the deck as if she expected an attack to come straight at her. A noise from below caused her to jump.

The crown sat askew on her curls, almost like she had thrown it on upon waking in a frenzy, though the sun had been up for hours. Which led me to believe she did, in fact, take it off in private. It wasn't yet moulded to her. It wasn't as comfortable or familiar as she pretended it was.

But biting her nails, that was familiar. That was the Evhen who wasn't quite sure of her place in the world, who took control in the only way she knew how when things seemed too overwhelming. She was struggling, and this small city of a crew moved around her like they didn't notice.

Because they didn't. Why would they expect their queen to be nothing if not in command at all times?

She noticed me watching her and froze, a fingertip between her teeth. Her stare had the opposite effect of its usual searing heat—my veins turned to ice, a chill cramping in the small of my back. She reminded me suddenly of the white sky, frigid and blank, instead of the blazing sun I normally associated with her. Cold breath shredded my throat as I watched her straighten her shoulders and approach the body thumping onto the deck.

A breeze like an icy kiss wafted over me. She was newly dead, and yet she looked like she had perished weeks ago, grey skin puffing around her face and hands, features unrecognizable around the peeling rot. Salty ocean water bulged under her skin, pushing her eyes out of their sockets. And beneath her clothes—a simple navy uniform that marked her as crew, not soldier—jagged flesh crossed her stomach in vicious slashes.

A familiar tug pulled at my own stomach. Magic swirled just beneath the surface of my skin, surging from a well deep within, but I knew if I called for it, it wouldn't come. That magic had died beneath a blood moon. There were no souls here, no glowing seaweeds to claim from the Dunes of Forever. No way to call upon the bones and move this bloated carcass. The only magic I had was tied to the bones in my skin, and they twitched in agitation at the sight.

As if affronted by death.

Insulted by it.

"Your Majesty," said one of the crew members gathered around the body, straightening to talk in whispers to Evhen, heads tucked close together, and bodies angled away from the curious crowd. Nerves pitched higher the longer they talked, and several people glanced my way, suspicion blazing in their narrowed gazes.

My skin crawled with the inability to do anything. Under different circumstances, I would have offered to bring her back on the next full moon, but I didn't even know when that was anymore. My entire paradigm had shifted the moment my connection to the moon was severed. I could hardly look up at the night sky without feeling sick.

This dead crew mate was going to remain dead, and it was becoming increasingly obvious who they thought was responsible.

Someone broke off from the crowd and strode across the deck towards me. I recognized him as one of the men who stood around while the older soldier attacked me a few days ago, and did nothing. Sensing a similar argument, or at least an accusation, I shifted my stance, prepared to use my fists if I had to.

"You're awfully quiet," he said, loud enough to draw Evhen's attention away from the body. She hesitated, glassy gaze unable to focus on me, her options limited. Would she be able to run across the deck before this man struck, or would they even listen to her if she shouted for him to stop?

It didn't matter. He didn't seem concerned with whatever Evhen decided to do.

Only what I had to say on the matter.

"Should I have immediately shouted *I'm innocent*?" I asked. The stench of death was beginning to reach me, overpowering amid the salty air and choppy waves. The smell and taste and touch of death had never bothered me before, but out here, it churned my stomach.

His eyebrows shot up. "Are you?"

"Yes." I tried not to sound as frustrated as I felt, but it was difficult when all I wanted to do was walk away from this interaction. Which would not convince them to the contrary at all. "Not that you would believe me."

"Maybe you're killing us off to help your father retake Vodaeard," he sneered, delusional in his theories. But maybe it wasn't so ridiculous to think. My father had seized Vodaeard once. Why wouldn't they believe he wanted it again?

But I knew the truth about their occupation there. Evhen had told them a secret that her parents had died trying to keep safe. And it had led my father to gaining the one thing he wanted more than power—immortality. He had everything he wanted. He didn't need Evhen's home anymore.

"He has everything he needs," I said, feeling my dead magic sour in my bones and course like poison through my veins. "He doesn't need me to help him."

It was a painful truth to acknowledge out loud. My whole life, my father said my power needed to be protected, and it took me too long to realize he didn't mean me by extension. It was never about me. It had only ever been about the magic, and the legend, and the moon—that impossible power. But a small part of me still wished he cared for me. Still hoped he had even a kernel of love for me, and not the power I granted him. He was still my father, but the truth was that I was scared to be the last.

The last Maristela. The last true Marama heir.

"Then why are you still here if no one needs you?"

I felt as though I reeled back, as though his words had physically shoved me against the railing, taken my breath away, but I didn't move at all, didn't breathe at all, only stared at him while a painful ache spread across my chest. When I blinked, the entire deck—the gathering crew, the sky above, everything around me—blurred through a curtain of tears. He seemed oddly satisfied with himself for eliciting such a response, a smirk tugging at the corners of his mouth as he stepped closer, towering over me. I felt the railing dig into my back without realizing how I had let him push me towards it.

"You're worthless," he said, lowering his voice now, barely audible over the rush of waves and clanging of thoughts in my head that agreed. "Just another mouth to feed on this voyage. Next time, maybe you'll throw yourself overboard."

He didn't know that I was already dying, that Death crept a little closer every day. It was hot breath down my neck and cold fingers up my spine. It was a constant effort to stay upright, when all I wanted to do was close my eyes. This wasn't the time, though. Evhen wasn't safe yet.

The bones in my skin were vengeful things. They wanted immediate retribution. And I didn't realize I had already unwound the bandage from my arm to peel back the scab until Evhen's warm hand landed on my shoulder, and my vision cleared. Red wavered at the edges, like the rage firing in my veins, but when I looked, it was only Evhen's hair, unpinned and wild in the death-saturated breeze.

She didn't seem affected that I had almost attacked this man. Instead, she turned her patient stare on him, authority etched into the planes of her face. "Princess Kalei has immunity on this ship. She is under my protection here."

The man shifted, grumbling beneath his breath in a wordless whisper. It took some effort for me to drop my hand from the wound on my arm, Evhen's warm fingers acting as an anchor to steady me.

The queen frowned. "If you have something to say, say it now."

"It's nothing you haven't heard before, Your Majesty," he said roughly. "She's a danger to have on board. She's a threat to us all. How do you know she's innocent?"

Evhen's hand fell from my shoulder, leaving me cold and hostile. She looked around the deck—a handful of her councillors had appeared during the commotion, huddled together to whisper among themselves. Icana perched in her usual spot at the helm, overseeing the ship as if it was hers to command.

Cazendra bent over the body to examine it closely, keeping most of the crew away from it—and despite the size of the ship and how many people had duties to fulfill, everyone looked back at her expectantly. A little less suspicious than how they looked at me, aware that she was their queen and I was an outsider. It felt strange to be on this side of Evhen, to see how other people looked at her, instead of being the one to look at her.

But where they all wanted her to do something, I had only ever wanted to be the one to do something to her. They all had their own doubts about her ability to lead, but I had always known she was exactly who she needed to be in order to rule them. Now, I saw the doubts landing like barbs against her skin. Her crown wasn't enough to barricade herself against them.

"Haret!" Evhen's gaze flattened as she called to her councillor, the one who seemed to be in charge. "Gather everyone on deck. I'm going to make an announcement."

A sense of dread flattened in my stomach. She wanted to let everyone know there was a murderer on board, and not to worry, because she was certain it wasn't me. My lips pressed together, a chill spreading from my core into my toes and fingers and the top of my head.

As Haret nodded and drifted out of sight to do as commanded, I brushed my fingers against Evhen's pale, freckled arm. Even with this change in the air, she rarely wore her brocade coat, preferring a simple tunic to anything else. Warmth shot through my fingers upon contact with her skin, but she shuddered like a shiver coursed up her back, eyes like embers meeting mine with a mix of surprise and shock and something else I couldn't quite name. Regret, maybe. Longing, perhaps. Something that we had once shared, but was now lost.

"Are you sure?" I asked softly, despite my misgivings about questioning her. She was queen—her decision was final—but maybe there was still some part of her that valued my input. That yearned for me to help her make those decisions. That wished for me to stand by her side through it all. That was the part of her I appealed to now, the Evhen who had said *All of you* in a dark cave surrounded by our worst thoughts, not the Evhen who said *goodbye*.

The Evhen I loved, not the Evhen I lost.

She reached up—almost hesitantly, as if unsure how to proceed with this brief display of affection—and tucked an errant strand of bone-studded hair behind my cheek. I ignored the way her finger twitched when it connected with the shard of bone, and instead leaned into her warmth, her palm cupping my cheek. Fire streaked across my skin where her thumb brushed a path. I wanted to stay in this moment forever, the sensation of her skin on mine silencing the darkness in my mind. There was only us, a sunless white sky above and an endless, depthless sea beneath. Nothing else mattered but this moment, fragile veins of gold mending the chipped porcelain of our lives.

"I have to do this," she answered, and I hated how that was her excuse for everything.

Hated that I hated it. She didn't *have* to do anything, and she certainly didn't have to do it alone.

Her hand fell from my face, leaving a searing mark in its place on my skin, and she walked away without another word, another promise, another touch, the light in her eyes snuffed out like a torch.

Heart thumping painfully in my chest, I looked around the deck, searching for I didn't know what.

Something to hit, something to hurl. Something to hurt.

Heart thumping painfully in my chest, I looked around the deck, searching for I didn't know what. Something to hit, something to hurl. Something to hurt.

No one came close to me as they passed around the word to gather, suspicion keeping them far away. But their whispers reached me regardless, carried on a salty breeze over the dead body.

I did the only thing I could think to do when the whispers became too loud—I settled into the one thing I knew, the one thing I understood. Death. The pull of it, the promise of that dark tunnel leading to the door and the shore and the dunes and the souls, drew me towards the body, and like a wave, everyone gathered around it parted, moving aside to slot me in the empty space they left behind.

I crouched next to her, this body that used to be alive, a shell that once breathed, and didn't recognize it. Up close, there were only the signs of death—pale blue lips, sunken hollow cheeks, gouged bloated stomach—and none of it felt familiar. With the bodies I used to bring back, there were always glimpses. Fragmented images of the lives they had, spiralling in the tunnel, cascading over me like waterfalls of grief and agony, love and bliss. Their lives were simple to imagine. But this—without my power, I didn't see the woman she used to be. I didn't see a life lived.

I only saw the aftermath of one cut short. Fingers curled like claws, legs bent at odd angles, a torso torn to shreds. She had died, and I felt no connection to her, as if she'd never had a soul at all. It was the first time—I realized with a pang—that I'd seen a dead body since I lost my power. The severed arm had almost felt the same way, a useless artefact of something long lost, but I'd thought that feeling was just because it was only a limb, not an entire body. Seeing this woman now, this husk, emphasized that empty feeling—that lack of something intrinsic.

The lack of a soul.

Under the light of the full moon, I'd been able to bring bodies back from the dead just by seeing them. As if in the depths, they were still connected to their souls, and by seeing them, I could reach for their lives in Death's domain. Maybe, with this new power that answered blood instead of the moon, there was something else I had to do in order to reach their souls. Maybe touch, because sight and smell certainly weren't helping.

I placed a hand over her chest and shut my eyes, pushing out all other thoughts, focusing on the singular sense of touch—the skin beneath my fingers, the lumps of her chest, the solid layer of frozen innards that didn't budge. It all felt wrong. Not soft like bodies should be. Like she was made of rock, or ice.

Or bone.

"Kal!" a shrill voice speared through my thoughts.

A wave of darkness rolled through my mind, peeling away like shadows dispersed by morning light. A gasp clawed up my throat as the darkness took on the shape of wings and then vanished, and I felt warmth oozing over my hand.

I shook my head and looked up to see Evhen above me. Haloed by the red sun, she looked like a portent of Death itself. A sea of bodies surrounded her on the deck, everyone staring in horror at me, at her, at the cutlass in Evhen's grip. Tipped down towards me. My heart.

No, not at my heart. At my hand, which had pushed through the woman's chest like she was made of glass, my fingers folded over a piece of her rib cage.

No, not at my heart. At my hand, which had pushed through the woman's chest like she was made of glass, my fingers folded over a piece of her rib cage.

Nausea bubbled in my belly. Evhen looked disgusted by the scene, and I slowly pulled my hand out of the woman's body, her thick blood squelching between my fingers

My palm caught on a jagged piece of her breastbone, broken so easily beneath the weight of my hand that I hadn't even realized I'd done it until it was too late.

A drop of my black blood dripped into the cavity of her chest, and the rib I'd grasped not a moment ago snapped apart. The broken shard shot out and up, straight through my palm, and I fell back against the deck with a groan, flinging my arm out as if to toss the bone away.

While it wiggled and settled beside the other pieces of borrowed bones, memories of a life that wasn't my own scrolled in disjointed flashes across my vision, until it all went dark.

NINETEEN

Kalei was still unconscious, laying on the bed in my quarters, when I addressed the ship.

I stood where I had only days ago to accept my crown, but this time my council wasn't behind me, and I stared out at a sea of bodies, seeing only suspicion. Distrust. The people who were meant to follow me did not believe in me. And it was evident on all their faces.

"Yesterday, the soldier I sent to the brig for attacking Princess Kalei was found dead in his cell," I started, letting my voice carry to the far end of the ship. Out here, there were no gulls to contend with, no sounds of fishing or masonry, only the ceaseless rush of waves splitting around the hull. It allowed my voice to carry with ease, but it also allowed their voices to carry back to me, hushed and urgent, whispers of doubts and accusations.

I raised a hand for silence. "Today, another member of our crew fell overboard."

"Fell?" someone shouted from the deck below. "Or was pushed?"

A murmur of agreement rippled through the crowd. At this moment, they were all the same to me, crew and soldier alike, people whose homes had been invaded, who had lost friends or children or parents on that bloody beach. They were people who saw me as a failure, as a disappointment to my parents' legacy.

"We don't know yet," I answered, raising my voice to be heard over their grumblings. "There were wounds on her stomach that looked intentional, but that's all we know. At the advice of my council, I am investigating these two deaths as murders. Possibly by the same person, but I do not have any more information than that. I can assure you—"

"Are there any suspects?" someone else shouted, and then several people were yelling at once, a clamouring of voices like rocks being thrown at the inside of my skull. My mouth hung open as I stared at them, unable to find my voice among theirs, the breath sticking in my throat. A heartbeat drummed in my ears, frantic and anxious, until that was all I could hear. Worry echoed in each beat. The sour sense that I had failed, was failing, would continue to fail. I didn't know how to be queen. This was only a small portion of Vodaeard. What would the rest of them think when they learned I couldn't even talk during my first official declaration as queen?

Until, "It was the Princess of Bones!" a deep voice rose above the rest. A new name, a new title, that startled me enough to drag my attention back to the crowd. "You saw what she did to Relyna's body. And the other victim—he approached her, too. It has to be her."

Disappointment settled over me like a well-worn blanket. A tiring complaint that I'd heard over and over again. Part of me had wished it would be different out here, that these soldiers had left their prejudices on the beach. But they'd only brought them here, sharpened them into weapons. And Kalei, of course, wasn't making it easy. It was as if she wanted to be guilty. She had plunged her hand through Relyna's chest like the bloated skin was paper. Nothing had terrified me more, and too many people had seen her do it. I could only defend her for so long before they started calling me a traitor, too.

The crowd was shouting again, calling for retribution. For Kalei's blood. They were all brave when they spoke as one, and that was the problem—I couldn't distinguish one voice from the next, which meant I didn't know who to punish.

And I couldn't punish the whole crew.

Their shouts were indiscernible now. They didn't care what they said anymore. Their voices had drowned out mine. As panic clawed through my chest, I scoured the crowd. At the edge, I spotted Breva and Akev, with very different expressions on their old and young faces. Breva appeared concerned, wizened hands fidgeting beneath her cloak, wispy strands of grey hair flitting in the wind. Akev's frown deepened with every passing second until he was scowling at the crowd. His hands balled into fists, and I recognized the familiar gesture, the heat of anger in his gaze. Despite the chilly northern wind, it warmed me, and lessened the panic in my chest.

I didn't see Haret or Aunt Caz, but I didn't need their authoritative voices in order to be heard now. I was their *queen*, and they were going to listen to me.

"Silence!" I shouted. The wind carried my voice across the deck, flinging it to the bow and back, crashing against the mainmast where the chimes sang in the ensuing quiet. The only sound for a long moment was the ring of the bells and the hush of the waves against the hull as we cut north. Finally, I had the attention of the whole ship, and I didn't quite know what to do with it.

"Say something," Eiramis prodded quietly, standing behind me at the helm. "You are their queen. Don't take their silence for compliance. They're angry"

"I'm angrier," I growled. And I was. For too long, I had been the silent, compliant one. I'd been too scared to be angry, thinking that part of me had been lost beneath the waves along with my life. I wasn't scared anymore.

Suddenly, I didn't see the crowd before me as a mob full of hate. They weren't just a show of force, a farce. They had joined an army, and I was going to need it together when we landed in Geirvar. We were going to show the Chief of Marama that we were not going to be intimidated by him anymore. And that started here, on this ship, with me taking charge.

"Four months ago," I started slowly, letting the weight of grief echo in my voice, "the Chief of Marama came to our shores and killed our king and queen. I was there in the throne room when it was painted with their blood. I was there when he cut out their hearts and turned to do the same to me. I survived him. And with your help, we can survive him again, together."

I paused, holding their gazes for a long moment. My palms itched, the crown heavy between my curls, but I could not let them see weakness right now.

"My brother was taken from me, and the chief wants my life in exchange for his." This caused a ripple through the crowd, a murmur of surprise that grew and grew until one voice sounded above the noise.

"Give him the princess instead!"

I quickly lifted a hand for silence again, my breath catching. "If you feel so strongly, step up so I can address you properly." Rage clipped the edges of my voice, but no one moved. No one spoke. "Don't hide yourself in the masses. I know what you all think about the princess."

"She did her father's bidding," another voice added.

Several more chimed in with agreement.

"So did I," I snapped back. That was enough to silence them, though in shock and suspicion instead of respect. "For three months, he sent letters asking me to do things. Demanding information about our political neighbours, funds, anything that could help him. And I did it all, because he had my brother. Because every single one of you would rather have Alekey as your king instead of me as your queen."

Someone at the front of the crowd scoffed, the sound biting. "The prince would never do what you did. He wouldn't risk his kingdom's safety like that."

"He already did!" I shouted. The pain and anger I had felt about Alekey's betrayal swelled in my chest again, burning my throat. I had wanted to let him rot for what he did, the suffering that Talen and Icana went through because of him.

But that was before he had been taken. That was before the chief of Marama threatened the last bit of family I had. As angry as I was at Alekey, I couldn't fault him anymore. He had been deceived. He only wanted to save his friends. And I was doing the exact same thing, only on a grander scale.

I took a breath that rattled on the way in and out. "My brother made some decisions that put our kingdom at risk to save my life, and now his is at stake. The decisions I've made haven't been any better, but I'm not giving in to the chief's demands anymore." I glanced at the deck boards beneath my feet, trying to imagine my father standing here and making a speech to his loyal crew.

When I lifted my head, the crown shifted, throwing the sun's light in an array around my body. "I didn't want this crown. Not really. I didn't think I was worthy of it. I only put it on so you would remember me as a queen who sacrificed herself for her country. But I don't want to be remembered like that anymore. I want to be the queen who does whatever it takes to keep her kingdom safe. And if that means war with the Chief of Marama, then are you sailors or soldiers?"

"Soldiers!" came the cry from behind me. I glanced back at Eiramis, who winked, and then the call was echoed below, until it was louder than the voices in my head telling me I wasn't good enough.

When the cheering died down, there were a few faces in the crowd who did not look pleased. My stomach twisted at their heavy stares, as though they were not satisfied with this outcome. But I let my gaze slide over them, looking instead to the dozens more who were on my side. People who had bled and fought for Vodaeard.

People who had loved my parents. Who loved my brother. Who had volunteered to go on this voyage to rescue him. Who knew they might die along the way. People I was going to protect.

"Back to your duties," I called out when the deck was quiet again. "We'll be landing in a few days. Some of you need to train."

As they dispersed, two figures at the base of the quarterdeck caught my attention. Aunt Caz watched the thinning crowd, back turned to me. Haret gestured to someone I couldn't see and started climbing the steps towards me. A smug expression crossed his face when he caught my eye, and a sense of warning blared through my body.

I tensed, moving closer to Eiramis, when five more people climbed the stairs behind Haret.

The helmsman's hand fell to his sword, one eye on the sea, one eye on the swarm.

"Haret," I said tightly. My fingers itched towards my hip, but there was no weapon sheathed there.

"Princess Evhen," he replied lightly.

My veins prickled. "*Queen*," I reminded him. The five other men, brutishly tall and thick, moved into a loose circle around me. They each wore a pin on their collars, crossed swords through a gem, and I tried to recall where I'd seen the symbol before when a scream pierced the air.

The sound froze my blood, and I made one halting step towards my quarters when Haret blocked my path.

"Haret, what are you doing?" I asked, voice low, but lacking any of the danger. Instead, terror gripped each word.

His eyes gleamed in the blazing sunlight. "Putting the Princess of Bones behind bars," he answered. "Something you should have done a long time ago."

The world tipped around me, though the boat remained steady. "You can't." The words rang hollow, with no authority behind them, lost to the horror of his actions against me. Against Kalei. "Haret, let her go. That's an order."

"I don't take orders from you," he said, too calm and sure of himself. "This has been too long coming, Princess. A government that *we* can control."

My gaze swivelled to the other men. Though they looked like sailors and fishermen, there was a different shade to their skin tones. Not the pale, ivory tones of most Vodaeardeans. "Who's *we*?"

Haret folded his hands behind his back. The pin gleamed wickedly. "Your father almost found us out too soon. Luckily, he was silenced quickly, and now my king is in a position to take Vodaeard."

Fear washed over me. My knees nearly buckled, and I grabbed the helm to stay upright. Eiramis's grip tightened on the wheel, knuckles white as he eyed the men.

"Your king…" I whispered, the symbol on their pins flashing in my mind. I had seen it four months ago, in a glittering castle built on a graveyard. The jewel of Xesta. King Ovono's realm.

"That's not possible," I said, shaking my head as if I could stop this revelation from hitting my ears. "King Ovono died when Xesta fell. Kalei killed him."

"Did she?" He raised a brow, posing the question in a way that made me rethink what I had seen.

"You're Vodaeardean," I said, scrambling for anything to say. "Why are you doing this? Did he promise you something? Believe me, Haret, it's not worth selling out your country for."

"You would know, wouldn't you, Princess? That was a pretty speech you made, but the farce ends here. Your reign ends here." Haret waved a hand, and one of the men behind me surged forward, seizing my wrist.

Eiramis's sword sang as he unsheathed it, but one of the other men slammed the blunt end of their own sword into his skull, and he went sprawling across the deck.

I screamed his name, the first syllable barely out, when a meaty palm covered my mouth, cutting off my cry. I thrashed, but the man was a mountain, pinning me against his chest with an arm the size of a barrel over my ribs. I frantically looked around for someone, anyone, to see what was happening and intervene, but everyone had returned to their duties or cabins. The only person who watched us was Aunt Caz, standing at the top of the stairs, and I growled her name, muffled behind the man's hand.

Pain lanced up and down my side. Stars dotted my vision, the heavy arm pressing up into my abdomen. This was all wrong. They were hauling Eiramis away. Someone from the circle took his place at the helm, and I knew it was over. My strength failed, and I sagged, but I had one clear thought before the darkness swooped in. Haret had cut my reign short, but I would make him regret ever stoking the fire of my anger with his fucking pride.

TWENTY

Shadows coalesced in the corners of my mind. They took on the shape of winged creatures. Lunging, gnashing, thrashing. Between their teeth flashed images of a life I hadn't lived.

The woman. The sailor. She had been happy. Married. Pregnant. Lost the baby, and her life lost its joy. Each memory after was carved with pain and grief. I knew those emotions. Knew them well.

The shadows materialized into one. I couldn't escape it, couldn't free myself from my own mind, and it snarled at me with jagged teeth. Blood oozed from its mouth. Wings stretched behind its back, wrapping around my mind, and I tried to scream.

Death, it was called.

The creature I had stolen from countless times. Who sent a messenger after me when I spent too long in its realm.

I had survived the ritual, and now Death had finally come for me.

You took what was mine, it said in a voice like knives, waves, flames. It burned as it washed over me, sliding between my ribs and lungs. *Now I will take it back.*

No, I wanted to say, but the word didn't come. No words came, only a pained scream, endless.

I will take it all back, it promised.

Twenty-One

They confined me to my quarters.

I paced the small cabin, from window to door and back again, wearing a trail in the carpet. We were only a few days out from Geirvar, and I had lost command as quickly as I had taken it. What bothered me more than Haret's betrayal was the fact that Aunt Caz had stood by and done *nothing* to stop it. She hadn't looked pleased—Aunt Caz *never* looked pleased—but she was involved. She had known. I just couldn't figure out why Wystan was working with Xesta to overthrow me.

It had been one day since the coup, and I was already unravelling. They didn't allow visitors. They wouldn't tell me if Kalei was all right. I was forced to live with the impression of her in my bed and the horrid memories of her reaching into that dead sailor's body. She must not have known what she was doing, but it still jarred me every time I closed my eyes and saw it happening again. Her hand, plunging straight through bone and heart.

A scream built up in my chest. I clamped my mouth shut, digging in my heels. Even if I screamed, the guards outside my door wouldn't come in. But there was no other release for this restless, angry anxiety that clawed at my throat. I wanted to bite my nails or scratch my arms until they bled or rip my hair out from the roots. Everything I wanted to do to hurt myself would be too fleeting. It wouldn't sate this energy in me.

Instead, I closed my eyes and found my father's ring. When I had first received it a few months ago, the band felt heavy and hollow at the same time—a weight I couldn't carry because it had lost its meaning. I had tried for days to find a connection to my father in its warped shape, only to toss it away with all the other things that brought me shame—the letters from Kalei's father, the crown I never wanted to wear. It sat in a drawer and collected dust.

Until last week, when that final letter arrived. If I was going to leave my home for the last time, I wanted a piece of my father with me. The remaining bit of family I had left. Spinning the ring on my finger now, I sensed him in the grooves. It was strange to feel his presence when most of my memories of him had been lost to the sea with siren magic—when I gave up my cutlass in exchange for Kalei's life. The memories associated with that sword were murky, as if they didn't happen to me, but nothing could fully erase my parents from existence. The band of his ring was warm now, and it brought me a small amount of comfort—enough to ease the tension from my shoulders and get rid of the urges to hurt myself.

I opened my eyes when a knock sounded at my door. There were no voices on the other side. Unease crept up my spine. Why were the guards letting someone knock?

I padded across the carpet. Before opening the door, I touched my father's ring again, and told myself it was nothing.

When I opened the door, a dark figure lunged at me. All I saw was a cloak, a hood, and a mask before white-hot pain seared between my ribs. My vision wavered with bursts of light, and I grabbed the edge of the door, trying to shut it on the assailant. With one hand pressed against my side, warmth leaking between my fingers, I shoved all my weight into the door, and it slammed shut. The bolt fell into place.

Pain like fire licked along my veins with every frantic beat of my heart. I looked down at my hand, covered in my own blood, and felt the world tilt around me.

My body slipped against the door.

A thought slipped through my mind, there and gone. It seemed important, but fleeting. My head spun. This was more than just a knife between my ribs, more than just my blood spilling onto the floor. Something else moved in my veins.

I slipped again, my body dragging itself down the door. The door. That was it. I had to open the door. Someone had knocked.

Throwing all my strength into the action, I slid the bolt back and pulled the door open, falling against the frame to keep myself upright. A figure stood at the end of the short hall, outlined by the glow of a harsh sun streaming onto the deck.

"Aunt Caz?" I mumbled, and then sank to the ground as she sprinted forward, the hallway going dark.

Pain. Excruciating, alarming, white-hot pain. It tore through my limbs, set my lungs on fire, turned the inside of my mind red, and then...it was gone. It didn't vanish in an instant, but gradually lessened until I wasn't screaming into the confines of my own nightmares. Until I could feel my body settling against soft blankets. Until I could open my eyes again, and it didn't feel like a thousand knives stabbing my eyeballs.

It hurt. Everything hurt. My joints, my limbs, my ribs—black seas, my ribs felt like they were missing—but it was bearable. I grit my teeth as a groan rose in my throat.

"Oh, thank the seas," Aunt Caz murmured beside me. She grabbed a glass of water from the side table and lifted it to my lips.

I stared at her, then the cup, and my thirst won against my suspicion. I gulped down the water, wincing as the movement jostled my side. "What happened?" I asked thickly, looking around my room. The only other person was Icana, stationed by the door, arms folded and eyes narrowed at Aunt Caz.

"You were stabbed," Aunt Caz said, pointedly ignoring Icana's glare. "The blade was poisoned. You're fortunate your weapons master knows a great deal about poisons." As she said this, she looked across the room at Icana. There was a glimmer of something dark in my weapons masters' eyes. I knew that look. Felt it myself. Suspicion.

Gritting my teeth, I pushed myself up until I was more or less sitting against the wall, pillows bunched under my lower back.

"I'm fortunate you were so quick to find me," I said, hoping my tone conveyed my message. I didn't want to suspect my aunt of anything, but why had she been in the hall, anyway? Even though my mind had been addled with poison, I was sure not enough time had passed for my attacker to disappear. Surely, Aunt Caz had seen something.

Aunt Caz frowned down at me. In that moment, she looked so much like my mother. My heart ached at the familiarity. We could have been closer, had she chosen understanding over jealousy.

I was eleven, and it was my first time meeting the girl who would become my weapons master and best friend and skilled navigator. She was tall, with fair hair and fair skin and fair eyes, and I had never been more terrified of a person before. She looked angry, twirling a pair of knives between her fingers. The blades caught the rare glimmer of sun and scattered the light in all directions. Like it was also too scared to get close to her.

My father put a hand on my shoulder. He had always seemed large to me—I didn't have Alekey's height. Even though my brother was two years younger, he already loomed over me. It annoyed me to think I might never be tall and intimidating like that. But I had been practicing my scowl in the mirror, and matched the girl's across from me.

"Evhen," my father said in his gentle voice, the one he reserved for me and Alekey. I had heard snippets of his other voice before, the one he used with his council and kingdom. And, behind closed doors, the voice he used with our mother. Softer even than this one.

"This is Icana," he continued, gesturing to the girl, though who else could he have been talking about? We were alone in the courtyard. "She is going to be your weapons master."

At the time, it was just a fancy title for trainer. I didn't need weapons yet.

I looked up at my father. The crown he wore looked like the sun's rays came out of his head. And with the glow of the sun behind him, I could almost imagine he was the morning light itself.

"Why can't Aunt Caz train me?" I whined.

His mouth turned slightly down at the sides. He didn't like it when I whined. *Queens don't whine to get what they want*, he'd said.

"Aunt Caz doesn't live in Vodaeard," he told me. "Icana does now."

I didn't know what he meant by *now*, and didn't ask. I didn't want to train with someone who looked like she could kill me with her little finger.

Then my father bent down to my level, hand still pressed into my shoulder. It wasn't a heavy weight, but it would become one later. *Responsibility*, it would be called

"You're going to be queen one day, Evhen," my father said, his voice shifting out of the soft tones to something firmer. "One day, this crown will be yours. And you'll need to learn everything that comes with it. That means training with people outside of your family. Outside of your comfort zone." He poked me in the chest, a silly gesture that made me squirm, but one that made me think about how far my comfort zone extended. It had never been very far.

"But who is she?" I pressed, eyeing her. She hadn't moved, continuing to watch us with keen eyes that unnerved me. "Where does she come from?"

When my father answered, it wasn't in response to my question. "In time, you'll learn that you have allies in other countries and enemies in other countries. And sometimes, you'll have enemies much closer to home that look like allies. You'll need to learn how to recognize them. Who to trust."

I bit my lip, a nervous habit. "So what is she? An ally or an enemy?"

"Come find out for yourself," the girl answered, lips drawn back into a wolfish grin.

"Aunt Caz," I said, hating the way my voice wavered, "please tell me you're not working with Haret. With those traitors."

Aunt Caz set her jaw and leaned back in her chair. She took a breath, one I recognized as a grounding motion. I braced myself for a horrible truth.

"A few years ago," she started, "one of our border guards intercepted a letter from Xesta to Vodaeard addressed simply to *The Crow*. Thinking it was a misspelling of *crown* and it was meant for your father, the guard let it go. I did not. I had one of my spies track the note and learned that it had been received by Haret. Over the years, he had received dozens of these notes from Xesta, always addressed to The Crow. I didn't like it, so I did some investigating."

She paused. "Crows were used in Xesta for centuries to send coded messages to their allies, but it was also a name given to their spies planted in other countries. The last mention of the name was over a hundred years ago, around the time that Xesta became a prominent hub of trade on the continent. A peaceful time. Then King Ovono comes into power, and the name starts travelling around again?"

Aunt Caz shook her head, fury sparking in the lines of her face. "I begged my commander to let me look into it further. I discovered Haret had a growing circle of followers in Vodaeard, but when I was going to confront them, the chief of Marama had launched his first attacks." Her gaze collided with mine, soft and sorrowful. My parents had died before she could warn them about enemies in their own nation.

"I'm not here working with Haret," she told me. "I'm trying to bring him down. The corruption in Xesta has gone too far. I won't let it ruin what little family I have left."

"He doesn't suspect you?" Icana asked from the door. She hadn't lowered her arms, but her glare wasn't as harsh.

"Would I be here, alone, otherwise?" Aunt Caz shot back. "He thinks I'm here patching up my niece and trying to get information out of her."

"Well, you can tell him I didn't talk," I grumbled.

Aunt Caz opened her mouth to say something, then thought better of it. She rose and rounded the bed.

"Whatever happens next," she said, "I'm your family, Evhen. Remember that. Haret thinks Wystan is on his side. It's the only reason he trusts me right now."

Icana moved aside as she approached the door.

"Aunt Caz," I called before she could leave. She glanced over her shoulder at me. "Did Haret try to have me killed?"

The crease between her brows disappeared. "I don't know. But I'm going to make sure it doesn't happen again."

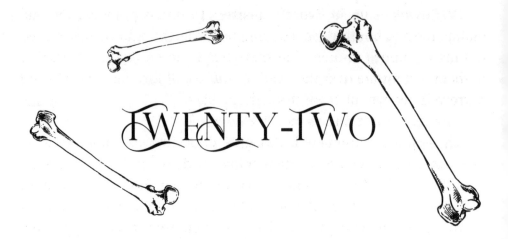

Twenty-Two

I spent three days in a cell that smelled of blood and death.

No one was allowed to visit, except to bring food and water, and no one spoke to me. Still, I'd gathered bits and pieces—Haret had staged a coup against Evhen. She was confined to her quarters, the helmsman was locked up somewhere else, and we were very close to Geirvar. Very close to my father. And I still didn't understand why I was in a prison cell.

Though I had my guesses. There was a murderer on board, and too many people had seen me shove my hand through that woman's chest, though the act had been entirely unintentional. I had simply meant to see what she had seen, in life, to know if there was still a soul attached to her body. Grabbing a bone, being flooded with her memories, had been unexpected. But it was damning enough.

Shivers wracked my body. It was cold and damp in the belly of the ship. The only lantern had guttered out a day ago, and no one cared to revive its flame. So I was sitting alone in the dark, hugging my knees to my chest and pretending I didn't see the shadowy creature in the corner when Haret stomped down the stairs.

Three men followed him, their heavy footsteps echoing loudly against the beams above me and the bars around me. I flinched at the sounds, watching them approach. It was the same men who had first brought me down here.

I had woken up in Evhen's quarters to hands grabbing me and pulling me and binding me. I'd screamed, tried to fight them off, tried to fling my bones at them, but there had been no blood to use. One of them had hit me over the head. A bruise still throbbed there, and I narrowed my eyes at them through the bars.

"Get up," Haret said to me. "We're here."

My stomach plummeted, though I didn't move. Couldn't move. The last thing I remember happening on deck, with that woman's body, had drained all the energy out of me. For three days, I'd been tormented by memories of a life that wasn't mine playing through my head. It was exhausting to hold back her memories, to stop them from impressing themselves on my own. It was confusing, what was and wasn't real, and I was so very tired of fighting it.

"Get up," Haret said again, motioning to one of the men. The man unlocked the cell and reached in. My head swam as he hauled me to my feet, but I didn't struggle, swaying. He shook me as he wound rope around my wrists, and I bit my tongue against the surge of bile in my throat.

"Please don't," I begged, and I wasn't sure if I was begging Haret or the man or my own body.

Outside, my first view of Geirvar was the imposing grey mountains spearing the sky. My breath hitched at the sight, and I strained to see more, but they were already dragging me down the ramp. My feet slipped over the wood and then hit stone, and I gasped at the first sensation of solid ground in over a week.

Geirvar was all rocks. A cold sun disappeared in the grey clouds that had rolled in once we landed. The shore curving around us was sharp, jagged stones slicing into the sea like swords. A thin layer of ice coated the water, breaking into tiny shards around the hull of the bulking ship, and a gust of wind blew off the sea to welcome us, cutting through cloaks and coats. I shivered and burrowed deep into the collar around my throat—no one had thought to give me a cloak or jacket, so the frigid wind bit into my arms and chest.

Haret left me on the pier with one of the men while he went back on board. I craned my neck to take in the height of the ship. I hadn't fully appreciated the vessel when I went down to the dock that day. Its hull was scraped, water-stained, and covered in a sheen of ice. A strange mirror to the people it had carried across the sea. Hardened but resilient.

It was very similar to the land we were on. Geirvar shot out of the sea like a defiant beast, rising into the sky. Sparse trees prickled the foothills in the distance, jutting up between black and white rocks, barely bending in the wind that sliced over the ground. It was a land determined to be seen and felt. To be feared. As if, by sheer will and association, it had bred such monsters as Evhen described simply because that was what nature demanded. It was a tough landscape, so only the toughest could survive here.

There was beauty here, hidden, a secret only for those who knew where to look, but I didn't have the energy to look hard enough. Instead, my gaze drifted to the ship again, the hull bulging with swords and cannons, dipping in the shallow waters like it was going to run aground when the tide ebbed.

Noise erupted on the deck, and my chest tightened with panic.

Evhen's voice, shrill and venomous, rose over the side of the ship and fell like fog over the docks. A pair of guards led her down the gangplank, and she cursed and spat and roared in indignation when her feet landed on solid ground. Haret stepped in front of her and nodded at the soldiers, and they pushed her to her knees just so they could twist her arms and tie tough rope over her wrists. Wild curls fell into her face, turning her a stunning shade of crimson in the white light of an early winter sun, and she looked up at Haret through a curtain of fire.

And spat on his boots.

Haret frowned at the globule on his foot. "Evhen, please," he chided with all the muster of a father scolding his disobedient child. "That was undignified."

She surged up, nearly wrenching herself out of the guards' grips, but they tightened their hold on her. "You stripped me of my dignity the moment you staged a coup against me," she snarled. "I will act however I want to act, and when we get back to Vodaeard, I'm going to watch your body sway in the courtyard."

He chuckled at that. "You misunderstand your position, Princess."

The anger bled out of Evhen's face as she realized what was happening. My stomach churned as the same realization dawned on me, not gentle like the rising sun, but quick as a tidal wave.

Haret leered at the queen. "This isn't to prevent you from stopping me when I hand the princess over to her father," he continued, a grin pulling at the corner of his lips as the colour drained out of Evhen's face. "This is to prevent you from stopping me when I hand you *both* over to her father."

Our gazes met over the short distance, a broken soul and an empty one colliding, her cracks filling my crevices. She bled into me, that one bright soul who didn't belong on Death's dark shore, who came back wrong. Chills ran along my spine.

"*No*," I whispered, the pieces tumbling in fragmented shards through my mind. It didn't make sense. Evhen had already made the decision to sacrifice herself. So why did it look like the betrayal went further than Haret's coup? My eyes widened a fraction, then burned with tears as the wind knifed down the pier. "You changed your mind," I whispered.

Her lips pulled back, anger thrumming off of her in waves. "I had to," she seethed, still pulling against the men who held her fast. "They were turning against me. They were turning against you."

I shook my head, as if that simple action could stop all of this from happening. "No. No. I was going to handle it. I was going *in* your place. I was going to let him have me instead!"

"Oh, that's sweet," Haret mumbled, while Evhen's eyes brimmed with tears. She didn't cry often, so the sight of it shocked me, but then they were pulling her away.

"*Wait!*" she cried, straining. Beneath her cloak, I glimpsed red skin where her wrists chaffed against the rope. "Kalei, you can't do that! Please don't do that for me!"

They hauled her down the dock, letting her scream the entire way, towards the road winding into the port town where roofs peeked over the crest. When her screams finally faded, my legs buckled, and I hit the dock with bone-jarring force. A sob burst out of my chest. No one moved to help me up. Haret had already disappeared into the harbourmaster's house, and we were to wait for him.

A peculiar scent wafted down the shore, almost like the salt air that rose over Vodaeard, but colder. More metallic. A few fishermen nearby glanced over, huddled together with their nets and hooks, items so familiar to me. Those were the tools I used when I dived into the depths—nets and hooks to scrape the souls like seaweed off the shores and cast them back into their waiting bodies. But these frayed nets, these rusted hooks, had no higher meaning. No greater purpose than to catch fish. But the fishermen watched us like they knew, suspicion gilded in blue eyes.

Behind me, Icana stepped off the gangplank, punctuated by the thud of her cane. She promptly raised her middle finger into the air, and unease spread like ice across the pier and its workers. The fishermen straightened, mouths down-turned, and the sailors and message boys paused in their clamouring across the boards to stare. Not in disapproval at her gesture, but in contempt at her presence.

I raised my head to look up at her. Those blue eyes, like the eyes of men around us, and hair so pale it looked like bleached wheat in the harsh light. The angles of her jaw were like the sharp peaks of the mountains. She could have been carved from the same stone.

My chest heaved as I opened my mouth, voice catching on another sob when I asked, "What is this place to you?"

"Home," she answered with a scowl twisting her features.

My heart jumped in my chest. *Home.* Once, I had known what that word meant. Endless sun and warm beaches and glowing volcanoes. Fruit trees and glittering palaces and strong lighthouses. Now, I wasn't so sure where home was anymore. But for Icana, it was here.

"This place smells worse than when I left it," she grumbled to me. Her sharp gaze locked on the sailors and fishermen and workers along the dock, as if the twin blades at her back were not enough to keep them away.

I sensed them drawing closer, but since my only reputation here was the Princess of Death, I kept my head down, not eager to see recognition spreading like wildfire through the country so soon. Maybe they didn't know me, but I wouldn't take that risk.

"What did it smell like when you left?" I asked, trying to focus on anything other than the look on Evhen's face when she'd been pulled away from me.

Icana frowned, sensing the question I didn't ask. *Why did you leave?* I knew better than to prod the weapons master for an answer she didn't want to give.

She was quiet for a moment, debating how much to reveal, how much mattered now that we were already here. Now that people were already starting to recognize her. "Like fire and fish," she finally answered. "The country was burning when I left. I set it on fire to cover my escape, and this port smelled like charred fish. It's not a pleasant smell."

I wrinkled my nose, trying to imagine such a stench. Fish was familiar, but fire…fire was too wild. My days on the island consisted of cold crypts and sandy shores, warm winds, and balmy breezes. Fires of woodsmoke and char on our island were contained, not the sizzle of burning flesh or scorching land. I could not imagine a whole country on fire, certainly not this one, now encapsulated in ice, white and grey and blue like winter storms.

"What does it smell like now?" I asked, wondering which had changed more—the country or the woman.

Icana tipped her chin up to sniff the air. She made another face. "Diseased. And desperate."

The disease must be my father, a man determined enough to have dominion over the world that he would try to slaughter his daughter for the curse of immortality. Maybe he had also sailed into this port, marched his way across the land, made himself a throne in the heart of a lawless place. But was it his desperation, or theirs, that she could smell now?

Now, she sniffed derisively and lowered her gaze again to glare at the men gathering at the end of our dock.

"How many of them do you know?" I whispered. They formed a line at the end of the pier, not saying a word, not yet threatening, but an invisible thread seemed to connect every one of them to her.

She reached down to help me up. "All of them," she said into the narrow space between us. "I only left six years ago. That's not nearly enough time to erase memories of this place."

As we waited on the dock, a collection of guards huddled around me and Icana, hands resting on weapons, and I didn't know if it was because they thought I would try to escape, or the dock workers would try to attack. The rope bit into my wrists. The threads sucked in the icy air from around us, and magnified it against my skin, searing pain from the cold lancing through me with every cutting breeze.

"Do they all know you?" I asked, looking everywhere but at the crowd forming around us. A whisper had begun to travel up the road into town, insidious ahead of us, and the air was changing with the announcement of our arrival. I squirmed as I did in King Ovono's kingdom, when my face had been plastered around the city with a grand reward for news of my whereabouts, becoming increasingly worried that our arrival had set in motion something that couldn't be undone. Something that would change the very boundaries of the world. An immortal man and his Death-defying daughter, together at last, war tearing them apart and bringing them back again.

Icana's sword-sharp smile was bitter with secrets. "Of course," she answered without an explanation. This was the one thing Icana wouldn't divulge, not without blood and teeth. She seemed strangely pleased with their reactions. As if she had predicted they would be nothing but enraged by her return.

Haret reemerged from the harbourmaster's house. The hazy light from the hidden sun leeched the colour from his skin. Soon, the storm sweeping over the mountains would reach us, and I hoped Haret had shelter prepared for when that happened.

"Come along, Princess," he said, curling his fingers at me, a yellowed parchment in his grip. A grey seal twisted into view, and my stomach plummeted with all the grace of the world falling out beneath my feet.

A full moon and crossbones.

"Your father awaits."

Twenty-Three

Night crashed over the port town with a storm as violent as the one raging in my head. Betrayal sunk teeth deep into my bones, draining me of everything but burning anger.

Ever since that day on the beach, Kalei had been cold—life leeching from her as a part of her was lost to the depths when her father spilled her blood. Meanwhile, I had been growing hotter and hotter, feverish in my need to save my brother, save my kingdom. Now, I was on fire, and there was nothing I could do to stave off the flames from leaving a charred corpse in their wake.

Except now, the world was going to feel my wrath. Someone had tried to kill me, and I was going to make sure they felt the flames before the end.

My skin peeled and cracked—at least, it felt like it did, with every movement, every scratch of the rope against my wrists, the cold threads flaking away more and more until only bone remained. It would be a relief, I thought, to have nothing left but bone, no skin, no heart, no mind, nothing to cause me to feel everything all at once.

A scream built in my chest, raw and ripping, filling my mouth with blood when it erupted out of me. The windows in the small room they locked me in rattled, and I imagined it was my anger, stronger than the storm outside, lashing against the panes.

Only when my lungs ached for air did I take a breath, and buckle, sinking to my knees on the carpet. I was alone—there was a guard posted outside my room, as there had been on the ship, but my lack of company wasn't the only reason I felt truly and utterly alone. I'd lost *everything*. My parents, my brother, my kingdom. There was nothing for me anymore, no war to wage, no crown to claim, no throne to take. For so long, I felt as though I'd been fighting a losing battle. Now I knew there was no way to win.

My throat ached. Every emotion I'd pushed down since that bloody day in the throne room came rushing up—sorrow and grief and anger all mixed together, finally overflowing, pouring out of the cracks in my exterior. My masks, finally fractured, drawn down to reveal the broken girl beneath.

Sharp pain lanced across my chest with every shuddering breath, and I pressed a bound hand against my heart, feeling it thud a painful beat in my ribs, as though it pushed on in defiance of my will to make it cease. Stubborn things, hearts. So fragile, so easily broken, and yet they maintained a life force that couldn't be diminished into such simple terms as blood and soul. They beat, strong against storms, even as walls of fortified stone crashed down around them. Much too small to carry the awful weight of so many emotions.

Better, then, that I could carve it out.

My breath hitched at the thought. My fingers, which had been curled into a claw against my chest, slammed into the ground. I had seen ribs split apart to reveal that hideous lump within, blood sprayed over stone and throne, that defiant little vessel still beating while a monster ripped it free. The shock frozen on my parents' faces, glossy eyes locked on me across the chamber, mouths hanging open in screams cut short. Those hearts, my parents' hearts, crushed in a gloved fist. Ceased. Deceased.

The memories came unbidden, unbridled. Wild like fire across my mind, and every bit as painful. I hadn't let myself mourn. I hadn't grieved them properly. I'd ran. I'd ran, and I'd been running ever since. Even after the Marama army had left our shores, I hadn't stopped to grieve. There had been too much to do in their absence, a kingdom to rule, a coronation to plan, a brother to save.

I hadn't even gone to visit their graves.

A whimper, soft and sad, broke through the echo of my scream. Tears rolled down my cheeks and splattered next to my bound hands, seeping into the carpet and disappearing without a trace. Even in this horrible little hovel, I couldn't leave a mark. I was a ghost in this world. Solid and alive, flesh and bone, but a ghost nonetheless. I had become one of those stories I feared as a child, tales of sailors drowned at sea, ghosts haunting the bellies of fishing vessels.

But this story would be told differently—I was a cautionary tale against foolishness and stubbornness. Against selfishness. Against wearing too many masks.

I wasn't just the ghost of Evhen, queen of Vodaeard. I was the ghost of Vodaeard itself, a once-great kingdom reduced to nothing because its queen had a heart that was at once too large and too small. A foolish heart that wanted to do selfish things, consequences be damned, and that's where everything had gone wrong. The Chief was going to get his wish after all, and Haret was going to get Vodaeard.

Unless Aunt Caz could stop him in time, but the doubts were already there.

"Fuck," I swore into the tear-stained carpet. "Fuck, fuck, fuck!" My voice rose with every curse, until it was louder than my scream, until it was louder than the storm, until it was louder than the doubt. My heart had betrayed me, this thing that felt *too much*, but I couldn't carve it out. I couldn't stab it, couldn't empty it. Because I had seen what that did to my parents, and those memories were the sharpest ones left in my mind.

The thought of ending it all now, of stopping the pain and the anger and the sorrow, quickened my breath in panic. My parents had died out of love—for me, for Alekey, for Vodaeard. It would be a betrayal to them, to their legacy, if I cut it out simply because I was feeling overwhelmed.

Icana had once, in jest, called me self-destructive during a sparring match. Because I had been so angry that she won every match, so she goaded me further, and I inevitably lost, thrown straight onto my back with two blades crossed over my throat, lungs empty, and limbs achy. She said my anger made me self-destructive, clouded my thoughts, blinded me to the obvious ways she had feinted and dodged. She hadn't been too quick or too skilled. I had been too mad, and she'd used that to her advantage.

It was true, I realized, grinding my teeth until my tears stopped falling. Anger made me do irrational things. Desperate things. Stupid things. But it was the only emotion I could rely on. The only one that draped over me like a blanket. A comfort. Everything else felt hollow, while anger felt hot. I wouldn't let myself be empty of emotion, when I could feel this with my entire being.

It might be self-destructive, but it would bring me too much pleasure to see the world burn in my wake. I didn't need to cut out my heart. I needed to let the fire consume every useless emotion within it.

I shoved up to my feet. Blood burned the back of my throat. I swallowed and crossed to the single window on the other side of the bed. A haggard reflection glared back at me, cheeks sunken, eyes dark, hair unruly. She didn't look like the Evhen whose portraits lined her home's hallways, jaw proud, eyes bright, clothes suitable. This Evhen was a dark shadow to that one, someone whose eyes didn't quite spark in the same way, who had grown up much too fast. I could barely see the parts of me that were the same anymore. It was like I had been erased, replaced with someone new.

Rain lashed against the window, streaking down my reflection's face, as if trying to wash away that version of me. But she refused to go, trapped between panes of glass, frozen in the hazy glow of the candles behind her—red, like her anger.

That was the version of myself I recognized.

I touched the glass, cool beneath my fingertips, and tipped my forehead forward, breathing into the space between these colliding versions of myself. Then I slammed my fist into the window, gasping with delight at the first crack that webbed from the centre of impact.

My next hit widened the crack, the glass buckling in its frame, and my third shattered a small hole in the middle of the pane. Wind howled through the gap, whipping my hair around my face, icy rain stinging my cheeks as I slammed my elbow into the fractured glass, pushing out broken shards onto the gravel below.

Behind me, the door rattled on its hinges.

Urgency flared through me.

I shoved my shoulder into the stubborn bits of glass clinging to the frame, careful not to snag on the jagged remains, and climbed onto the sill as a key clunked into the lock. I had one leg through the opening when the door swung inwards.

Haret shoved past the guards, shouting something incoherent at me, as Aunt Caz leapt across the small room.

I angled towards the stormy night, gauged the distance to the ground below—hazy through the pelting rain, but not too far that it would cause damage—and leaned forward into the dark.

Aunt Caz's hand latched onto my wrist as something whipped out of the darkness.

I fell back onto the floor of my room with a startled cry, a stinging pain radiating from my arm. Metal clanged against the wood floor, fetching up against the wall with a heavy thud.

I fell back onto the floor of my room with a startled cry, a stinging pain radiating from my arm. Metal clanged against the wood floor, fetching up against the wall with a heavy thud. Dazed, my ribs twinging from the fall, I looked at my arm to assess the damage. My shirt was torn over a shallow cut, but it didn't bleed excessively—only a thin line. Relief washed over me, quickly replaced by the pain in my side from landing on my injury. I rolled over, groaning, as Haret crouched next to me.

"What exactly were you going to do?" he growled at me. "You wouldn't survive a day in this country on your own."

"Then next time, make sure your assassins don't miss," I snarled, fingers digging grooves into the ratty carpet.

He frowned. "Despite what you may think, Princess, I don't get paid if you're dead."

He stood and motioned for Aunt Caz to follow him out. I stared at his back, bewildered and not at all shocked, my annoyance turning to frustration as he left.

"Find that assassin," he barked at my aunt. And to the guards, "Bar that window!" His footsteps echoed down the hallway, leaving me with a broken window and a broken spirit.

One of the guards left in the same direction, presumably to find the innkeeper and something to board up the window, while the other pulled the door shut. A howling wind tunnelled through the small room, smashing against the closed door. I glared at it from the floor, a slew of choice words racing through my mind at the disrespect.

Then I pushed myself up. No one else was going to help me, and I had learned long ago to do most things on my own. I found fresh bandages in a kit on the wardrobe floor and took them to the desk with a bottle of medicinal alcohol. Slumping into the chair, I braced myself for the process to come and wiggled out of my shirt.

Fresh blood stained the bandages around my ribs. I grimaced as I peeled them away to reveal the torn stitches beneath. My blood shone ruby in the candlelight. Angry skin surrounded the gash, puckered and raw where the poison had spread. The cut itself was jagged, not deep enough to cause lasting damage. It wasn't the work of a skilled assassin. My attacker on the ship hadn't known what they were doing when they tried to end my life.

My gaze trailed up to the cut on my arm. Neat, precise, only off target because Aunt Caz had reached me first, pulling me off balance before the blade could plunge into my heart. I looked across the room to where it had landed—Aunt Caz must have grabbed it on the way out. Even though I wanted to trust her, it was awfully convenient that she had grabbed me when she did.

Muttering beneath my breath, I started sopping up the blood on my ribs with an alcohol-soaked rag. A hiss whistled through my teeth at the pain, nearly covering the sound of crunching glass. I whirled towards the window, fists raised as if that could ward off another assassin, and watched in bemusement as Icana swung her leg over the broken sill, cane clattering to the ground before her feet touched the floor.

"I used to be better at that," she said, glaring despondently at the cane before raising her gaze to me.

"It's definitely the cane's fault," I agreed, hoping the tremble in my arms didn't show. I wasn't about to let my fear show. I lowered my fists. "Why are you climbing through my window?"

"Because the guards won't let me walk through the door," she answered, wiping the rain from her face. "I left your aunt a gift."

I stared at her in blank confusion. Each thump of my heart echoed in the wound on my side.

"I was going to come visit sooner," she said, sinking into the second chair across from me. "But it took me too long to figure out which room was yours. When I did, I saw the assassin running away. I didn't give them a chance to talk. Your aunt will find them dead at the back of the building."

The candlelight flickered across her face, catching the tears in her eyes. She blinked, and they were gone, and I thought maybe I'd imagined them after all.

I sighed, rubbing my forehead. An ache blossomed behind my eyes. "Do you know who it was?"

"House Sword," she replied, voice clipped.

I wracked my brain for the different assassin Houses of Geirvar, but came up empty. I didn't even know which House Icana came from, if she belonged to any of them. It struck me, then, how little I knew of the girl across from me, who had come from this land and swore never to return.

"I'm sorry I brought you back here," I said, my voice dipping into a whisper.

She held up a hand. The gesture cut me off like a knife cutting my tongue off. Sharp and sudden and serious. "I told you I'd rather die than ever come back here." Her voice fell flat, arms folded over her chest as if she could chase away the chill in the air with sheer determination. As if she could protect herself from whatever she didn't want to face here in Geirvar.

"I know," I whispered, wincing at the wrath in her eyes.

"Then why did you ask me to come?" There was a subtle sound in her throat, like a crack forming, pebbles raining loose from the solid wall she had built around her past.

I met her pale gaze, so blue they were almost white, colourless except for the speck of black at the centre. Icana often looked unimpressed with the world, as if it didn't live up to her expectations, and angry, a continuous fire that burned long and hot in her soul. But rarely did she look like she was in pain, like this place was festering beneath her skin.

I straightened in my chair. Icana had once said I could look more intimidating if I didn't slouch, if I carried myself with the same confidence she did.

She didn't look confident now, so I assumed it instead.

"I need you," I told her. Her brows quirked—she had never been good at raising one of them independently of the other. "Needed," I corrected myself, already losing my confidence with the reminder of my position as Haret's bargaining chip. "I planned to stay here in Geirvar. The chief wanted me in exchange for Alekey, and I knew you would be the only person who would actually listen to me, and make sure everyone else left without me."

Her jaw ticked, the only reaction she gave me. Then she rolled her eyes, and where they landed on the beams overhead, it felt like she could break them apart with the weight of her pain in her stare. As if the entire room could come crumbling down on me in an instant.

"Gods, Evhen," she murmured, a curse that must have come from Geirvar, because in Vodaeard, we didn't believe in gods. Only the sea, its tempers, and its tides. "You can be so stubborn sometimes. What makes you think I would listen to you?"

I opened my mouth to respond, not knowing if she meant it in jest or not, but she cut me off with another wave of her hand.

"I may have been born and bred by assassins," she said, pinning me with the weight of her stare, "but I'm not heartless. This place might have once been my home, but I renounced it a long time ago. Do you know why I left?"

I shook my head, not wanting to give life to any of my guesses. They all seemed foolish—she was running from a bad marriage. She had gotten in trouble with a teacher for saying something inappropriate in front of the monarch. They were all childish games I made up to pass the time, because I never dared to ask.

Her lip curled. "I didn't leave because something bad happened. I left to *stop* something bad from happening if I'd stayed."

My brow crinkled. That hadn't been one of my guesses. What could have possibly happened if she'd stayed that was terrible enough for her to run away from it? I didn't ask now.

"Now that I'm here, that bad thing is going to happen, and I won't be able to stop it. But no matter what, remember what I'm telling you now. I don't care for this place at all. It isn't my home. I barely survived it the first time, and I don't want it to be the place where we both meet our ends."

My spine tingled at the words. She narrowed her eyes at me, gaze burning with blue-flamed determination. "So no, I would not have listened to your stupid wishes. Vodaeard is our home, Ev. We're going to save it."

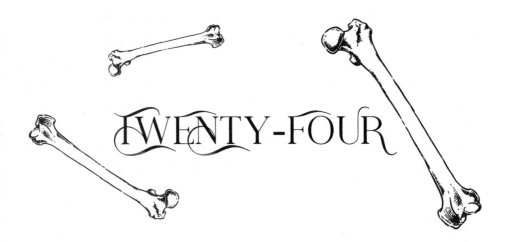

Twenty-Four

I sensed death. It was a blanket falling over the country. The fog rolling off the ocean. The rain lashing against the mountains. It hung in the air, thick and sweet, cloying in my throat.

I wanted to believe it was the history of this place. People like Icana born and bred to do one thing—kill. Or maybe it was my father's war, the remnants of his army creating a stain on this land.

Except there were no undead soldiers anymore, so I knew the death I sensed was much closer. Something had happened in the night, clamped claws around our company, and now Death loomed half a step behind as we prepared for the journey to the capital.

And then I saw it, as Cazendra ushered me into a covered carriage—Evhen, coming out of the inn, hands bound in front of her, bandages wrapping around her upper arm, stained with the unmistakable hue of fresh blood. Her eyes, discs of gold in the rain-softened morning, met mine for a heart-stopping moment before Cazendra guided me into the carriage and shut the door.

"What happened?" I asked the other woman as she settled onto the bench across from me, feet kicked up on the seat, back pressed up against the side. A study in serenity, as if nothing could touch her with so many weapons strapped to her body. I perched on the edge of my seat, unease rumbling through me, straining to see through the narrow window until Cazendra flicked the curtains shut.

"There was an assassination attempt last night," she answered, pressing her lips together, indicating she would not elaborate.

A forgotten power tugged at my abdomen, like a hook around my core, anchoring me to the spot while the rest of the world fell away. Death, cunning and mysterious and always one step behind, chuckled in my ear, a sound like souls wisping away across the Dunes of Forever, dry and cracked. Death, who watched me invade those dark shores, who sent his messenger if I lingered too long. I had always been a step ahead, the one who could cheat and steal from him, but without my power, he was toying with me. Letting me feel the promise, the pain, without any of the relief that came from using my power.

I hadn't sensed the death that rose like forgotten voices out of the soil of this country, like bones reaching to me from the crypts. I had sensed Evhen's, brief and bright, even though she hadn't died. But it was enough. The blood on her arm was a cruel imitation of how much she would lose if Death sunk his claws into her.

He was toying with me, and I felt sick in his suffocating presence. As chilling as the crypts, he filled the carriage with the lovely promise to take what he was owed. My soul, and Evhen's. In time, we would both lose.

Cazendra didn't seem to notice how cramped the carriage was, how stifling the air, how cloying the stench. She had never seen Death, didn't know how to interpret the signs. But it was everywhere here. The country was rife with murderers and sellswords. I could feel the bones of the people they'd killed clogging the dirt beneath our feet.

I scoffed at Cazendra's ignorance—her blissful lack of awareness—and that promising end drew back, letting light fill the carriage once more. Cazendra only frowned at me.

I leaned against the back of the bench until I was comfortable again. My neck stung as though champed by a monster's teeth, but I told myself it was only worry causing me to tense my muscles. I knew the darkness, the shadows, and creatures of nightmares, but in this realm, Death was only a concept. Only a figment of my imagination.

He had no dominion here. He couldn't hurt me here.

Except I had seen him. After touching the bones of that dead sailor, seeing her life before Death had come for her child. He was closer now than ever.

Cazendra cocked a brow at me as I studied her, the languid way she lounged, the confident tilt of her chin. She seemed to know something I didn't, and that bothered me.

"How is Evhen?" I asked, as much to know how the young queen fared after an attempt on her life and about Cazendra's relationship with her niece. If bonds borne out of duty to family were as easily broken as my parents led me to believe. They had never loved me, only my power. For the power it had given them. They would have burned down the world to find it if that moonstone had fallen into someone else's hands.

Cazendra tapped a hand along the ceiling, running a short fingernail over the fabric. It wasn't a fancy carriage by any means, no gold trims or plush cushions, but it was warm. Designed to trap in heat and keep out cold.

"My niece is resilient," she said. "She will be fine. And once we get her brother back…"

Outside, Haret gave the order to march, and the carriage lurched forward over the stones. My hands slipped to the edge of the seat to brace myself. "The prince betrayed me," I snarled. The word stung, even now. "His actions led to Evhen's death. I won't let you trade her for him, not ever."

Her eyes darkened, the cat-like yellow shifting to amber, but this was the warm shade of amusement, not anger. "And how do you plan on stopping Haret?"

My mind snagged on her phrasing.

The shade in Cazendra's eyes cooled to ice. "I promise to protect my family, no matter what. No matter who gets in my way."

The carriage rolled over a particularly deep rut, the wheels clunking as if they weren't quite sturdy enough to hold up the frame over this rocky landscape, and Cazendra planted her feet on the floor to maintain her balance, cursing softly. It was hard to hear her over the clatter, but it sounded like *Black seas.*

I thought about what Icana had told me regarding Cazendra, how she had been jealous of her position as Evhen's weapons master. Evhen's aunt seemed different, now that we had landed, compared to how she'd been on the ship. During the voyage across the ocean, she'd been hostile towards me. She'd acted poorly during our sparring match, but then again, I had dishonoured the rules of first blood, and that had landed like a personal offence to Evhen's aunt. But her actions immediately after had dug like nails beneath my skin, aggravating my already frayed nerves, angering me to the point that I wrote her name on our list of murder suspects.

Now that we were here, she seemed almost relieved. Buoyant. Sharing a carriage had sent nervous energy coursing through me, but looking at her now only made me confused. I didn't worry she was going to leap across the small space and sink a dagger into my heart. She seemed like a woman on the verge of victory, though over what, I didn't know.

I wasn't sure what to think, so I didn't. I simply moved. Closed the distance between us, and stabbed a shard of bone into her wrist, and brushed my finger against the hard joint. A surge of memories rose up in my mind, darkness sweeping across my eyes like a veil. I heard her cry in alarm as if from a distance, beneath water and pain, then felt the kiss of metal against my throat. My heart pulsed beneath it.

I blinked, and the inside of the carriage came back in sudden sharp clarity, the shadows of this horrendous power peeling away from my vision. Breath squeezed past the pressure of her arm over my chest, filled my aching lungs with icy air, as if I'd plunged into the ocean. A chill tapped along my spine as I stared up at Cazendra, and she stared down at me, horror flashing in her eyes. Blood, red like rubies, dripped from her wrist onto my neck.

"What the fuck?" she whispered. "What did you just do?"

Her memories are in my head. Her grief at losing a sister. Her fear for Alekey's life, and her hope for Evhen's. Death had come for her family, and now flashes of her pain and sorrow collided in my mind in a disjointed timeline of her life—glimpses of her past.

Except there was something I'd seen that hadn't happened yet. Fear for a future that hadn't come to pass. The kind of worry that gnawed at Evhen, anxiety deep in her bones, fear of the unknown. Cazendra's worry went so deep, she had already convinced herself it was bound to happen—she thought she was going to lose Alekey *and* Evhen *and* Vodaeard. All of that was carved in her bones.

In that future that hadn't happened yet, I glimpsed a warship. Cazendra's countrymen. A battle on distant shores. That was what she was worried about. If the ship would catch up in time.

"You want to save her," I whispered, realization crashing over me like the frigid waves on Death's dark shores. "You're not—"

She slapped a hand over my mouth, eyes flashing. "Watch your tongue, Princess. Ears less friendly than mine might be listening."

I fell into silence, time slipping away from me. Death felt even closer now, a shadow in the corner of my eye, a creature rising out of the darkness. By the time the terrain changed beneath the carriage and we were rolling over smooth stones, I imagined its teeth clamping over my neck like a tightening noose. I clutched the bench, sucking in breaths that felt too constricted, too shallow. A dull warning echoed in my head, a fear stemming from trauma too recent to be healed. No matter what I thought, no matter how much I had changed since that day, or stayed the same, nothing could erase the fear clawing up my throat at the thought of seeing my father again.

The carriage halted with a jolt. My knuckles white where they clung to the bench. I expected soldiers to swarm the transport, pull the door open, and yank me out. Maybe that's when I would fight, when I would thaw, but when Cazendra nudged the door open and hopped down and no one reached in to grab me, I still didn't move.

She looked up at me, annoyance flushing across her face. "Out."

My limbs moved, body unfolding from the bench, bones in my knuckles creaking in protest. Maybe if I just held on, I could stop this moment from happening. But she reached up, pulled me down, and my feet collided with the ground hard enough to rattle my teeth.

"Does she know?" I whispered to Cazendra, teeth grinding over each other as they chattered in fear.

"Yes," the woman hissed, shoving me forward.

A palace loomed ahead. The architecture was unlike anything I'd ever seen. Even King Ovono's jewel of glittering diamonds didn't compare to the monstrosity before me. Domed roofs topped towering turrets, each adorned with a rod that speared the sky. I had to crane my neck back to take in its height, mouth open in shock and surprise.

It was beautiful, yes, stone in varying shades of grey, heavy iron doors, and iron shutters on the numerous windows, but it was an imposing kind of beauty. A lethal kind of beauty. Fortified, archers visible even from below. This was the kind of place that could not easily be invaded. Which made me think they let my father walk right through the doors.

Those doors shuddered open now with a menacing boom that vibrated through my feet. I stumbled and considered running.

Then I saw Evhen, sliding off a horse. Her face twisted, pulling in pain, as the movement jostled her side. Someone had tried to kill her, twice now, and the strain was starting to show.

This was where we were always going to part ways. Either she was going to sacrifice herself for her brother, or I was going to sacrifice myself for her. One way or another, our crossed paths ended here.

Evhen lifted her chin with defiant pride, despite the erratic way her eyes darted around the frozen, empty courtyard. She expected another attack, and on the precipice of seeing my father again after losing her brother, she had every right to be anxious. Whatever happened inside this palace, our lives would never be the same again.

Inside, a battalion of soldiers dripping in metal weapons circled our company to lead us down the halls. We left many soldiers outside, and there were so few of us compared to those from the palace—Haret, Cazendra, Icana, Evhen, myself, and a handful of men bearing pins on their cloaks. The symbol seemed familiar, but my attention was pulled to the stone halls, and I forgot all about it.

Despite the spiky exterior, the inside was warm, decked in beautifully embroidered tapestries and thick plush carpets running the length of every corridor. There was a sense of urgency flitting through the air, nervous energy coursing through the stone and wood. I tried to meet Evhen's gaze again, feeling like time was racing forwards and slipping away from us, but she was tucked tightly between two guards. Instead, I looked at Icana.

The weapons master clenched her jaw. Icy flames flashed in her eyes. Short, shallow breaths filled her lungs. The nervous energy crackling in the air seemed to intensify around her, as if she was the centre of the brewing storm, and anyone who got too close would be caught in the maelstrom of her rage.

I looked away before her violent storm broke me.

We turned a corner, and the gilded throne room doors barred the way in front of us. Wood carved with straight and swirling designs, gold and bronze veins running through the pattern to create a mesmerizing image.

Evhen's breath caught in her throat, the only other sound in the quiet corridor aside from the shifting metal plates of armour. She had never spoken about that bloody morning, the one my father boasted about in the infirmary, but I imagined standing before these doors, about to face the man who murdered her parents, was dredging up those memories from a dark place within. She wasn't prepared. Neither of us were.

The doors creaked open from the inside. Towering pillars topped in red-capped domes lined the aisle towards the dais at the end. Between each pillar stood more guards dressed in black and red, chest plates gleaming. An insignia marked each one, but I couldn't see it clearly through the circle of soldiers marching us forward.

Rocks weighed in my stomach, making each step forward feel like a league through tar. I looked everywhere—the stained glass windows beyond each pillar and balconies running along the second storey and the painted murals set between each window—but not at the throne ahead, dreading what I would see there. Who I would see there.

Until we stopped, and my gaze dragged inevitably up.

Marble steps inlaid with streams of rubies—like blood—led up to the platform in the middle of which sat a throne. The arms ended in the shape of an animal I had never seen before—a face like a bear, spiky feathers sprouting from its head, with wings curling from its back. The top of the chair had two spears running up the length of the back, looming over the figure sitting on the cushions. Even at a distance, I could see the rusty brown residue on the sharp tips of the spears—as though they had been weapons used in war, and now decorated the throne.

The man who sat beneath the gory display of power was white—white beard, white hair, white eyes. Disease rotted his teeth and bent his back, but his clothes were fine. Red and black embroidery lined his cloak, which looked too heavy on his frail shoulders.

Here was a man close to death.

And standing next to him was my father, hand resting on the throne as if he already owned it.

TWENTY-FIVE

When the doors to the throne room opened, I expected a gory scene, like the one I'd witnessed that fateful morning when Kalei's father carved out my parents' hearts.

My throat had closed up over the fear that choked me with those memories, and I chided myself for being ridiculous—this was a completely different kingdom, on the opposite side of the world, under completely different circumstances.

Chief Mikala wouldn't be so brazen as to assassinate Geirvar's monarch. He would never have escaped the throne room, surrounded on all sides by a country of mercenaries and murderers, sellswords, and shieldmaidens.

So, of course, there wasn't blood. There was nothing in the chamber to indicate a battle had been fought and won—or lost. Only a line of people in shining armour with shining weapons, each one glittering in the light that filtered through the windows high above. Where the defiantly white sun caught the tips, they shone with deadly promise.

That line led straight to Alekey. To the cuts and bruises on his arms, the deep trenches in his gaunt face, the iron shackles weighing down his hands. He stood beside the chief, and rage burned off my skin at the sight of his untarnished frame, the slight glow in his veins, the smug tilt to his mouth.

He had been given an impossible gift, and he bore it like a well-fitted crown. He remained untouched by what had happened that day on the beach.

An enraged scream broke from my lips, and I lunged forward. As if I could fight through an entire army of guards to claw the chief's eyes out. To rip his own seas-damned heart from his chest.

Aunt Caz's hand tightened on my injured arm, and I buckled under the pain that shot through me anew. With ease, she pushed me down to my knees on the carpet. Marks that I'd thought were the design, but were actually blood stains, swam in my vision.

"Chief Mikala," Haret said, his voice carrying through the stony space. His mouth was fixed into a frown as his eyes roved over the dais.

"Who are you?" the chief asked, narrowing his dark brown eyes. In that moment, he didn't look anything like his daughter.

"The Crow," Haret answered. My skin prickled at the title. "I'm here to negotiate the safe return of Prince Alekey, in exchange for Princess Evhen *and* Princess Kalei."

My gaze slid to Kalei, but Cazendra and Haret both blocked her from my sight. I wanted to see her. Needed to see her. One last time.

Instead, I glared up at the chief, watching for his reaction. He barely acknowledged his daughter, eyes glazing over her like she was just another hostage.

The king of assassins hadn't said a word yet, but one of his guards stepped forward to guide Alekey down the stairs.

Words tumbled out of my mouth before I had the good sense to stop them. "What does torturing him bring you?" I snapped. "You had me in line for months! I did everything you asked, and you still tortured him."

"Evhen," Alekey pleaded, voice dry and cracked.

The chief's eyes bored into me, like knives in my bones. "You're still a child. Soon, you'll understand we all do what must be done."

"Yes, we do," mused Icana. Her voice surprised me. She was usually quiet, tending to stay out of politics altogether, but now she strode forward as if someone had addressed her at court. As if she was leading this conversation. One of my soldiers moved to stop her, but Haret raised a hand, a curious tilt to his chin, allowing her to do her thing.

The chief regarded her as one might regard a bug. "I see we left quite a mark on you."

"Oh, that's funny, because of the scars," Icana quipped dryly. The end of her cane echoed dully against the stone until she halted at the base of the steps, chin lifted to glare at the chief with as much distaste as he regarded her. "I assume you came to ask the king of assassins for an army. Because your daughter eradicated your undead bastards."

The chief scowled. There had probably never been someone who contradicted to him. Kalei had never been brave enough. "They gave their second lives to give me a power you could never imagine."

"You're right." Icana shrugged. "I can't imagine it. Gods know one lifetime is hard enough. How did you convince him to help you?"

The chief rested a hand on the king's chair. "It wasn't difficult," he said proudly.

The man in the throne didn't react, giving the impression that he was stone. Or dead already.

"Presumably, you thought because he's old, you could manipulate him into giving you an army you have no idea how to control. But my question is, do you know how succession works in Geirvar?"

The chief scoffed and opened his mouth to reply, but Icana cut him off again.

"An heir kills a monarch. A child kills a parent." Her tone chilled me, and suddenly, I realized this was a much larger situation than a simple hostage trade. She ran a nail over the top of her serpent's head cane, and I shuddered at the simple threat. "If he dies without an heir killing him, the country falls into civil war, members of every House vying for the throne. Even if he did promise you an army, no one would honour that once he's dead. Family blood means nothing here, but spilling blood? That means everything."

She mounted the bottom step. Unease spread through the soldiers standing around us—curiosity and suspicion blending together, making it impossible for anyone to move, to guess at her actions. Hands lay on weapons, but no one drew.

Me?" she continued casually. "I left before I had to make the choice. I wouldn't kill my father." She climbed the last step—*thud*—and stopped beside the throne.

The white-haired man lifted milky white eyes to her, raising a hand as if to caress her face. Or embrace her.

"Look at him now, taking his last breaths. Father, are you quite well?" Quick as a viper, a concealed blade slid into Icana's palm, and she buried it in the man's chest.

Her *father's* chest.

He coughed. Blood speckled his lips, and more of it spilled from the wound in his chest, spreading rapidly across the grey suit. Clarity shone in his eyes as he gazed up at Icana. A smile curved on his mouth, and he patted her cheek. A single word bubbled out of his throat: "Good."

My weapons master pushed her father out of the throne. She winced when he hit the ground before she masked it with her usual scowl before she took the vacant seat. I only saw that because I was watching her closely. Everyone else eyed the surrounding assassins, suddenly wary of their loyalties. No one else was looking at her the way I was, which gave me a clear view of the chief as he leaned away from Icana, like the throne was suddenly poisonous to touch. He gave a sharp gesture to one of his men. That man grabbed Alekey and pulled him back.

I lurched to my feet, free for all of two seconds, before Aunt Caz yanked me backwards. I hardly felt her hands on me, burning with rage as the chief's men bodily dragged Alekey out of sight.

"No!" I snarled, straining and hissing. "Give me my brother back!"

Chief Mikala hesitated. A glimmer of fear flickered across his face, gone just as quickly as it appeared, and he looked down at Icana with disdain. "How do I know you're not lying?"

Icana's gaze swept around the chamber, landing on each assassin. The room itself seemed to bow under her scrutiny. My heart stuttered as though the world had been knocked off-kilter. "What House do you serve?" she asked. The command in her voice carried through the silent chamber.

"House Snake," the assassins responded in unison, a sound like thunder. Like a proclamation.

"And who is the monarch of assassins?"

"The heir of House Snake," came the reply.

"Who is the heir of House Snake?" Icana pressed, a sharp edge to her smile.

"Icana Vipden."

SShe looked up at the chief with a vicious grin. He recoiled. Grim satisfaction warred with the urgency tumbling through my gut—he still had my brother. Perhaps he even still had an army loyal to him—only the assassins in this room were dedicated to the throne, it seemed, and I didn't know how many others he had already swayed. He looked uncomfortable at this turn of events, but he had still won.

Icana flashed her teeth. "Get the fuck out of my country."

As one, the assassin guards lining the walls withdrew their weapons, turning to face the chief and his soldiers. The man stammered, and the act of backing away—even though he was fleeing—reminded me of that moment on the beach, when he stole my brother from me. A pathetic sound rattled in my chest, clamouring to be free, but I wouldn't allow any of them to see weakness in me again.

When the chief and his retinue had fled, the assassins barred the door. I knew enough about Geirvar to know that everyone was a killer, but a select few were assassins-for-hire for the monarch, an elite squad of men and women that made up the guard. And now they were loyal to Icana.

I still didn't feel better when she set her eyes on Haret.

"A wise move," he said, stepping forward to humble himself before her. Already moving towards where the power was.

"Shut up," Icana snapped at him, leaving him to flap his mouth in shock. "You are not welcome here, Crow. Take your army back to Xesta and stay there. You have one day."

"Let's be reasonable," he argued.

"*You're* not reasonable," Icana replied. "This isn't a debate, Haret. This isn't a war or council meeting, or a fucking coup. You walked in here assuming you could trade two people for one, and that would be the end of that conversation. You failed. There is no reasoning with someone stupid enough to think they had the upper hand here."

Haret's lip curled, a clear sign of his discomfort at being talked down to by someone younger. Icana was a scythe, falling swiftly to cut the head off the snake, and a snake-like Haret did not like to lose.

I would have been proud if I wasn't still trapped.

"Leave, before I make you leave." Icana narrowed her eyes into slivers, but I caught a gleam of light as she glanced sideways. A ring of metal hissed through the air, barely a whisper against the stone and glass, and a body slid silently to the ground. Haret looked around, hand dropping to the short sword at his waist, and even our guards shifted back, twitchy in their makeshift armour, eyes darting around the room for any sign of movement.

"No?" Icana raised a thin brow—or attempted to. She had never been good at raising one, so both lifted towards her sun-whitened blonde hairline. Another body crumpled, folding to the ground like a piece of paper. Aunt Caz pulled me back from the pool of blood seeping into the carpet. "How many of these traitors have to die before you take me seriously?"

"How?" Haret growled.

She gestured to someone at the side, and one of our soldiers on the opposite side fell backwards. My heart quickened, fear racing through me. I didn't see anyone move, and Icana was terrifyingly good at turning our attention away from the danger. I thought I knew all my friend's tells, but she was unreadable now.

"The monarch's guard are living shadows," Icana explained. "You will never see them until it is too late."

"Haret," I snapped, "put your fucking pride aside for one second. People are dying. Listen to her."

"Spoken like a true queen." Icana smiled at me. The act, rare enough as it was without the sharpness of a dagger's edge, sent shivers down my spine.

"Fucking seas," he muttered beneath his breath, but I was the only one close enough to hear him. He finally nodded, a quick dip of his chin, and Aunt Caz pushed me towards the doors ahead of our guards.

"Kal?" I strained in my aunt's grip to look for the princess. She should have been next to Haret, but her ash-white hair wasn't anywhere to be seen. "Kal!" I shouted, pulling against my aunt. How had she simply disappeared? I cursed myself for being so focused on Icana and Haret that I'd forgotten about her entirely.

"She's gone," Aunt Caz hissed in my ear. "Left with her father."

Left. *Willingly*.

She had given herself up, just like she said she would. Teeth gritted, I swallowed my whimper of denial. Nothing had gone according to plan. My brother was supposed to be safe. I would have gladly traded my life for his, but now both of them were gone.

And without my star of the sea, without Kalei's gravity holding me in place, I was lost.

Outside, Aunt Caz hefted me onto a horse, and she jumped up behind me, swiftly kicking the beast into a gallop. At Haret's warning shout, the company outside mounted and rode out of the courtyard.

The winding, narrow streets were empty as we fled from the capital, the sun beating down on our retreat. The eerie silence was not a comfort. I'd had enough experience to know noise was preferable over quiet in dangerous situations like this. It felt like a collective breath was being held, and the unease it gave me spread like ice through my veins, until we turned a corner, and the chief's men ambushed us.

They burst out of the side streets, weapons drawn, cutting down our company before they had a chance to swing their swords. Some of them were Haret's men—I didn't feel sympathy as their bodies piled—but most were mine, and guilt burned through me. I knew it was only a matter of time before the chief's allies went to the harbour.

KAY ADAMS

An arrow hissed by my ear, close enough for the fletching to sting my cheek. Aunt Caz urged our horse into a narrow alley, and when we burst into the next street, we didn't look back. Cries of the dying filled the air behind us.

TWENTY-SIX

A red river ran down the road.

I paced between the bodies, aware that we didn't have much time before Icana ordered the assassins retaliate, but there was a presence hovering over the bodies that I couldn't ignore. Death, taunting me, a black shroud flitting between the dead. Snatching their souls away across the Dunes of Forever. Each one slipped from me before I could reach them. Each one screamed for me before I could rescue them. More Vodaeardeans dead.

Because of me.

That small kingdom was running out of people who would die for it. And Evhen was running out of people who would die for her.

My father watched me from a distance. He hadn't said a word to me since his new first mate escorted me out of the throne room while Icana and Haret argued. I didn't know the man—I didn't recognize any of his soldiers, because they were all alive. Noa had perished with the rest of the undead on the beach. This was a new army, as ruthless as the previous one, but they could still bleed. They could still die.

None of them had, though. They outnumbered the amount of men Haret had brought to the trade. The Vodaeardeans had fallen quickly.

And I worried Evhen was among them.

Ignoring my father's harsh glare, I scanned the bodies for Evhen's familiar red hair. The dead all looked the same, dressed in the grey and navy of Vodaeard's makeshift army, splattered with blood that was already starting to turn brown. My father's crew wore tan and blue, the colours reminding me of the ocean and land meeting on the shores of our island. They still bore the Full Moon and Crossbones on their chests, and the insignia stamped into the armour of the Vodaeard army was difficult to see beneath the blood, but I'd been living in Vodaeard long enough to know what it was supposed to look like.

A mountain peak rising out of the ocean. A sign of strength.

Of resilience.

It was a cruel joke from the universe that they were constantly being killed.

"Kalei." My father's voice drifted over the shroud of Death.

I raised my head, stomach twisting at the lack of emotion in his usually warm voice. It had been so long since he called me *Minnow*, and I was surprised to miss it now. Here was a man who had lied to me, who had tried to kill me, who had always been kind to me when Mother showed no love. What was the point in loving something that was going to die, anyway?

But he had loved me. I had to believe he did, once. It hurt too much to think that had also been a lie.

I carefully picked my way through the maze of bodies, wondering what kinds of stories their bones could tell me. But this wasn't the time or place to delve into that power. News of this attack would reach Icana soon enough, and I didn't want to imagine what would happen if she decided to send her assassins after us. My father had lost the king's support, which meant he didn't have the army he needed, but he still seemed determined to let Evhen know that he wouldn't stop until her kingdom fell.

"Why do you keep killing them?" I asked when I reached him. Evhen's brother sat on a horse next to him, and even though I dutifully ignored the young prince, I saw how he flinched. This was all his fault—I hoped he felt as much guilt as I did. I wanted him to suffer for betraying me. For betraying Evhen. For letting her die.

"Because the little queen needs to understand that her actions have consequences," my father answered. "And I wanted to send a message to the new monarch of assassins. She knows what happens to kings and queens who say no to me."

Of course Icana knew—she had been there when he slaughtered Evhen's parents.

"Why Vodaeard?" I pressed. "You already have what you wanted. Why is Evhen's kingdom so important to you?"

"Kalei," he said with an impatient sigh. "Get on the horse. You've served your purpose. Leave it at that."

His first mate lifted me onto the horse behind the prince before I had a chance to protest. I struggled feebly, kicking my feet, keenly aware of how thin and lightweight my body had become in the months since the Blood Moon. The movements only had me gasping for air. The beast rumbled beneath me, shifting under the weight. I had never ridden a horse before and immediately grabbed the saddle to keep my balance. My heartbeat sounded hollow in my ears.

"Don't do that to me," I muttered as my father took the reins in his hand and guided us in the opposite direction of the carnage. His first mate rode on the other side of us. As if we could get very far with our hands bound.

"Do what?"

"Dismiss me." A childish whine edged into my voice, the same way it had that day in the infirmary, when my father continued to lie to my face about his deeds on the mainland. *What war?* I had asked him then. And now I was in the middle of it. "Act like I'm too young to understand anything."

"You *are* too young," he argued.

"I'm not! I'm old enough to understand war and death." No one knew about death better than I did. Even after the moon had gone dark, that was the one thing I still understood. It was my domain. "What I don't understand is why you keep attacking Vodaeard. This isn't about the moonstone anymore, so tell me why."

In front of me, the prince was still silent. I wanted to shake him. Didn't he care about his sister at all? He hadn't even reacted upon seeing her in the throne room. I couldn't fathom what was going on in his traitorous mind.

My father's gaze raked over me, noting the bandages stained with black blood and the various pieces of bone sticking out of various bits of skin.

"Did they hurt you?" he asked, light flickering in his eyes as a familiar emotion rose to the surface.

I nearly laughed. Instead, it came out as a disbelieving choke, a sound that scraped my throat raw. "You killed me, and you're concerned with what those people did? Don't pretend to care about me now."

Beneath his beard, his mouth became a thin line. "You didn't die," he said, as if annoyed with my dramatics. "If you had, your mother would still be alive."

Anger churned in my stomach beneath the exhaustion. I had never felt my mother's love. She had been an emotionless rock, and I was glad she was finally gone, though I couldn't find the words to say it out loud.

"I loved your mother, Kalei," my father said, grief turning his voice hoarse. He looked ahead, and I wondered if he didn't want to look at me because I reminded him of her. I shared more of his features, but I had somehow survived when she didn't. She had been meant to share this gift with him. Maybe he thought I had stolen it from her. "We were supposed to spend eternity together."

"By killing me!" The black spot over my heart gave a twang. I dug my nails into my palms, heedless of the shards of bones. The woman's rib still curved through the heel of my hand, but I barely felt it now.

He glanced over at me, a spark of remorse glittering in his eyes for a second. "I would have traded the world for it to be anyone else, Minnow." The word was like a knife, bringing tears to my eyes. "We knew about the Blood Moon and the legend long before you were born, so when you found that piece of moonstone on our island and touched it and gained that power, we were heartbroken. We knew what had to be done, and we didn't want to do it."

I shook my head, as if I could stop myself from hearing the words. This couldn't be true. It was another lie, to make me feel sympathetic. "No, you said I was born with it."

"You weren't born with it." Sadness turned his voice raw. "You were cursed with it, Minnow. Your mother couldn't fathom the idea of killing her only child, so she became cold and distant. It was the only thing she could do so it wouldn't hurt as much."

"No," I snapped. My cheeks were wet, but I didn't move to wipe them dry. Pain and rage burned in my veins, replacing the icy touch of Death that had settled in my bones. My chest heaved. "I won't forgive her for that. All I ever wanted was her love! Her approval. I did everything right, and she still hated me in the end. I'm *glad* she's gone."

My father flinched. "She didn't hate you. She loved you so much."

"Not enough," I snarled. "And don't tell me you did, either, because you still tried to kill me!"

"You're alive, Kalei," he snapped. "Is that not enough?"

"I'm *dying!*" The word tore from my hollow chest, the place where my heart had turned to ash beneath the Blood Moon. "I have been dying since that day. I can feel my life chipping away, bit by bit every day, and every moment still breathing hurts because I shouldn't be here." A chill rattled down my spine, as if Death was there waiting. Eager. "I didn't come here to be traded for this traitor"—Alekey winced in front of me—"I came here to die."

"Kal," the prince gasped, twisting to face me. Dark bruises—fresh bruises—painted his pale cheeks in splotches of navy and indigo. A cut through his lip had bled recently and dried into a scab that pulled when he spoke. "Don't say that, please."

His pleas lit a flame in me.

"I promise," I said in a low voice, watching the fear bleed across his face, "that the next time you speak to me, I'll use this bone to cut your tongue out. And I always keep my promises."

He blanched, searching my gaze in silent horror, trying to gauge how serious I was. I kept my stare steady on his face, narrowing my eyes with every breath that passed into the cramped space between us, until he looked away.

"You came here to save your little pirate," my father snarled at me, reducing my confession to its barest truth, eyes flashing in the darkness. "And when you're gone, there will be no one left to protect her." His heavy gaze landed on me, full of promise, and I saw that he truly did not care whether I lived or died. As long as Evhen suffered

"Chief," my father's first mate said, a warning edge to his voice. We both looked at him, and then I followed my father's gaze into the distance behind us.

As the white sun sank, an icy breeze blew through the city, and a black shadow seemed to be stretching towards us from the capital. The spires of the palace were still visible, red roofs aflame in the dying daylight.

A grim smile pulled at my lips when I realized we were already surrounded. Icana's assassins had slipped out of the streets in wraith-like silence, and we only noticed when they wanted us to see them, on foot and black steeds, scarves covering the lower half of their faces.

Icana's blonde hair shone like glass as she dismounted her black stallion. In a short time, she had changed from her casual voyage clothes into black armour stamped with a red snake, the same symbol I had seen in the throne room. The emerald eyes of her serpent-headed cane gleamed between her fingers.

My father dismounted and approached her.

She looked around at our company, face twisted in her usual scowl. It was strange to see her in a position of power—I'd always known her to be the one standing off to the side while Evhen made the decisions, though she had always been observing. I couldn't imagine what growing up in a nation of killers was like, but I guessed she had learned from a young age to be suspicious of everyone. That made her the perfect guard for Evhen, who didn't take the time to check her surroundings before charging into battle. Icana always knew where to check, and this position suited her well.

"I thought I told you to get out of my country," she said. "Instead, I find foreign blood in the streets. Foreign blood not spilled by my assassins." Her piercing gaze cut to me. "I assume Evhen got away?"

I nodded, sharing her relief. Evhen didn't deserve any of this. I didn't know what I would have done if her body had been among the dead. I cared about her, more than I cared for my own life. She was supposed to have a chance to heal, to live and rule in a place that wasn't ruined by war.

"Good," Icana murmured. "I might have had to start a war if she was dead."

"You're already in the middle of this one," my father told her.

"Actually," Icana said, "you're in the middle of it. This is my country, and foreigners spilling other foreign blood is against the law. Only death paid for by a member of a House is allowed in Geirvar. We have fair laws here, Chief, and you broke them. Surrender your army to me, and only those with blood on their hands will die."

Steel flashed, my father's weapon sliding easily from its sheath. I had never seen my father fight before. Even on the beach, he had fled when his undead army fell.

I'd assumed they had fought most of his battles, but the man in front of me now looked like a commander. Someone who could lead armies. Someone who would have armies follow him. Frustration turned my awe into something sour as I realized there were things I clearly didn't know about my father.

For my whole life, I had thought he was a sailor, making connections on the mainland to support our small island. I'd wanted to be an adventurer like him.

Meanwhile, he had been leading an army to hunt for immortality.

And I'd given it to him.

Icana sighed. Her nail tapped the top of her cane. "Hardly fair, is it?" At a gesture from her, someone broke away from the line of horses and trotted forwards. A man jumped down, only his eyes visible behind his mask, blue glittering like gems in the dying light. He held a sword twice as long as he was tall.

"Oh, I'm not going to fight you," my father said. He reached up and dragged the prince from the horse. Panic rang in my bones, and my fingers scrabbled to hold onto his sleeve, but they couldn't find purchase before my father angled his sword at the prince's chest.

Icana held up a warning hand. It looked intentional, but I recognized the hesitation in the gesture.

"Do you really want to start a war with me?" she asked in a low voice. She had the same kind of scary silence that my mother had commanded so well. The same one I had used in the brig. We were the kind of people who wielded whispers better than weapons, better than shouts, but my father was the opposite.

He was the tempest.

"Your speech in the throne room might have fooled your assassins," my father said, the tip of his blade carving a hole into the prince's throat. He squirmed, eyes locked on the steel that could end his life. "But I know your kind better than you think. Family means quite a lot to you. Specifically, this one. His sister is the same. She was willing to do whatever I asked. It's the same reason he betrayed you. *Family*." He sneered the word, and I felt the lack of love like a knife in my heart.

Everything he had said only minutes ago rang false now.

"You're right." Icana dipped her chin at the man next to her, and he stepped back, strapping his weapon to his steed as she continued speaking. "He made the wrong choice. But he didn't betray us. You lied to him. And family isn't just the people who share our blood. I chose Evhen as my family, and she means more to me than the man I just killed in that throne room. I would be betraying her if I let you kill him."

She spun and swung up onto her horse with ease, resting the cane across her thighs. "Take your war out of Geirvar. I won't ask again."

As she turned away, I called out to her, helpless. "Icana!"

Her shoulders tightened, a subtle indication that she had heard me, but she didn't look back. The assassins bled back into the shadows with the final rays of light, and night fell over the city.

A shiver trembled in my neck. Even though the streets were empty again, I felt a presence pressing down on us, wrapping us in an icy vice. Death was so close.

TThe young prince breathed a sigh when my father pushed him away, and the overbearing pressure inside my head dissipated. Once more, someone had escaped Death's claws, but he continued to brush against the base of my skull, a tap tap tap like he was knocking on the door to my soul.

I ignored him as my father's first mate hefted Evhen's brother onto the horse. For as long as I had known the prince, he had always been lanky, maybe too tall for his frame, but now he looked starved. Beaten. He bent over the saddle, shoulders hunched to ward off the plunging temperatures. He looked the same as I felt.

My heart gave a twinge. It was true—Evhen would be heartbroken if her brother died.

Maybe Alekey deserved to live. But I couldn't find in it my hollow shell to forgive him.

Twenty-Seven

"Aunt Caz!" I panted after nearly a half-hour of hard riding. Our shadows stretched behind us as the sun sank towards the horizon. My hands were frozen on the saddle, knuckles sore from gripping it so tight. Icy tears clung to my cheeks and stung my eyes when I lifted my head into the whipping wind. "Aunt Caz, stop!"

I yanked back on the saddle, causing her to pull sharply on the reins, and I nearly fell off the horse in my haste to dismount. Pain sparked across my ribs when my feet hit the ground, and I listed sideways into a wall, fetching up against it with a gasp. Chest heaving, every breath more painful than the last as heat seared through my wound, I sank to the ground, knees folded, forehead dropping until sobs filled the small space between my legs and my heart.

Aunt Caz's boots pounded onto the cobblestones. "Evhen, there are two armies at our back and an immortal man who wants you dead. We don't have time."

"*Make* time," I snarled. Her looming presence fell over me, no different than the shadows shrouding my mind. I lifted my head to glare up at her. "Why did you let them take her?"

Her eyebrows knitted together. "Who?"

"Kalei!"

She rolled her eyes towards the sky. Streaks of red and pink ran overhead. "She *wanted* to leave, Evhen. She told me on the ship."

The adrenaline was bleeding out of me, along with the initial pain in my ribs, fading to a dull ache. But without pain, without fear or grief or anyone left to lose, anger wove through my veins, a burning fire that stole my breath. "What do you mean?"

"She was always going to go with her father in your place," Aunt Caz explained, though Kalei had already said as much and I'd begged her not to. "She wanted me to make sure you got out of there."

I raised my bound hands to pound them against her chest, but she hardly moved. "You should have stopped her! You should have grabbed her, not me!"

She grabbed my arm, drawing me close. A thick knife, like the one she used in her match against Kalei, slipped into the space between us, but before I had a chance to react, she swiped it through the rope on my wrists. "She's not my family, Ev.."

I rubbed some warmth back into my hands, staring at the raw skin banding my wrists where I had struggled, and then slammed my fist into the side of Aunt Caz's jaw.

She yielded two steps, surprise flashing across her face before she frowned. "Did you hear me or did you willfully choose to ignore me?"

"What do you think?" I spat. Blood speckled my knuckles, but it was my own, seeping through the cracks in my frozen hands.

There was only a red mark on her jaw when she flexed it.

"YYou've never been good at listening, have you?" she muttered. She swung up into the saddle, knife tucked away in her belt, and held out a hand towards me. "Get—*seas*," she swore suddenly, gaze flicking past me. "*Run.*"

Without thinking, I shoved away from the wall, sprinting down the middle of the street. With each slap of my feet against the cobblestones, the bandages tugged over my wound, making every step hurt more than the last. Teeth gritted, pain flashing like bursts of lightning behind my eyes, I slipped around a corner, nearly colliding with the opposite wall. My wrist snapped as I pushed away from it, a sharp cry hissing through my teeth, but I didn't stop to breathe, to think.

I barely made it to the next cross-street before hooves beat on the stones behind me.

Aunt Caz shouted, and a shrill ring of metal cut through the air next to my head. I ducked, tripping over my feet to avoid Aunt Caz's sword. When I straightened, her foot connected with the centre of my chest, and all I could do was stare at her with wide eyes before she shoved, and I sprawled into the middle of the street, head smacking the stones. Momentarily forgetting how to breathe, I gasped, blinking up at the deep night sky. Head spinning, lungs screaming, blood spilling from several scrapes on my arms, I lay there until a second pair of boots approached me.

Haret leaned into my field of vision, and sensation flooded back all at once. Air filled my lungs, pain filled my head, and anger filled my heart as I scrambled to my feet. Too fast. The world tilted around me, the buildings a blurry sheen of grey and tan, and bile filled my mouth. Everything else dimmed to that one bright ember of burning pain in the centre of my chest, and before I could stop myself, I was on my knees, vomiting.

"What happened?" he asked, displeasure making his voice sound even more sour than usual.

"My niece has a sharp head," Aunt Caz explained. *Lied.*

Through strings of sweat-drenched hair, I looked up at her, confusion twisting my features.

"She's not particularly good at punching, though."

"Get her up," Haret ordered.

Aunt Caz hopped down, hands under my arms to haul me back to my feet.

I swiped at my mouth and spat at Haret, a halfhearted attempt at a snarl due to the nausea roiling in my stomach. The base of my skull burned, and when I reached to touch it, my fingers felt slick. The only clear thought that passed through my head was grim relief that the blood was hidden by the colour of my hair.

"How many dead?" Aunt Caz asked, holding the horse steady as I climbed up. She swung into the saddle behind me, hands wrapped around my torso to grip the reins. A strand of her dark braid brushed my cheek, a comforting scent wafting from her. I hadn't noticed it before, but Aunt Caz wore an achingly familiar perfume. One that reminded me of my mother.

"TTwenty," Haret answered. The number clanged through my dazed head, a sentence as damning as the rope that seemed to be tightening around my neck.

We had brought thirty of our pitifully small army, leaving about fifty people on board the Midnight Saint. We didn't even number one hundred in total, and twenty-five were already dead—including the three Icana killed in the throne room and the two who died during the voyage—though at this point, I didn't know who were Haret's men and who were my own.

I had led them all into a trap.

Aunt Caz made a noise in her throat. She was a military commander. She understood the implications well enough—we didn't have enough people to fight against the chief's army, and we weren't going to find help from Icana's assassins. My weapons master would never put her country in that position, especially when it seemed everyone in her country was divided by her unexpected return. I hadn't missed the way they glared at her when we departed.

"And the chief's men?"

"Escaped," Haret replied. Anger reverberated in his voice. "With the princess and the prince."

I pinched my eyes shut, as if I could stop his words from hitting my ears. Chief Mikala had won, again. I was no closer to freeing my brother than I had been at the start of this voyage, and now Kalei was with him, too.

Helplessness crashed over me, a violent storm that dragged me under the waves and filled my chest with panic. Dark thoughts collided in my head, swirling into oblivion, pressing on my lungs until it hurt to breathe. I was aware of Aunt Caz's body behind me and the horse beneath me, but the rest of me was drifting farther away from the only shore I had ever known. The ebb and flow of panic was familiar to me, chest tightening, a tremble beginning in my core that spilled into my hands and legs. The last time I had felt this way, unspeakably terrified by things I couldn't control, Kalei had been there to take some of my anxiety away.

She had chased away the darkness, wore it like stains on her heart. BBut she was gone now. And I couldn't run away from it, either. There was nowhere for me to go in this seas-damned country, nowhere to escape the betrayals and bastards that had ruined my life.

Aunt Caz tapped my hand, as if she sensed the tremors, and the simple motion drew me to the present, bringing the city back into clarity around me. I twisted around in the saddle to face Haret.

"Their blood is on your hands," I told him. "Those innocent people that you killed because of your fucking pride."

He glanced over at me, and it was with discomfiting shock that I realized he looked at me the same way Chief Mikala did. Like a petulant and disobedient child. "YYou are the one who switched course, Princess. You convinced those innocent people that they were an army who could fight an immortal man. If you had stayed your course, gone willingly with the chief, we wouldn't be in this position."

"Their lives weren't yours to gamble with," I shot back. "They died for nothing."

"They died for their country," he said dismissively. "They were honourable deaths."

"What country?" I shouted, my voice pinging off the stones around us. Aunt Caz hissed a low warning, but I ignored her.

His hand fell to the sword at his hip before he responded to me. "You created an army out of fishermen. You brought them here to die. Don't deny your role in all of this."

My lip curled. Warmth flooded my cheeks—shame, yes, but there was also rage. "You took my crown, Haret. You took my command. Their deaths are your fault."

"Shh," he whispered, holding up a hand as if such a gesture could silence me.

A scathing reply burned the tip of my tongue, but Aunt Caz clapped her hand over my mouth and murmured in my ear to be quiet.

When she lowered her hand, I kept my mouth shut, eyes darting to our surroundings. We were at the edge of the night-veiled city, roads rumbling away into farmland and foothills. A range of grey mountains smudged the sky in the distance.

Figures in black peeled away from the shadows and the alleys around us. A shiver curled up my spine at their sudden and silent appearance. In the dark, there were no defining emblems on their clothes, only the eerie silver glow of their weapons and blue gleam of their eyes.

"Who do you serve?" Haret asked, watching them closely. He would never get his weapon drawn in time if they decided to kill him.

"House Sword," one of them responded. My heart pounded madly against my ribs, each beat sending a jolt of pain through the wound in my chest. Icana said the assassin who tried to kill me was sent from House Sword. Were they here to finish what he couldn't?

"House Sword," Haret murmured, and I could almost hear his mind whirring through the different Houses. He must not have known my attacker was from that House. "And who is House Sword loyal to?"

Dozens of eyes raked over me, small pinpricks of light in the dark. "The highest bidder," one of them answered.

Next to us, Haret allowed a smug smile to pull at his mouth. I wanted to take Aunt Caz's sword and cut it off along with his head. "Then, perhaps, we might come to an agreement."

"And what's to stop them from turning on us when someone comes along with more money?" I argued.

At home, Haret had understood politics. He had been a valuable member of my council, and my father's before me, but now it seemed he was faltering, making hasty decisions just to keep his head above the rapidly rising waters of this war.

"Would you rather they kill you now?" He raised a brow at me, the gesture mocking.

The hint of a smile appeared under one of their masks, eyes crinkling in the shroud of night. "You will help us depose the new queen?"

"Fair enough," Haret said with a dip of his chin. As one of the assassins stepped forward to shake his hand, my heart quickened, skipping several beats as panic squeezed, and squeezed, and squeezed. When they shook on their agreement, and Haret invited them back to the ship, it felt like an executioner's blade swinging at my neck.

House Sword seemed to be a rather larger house, or at least the assassins loyal to them had lofty numbers. They fell into line with our meagre survivors, and Haret aimed a proud grin at me.

"You live to see another day, Princess." He said the title like the ending to a joke.

Instead of rising to his bait, I swallowed my retort. "Icana won't be easy to kill. Not if she has most of this country behind her."

At least, I hoped she had most of the country at her back. She had been gone for so long. Maybe the assassins of House Sword were right, and the others wouldn't stand with her.

"Your friend isn't a leader," he whispered back. "Her position here is precarious at best, and soon enough she'll realize she doesn't have the support of her people."

A scowl nestled between my eyebrows. "Are you talking about Icana, or me?"

"Oh." He feigned surprise. "Both, I suppose."

"Haret," Aunt Caz said before I could reach between our horses and pull him off his saddle.

But that was exactly what he wanted, and it angered me more when I had to bite my tongue. His coup had been frustrating, to say the least, but he wanted me to do something unforgivable. To prove him right. That I was unfit to lead. And I wouldn't give him the satisfaction of seeing me react like that. Not until it mattered. Not until my brother was safe.

Their quiet murmurs filled the night around me, but I didn't care to listen to them talk. I had to trust Aunt Caz knew what she was doing. This whole time, it seemed like she had been waiting for something, but I couldn't discern what.

Haret's voice finally needled through my spiralling thoughts. "It's time to turn those fishermen into fighters."

"I hope you're ready for them to hate you," I said quietly, glancing sideways at him.

Shadows concealed his face, twisting and dancing with the movements of his horse, but his frown was still visible, tucked between his brows. "You weren't," he told me.

My mouth twitched in a tight-lipped smile, but there was no fondness in the gesture—only grim truth. "I grew up with their hatred," I replied. "That's why I'm here, Haret. I only want my brother back. Can you do that for me instead of plotting how many different enemies you can pawn me off to?"

He must have heard the desperation in my voice, the hard truth of our presence here, because he turned to look at me, searching my face. I didn't know what he was looking for when all I felt was cold dread. His coup hadn't been the big betrayal he expected, because I was going to die here—one way or another. It was only a matter of who tied the noose and who pushed me off the ledge.

"I'll try," he finally said, and even though I believed him, it wasn't the reassurance I wanted. I didn't want him to try. I only wanted my brother safe. But Alekey's safety was a mild concern in comparison to his grand scheme. What was the point in protecting my brother if there wasn't a world left for them?

Ahead of us, night spread across the land, blurring the horizon until only the stars were visible.

They winked and sparkled, and a second later, the points that I thought were stars fell out of the sky as arrows.

One pierced our horse through the leg, and the beast reared back with a cry of pain, throwing us off before darting into the darkness. When I landed on the cold-packed dirt, I bit my tongue, barely noticing the pain as I scrambled away from Aunt Caz. Blood swirled in my mouth. I spat it out, sweeping hair out of my face to look around, the world spinning around me in a dizzy array of stars and arrows.

Haret had been knocked off his horse, and was currently swinging at a black-cloaked figure wielding a massive sword. My councillor ducked under the weapon, but I didn't have a chance to watch for long before an arrow slammed into the ground close enough to my hand for me to feel the dirt it disturbed. I jerked my arm back, pushing myself to my knees.

Aunt Caz was already on her feet, engaged with another figure in black. It was easy to distinguish my people from the assassins, dressed in shades that didn't blend into the night, and they didn't fight well. Several were on the ground by the time I bounced to my feet.

Someone ran towards me, a smudge in the dark, and I barely slipped under their attack. Metal hissed through the air next to my head, but when I turned, arms raised as if I could punch my way out of a sword fight, they were already gone.

Light glimmered off of something in the dirt. Aunt Caz's knife. I scooped up the thick blade, testing its weight as I scanned the area. The buildings were too far behind us, and there was nothing ahead but open fields. I wouldn't be able to make it back into the winding streets before someone cut me down.

I needed a bigger weapon. Preferably the one I had given to the sirens as an offering. Instead of lamenting its loss and succumbing to sorrow once more, I raised my head and adjusted my grip. I was going to die here one way or another, so I might as well fight until my last breath.

A rider on a black horse charged towards me, but I didn't see the telltale gleam of a weapon in their hand as they approached. Instead, I saw something even better. Short blonde hair peeking out of a hood, pale as wheat, and the familiar serpent's head of a silver cane.

I didn't hesitate when Icana reached down and pulled me onto the horse behind her. Breathing shakily, I leaned my head against her shoulder as we fled back towards the palace.

Twenty-Eight

A familiar sight greeted me when we approached the beach. We'd ridden through the night to the far side of the country, and my bones ached with exhaustion. Light caressed the sky as the sun climbed over the horizon, and I recognized the figurehead at the front of my father's ship. A siren, with a gaping hole in its chest and bony tail rising out of wooden waves. Longing pain tugged at my stomach.

The first time I had boarded this ship, I'd seen my father wounded in a war I knew nothing about. I had later learned that Evhen's crew had planted the explosive that caused him to return a day early from the mainland.

The figurehead was still burnt and broken.

The ship swayed beneath my feet when we climbed on board, as if it recognized me, and knew I wasn't supposed to be here. It was a bitter comfort to be back here now—I didn't want to be here, not with all the pain and death associated with this ship, but it reminded me of home, and no matter what had happened, I missed my island terribly.

My father's first mate guided Alekey and me across the deck, down into the depths of the ship, and to a room at the stern. Movement flurried all around us as orders passed from mouth to mouth as the crew prepared to drop the sails. Even though Icana had warned us about staying in her country, I knew my father wasn't going to listen.

We weren't fleeing. We were fighting.

Two hammocks swung in the corners of the small room, one of them recently occupied, judging by the blankets and pillows. Without a word, Alekey turned to the man and held out his wrists. My father's first mate unlocked the shackles, and Alekey climbed into the hammock, rubbing what looked like a fresh wound.

"What's your name?" I asked as the man turned to me and gestured. I held out my arms, watching his face closely for any sign of disgust or distrust—lately, people had recoiled at the marks swirling up my arm or the bones protruding from my skin. His face remained neutral as he hacked through the rope.

"Why do you want to know, Princess?" he asked, tucking the rope into his coat along with his knife. Amusement flickered across his face in the dim lantern light, making him appear younger than I initially thought. He might have been younger than Noa, before Noa came back to life and stopped aging, but the way he said *Princess* reminded me so much of my father's previous advisor that I could almost imagine they were the same person.

"I knew all the names of everyone in my father's old crew," I said with a slight shrug of my shoulder. His army was another matter, but I had known his crew—his closest friends, the people who regalled me with stories of adventures when my father wouldn't talk about what he did on the mainland. Now, I knew all those stories had been lies, but some fond memories couldn't be erased so easily.

"It's Seaglass," he said.

My lip quirked. "That's not a real name."

He chuckled, a warm sound in this cold place. "It's the only one I've ever known. Your father liberated me from a slaver ship a few years ago, before he sank it. That was the fifth ship I'd been sold to since I was old enough to talk, and now I'm a free man. Kept the name, though."

A strange mix of emotions warred in my chest, bouncing in the hollow emptiness inside until something stuck. Sadness, that people were being sold and traded. Pride, that he had reclaimed a name that carried such awful memories. Anger, that he could have been a free man anywhere but chose to stay with my father.

And the barest spark of sympathy, that my father had done a kind thing for a stranger.

After everything I had seen him do, I didn't want to believe him capable of kindness anymore.

"How come I've never seen you before?" If he had been freed a few years ago, why hadn't I seen him on our island?

Seaglass shrugged. "Chief Mikala freed me. He didn't buy me. I wasn't in service to him until he asked for it a couple of weeks ago."

Of course. Most of my father's crew and army had perished on the beach—everyone who had once been dead, turned to ash when my power stole their lives and gave it to my father. He had needed a new crew, a new army. It made sense that he would send a message to the people he had come across on his journeys. The people he helped. Because they would be the ones most likely to help him in return.

The hammock behind me creaked. "Why would you agree to work for a monster like him?" Alekey asked, his voice hoarse and thick with emotion.

Swallowing my anger at the prince, I twisted to look at him in the gloom. The bruises on his face were more prominent in the low light, sharp cheekbones cutting high across his face. Dark eyes glared across the small space. Once, they had been golden, a melting sun like his sister's, but there was no light left in them now, only the fear of pain. He held it in his entire body, shoulders tight as if braced for another hit, gaze darting around as if wondering where the next strike would come from. How many times had my father tortured him in the last month?

How many more times would he have to endure it?

Seaglass averted his gaze from the prince, looking instead at me with eyes like chips of emerald and sapphire, onyx and pearl—a myriad of colours. I wasn't sure about the emotion on his face, shadows obscuring most of his features. He wasn't ashamed by Alekey's question, but he seemed to understand the prince's position well enough. He had been a slave, once—maybe he sympathized with Alekey's plight, the cuts and bruises that marred his soft face.

"To some of us, he's not a monster," he murmured. And there it was. The kind of forgiveness I couldn't give to my father. The kind of understanding that didn't mesh with the reality of his actions. He had done awful things in his search for immortality, and I couldn't empathize with the few good things he had accomplished—like freeing slaves—in doing so.

"Then you're a fool," Alekey muttered. "You're just as bad as he is."

Brows pulling together, I watched Seaglass for a reaction. For a denial, for a spark of anger—anything.

Instead, he shrugged. "Maybe. But we all do foolish things to survive." The words seemed pointed, a knife's tip, and Alekey flinched, but not before they cut deep.

"I was trying to protect my friends," he snapped, eyes flashing with hurt.

Shame.

"Her father might have freed you, but he caged me."

His anger slammed into me with the force of a gale, but it only fanned the flames inside my chest. Seaglass responded, but I didn't hear him over the rush of anger in my ears. To Seaglass, my father was a saviour. To Alekey, a slaver

But I knew my father better than either of them. He wasn't any of those things—he was simply a survivor. Seaglass had said it—*we all do foolish things to survive.* And my father had done them without remorse. They all spoke as if trying to justify their own actions, but there was a clear distinction between them. My father had done what he did simply because he could, and would do it again for the same reason. He craved power, and he didn't care who he hurt along the way.

Alekey had done what he did because he was weak, and in the end, he would do it again for the same reason. He was broken. And broken things couldn't fix themselves.

It was only a matter of time before he surrendered again. This brief glimmer of anger was fleeting. I didn't want to see his false bravery now, knowing what lay beneath. So I looked away, kindling the anger in my bones.

"Settle in, Princess," Seaglass said to me, drawing my attention back to his face. "It's a long journey back home."

Home. I knew he meant Marama, but my mind pictured Vodaeard. Its black cliffs, grey rocks, and the cold stone castle filled with ghosts. Warmth had seemed impossible to find in Evhen's country, whereas it flooded my island nation in abundance. But *Vodaeard* was home, because that was where the one person I still cared about lived.

A strained noise rumbled in Alekey's throat as Seaglass locked the door behind him. He hopped down from the hammock, fingers tangling in his hair, while he paced from wall to wall. There were no windows in this small room, nothing to indicate time or direction, the only light source being the lantern swaying overhead.

Frustration rolled off the prince in waves. With each pass under the lantern, before his face fell back into shadows, splotches of red that had nothing to do with the bruises spread across his cheeks. When he finally stopped moving, on the other side of the room, shoulders hunched, tears rolled from his eyes.

"I'm sorry," he blurted, voice breaking. He swiped at the tears, but they continued to fall, smearing through the dried blood on his chin. "Seas, Kalei, I'm so sorry. I know you hate me, and I deserve it. I hate myself too, but I thought if I just surrendered, he wouldn't hurt them. I didn't want any of that to happen, Kal. You have to believe me…"

He continued rambling, a string of apologies falling as fast as his tears. Each word landed like an excuse, sparking against the fuse in my chest until I burst. *Weak, naive fool.*

"Alekey!" I shouted, startling him into silence. "Stop. I don't want to hear anything from you. Your sister died because of you. *I* died because of you. Do you understand? There's nothing you can say that will earn you my forgiveness."

He gaped at me, chest heaving. Uncomfortable silence stretched to fill the space between us. A previous version of myself might have felt guilty for snapping at him, might have even tried to understand what he was going through, but everything that had happened since I last saw him only made me an empty shell of the girl I'd been. That girl had died in the depths, had left all her kindness and warmth there. The version of me that stood before Alekey now only saw him as a traitor, and my black blood boiled at the sight of him looking so pathetic.

"He's going to kill us," I told him, crossing to the other hammock so I wouldn't have to see his face. "Evhen can't come save us because her councillors have her in chains, and there's nothing either of us can do about it. So don't apologize to me. Don't waste your last breaths making excuses."

Hours later, Alekey shot up out of sleep with a scream. I hadn't realized I'd fallen asleep until he cried out, and I lurched upright in a panic, grabbing for a weapon I didn't have. My fingers closed around the edge of the hammock to steady myself as it swayed against the wall. Bones pricked my palms.

Heart thumping, I looked over at the prince.

He sat in his hammock, wide and wild eyes staring back at me, unblinking until the last remnants of sleep faded. A breath hissed between his teeth. He shuddered and slumped forward to rub the dregs out of his eyes. Sweat-slicked dark curls to his forehead.

"Sorry," he mumbled into his palms. "I forgot where I was."

How many times had I woken up like that in the last few months? How many times had I avoided sleep in fear of what I'd see behind my eyes?

And every time, there was only one thing I blamed. He sat across from me now, the hammock bowing under his weight as he shifted into the light.

I didn't say anything as I swung my legs over the edge of my hammock. The floorboards rose with the rocking of the ship to meet my bare feet and fell away again a moment later. Muffled shouts seeped through the ceiling. We must have set sail sometime while we slept.

I hopped out of the bed and crept to the door, testing the handle. If we were already sailing away from Geirvar, there was no telling how far from Evhen's ship we were by now.

The last thing I remember from the throne room was how angry she had been, and that was familiar. That was the Evhen I had fallen in love with, not the shell of a girl who had come back from the depths without her hatred and anger. She had wanted to fight, and I would never get to see that again.

She was supposed to be happy. She was supposed to rescue her brother, and her happiness was the emotion I was supposed to be left with when I died. Not the fire of her rage and hate turning my insides to ash.

"Kal," Alekey's voice startled me, and my hand slipped on the doorknob. Its rusty edges cut through my palm, opening the skin, and I closed my eyes at the rush of power rising to the surface along with a thick stream of black blood. "Kal, please don't ignore me."

"I wish you had died instead of her," I muttered. My voice sounded distant, faint. It didn't sound like my own.

"*Kal*," he said, pained at my confession. Even his voice sounded far away, like it was coming to me from across the seas.

A rushing, like pouring water, pressed against my ears. I inhaled, tasting blood in the air, letting the power wash over me. Every breath was deep, calm, nothing like the icy shards that had been filling my lungs for months.

"She should have lived," I answered, raising my stained hand to examine the bones. Swirling threads of black wound through my fingers, but the bones themselves were untarnished. They twitched in anticipation, sensing release. "She deserves to live."

Ahead of me, Alekey shook his head, but it was as though I saw him through a veil. He was a blurry imitation of the dark-haired prince I knew.

As I stared at him, watching his mouth move but hearing no words, the darkness behind him lurched with the swaying light from the lantern, filling the corners with wings made of shadow. Claws scraped along the walls.

Death's messenger loomed over Alekey's shoulder, pale eyes rooting me to the spot. Hot breath fanned my face. It let out a guttural growl, revealing a mouth crammed with teeth, and I smiled back. For the first time in my life, this creature didn't scare me.

It leapt over the prince, and my bones shot forth. The sensation was less like cutting my skin and more like releasing my breath. When they rushed back into my hands and arms, settling against my own bones, there was only the sweet relief that came with knowing they were back where they belonged.

The veil over my gaze lifted to reveal Alekey on the floor, staring up at me in horror. He looked from me to the dozen marks embedded in the wall behind him, and back again, mouth flapping until he shouted, "What in the great black seas was that!?"

In the same breath, movement shuffled behind me.

"What are you?" Seaglass murmured.

Recognizing the tone as awe instead of fear, I glanced back at him. His brows pulled together over his blue-green eyes, but he wasn't looking at me. He studied the marks on the opposite wall, assessing the damage before his gaze flicked to my face. For too long, people had looked at me with hatred in their eyes, so I was surprised to see nothing but respect in the way he viewed me.

It kindled a strange, greedy emotion in my chest.

"A nightmare," I replied with a crooked grin, before a wave of dizziness crashed over me. I swayed, hand flailing for purchase, grasping only air.

Seaglass stepped into the room, catching my arm and steadying me with graceful strength. "Don't let your father see that," he said, the casual warning brushing against my spine. "Come on. He wants you both above deck."

Two sets of chains rattled from his hands. Frowning, I fought to remain upright and silent as he clamped them over Alekey's wrists first, but when he turned to me, I asked, "Why?"

"He's meeting someone, and he wants you beside him," Seaglass answered cryptically.

"In chains?"

He shrugged.

The cold metal bit into my skin. Numbing ice spread up my wrists into my fingers. Beneath one cuff, a shard of someone else's bone dug painfully into my own, and my teeth gritted together at the sensation.

"Kal," Alekey whispered behind me when we were in the hall, following Seaglass towards the stairs. "I know he's your father, but please don't say anything that will make him angry. I don't know how many times I have to apologize."

"Are you worried he'll punish you instead of me?" I growled beneath my breath, glancing back to catch his reaction.

He nodded, throat bobbing.

"Good," I snarled, curling my hands into fists. The bones had settled in places other than my palms, which meant I was able to dig my nails in as tightly as possible. With each step, the dizziness in my head faded to a dull throb, and I relished the pain and clarity it brought.

Above deck, a heavy mist shrouded the ship, almost too thick to see through, but as we were guided towards the captain's quarters, I caught sight of a shadow hovering on our port side. The shapes gave me the impression of a ship anchored next to ours, but a freezing gust of wind pushed the fog to obscure it before any crests appeared through the gloom.

My bare feet slid over the wet boards—I focused on the deck before me instead of the shapes bobbing in the ocean next to our ship, but the questions didn't stop tumbling through my head. Who could my father be meeting all the way out here, and why?

The door to my father's cabin was ajar. Voices floated out, catching me off guard when I recognized both of them.

Without thinking, I glanced at Alekey. The bruises on his cheeks darkened against his pale skin as the blood drained out of his face.

Seaglass pushed the door open, and my father looked up.

The other figure sat on the other side of the desk with his back to us, but I knew that posture and that crown. Had stood in this man's throne room while he declared his hatred for me in front of Evhen. While he said he'd rather kill me himself than let my parents have any more power.

My vision blurred as he rose and faced me.

"King Ovono," my father's voice droned through the warning buzz in my head, "allow me to introduce my daughter, Kalei."

TWENTY-NINE

"I don't understand," I said when the palace came into sight. Light bled across the horizon, and I stifled a yawn, surprised to see the night was already behind us.

I'd lost track of the hours.

Icana made a questioning noise. The stony courtyard echoed the horse's steps back to us as we approached the doors.

"You're queen of assassins," I said, letting the awe seep into my voice. "How come you never told me?"

My weapons master glanced over her shoulder. "You never asked."

"I didn't think *this* was the past you were trying so hard to hide."

"You knew where I was from," she said, a hint of annoyance in her tone as she slipped from the saddle and handed the reins to a waiting guard.

"Yeah," I murmured, sliding down with less grace, grimacing at the aches covering every part of my body. "But I just thought you had done something horrible and ran away from your training. I didn't think you were running away from this." I gestured to the palace, its turrets and domes with red shingles.

"Killing my father?" She scoffed, the sound cold among the dripping morning dew. Everything seemed frozen here—in place, in time, in memory. At least in Vodaeard, there was movement.

Despite how ghostly my home had become, there were sounds of life everywhere—sea birds calling to one another, fishermen selling their daily catches, old boats creaking in the harbour. Here, there was eerie silence, tension in the air, and eyes everywhere. My skin crawled with the sensation of being watched as we climbed the steps and crossed the threshold into a surprisingly warm interior.

"I wish I had done something awful," Icana added, ducking her head from the heavy stare of her father's portrait hanging in the hall..

I hurried to match her pace without stopping to look for signs of her past on the walls. "With the assassins, you're the most powerful ruler in the world," I argued, excitement jolting through my fingertips. Icana could single-handedly topple nations. She could stop this war. "Why don't you want that?"

"Would you?" she shot over her shoulder. The comment caught me by surprise, and I paused in the middle of the corridor, staring at her back until she realized I wasn't following her anymore. She turned, both brows lifting in question, her short braid swinging. Even after a long night of world-tipping changes, Icana didn't look frazzled, not a hair out of place.

She sighed. "Ev, you're the queen of the smallest nation in the world that still has a monarchy, and you don't even want that." The reminder that Vodaeard was slipping into obscurity found the only spot in my heart that hadn't completely turned to stone yet. "Why would you want this one? Why would anyone want this?"

"You could stop the war," I said, voice soft. Pleading. There had come a time in the last month when I realized I couldn't win this on my own—I had known it for a while, ever since King Ovono imprisoned us, but I'd seen how Kalei wanted to pretend the war wasn't happening, and that was when I understood it was never going to end. Not on my terms, at least. And maybe at that point, it would be easier to surrender than to keep fighting. I had lost everyone—what was the point anymore?

But Icana's position here could change the tide. She was right—my nation was too small to make a difference. But the assassins were feared all over the world. Even Chief Mikala had seemed frightened by the idea of my friend leading them.

Icana's gaze softened. "There will always be war, Evhen," she said. "I can't fight in all of them. Not when half of the Houses won't follow me." A knowing look passed between us as she pushed open the throne room doors. "I know House Sword pledged itself to Haret."

"Why won't they follow you?" I asked in her wake. The long aisle to the throne stretched ahead of us, and every step closer felt like a rope cinching around my neck. Between every other pillar stood a guard in black, eyes watching our progress. There seemed significantly fewer than last night.

Dropping onto the gruesome throne, she waved a hand around the room. "You've already noticed my own guard abandoned me," she said bitterly. "Those who did are already dead. The problem with assassins is that there are no traitors. Only cowards. And when I left, that's what they saw me as. I didn't betray my father when I killed him. I was a coward for not doing it sooner."

"You're *not* a coward, Icana," I insisted. "You said it yourself—you're not heartless." It took a certain kind of person to kill their own father, and even though Icana was the scariest person I knew, I hadn't imagined she was that kind of person.

She slumped in the chair, lips pursed, as she surveyed the room. "Gods, I hate this place," she muttered. "I never wanted to come back here. It could have destroyed itself with civil war for all I cared."

"Will it? Destroy itself?"

She heaved a sigh and sat up. "My family has ruled Geirvar for three hundred years. Three centuries years of children killing parents, and not a single other House vying for the throne. With one choice, I ended that tradition. I wanted them to destroy each other. And yet…I still killed him. I still inherited this fucking hunk of iron." Her fingers curled into the throne's armrests. "But now the other Houses have an excuse. War is coming. If they decimate the country because they want me off of this chair, then I'll watch it burn again with a smile."

A chill skittered down my spine. If Icana's choice all those years ago caused civil war now, then the most powerful nation in the world was on the brink of destruction. The rest of us weren't prepared for the outcome. Who would emerge when the dust settled?

Icana glanced up at me, her own zeal forgotten as she looked at me—truly looked at me—for the first time all night. "Gods, you look awful. Do you want a doctor or something?"

"Just a bed," I mumbled, fighting another yawn. "I'll be fine."

She gestured to one of the nearby guards and told them to escort me to a room. When I hesitated, not willing to follow a stranger, she patted my arm reassuringly. "I know it's not the answer you hoped for," she said quietly, "but this is the best I can do under these circumstances. You're safe in these walls, Ev. Get some sleep while I figure out how to save your princess and your brother."

Surprised tears pricked my eyes. She was still thinking about Kalei and Alekey. Despite her tenuous grasp on Geirvar, she still wanted to help me. Even if it wasn't in the way I wanted.

Nodding, unable to find my voice to say *thank you*, I followed the guard out of the throne room and through the twisting labyrinth of halls to a warm chamber with a soft bed. He said something about being posted outside the door, but my mind was foggy the moment I slipped beneath the covers.

Weak light trickled through a gap in the curtains when I awoke hours later. I pushed the covers aside, inhaling the sweet incense that wafted from the burner on the sill. For the first time in months, my sleep hadn't been plagued with nightmares, and I felt rested.

I did not, however, feel less sore. The simple act of stretching pulled at my wounds and bruises and bandages. A long groan rumbled in my throat—the first time I allowed myself to feel every ache. There was no one around to judge me based on how well I handled my pain, and I relished the peaceful quiet.

Ambient noise surrounded me, a welcome reprieve from the constant anxious buzzing in my head—the soft hiss of the incense, light rain pattering on the window, the tap of passing feet through the halls. Everything seemed stifled, muffled, so the creak of the bed when I slipped out sounded almost too loud. I cringed and held my breath, expecting an immediate knock on the door—someone to tell me I was needed somewhere to do something. But, after several moments passed, and no one came for me, I released my breath and crossed to the window.

Outside, a heavy mist shrouded the capital city. I wasn't sure which way I faced, but it didn't matter—I couldn't see anything beyond the balcony. The glass was cold beneath my fingers when I traced raindrops through the pane.

Longing speared through me so suddenly and painfully that I gasped, clutching my chest. I hadn't been able to sleep in my own chambers at home, finding solace instead in my council room or the kitchens, but waking up in a similar room and watching the rain fall like it constantly did in Vodaeard reminded me what I had lost. Alekey and I used to race raindrops on our bedroom windows—he had always been scared of the violent summer storms that lashed our shores, so I would stay up with him and make games out of it until he fell asleep.

Wherever he was now, I hoped he was okay.

Turning from the window and my dreary reflection caught within, I trudged barefoot across the plush carpet and pulled over the door. The guard acknowledged me by giving me a rather judgemental up-and-down glance.

"We brought clothes earlier," he said, nodding to the low table next to the door.

Shutting the door in his face, I quickly stripped out of the sweaty, dirty, bloody clothes I'd fallen asleep in. The bandages across my chest would need replacing, and my hair stuck to my neck, but I didn't have the patience to deal with a bath right now.

Wakefulness had brought worry, anxious thoughts thrumming noisily in my head. I needed to move.

The clothes were black, with red detailing along the hems—serpents twining up and down the arms and legs. A guard's uniform, then, but at least it fit comfortably. I knotted my hair into a loose bun and wiped the remaining dregs of sleep from my eyes before opening the door again.

"Do you have to escort me everywhere?" I asked the man outside. The idea of being led like a prisoner made my skin itch.

"No," he answered, voice flat as if he didn't care. "You are free to roam the castle. My post is here."

"Okay," I said, half to myself, turning aside to hide the mischievous grin that pulled at my lips. A whole castle to explore, and no one telling me what to do or where to go.

My urgency to find Icana faded the farther away I wandered from my room. It was still there, trilling at the back of my mind, but it wasn't as loud as the curiosity that pulled me through the hallways. This was Icana's home. She had spent sixteen years within these walls and hated every second of it. Even though I had never asked about her past, I wanted to know more, and thought I could sate my inquisitive nature now.

When I ended up in the library, my questions were no closer to being answered. Tapestries and portraits covered almost every wall, but none of them depicted Icana. At least, they didn't anymore. She had clearly been included when the artist did the original work, but someone had erased her with strokes of black paint over the portraits, or removed the thread from the tapestries. She was a ghost, her presence as clear as her absence.

Inside the library, grey light spilled through a massive dome high above the floor. Beams like ribs curved towards the peak, holding the thick panes of frosted glass that were mottled with rain. Balconies circled the room, three levels high, all of them crammed with bookshelves. I wasn't sure what I expected from a library in the land of assassins, but it certainly wasn't *this*. The dark wood and marble floor took my breath away.

In the middle of the room, away from the dusty old tomes, an open fire roared on a stone pyre. Chairs and couches surrounded it, with low tables placed between them.

And slumped in one of the chairs, Icana dozed, head propped on her hand. As I stepped closer, her cane slipped and clattered to the ground, startling her awake. A knife appeared in her palm before I even saw her move, but she lowered it when she noticed me.

"I don't know why I'm expecting someone to murder me in my sleep," she muttered, picking up her cane and a piece of parchment she dropped.

"Trauma," I suggested. We had been attacked too many times on the road to Xesta, and after, for it to be anything other than suspicion that everyone was trying to kill us.

She didn't respond except for a breath of air I took as a laugh.

I sank into the cushions of the chair next to her. A small pile of bool sank into the cushions of the chair next to her. A small pile of books teetered on the table between us, all of them open. The top one bore images of ships and seas. "I've never seen you touch a book in my life. What are you doing in here?"

"One of my spies told me what kind of ship the chief is sailing," she explained, scooping the book into her lap. The one beneath it showed a crest I didn't recognize, along with blocks of text in a language I didn't know. "I was reading up on that style of ship to figure out a way to stop him from going back to Vodaeard. There are weak points we can exploit."

Once, I would have suggested a bomb. We'd caused damage to the Marama fleet. Any closer to the helm, and we might have been able to stop the war then and there. But the chief had both my brother and the princess. I wouldn't risk it.

"Has he set sail already?"

"Yes, but..." Icana hesitated, running a finger down the illustrated page. "According to my spies, he hasn't gone far. He's anchored just off the coast, in a small cove up north."

My eyes narrowed in confusion. "Why?"

She shrugged. "They won't row out to investigate. As far as they're concerned, it doesn't concern them." She scattered the pile of books until she reached one close to the bottom. Freeing it, she withdrew a folded piece of paper from its pages. With one hand, she spread it out on the table, and pointed to a spot on the map it contained. "Haret is here. As far as I know, he's still there. Chief Mikala is up here. There's a boat waiting here, and I have a horse that can get you there by nightfall."

I followed her finger across the map, judging the distances and weighing the options. We were balanced on a precipice with only deadly waters below and enemies all around. "You're not coming with me?"

"Ev, the crown doesn't choose sides. I can't be seen helping you."

"I thought the assassins worked for whoever had the most money," I argued, feeling my frustration spark like the fire next to us. "Doesn't the crown have the most money?"

"Then everyone would be working for me, wouldn't they?" She sighed, rubbing her eyes. Exhaustion clung to her in ways I had never seen before. "Besides, there's…something else."

The scrap of white parchment dangled from her fingertips. She held it out to me, gaze focused on the fire. Flickering shadows danced across her face.

I took the paper, unravelling it as she spoke.

"That arrived shortly after we came back this morning. It was intercepted before it reached your ship."

Talen's familiar handwriting slanted across the page.

I scanned it quickly.

Warships were spotted leaving Wystan a day after you left, following your route. There may be a spy on board your ship. Be careful.

I swore, chest constricting with the familiar feeling of betrayal.

Aunt Caz might have been telling the truth about Haret, but she hadn't told me about the warships from our northern neighbours.

THIRTY

When King Ovono smiled at me, that same leering smile he gave to Evhen in his throne room, I wanted nothing more than to send my bones straight into his chest and kill him where he stood. But with my hands bound, I couldn't reach the cut on my arm to reopen it, and Seaglass's warning not to show this power to my father stilled my movements.

"We've met," I said, glaring at the man who should have died when his kingdom collapsed. "He tried to kill both of us."

Beside me, Alekey was silent, but I felt his nervous energy. Likely he hadn't expected to see the king again, not after the city fell to dust and rubble and bones.

Bones which now belonged to me. The ones that studded my hair and marked my arms and even the extra one in my leg were all from his city. A glittering jewel built on ugly truth, and I had set that truth free. As his gaze raked over me, noting the bones, I hoped he realized where they had come from.

He had made me this.

"Kalei," my father said, his tone scolding, "you are talking to a king. Be respectful."

I choked on a laugh. Tired of being the perfect daughter, I was going to be the monster he created instead. That meant I didn't have to bite my tongue anymore.

"Respectful? *Respectfully*, I wish he had died when I decimated his kingdom. He said he'd rather kill me himself than let you have any more power. He betrayed Evhen, tried to assassinate Alekey, and then threw us in prison to die. You didn't know I could wake the bones beneath your city, did you? I saw it all. Generations of trauma and pain while your family sat in your shiny palace and ignored their pleas. You let half your city die so you could cater to tourists instead of your own citizens."

"And you killed the other half," he shot back, dark eyes glittering. "Including my son. Yet here we are again." He looked at my father. "My spy delivered."

My stomach sank with the realization. This was a transaction. Haret had been working with King Ovono to deliver me back to my father. That's where I had seen that symbol on his men's cloaks before—crossed swords through a large gem. It had been everywhere in Xesta, before the palace collapsed.

Before *I* had brought it down.

"What do you gain?" I asked the king, straining forwards, chains rattling around my wrists.

Seaglass put a hand on my shoulder, and the weight felt excruciating, but neither man seemed fazed.

"Your kingdom is in ruins. What do either of you gain?"

"Xesta has been poised to invade Vodaeard since before you or the princess were born," King Ovono said. "My spies were everywhere. On the council. In the king's ear. That little kingdom was going to become another city under Xestan rule, giving me control over its ocean trade routes. With your father's army, I can finally take it."

"I don't need Vodaeard," my father added at my questioning look. "It's small. Insignificant. Its royal family will end."

Beside me, Alekey made a small noise, but I didn't tear my attention away from my father. "Then what do you need me for?"

This had always been my plan. Save Evhen by sacrificing myself. But, for some reason, my father wanted me alive.

He leaned forward, elbows resting on his desk. "You should not have survived that night," he said slowly, dark eyes drilling into me. "If your blood continues to give you power, I will drain it all until I know what that power is."

I staggered back, sickened by the bloodthirsty tone of his voice. Seaglass had been right to warn me not to show my power now.

"You know I'll stop at nothing to prevent you from getting what you want," I said to my father, all those years of false love turning my heart cold against him.

A hint of amusement danced across his face, as though my bravery were a facade. Something that wasn't real.

Anger burning in my throat, I looked at King Ovono. "I thought you hated my father. Why would you work with him now? He's immortal. He doesn't need you."

He smiled. The kind I associated with snakes and liars. The one men liked to use when they talked down to people like me. And they loved to talk.

"It seems our goals are more closely aligned now. Evhen made a mistake when she chose you instead of my son."

My heart fluttered at his choice of words.

Evhen chose me.

She had chosen a miserably short life with me instead of a long future where Vodaeard could flourish.

She had made her choice, but I wasn't dead yet. I still had anger. I still had power.

My father shuffled and organized some papers strewn across the desk. Maps and letters. Some of them were still sealed with wax—important missives from kings and queens across the world. I could only guess their contents—declarations of war or peace or surrender.

"Once I send her both your heads, she'll have no choice but to surrender," he said without looking up, distracted, dismissive.

As though we weren't even worth his time, since he had already made the decision to execute us.

Alekey made a sound, halfway between a whimper and a wail, when Seaglass started pulling him towards the door. As he reached for me, I stepped out of his grasp, planting myself in front of my father's desk.

My heart beat unevenly against my aching ribs, but it was a reminder that I was still alive. And if I was alive, if my heart continued to beat stubbornly when it should have stopped all those months ago on the beach, then I still had some fight left in me. "It's not Evhen you need to worry about," I said, forcing him to look up at me. His daughter. His Minnow. I'd make him remember my face.

Elbows on the table, he narrowed his gaze at me, and I caught a glimmer of hesitation when he looked past me to King Ovono.

"Leave us," he murmured, waving a hand for Seaglass to escort Alekey and me back to our locked room.

His first mate pulled me away from the desk, but this time I went without struggle, all my energy spent on hating my father with my final breaths.

His first mate pulled me away from the desk, but this time, I went without struggle, all my energy spent on hating my father with my final breaths. I cast a look back as I crossed the threshold. "She chose me, not Vodaeard." My heart flared with warmth, for once, instead of ice. "It's Wystan you have to worry about. You'll have to fight for that land and those seas. They own half of Vodaeard. They won't give it up without a fight. Your war means nothing to a centuries-old treaty."

"Get out," Father snarled. The anger in his voice felt like a victory.

Seaglass pinched the tender spot of my elbow until tingling numbness spread into my fingers.

When we were out on the deck again, light filtering through the mist in weak streams, Alekey shuffled next to me.

"Is it true?" he whispered. "Is Vodaeard doomed?"

I glanced sideways at him, wishing he wasn't so desperate for my forgiveness. Wishing he didn't insist on talking to me when I'd made my feelings clear.

"It doesn't matter," I said. "We're going to be dead."

He bit his swollen lip. Tears shimmered in his eyes, but they didn't fall. Maybe they had all been shed already, and he was resigned to his fate. Perhaps if he thought we were both going to die, he would stop begging me to forgive him.

The guilt would eat at him until his final breath.

It was cruel to wish something like that on someone like him, but I was tired of looking for the good in people and finding only disappointment. My father was cruel for the sake of being cruel. He didn't need Evhen's surrender—he only wanted to hurt her. After all, she had been the one to kill my mother.

I knew what she had done after. Torn her heart out as they had torn out her parents'. It was her heart that had restarted mine. For that I was grateful, but now my father wanted revenge. A cycle, over and over, until the entire world burned.

And I was going to be the one left standing in the ashes.

In our cabin at the end of the ship, I slipped the letter opener I'd swiped from my father's desk into my pocket before Seaglass unlocked the shackles around my wrists. He bent his head to avoid my gaze, but not before I saw the guilt in his eyes and felt the hesitation in his movements.

I caught his wrist when the metal cuff fell from mine, startling him enough to make him look up at me. "Don't pretend like you agree with this," I said.

"I have no input on the matter, Princess," he replied quietly. Emerald eyes dropped to my pocket, shifting to darker jewel tones in the wan light. He leaned in close and lowered his voice further. "Be careful with that."

Eyebrows knitting together, I didn't respond. Pretending to act like I didn't know what he was talking about was safer than admitting I had a weapon. He had seen what I could do with the bones, so he knew the small letter opener was the least of the weapons I possessed. But why didn't he take it, unless he wanted me to use it?

He gave me a knowing look before he left.

The key in the lock sounded like waves crashing against a rocky shore. Familiar, but threatening all the same.

When his footsteps faded down the hall, I pulled the unassuming object from my pocket. It was shaped like a piece of bone—I nearly laughed at the irony of my father appropriating such a symbol—the knobby end forming the grip, the tip sharpened to a point. Even though it was metal, it was clearly modelled after a leg bone. Like the extra bone in my shin, the broken edge protruding from my skin.

"What are you going to do with that?" Alekey asked when light bounced off the bronze.

"Cut your tongue out if you keep asking me questions," I muttered, twisting away so my back was to him. There was no reason why I had taken it, other than to prove to my father that he kept underestimating me. But a letter opener wasn't going to cut a hole in the hull for us to escape through.

Maybe I had simply taken it because it looked like a bone.

The prince mumbled something beneath his breath, too low for me to hear, but it sounded annoyed.

I glanced back, raising an eyebrow at him. "Repeat that," I said in a low voice. Anyone else might have been frightened, but Alekey had never been scared of me. Not when I was the Princess of Death. And not now when I was the Princess of Bones.

He looked up at me with a glare in his bruised eyes. "I said for fucking seas' sake, Kal," he spat.

The curses thrilled the bones in my skin, as if they were excited to hear him talk with such vitriol. As if they understood. I fought to hide a sinister grin. Finally, he wasn't begging or pleading with me. This version of Alekey—angry, hateful, vicious—was easier to handle than the broken and beaten boy who wanted my forgiveness so badly. This boy knew what it was to be angry.

"If you're going to keep threatening me, then put my head on the executioner's block yourself," he said. The light swayed gently overhead, but it cast his face in shadows that darkened the mottled bruises under his eyes. "You changed. I'm sorry for thinking I needed *your* forgiveness."

His anger tugged at my own in my chest, weaving through the threads that connected me to the only other person whose forgiveness he needed. But Evhen had already forgiven him—that was the whole reason we were here.

"I didn't change," I snapped. "You just didn't know me that well."

He shook his head. I noticed his unwashed hair stuck up in places, gleaming like oil on fire in the lantern light. "No, I *did* know you. I knew you better than Evhen did. I was always honest with you. I was kind to you."

Annoyance flared like a spark. "My *father* was kind to me, Alekey. And then he killed me because you led them to us. Evhen *died*! I had to pull her out of the depths."

"And I've hated myself every day for that," he exclaimed, voice hoarse with emotion. "You're not perfect either, Kal."

"So, why do you want my forgiveness so badly?" Shadows crawled up the wall behind him, but this time, it was only the lantern light swinging back and forth. Death's messenger hadn't come for us yet.

"Because I don't want to die with you hating me," he said, visceral pain in his words. "What I did was wrong, and I've paid that price, over and over again. He already took my parents from me. I won't let him take Evhen and Vodaeard as well."

"You're a prisoner," I reminded him through gritted teeth. "How are you going to do that?"

"You're the one with power in your blood," he said, bringing to mind what my father had said.

He would bleed me dry just to understand why I was still alive.

I might not have been able to dive into the depths and bring the dead back to life anymore, but I had control over the bones in my skin. Death was closer than ever now, but maybe he had been trying to tell me something on the ship with the dead sailors.

KAY ADAMS

Maybe instead of coming after me, I was sending him after *others*.

My jaw clenched. A heartbeat like thunder crashed in my ears.

If this thing wanted to beat so badly, I would give it something to beat for.

THIRTY-ONE

"Where are you going?" Icana called out behind me when I shoved up from the chair, accidentally toppling her collection of books, and hurried for the doors. She scrambled to gather the map and her cane. The end of it thumped a few paces behind me, but I didn't slow down.

Not when I finally had an excuse.

"I'm going back," I said over my shoulder, teeth grinding together. Pain rippled through my jaw and radiated from the centre of my chest, but my blood ran hot in my veins and made me forget about the aches in my bones. Anger swallowed me in a fiery maw. "She sent warships after us. I don't care if she's family. She's going to regret ever leaving Wystan."

"How, exactly, are you going to do that?" Icana was a bit slower on the stairs, and when I reached the bottom, I whirled to face her.

My nails bit into my palms, clenching and unclenching, shooting savoury pain up my arms. "I have to do this," I said, evading her question. It was the same thing I told myself when we left Vodaeard for the first time. Back then, I had a single-minded focus, and no escape plan. This time, I wasn't even sure how I would confront Aunt Caz.

Had she been telling the truth at all? Or was I marching into another trap?

"Fuck this place and fuck its rule. You're my friend, and your allegiance is to me. To Vodaeard. Your assassins are going to try to kill you anyway, so why not help me destroy my enemies?"

She looked around at the castle—its stone walls and mahogany banisters and diamond chandeliers. It was much warmer than home had ever been, but that was because Geirvar thrived while Vodaeard was barely surviving. We were hardened by climate and ocean and pressure from Wystan.

Geirvar had been allowed to grow.

But to Icana, this had never been home. It was unfamiliar to her. And she was starting to realize that her claim to the throne was going to be contested one way or another.

To the assassins, there were no traitors. At least if she helped me, despite the outrageous odds against us, she could prove she wasn't a coward before they tried to dethrone her.

She sighed deeply. "Why the fuck not? This place can rot."

A glittering mosaic of gems and gold covered the floor of the entrance. There were seven icons, haloed around a central image of a bird with one wing of fire and one wing of water—a sword, a spear, a whip, a cup, a snake, a fist, and flames—and she purposely dug the tip of her cane into every symbol as we crossed into the falling night.

"What do they mean?" I asked her. The passing guards gave us curious looks as Icana led us around the side of the palace.

"They're the symbols for the Great Houses," she explained. "Sword, Spear, Whip, Poison, Snake, Fist, Fire. Each House is named after their specialty—their method of killing."

"House Snake kills with snakes?" I raised an eyebrow, half in jest, but I was keenly aware of Icana's reflexes. She was quick, like a viper, always poised to strike.

She gave me a dry look as the stables came into view through the pressing mist. "The assassins of House Snake kill with whatever is closest," she said. "Our specialty is that you never see us coming."

As if to prove her point, a blade she hadn't been holding a moment ago appeared in her hand, flipped across her arms, landed in her opposite palm, and fell across my neck in the span of a breath. The cold metal felt like a kiss of death, but I was still trying to figure out when she moved her cane to her other hand. She moved like lightning and struck just as hard.

Chuckling, she tucked the knife away again. "Maybe I'll teach you that when we get back."

Following her into the stables, I shook my head. I knew my limits. No amount of training could make me move any faster. Besides, I enjoyed the thrill of fighting face-to-face. Swords felt real in my hands, as compared to daggers or poison. But Icana could turn anything into a weapon. With her by my side, getting past Haret would be easier.

Inside, the stables smelled musty and dusty. A wet horse stench clogged the air, and I scrunched my nose as we moved towards the back row of stalls. Around us, stallions and mares huffed and whined. The wooden rafters echoed the sounds back to us, making the building feel much larger than it was. We didn't have horses in Vodaeard—so many trampling feet and chomping teeth made me nervous, but Icana seemed comfortable, so I trusted her instincts and followed her to a stall at the back.

We stopped at the small door. A black mare with a white streak down its nose nudged its face towards Icana's outstretched hand. "This is Sylda. Named after our brightest star. My father bought her for me when I turned sixteen. The same day I left."

"Does she remember you?" I asked quietly, eyeing the mare. Icana never spoke about her youth in Geirvar, and I was worried she would startle like a caged animal if I raised my voice too loud.

She shrugged, stepping aside without a word.

After a moment, I realized she was expecting me to stroke its nose. I'd already been much closer to a horse than I ever wanted to be, but those instances hadn't been by choice. There was a reason we hadn't ridden across the mainland after the *Grey Bard* sank, and it was because the creatures terrified me. Haret had made me ride across Geirvar just to make me uncomfortable. I was annoyed it had worked.

But this—this was letting me become familiar with the creature before getting on its back. This was easing me into a relationship between ride and rider. Horse and human.

Just to appease her, I reached out, fingers uncurling from the tight fist I had made with my hand. Warm air brushed against my knuckles as I rasped them lightly over the mare's nose. She stood still, as if sensing my hesitation, ears flicking merrily. When she scuffed a hoof into the hay, I drew back with a sharp gasp.

"Okay, enough," I said. "Let's go."

Stifling her laugh, Icana unlocked the door and guided the mare into the aisle. She worked quickly to fit a saddle onto the horse's back, adjusting the straps before swinging up. The reins looked so natural in her hands, and I realized, not for the first time, that Icana would have been trained from a young age for something like this. She'd had a whole life before she came to Vodaeard, and I was only getting glimpses of it now.

"Beré!" Icana called into the depths of the stable. Feet shuffled over the hay in the distance. Icana called again, adding something in a language I had never heard her speak.

Moments later, a young boy skittered into view at the end of the aisle, pulling on the reins of a horse already fitted with a saddle. The grey beast huffed in protest, stamping its hooves, and I flinched at the sharp sound it made against the cold stone path.

"What did you do?" Icana muttered, noticing the horse's distemper.

The boy responded in the other language, looking from me to Icana and back again. He bowed his head, dropped the reins, and ran away.

The horse huffed in my face, but seemed immediately calmer. Calm enough for me to snatch up the reins and hold them at a distance. Little good it would do, though, if the horse decided to bolt.

I jammed my foot into the stirrup and hoisted myself up, trying to orient myself with the jarring sensation. The rise and fall of ships over waves was familiar, but this was a living animal, breathing and moving on its own.

I could predict ships based on the water and weather. This thing could throw me off without warning.

We rode out into the courtyard, where Icana whispered to one of the guards adorned in the crest of her House, the red serpent gleaming on her breastplate.

"Let's ride," she said when the guard hurried back inside.

"What did you say to her?" I asked.

"I told her to send redbirds to the assassins. A call from the crown. We'll know who answers when they show up."

"Where?"

"Your ship," she replied.

Grimly, I nodded, stomach in knots. This was another reckless, hasty plan put into motion without much thought. I needed to know the truth about Haret and my aunt. Who was she *really* working for?

The snap of leather cracked off the stone around us, and our horses lurched into a rapid trot across the drawbridge. Mist clung to our cloaks and steamed against our skin, parting around us as we charged through the winding streets. It unnerved me to see nobody, but still feel their eyes on me, as if they were lurking just beyond the edge of the mist, just out of sight.

The city fell away behind us, swallowed by gloom and cold, the beginnings of a storm churning in the clouds. Darkness crept in at the edges, crawling over the landscape towards us, moving slowly but steadily. Even as the wind whipped around us, howling against my ears, I felt like we were standing on a cliff, leaning into the unknown. Bracing ourselves for the fall. Enemies surrounded us on all sides, pushing us closer and closer to the edge with sharpened knives and poisoned words, and some great beast was hiding in the shadows below. Ready to ravage. If we didn't get our feet beneath us in time, we'd be devoured.

Tears stuck like icicles in the corners of my eyes. I drew my hood down, bent my head, and rode hard. The sound of Icana's horse panting beside me drowned beneath the rush of wind past my ears.

When I looked up again, the world was like pitch, ink-black ground hardening under our horses' hooves. Rain pelted down from the sky-obscuring clouds. Soggy curls fell limp in my eyes as I glanced over at Icana and noticed the line of horses next to her. Straightening in surprise, I looked around. Fifty or so steeds made a half circle around us, with Icana at the forefront, but she continued to stare straight ahead, eyes sparking like gems in the crack of lightning that forked above. For several minutes, we galloped in silence, the pound of hooves against the ground as loud as the thunder rolling in from the mountains.

If I believed in any gods, I would have said they'd all come down from their thrones to join us. Thunder boomed in the clouds, shaking the ground, and the sound was like a tidal wave rushing over the land. I didn't believe in the gods of these people, but I *did* believe in the Endless Seas, and this was how I imagined they sounded.

It quickened my heart. Not in fear, but in determination. The Endless Seas were not going to wash me away yet, and people like Haret and my aunt had no place among those waves. They were going to drown here. They were going to join the ghosts lost at sea.

Icana held up a hand, and our company stopped as one. She peered through the gloom, and like a hand peeling back a veil, the rain and ice and mist parted to reveal a stretch of black sand beach. The *Midnight Saint*'s mainmast speared the low-hanging clouds, poles and sails rising out of the fog with every violent toss of the waves against its hull. Wood creaked loudly between claps of thunder. Lightning briefly illuminated the deck, the huddled forms of sailors and soldiers running to and fro to tie down anything that might be disturbed in the storm. When the shroud of darkness settled over the ship again, I slipped from my saddle.

"Cazendra!" I shouted. The wind immediately snatched my voice away. Spray from the ocean and rain from the sky burned my throat.

Icana appeared next to me. "Do you want me to find her?" she asked, a thin blade twirling between her fingers.

I hesitated. "These are still my people, Icana," I whispered. "Just bring Aunt Caz to me. Don't hurt anyone else."

Her eyes glittered, twin blue flames against the storm. "Not even if I have a chance to kill Haret?"

The grim reality of Haret's betrayal weighed on my shoulders. They had taken my crown, but even without it, I didn't know what kind of queen I wanted to be. Killing my own citizens, reducing Vodaeard's population even further, didn't seem like the right course of action. Not when I had to consider Vodaeard's dwindling future. But did they even deserve a trial? Keeping them alive felt like a failure. A weakness. Something that other, more powerful nations could exploit. I was too young to rule, but if I started killing anyone who disagreed with me, I wouldn't gain the respect so desperately needed from my country.

I shook my head. Haret deserved to die for what he had done, but I would be the one to swing the sword. The decision had been made long ago.

"If he wants a fight, I'll give him one," I promised. "Just bring me my aunt."

She nodded. Tucking her braid beneath the cowl, she faded into the slinking darkness. Her cane never made a noise.

I shuffled back to my horse. Like silent sentinels, the assassins remained in position around me, wraiths in the dark. Living shadows. Only their eyes were visible above their scarves, a thin strip of skin. Even their hands were obscured by gloves, and now I understood why Icana always carried hers with her. None of them moved, giving the impression that they were statues, though their horses swayed and shifted and snorted and stomped.

Anxiety wound through my bones as the minutes dragged. My body thrummed with the urge to move, to act, to run. I stuck a finger in my mouth and bit the nail, scanning the shadows as if expecting another ambush. The thunder and lightning seemed to be coming from within, jolting through me with every breath, and every other noise made me jump. This was taking too long. Maybe Icana had been discovered. Maybe Haret was torturing her.

Why had I let her go? Why hadn't she sent one of her assassins? But Icana knew the ship. She knew where Aunt Caz would be. I had to trust she would be safe.

It didn't stop my stomach from twisting in knots.

I closed my eyes, face tilted to welcome the cleansing rain. I tried to remember the soothing motions of Kalei's leg bouncing against mine, the way she healed my fear with her small arms around my chest. The scent of her hair and sound of her voice. Before everything had burned between us.

When I found the courage to open my eyes again, a figure was marching down the gangplank, made of mist and fog, rain and sleet. The sharp clack of boots on wood echoed between each boom of thunder. Heart in my throat, I scrambled backwards, fumbling against the saddlebags for a weapon of any kind.

Icana would never walk so loudly.

She had also taken the only weapons.

One of the assassins sidled up next to me and silently held out a curved sword. I took it with shaking hands, mumbling a thanks that was snatched away by the vicious winds.

Haret emerged from the gloom with a billowing cloak of black leather snapping like a pennant in the storm. A broadsword extended from his hand, its tip nearly scratching the pier as he stalked towards me. When he stopped mere paces away, I fought to steady my breathing, focusing on each inhale so I wouldn't faint.

"Where is she?" I called, humiliated by the waver in my voice. Even Chief Mikala didn't frighten me as much as Haret did. Kalei's father had always been an enemy to me, but Haret had been a councillor. An advisor. A friend to my father. He knew me better than anyone. He could exploit me.

Because he knew my weaknesses.

And there were so many of them.

"The assassin with the limp?" He forced out a dry laugh. "She's safe. For now."

"And my aunt?" The curved blade, like a sliver of the moon trapped in metal, looked promising. I just didn't know if it was my neck or his that it curved towards.

"Alive," he said, sounding annoyed, though I didn't stop to question why he would be.

They had been waiting for us.

"I just want to talk to her," I said, reaching for the authoritative voice that had faded into low embers since Haret's coup. My captain's voice. The voice of a queen. "I need to know who she was working for. You or Wystan. She sent warships to follow our route. I just want to know the truth."

Nothing else mattered now. Vodaeard didn't have a future with me as its queen. Icana was right—we were the smallest sovereign nation in the world that still had a monarchy. Every other nation had already been consumed by larger kingdoms. We were clinging to our cliffs with splinters in our fingers, and the tide was threatening to pull us out to sea.

Part of me wanted to let it crumble. Let the ocean wash away the memory of the worst queen in history.

But there was a part of me that wanted to fight. It was an urge threaded through the very marrow of my bones, the reason I continued to act and act and act without thinking—an insatiable need to prove everyone wrong.

It was going to kill me one day. But not today.

Haret didn't respond, but he wasn't quite so good at hiding his reactions—for a brief moment, between flashes of lightning and the following patches of darkness, he looked surprised by my accusation.

"I won't humour unfounded rumours," he said, jaw tightening. "Not when you are so clearly desperate to say anything. I am—truly—sorry it had to come to this, Evhen. Your father was wise. Unfortunate that wisdom skipped a generation."

"Oh, fuck you," I snapped before I could hold my tongue. His words shot through me like a hot poker, stoking that angry fire in my core. "Don't disgrace my parents in the same breath you talk about overthrowing me. You're a traitor, Haret. I wanted to give my aunt the benefit of the doubt and talk to her, but you…I was always going to kill you."

With an enraged scream ripping through my throat, I lunged forward, angling the blade towards his head.

Panic marred his features between ripples of mist, obscuring and disfiguring his face in equal measure. Through it, I glimpsed his own rage as he brought his sword up to meet mine. The clash reverberated in my bones, rattling the teeth in my jaw. Pain scoured my shoulder.

I drew back, shaking out my arm. Even with an injured leg, Icana was better in a match than I was, and my entire body ached, scraped raw from falling off a horse and catching a knife in my arm. It wouldn't be a very long fight, and Haret was obviously skilled with a sword.

I needed the assassins.

Haret watched me, assessing. He didn't move to strike, which annoyed me—he wanted me to exhaust myself by attacking first, and then he would land the final blow. And the worst thing was, I would do exactly that. It was the same thing I'd done when sparring with Aunt Caz.

I didn't know when to stop. I'd stop when I was dead.

I glanced over my shoulder at the army behind me. Shadows dancing. Darkness swirling. The assassins were silent, but watchful. Eyes skittered over me.

"You answered Icana's call," I said, shouting to be heard over the storm. Rain streamed down my face and made the sword slip in my grasp. "She's in trouble now. Help me and help her!"

One by one, starting with the assassin who had handed me a weapon, they dismounted, feet pounding the sand in a thunderous echo. Various weapons caught the rapid bursts of lightning—lances and swords and whips that ended in metal spikes.

Beneath the sheen of rain and rage, Haret paled. Then he snarled.

Before he could take a step, a sound like rockslides and avalanches broke the rhythmic rumbling of thunder.

Instinct took over, and I ducked, the sound of cannon fire distressingly familiar—it was the same noise I heard that morning, the one that shook me from my bed and sent me running to the throne room.

Explosions turned the fog to fire. And out of the shroud of smoke sailed an armada flying the Wystanian arrow.

THIRTY-TWO

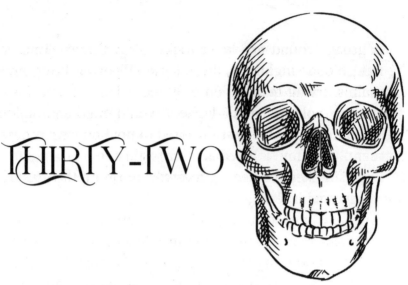

The air inside the windowless cabin tasted like metal.

Waves lashed the hull, and wind howled through the slats. My stomach lurched with the motions of the ship in the storm, the rise and fall of cresting waves, and the terrifying moments where it felt like the entire world disappeared from underneath my feet. Alekey and I crouched in our separate corners, the hammocks swaying over our heads. The lantern, the only source of light in this pitiful room, swung wildly from the rafters.

When there was a brief break in the violent thrashing, Alekey crawled out of his corner into the centre of the room. Standing shakily, he unhooked the lantern and blew out of the flame, moments before a wave slammed into the side of the ship and he flew into the wall next to me, landing in a heap of tangled limbs and broken glass.

"Ow, *seas*," he grumbled as the scent of blood spiked the air. In the darkness, I heard him brushing aside the glass, pieces chiming together like wards. He finally sat back against the wall with a huff. Warmth transferred from his skin into mine. "You can't heal anymore, can you?"

I didn't respond, eyes closed to focus on my breathing. There was no difference in the black between having my eyes closed or open, but a piece of glass had landed in my thigh, and I feared seeing Death's messenger if I kept my eyes open. Air whistled through my nose, trapped behind my teeth, and hot blood rolled down my leg.

Crowns of Blood and Salt

A groan ground like loose rocks in my throat. Bones strained to be free, blood singing for the release of power. I dug my nails into my palms, trying to focus on a different kind of pain instead of the pressure of holding back. I knew it would build and build and build until it burst out of me, but I wanted to hold on until the last possible moment. Until my father was in my sights.

"Kal?" Alekey pressed, though the storm raging outside drowned his voice to whispers.

His hand landed on my thigh—he probably meant to touch my arm instead—and slipped in the slick blood. With his hand in such an intimate position, my skin sizzled like his touch was fire, but it was not the pleasant kind of warmth I usually felt when his sister touched me. This was thousands of needles jammed under my skin, scratching through my veins like pricks of ice—a cold, burning sensation that shot through my senses, numbing me to the pain in my limbs.

I was frozen, likely to shatter with one wrong move, unable to drag a breath down my raw throat.

Something uncoiled in my core, waking.

"Did you get cut?" the prince asked, worry making his voice sound small and distant, reaching me through the churning winds of panic in my head.

Something tried to claw its way out of my skin, taking bone and marrow with it, and I screamed, head falling back against the wall sharp enough to daze me. Sparks danced in front of my vision like lightning, and through the patches of darkness, I saw a figure rising out of the shadows, leathery wings unfurling. Teeth gnashed, hot breath singeing my face. Sweat rolled down my cheeks like tears.

Alekey's concerned voice was far away, and I saw him in my periphery, as if through thick panes of glass, slightly distorted and hazy, but the creature in front of me filled my vision. It opened its maw.

It was becoming more and more real.

A wet cloth landed on my leg, and the illusion faded into smoke, into shadows, into silence but for the winds and waves outside.

A ragged breath scraped my throat. I blinked furiously to clear my vision, glancing down. In the darkness, I felt Alekey pressing a cold strip of fabric to the cut on my leg, stanching the blood. Chills cascaded down my body. Every bare patch of flesh prickled.

Alekey's fingers were suddenly on my face, tender and hesitant, gentle and searching. "Are you all right?" he asked.

Without realizing it at first, I leaned into his hand, eyes fluttering shut. Maybe in my final moments, I didn't have to hate him so much. Maybe, beside all the anger and heartbreak filling the empty void in my chest, there was still room for kindness. For fondness.

Not for love. Anything left in me that was still capable of love was reserved for his sister. It was her arms I wanted to be around me now. It was her voice I wanted to hear when the executioner's sword came down. It was her face I wanted to see when I finally greeted Death like an old friend.

But Alekey was the only one here now. Evhen was far away, her fate uncertain. Even if I could raise the dead bodies beneath the waves, there was a chance I'd never see her again.

So I leaned into Alekey and closed my eyes.

And cried.

Too soon, Seaglass appeared.

The storm continued to rage outside, threatening to turn the ship into splinters, and the door was wrenched out of his grasp by the force of a wave hitting the side. It smashed into the wall, metal knob grinding into the wood, and a soaked Seaglass peered into the gloom. Water doused his frame, dripping from his wavy hair and creating a pool around his feet. He held an orb of contained fire. The facets cast flickering prisms of light around the room.

"Your father requires your presence above deck," he said, defaulting to the same kind of formality the previous crew used when I asked too many questions. They had been willing to make up stories, when I was younger, before curiosity became too much of a burden to them.

So, in later years, when they spoke to me, it was so formal as to be detached. The tone now made me grimace.

"Say it as it is, Seaglass," I murmured, pushing myself away from Alekey. My limbs creaked from sitting for so long. "He means to cut off our heads. He means to bleed me dry."

JJaw clenching, he said nothing, dangling a damning pair of cuffs between us. I wiped my face first—if this truly was going to be the last time I died, I would do it bravely—and held out my wrists. The metal didn't feel as heavy this time.

After he had clamped iron on Alekey as well, he gestured to the hallway, which tilted sideways in the thrashing waves. I banged my shoulder into the door frame, wincing as a splinter pierced my skin.

As we walked—slowly, carefully, to avoid falling in the lurching corridors—Seaglass's mood returned, though when he spoke, his tone sounded strained. As though he was trying to stay positive for his own sake, and not ours. "I didn't think the Princess of Death was actually scared to die," he said lightly, but an undercurrent of worry wound through his words, caressing my spine with hidden truth.

"I'm not," I whispered. The lie weighed heavily on my tongue. No one knew what lay beyond the Dunes of Forever, if souls of the damned ceased to exist at all, and that is what frightened me. But I had become Death—I had walked those dark shores once and knew I belonged there—so perhaps there was something for me on the other side. Maybe the creature I kept seeing was only a guide, and not a beast gathering strength to devour me.

But I wasn't going to die with fear in my heart. Not when I had the power of blood and bones to command.

And if I fell victim to this power, if I couldn't control it, I would drag my father into the depths with me.

Rain plummeted from the sky as we emerged on the deck. Eerie green clouds churned overhead, broken by patches of writhing darkness and flashes of blinding light. Waves frothed against the hull, crashing over the deck.

In an instant, I was drenched. Bone-studded hair tickled my neck, and my clothes clung to my figure, making every step harder. The rain washed away the black blood that had crusted over every wound on my body.

Rope tightly bound the sails in place and held the cannons firm so they wouldn't careen across the deck. Through the sheen of rain on my face, King Ovono's ship rocked next to ours, tossed about just as violently. One strong wave could send it crashing into us.

I couldn't see King Ovono through the sheets of rain, but I sensed he was close by based on the way my skin crawled.

Lightning ripped the sky in half and illuminated my father standing in the middle of the deck. Rain plastered his hair to his face. He looked stern beneath his beard, furious in a way I had never seen him before. The sight terrified me—a man so enthralled with revenge that he would kill his own daughter a second time.

In his hand, he gripped an axe.

My feet rooted to the spot. The storm beneath my skin refused to allow me one more step closer to my father, even as Seaglass placed a firm hand on my shoulder. I couldn't move, couldn't allow my father to use such an ugly weapon against me—such a definitive way to die.

Alekey was already on his knees in front of my father. Seaglass lifted me off the ground—I yelped in surprise, the humiliating sound snatched away by the torrent—but the act was enough to jolt the desperate creature within to life.

Blood racing through my veins, rushing in my ears as loud as thunder, I thrashed against him, kicking and growling until he dropped me on the deck. I crumpled, elbows tucked in, to lessen the impact. Before he could pull me up onto my knees, I slipped the letter opener from my pocket into my palm. Hands clenched in my lap, I hid the bone-shaped object between my forearms. My heart pounded frantically in my neck, in the soft space between my throat and shoulder, but neither Seaglass nor my father noticed the thin blade pressed against my skin.

Strands of bone-beaded hair fell into my eyes. Rain dripped off my chin. Between blurry blinks, my father crouched in front of me and pushed the hair out of my face. He wiped some of the rain away with the pad of his thumb.

I jerked away with a curled lip.

Frowning, he stood, lifting the axe with both hands.

"This could have been avoided," he said without a trace of emotion in his voice. Thunder boomed in echo.

"No," I said, scowling up at him. The last time I had been sacrificed for his immortality, I had cried and begged for mercy. There would be no begging now. "You always meant to kill me."

"Yes, but it should have been months ago." He looked at Alekey beside me, silently hunched against the lashing rain. "*He* never had to die for your mistakes, Kalei. He could have lived if you had only left his sister to die."

The reminder cut through me faster than any blade. Tears welled against the bottom rim of my eyes, hotter than the rain falling around us. Evhen's soul had been so bright, so sad, so lonely. The depths were no place for someone like her, someone who burned so hotly and loved so fiercely. I hadn't been thinking of myself when I pushed her out, only that she should have the chance to live.

That choice shouldn't have condemned Alekey. It wasn't fair for one sibling to die while the other lived because of the decisions I made in their favour. They could both survive.

I owed them that much.

When I didn't respond, my father turned to his crew. His voice rose over the crashing ocean and booming thunder, but as I sliced through the wound on my arm with the letter opener, his words became muddled in the wave of power surging through my blood. Swatches of darkness flitted across my vision like a veil, and I sank into the comfort of Death's arms, the familiar pull of the depths at my bones.

A shudder ran through my body. I bent, ducking my head, as if accepting the axe. While blood oozed from my arm, hot and thick and acrid, I clenched my teeth and braced for the next cut. A poisoned stench filled the air, clogged my nose with the scent of blood and salt, and I bit on my tongue to keep from crying out loud as I pressed my unmarred arm into the sharp tip and swiftly dragged it to the inside of my elbow.

The letter opener clattered to the deck between my legs.

Blood spilled over my arms, pooling around my knees. My fingers shook as they stretched towards the sea, towards what lay beneath.

An unfamiliar sensation slithered up my back, like the spindly legs of thousands of spiders crawling beneath my skin. Nails scraped along the ridges of my spine, a *bump bump bump* of claws knocking at the base of my skull. Hot breath brushed across my cheek like a tender touch, and a voice made of rotting dirt and decomposing flesh whispered in my ear. *YOU'RE MINE.*

I lurched forward to vomit, palms slipping through pools of water and blood. Curling my fingers into the wood, I opened my eyes to stare Death in the face. Then I reached past him into the depths of the ocean.

Wings beat at my back, churning the air around my body into a maelstrom. A cyclone of dark clouds and cold rain swirled in the middle of the deck, my prone frame at its centre. For a brief moment, I was outside of my body—I was the creature behind me, watching through colourless eyes, beating the wind into a torrent. My father leaned into the winds, trying to reach me, but the gale forced him back.

I *was* the storm.

Time ebbed and flowed. In the middle of the cyclone, it appeared to stop altogether.

My heart thumped loudly in my ears, defiant and strong, and every breath was deep and fresh. Droplets formed on my skin, the rain no longer running in rivulets, and instead rose off me like steam.

But outside, panic snared the crew as the storm-tossed the ship to and fro. My father shouted orders, but no one heard him over the crashes of thunder that shook the boards and splintered the masts.

Crowns of Blood and Salt

The crew scrambled. Some fell overboard as the ship tilted to one side and then slammed back into a valley between tides.

Death grabbed my chin with claws that pierced through my jaw.

Sour blood filled my mouth with a scream of agony.

YOU ARE ALL MINE, he said again.

The sound broke a bone in my chest, and I gasped at the sudden pain skittering along my side.

I gritted my teeth and spat at him. "Take them," I growled.

A scream jostled in my throat, first of pain, then of determination, and I let the wind whisk it into a thunderous echo high above. My power dove beneath the waves, yanked back the veil into the depths, and gathered the bones at my behest. Like drawing from a well, I pulled on the threads that connected me to the bones and bodies. The ones in my skin ripped free and hovered in the air around me.

The creature howled and swept across the deck at my command. It drank like it was dying of thirst. It consumed like a creature starved.

My father's crew collapsed to the wet boards, bones exploding out of their bodies to join the ones shielding me. Blood spurted from their wounds, staining the fresh pieces. Some died instantly as their spines tore open their backs. Others writhed on the floor, dreadful moans creating a symphony with the deep boom of thunder and roar of water against the ship.

Death came for us all in the end, but now I commanded it. I gave it what it wanted.

I let it feast.

Thirty-Three

An anchor dropped into the frothing waves with a mighty splash. I looked up at the ship, the figurehead of arrows piercing mountains, and scowled at the man standing at the prow. Even in the torrential downpour, his gold buttons gleamed, and the markings on his brocade coat denoted him as the captain.

The rest of the fleet sailed into formation around the *Midnight Saint*, sails spearing through the storm. I knew without seeing all of them that they numbered more than the chief's armada had the morning he killed my parents. The Wystanian navy was famous worldwide for being the largest. And one of the deadliest. Even if those cannons had been warning shots, I had no doubt they would demolish my ship in seconds.

"Queen Evhen," the captain called from the deck. "Wystan offers its aid."

My mind spun. *Aid?* Aunt Caz had been telling the truth? But what good did aid do now? I needed them long before Haret betrayed me.

Ignoring the captain, who was still trying to get my attention, I lunged at Haret again, swinging madly at his head.

He scrambled back and slipped on the rocks, yet still managed to lift his sword in time.

My bones ached after the impact, but I pushed forward ferociously, refusing to allow him a breath. Both hands tightened on the hilt of my blade. Every swing was erratic and fierce. Determined, though a little unfocused. Icana would be disappointed in the way I moved, the anger guiding my actions instead of rational thought, instead of the way she had taught me to predict my opponent's next move, but Icana wasn't here to call out my mistakes now.

A melodic sound rang out from behind me, and I glanced back down the beach to see sparks flying as metal clashed against metal. Dark shapes moved through the rain, living shadows in the storm. The assassins who had pledged themselves to Haret—House Sword—descended upon the assassins who had answered Icana's call. Between flashes of lightning and sheets of rain, I couldn't discern the difference between the two groups.

"Your people were always going to die," Haret said, drawing my attention back to him with a boasting tone that slammed into me as painfully as the pelting rain. "You tried to turn fishermen into fighters and led them here to be slaughtered. At least I took that power from you before they could die needlessly."

His words, aimed like daggers at my fragile mood, found the parts of me that doubted myself, making them twinge with shame and guilt. I had been battling those doubts for years, and he wasn't going to bring me to my knees now. Not when I knew my reasons were valid, and his were entirely selfish.

"*No.*" I pointed my sword at him, its curved edge reflecting the dark sky above. "I didn't force anyone to come here. They came because they wanted to help Alekey. They came because they needed a king, and they were going to fight for him. I didn't lead them to their death. I brought them to their future."

"Look around, Princess," he replied, gesturing to the beach.

It wasn't like the sandy shore where the moon bled into the ocean, but it still reminded me of that night. Instead, boulders tumbled down the crags into the ocean, leaving no room for sand. We were balanced precariously on slippery stones, waves lashing around us. One wrong step, and the sea would smash us against the rocks.

Unforgiving.

"There is no future for Vodaeard. Not with you as its queen."

How many more people would I have to fight through until they realized I never *wanted* the seas-damned throne?

"I came here for Alekey!" I screamed at him. "So he could rule! You came here with your bloated head full of fantasy. You led a coup against me to bolster your own fucking pride. Two people died while I was still queen. How many more did you let die because you wouldn't listen to Icana?"

His eyes flashed, like lightning was caught in their depths, and leapt across the boulders at me. Light crackled in fractured bursts along the edge of his blade as he swung at my head.

I slid down from the rock, angling my body towards him while his momentum continued to carry him forwards. My curved blade caught him under the arm. Blood streamed onto the rocks, mingling with the saltwater and grit, darkening the stones.

He swore, gripping the wound. Fingers slick with blood, he shifted his sword, face twisting in pain. "You're not a killer, Evhen," he said.

I scoffed. He clearly didn't know me if he thought I wouldn't end his life here.

"Let's go home. Let's be civil about this and come to an agreement that benefits both of us. You wouldn't be able to live with yourself if you do this."

"Fuck civility," I spat, causing him to flinch. "I've killed, and that's not what keeps me up at night, Haret," I said.

He seemed surprised by the confession, and suspicious by the glimpse I gave him into my personal life.

"I lay awake wondering if I should have died alongside my parents. Alekey could have carried on their legacy without me ruining everything. I lay awake with regret and shame and guilt, but do you want to know why I won't listen to your shit?"

He frowned.

"Because I am trying to save what is left of my family. If that is what makes me a terrible queen, then at least it proves the difference between us."

"What's that?" he muttered.

"You have nothing to live for," I said. "I have *everything*."

Curling his lip, unable to deny the truth or hide from it, he lunged at me again with his non-dominant arm rising into the air.

My blade met his with sparks and a screech of metal, but the curved tip allowed me to knock his down with only a flick of my wrist.

He stepped back with a grunt.

Behind him, the beach crawled with shadows. The captain of the Wystanian ship had ordered his infantry to disembark and engage the assassins, but Haret and I were alone in the gathering dark.

I narrowed my attention on him as he advanced, shifting his weight to account for the imbalance.

He wasn't as skilled with his other hand, which made him sloppy and hesitant.

A storm raged through my veins, as violent as the thunderous beats around us, but it was a familiar kind of storm—nothing like the darkness of panic that seemed to perpetually cloud my mind. I moved with purpose, dancing across the rocks with the wind forming wings on my back, and struck at Haret with vigour. Every hit weakened him, pushing him closer and closer to the water's edge. The ocean lashed at his feet.

When the waves hit his knees, he looked down. "Are you going to drown me?" he asked with a bark of dry laughter. Sweat steamed off his skin as the rain pelted sideways.

"Drown you, cut off your head—I haven't decided yet." I braced for the next wave, feet steady on the rocks.

He swayed, and glanced back into the roiling waters.

Clouds the colour of jade churned in the sky as navy waves frothed with rain and hail. Small icy pellets broke against the rocks with a ringing sound and pinged off our blades.

My cheeks stung, but I didn't move, my cloak whipping around my legs and getting caught in the gale. I wanted Haret to remember me, for as long as he had the ability to remember anything before I killed him, as someone who didn't cower in any storm. Not the one inside my head, not the one he tried to throw against me.

I raised my sword.

"Evhen!" The voice cut through the roaring atmosphere, sharp as a knife. Thunder responded with a crack over the world, and lightning speared the ocean. The beach plunged back into darkness a heartbeat later, but light continued to dance erratically through the clouds, green and yellow amid swaths of black and grey.

I twisted to see Aunt Caz breaking through the clamouring bodies near the two ships. The sounds of battle were muddled in the downpour, distant and hollow, but Aunt Caz was a commander and knew how to make her voice heard over anything. Even the thunder reduced to whispers when she spoke.

"Evhen, don't end it like this," she said, stopping far enough away that I wouldn't be able to reach her before she reacted. Though, I noted, squinting through the rain collecting on my eyelashes, she didn't have any visible weapons in her hands. That didn't mean she was unarmed or vulnerable.

Where is Icana?" I shouted. In my periphery, Haret shifted, but I forced him to stay where he was with my curved blade aimed at his heart. Aunt Caz wasn't going to take this away from me, either..

"She's safe," my aunt replied. Rain sluiced off her shoulders, dripped down her braid, but she looked invincible against the storm. "Trust me. I told you the truth, Ev. I called on Wystan for aid. Haret is the only one you have to distrust."

She took a step forward, and I moved sideways to keep our distance. The three of us formed a triangle at the edge of the water, but only one of us seemed to be in control, and I knew it wasn't me.

"What?" Haret blurted, and I felt a grim sense of satisfaction at his outrage upon realizing Aunt Caz had been lying to *him.*

Guilt for doubting her rose in my stomach, sour and swirling, the familiar sense of being knocked off balance as the waves crashed closer and closer to where I stood.

CROWNS OF BLOOD AND SALT

Aunt Caz glanced over her shoulder into the flurry of movement on the beach. The ships were obscured by low-rolling fog, but I had no doubt the *Midnight Saint* was crawling with Wystanians by now. Her eyes narrowed, as if she could tunnel through the gloom and pin her glare on someone aboard the warship.

"I wanted to help you, Ev." She looked at me again. A crackle of lightning illuminated her face, making the gold specks in her dark eyes more prominent—the same eyes as my mother.

A painful stitch rippled like an undercurrent through the rage in my veins at the similarity, the reminder that Aunt Caz was family.

"I had hoped they would arrive sooner, though, so that we wouldn't lose Kalei too. Everything I've done was to keep this family together."

Salt air stung my nose as I fought to control my breathing. This was why I had come here—to get the truth. To know why she had led the Wystanians here. But now that the truth was out, I didn't feel better. Aunt Caz had let them take Kalei from me. But if I didn't trust my own family, then there were few I could trust. I knew family wasn't always trustworthy, and didn't always deserve it either. Kalei's had killed her for the truth hidden in a legend.

My legs wobbled.

This was too much.

There were too many factors, and I was tired of looking the fool. Tired of others taking advantage of me and my naivety and my weaknesses. All of this, just to get my brother back.

I looked back at Haret, silent through the whole thing. "Did you kill those people?" I asked. The wind nearly snatched my voice away. "To make me look weak?"

"You *are* weak," he snarled. "Vodaeard is weak. It will fall."

"Did you kill them?" I shouted.

He sniffed, as though my outburst was unwelcome and unwarranted. "I was testing a theory," he answered. "The Princess of Death was on board our ship. I was tasked with learning as much about her as possible. If she still had power. What would happen if she was surrounded by death in such close quarters. She brought about those deaths, not me."

Spinning on the slick rocks, I charged at Haret, and caught him by surprise. I bent low, dropping my curved blade to tackle his legs and knock him off his feet. His sword fell with a splash and vanished beneath the tar-like waves as we both crashed into the ocean. Water rushed over my head before I shoved up. I broke the surface with a gasp, nearly falling backwards as another wave slammed into me.

For a moment, I was back in Vodaeard, chains around my ankles, saltwater filling my lungs. Drowning.

Dying.

But then I straightened in the shallow water, feet between two sturdy rocks, and waited until Haret came up, coughing and spluttering. I immediately shoved him back under, fingers tight in the collar of his shirt to brace myself against the next wave. Limbs thrashing, he fought, trying to throw me off. The water drew back, allowing him to gasp for air again, and I slammed my fist into his jaw. Pain seared across the top of my knuckles, and when I hit him again, blood smeared across the top of his cheekbone. Another wave crashed over him. With my hand clenched in his collar, I felt the impact when his head smashed into a rock beneath the surface.

His body went limp under me.

Panting, I scrambled backwards, scraping my hands over the rocks for my sword. The waves churned and frothed and then went still as a mirror. I held my breath, a chill erupting over my body that had nothing to do with the icy hail pelting down from the sky that seemed determined to tear itself in half.

A face appeared out of the still waters by my feet. As it had done in Vodaeard, the siren grabbed my free hand and pressed its slimy lips to the cuts on my palm.

I hadn't even realized they were bleeding, I was so cold and light-headed from the adrenaline quickly seeping out of my veins. My chest rose and fell with the unsteady beating of my heart.

"You bring us a sacrifice," it said, showing its teeth in what passed as a terrifying grin. Two eyelids blinked at me.

"I just wanted him gone," I said, throat suddenly parched.

"A death is a death," it said, and I remembered what it had told me before we left Vodaeard. Someone's death would bring me peace.

This didn't feel like peace.

It pushed away from the rocks. Webbed hands searched beneath the waves until it found Haret's body and dragged him to the surface. Its tail flicked, and the ocean resumed churning and bubbling. Forked spears of lightning sparked off its scales as the siren sank below the waves again.

A moment later, it returned to the surface, further out beyond the shore. "There is another," it called. Its voice, like the screech of metal and melody of stones, tingled the base of my skull. "She is not dead, but Death comes for her." With one final smack of its tail against the surface of the ocean, the siren dipped beneath the waves.

Haret's body disappeared with it.

Breath rushed out of me in one long gasp.

Kalei. She was still alive.

Heart clamouring, I hurried down the beach towards the Midnight Saint. Haret was dead, which meant the ship was under my command again. If Aunt Caz was telling the truth, then the Wystanian armada was here to help. And with Haret gone, I had the opportunity I needed to take my army to Chief Mikala.

With Wystan coming to my aid, I could save both my brother and my princess.

"Ev!" Icana's familiar voice, cold as ice, reached me on the wicked wind. She appeared as a wraith against the backdrop of the storm, a figure of slithering shadows. Her cane waved in the air as she hobbled towards me. Behind her, the fighting had stopped, nothing but smoke and fog covering the beach.

I scurried over the stones towards her, shivering beneath my cloak. "Where's Aunt Caz?" I panted.

"She's talking with the Wystanian captain," Icana explained, bringing her cane down to lean on it. "They're here to help. What happened to you? Where's Ha—"

Hot blood splattered on my face as an arrowhead burst out of my friend's neck. She blinked in surprise and tipped forward.

I caught her, a scream trapped in my own throat, and lowered her to the stones. Blood pulsed in steady streams down her chest, pooling in the hollows of her collarbone. It stained my arms as I cradled her head. Looking up wildly, I scanned the beach.

A lone figure stood amid the swirling darkness, wind tugging at their clothes. A crossbow hung from their hand.

"Long live House Poison," the girl said before walking away.

Icana coughed, a wet, gurgling sound that filled my ears with the horrific images of a throne room painted with blood and gore. I pushed strands of wet hair out of her face, trying to ignore the rapidly spreading stain over the tips of her blonde bob.

"Shh," I said. My hands shook as I examined the wound. The bolt was short, meant to enter and exit completely, but it had stuck. The metal rod was the only reason Icana hadn't died immediately, but she was losing too much blood. "You're okay. You're *not* going to fucking die on me, Icana. Come on. The doctor will—"

"Ev," she choked, the word more like a gasp.

I shook my head, swallowing the bile that came with the tears. "No. You don't get to have any last words with me right now. That's not how this ends. You survived this place once. You are not dying in this seas-forsaken country. I am your queen. I won't *allow* it."

A weak laugh bubbled over her lips with a stream of blood. Tears streamed down her cheeks, a pattern of salt-encrusted freckles that I tried to wipe away. Blue eyes, like the palest sky at noon, mirrored the storm raging above us.

Footsteps approached from the side, and I looked up to see Aunt Caz and Eiramis. I hadn't seen the helmsman since Haret's coup, and my joy at seeing him unharmed was short-lived.

The Wystanian captain filled the space behind them. The three of them were hazy figures in my vision, blurry with tears, slightly out of focus through the falling rain.

"House Poison," I said, the words sticking in my throat as realization dawned on me. She had not only been shot, but poisoned too. Even if she survived the bolt through her neck, chances of finding an antidote were slim. "Get the doctor. He might have—"

"Captain," Eiramis said quietly. The title was a nail to the inside of my chest. "She's gone."

THIRTY-FOUR

Emerald eyes wavered in front of me. Hands on my shoulders dug into my flesh, pulling my attention away from the dying crew to a sea-kissed face.

"Stop this," Seaglass begged, blood dripping from the corner of his mouth.

My vision rippled like water over stone, then fractured, as if lightning broke my sight in half and made me see two realities at once.

Death crouched before me. Once more, it was his claws that pierced my shoulders and his eyes that flashed like colliding stars. *CEASE THIS*, he said with a brittle voice that transcended this realm. The command wrapped around my bones, squeezed tight to force me into compliance. Dry laughter caressed my spine, as if he knew my resolve was crumbling. I wasn't made to hold power over Death, and every part of me wanted to bend. To surrender.

The boat around me faded. The screams and the storm faded.

Alekey shifted on his knees, facing me sideways, in a part of my vision that hadn't yet broken.

Everything else was dark, strokes of black replacing the grey and green clouds.

Death himself, painting over my vision, until it was only him I saw.

But Alekey was there, not yet blotted out, and he put a warm hand on my cheek. "Survive," he murmured.

Survive, little moon.

The sirens had known, even then, what I was capable of. Had they always known it would end like this, with a battle of wills against Death himself?

Hot winds blew against my back. Teeth gnashed at my ankles, but until I surrendered my soul, the creature couldn't touch me.

"Move, Seaglass," I whispered, watching him fade in and out, Death hazing over him like an image painted on glass. My tone didn't leave room for argument, and Seaglass shifted to the side, leaving only Death in front of me.

I screamed.

The bones that swirled like a shield around me against the storm shot forward. More ripped from the dying crew, their screams silenced. The tornado of bone shards slammed into Death, forcing him to relent a step. A cage of ribs and spines wove around his frame. Shadows leapt from him in agitation, seeking, searching for a weakness, but the bones fused tight. Pieces from different people formed a skeleton around his incorporeal body and trapped him, dragging him towards the edge of the ship.

"You're *mine*," I snarled at him, pushing myself to my feet. Burning pain lanced up my arms while thickening blood oozed down my fingers. The world tilted with the motions of the ship, but I remained standing, staring at Death, when a sound like breaking glass shattered the night.

Waves frothed over the side of the ship, staining the boards with fish guts and a flurry of other deep sea refuse. A rotting smell clogged the stale air. Webbed hands grabbed the edge of the ship and pulled it towards the waves. My feet slid over the boards, losing purchase as rain pelted my face.

Alekey yelped, sliding towards the railing. Several dead bodies followed. His fingers scrambled for a hold, and I distantly heard him calling out my name, but the only thing that reached my ears clearly was Death's low chuckle.

Heart thumping loudly, I reached for one final bone and slammed it into the cage surrounding Death's body. The force caused him to stumble back, and a siren snared the top of his spine, holding him in place. It dragged him over the edge.

At once, the other webbed hands pulling at the ship disengaged, tails flashing like lightning sparked in their scales as they leapt back into the ocean. The ship lurched into place against the waves. Wood creaked and snapped.

Alekey fetched up against the side, chest heaving.

My knees scraped the deck, breath shuddering in and out until the sound slowly returned to normal.

The storm continued to howl around the ship. Rain and blood coated the deck in a gory display of power.

Sickness roiled in my stomach at the sight of mangled bodies, and I gagged, a whimper building in my throat.

Alekey scrambled across the deck towards me. Warm hands brushed my shoulders in comforting circles. "What did you do?" he asked, half in awe, half in horror.

"I don't know," I whispered, hand pressed against my mouth to keep the sickness inside. Blood smeared my face, but for the first time in months, there were no bones pressing into my skin.

Startled, I flipped my hands over. Circles of blood were the only indicator that they'd ever been embedded in my skin. I searched for the chip in my jaw, the femur in my leg, the extra rib. They were all missing, toppled over the edge with Death.

There was no rising swell of power in my veins. An empty feeling coursed through my body, but I didn't mourn its absence. I felt free.

I lifted my head to look across the deck at my father.

He had lost the axe in the ship's violent tumbling, but not his anger. It shone even brighter on his face, a sheen of red with every lightning strike around us.

Veins on fire, I tried to get my feet under me, but my limbs were too weak to carry my weight. Alekey held me upright, staring down the man who had slaughtered his parents with the same kind of bravery I admired in his sister. They were both so young, but Evhen had been right—this world trampled those it viewed as weak. They had to be brave in the face of certain death if they were going to survive.

"Chief," Seaglass said suddenly, urgently, but it wasn't to plead with him. We followed his gaze out beyond King Ovono's ship, to the pale specks of sand-coloured sails creeping through the fog.

As the sails multiplied, an entire fleet filling the cove, a burst of red light illuminated the gloom. Rain turned to fire as cannons boomed. The mainmast of King Ovono's ship exploded into splinters.

"Get them below deck," my father ordered. "Now!" He spun around to the pitiful remains of his crew and started shouting orders, though many of them still writhed on the floor. Arms hung at odd angles with missing bones. Legs dangled uselessly from their hips. A few of them clutched their sides.

Seaglass swept me into his arms, gentler than before. A line of red stained the side of his mouth.

"Did I hurt you?" I asked.

"Just a tooth or two, Princess," he replied with a crooked grin, revealing the gaps in the back of his mouth. "Not like some of them," he added grimly. At a nod from him towards the side of the ship, I directed my attention to a body slumped against the railing.

King Ovono, chest torn open, missing sternum allowing his innards to spill out. His had been the last bone, the breastplate that completed the cage around Death. The one that pushed him back into the depths.

The one that locked him in his realm, taken from the man who had ultimately led to the discovery of this power.

"Is that Evhen?" Alekey exclaimed as we reached the steps descending into the dark belly of the ship.

I twisted around in Seaglass's arms to scan the approaching armada. At the prow of the leading ship, blazing red hair haloed a sun-touched face.

Cazendra stood next to her, severe in a black uniform I had never seen before, braid stiff despite the wind cutting across the seas.

Fog curled up the sides of both ships to obscure them from view as they sailed into position next to us. Alekey bolted across the deck without a moment's hesitation, sweeping up a sword from one of the fallen soldiers before disappearing into the thick torrents of rain.

"Shit," Seaglass muttered. He set me on my feet, one hand tight on my elbow, when the deck lurched beneath me.

"Let the prince go," I whispered. "Please."

"What about you?" The question surprised me with how genuine it sounded. He was still my father's first mate, but he was giving me the choice.

My breath hitched. I wanted to survive. I wanted to see Evhen one last time.

I didn't have a chance to make a decision. My father strode out of the obscuring veil of smoke and ash, a menacing figure of reckoning. Shadows marred his face as he clamped a bruising hand over my arm.

"If this ship goes down, you go down with it," he snarled at me, his fingers digging into the fresh wound.

I cried out in pain, and struggled, but I was too weak to thrash in his spine-tingling grip as he hauled me down the steps. Every little move jostling my wounds. Pain burst along the base of my skull. The labyrinthin halls twisted into darkness.

There was little I could do as he yanked me through the open doorway of the small cabin below deck. Without any light, darkness gathered in heavy folds against the walls. In the centre of the room, he pulled my arms above my head, looping the chain that connected the metal shackles around my wrists to the hook where the lantern had hung earlier. It was in such a position and just high enough that I couldn't jostle it free, no matter how much I struggled.

My father's boots crunched through the broken glass.

"Wait!" I cried as he stepped out into the hall, struggling to free myself from the chains. "Please don't leave me here!"

The door slammed shut.

The darkness in the room didn't move to devour me.

Nothing slithered out of the shadows to taunt me.

I was alone for the first time in my life, so far away from the light of the moon. The well of power had gone dry in my bones. There were no whispers in my ears. I could breathe without pain for the first time in months.

Distant explosions rocked the ship for some time. I remember being so afraid when I saw the damage to my father's ship for the first time. Evhen's crew had planted the bombs, and forced the Full Moon and Crossbones to flee Vodaeard, but not before my father had slaughtered their monarchs. And now she had returned to have her revenge.

Most of my father's crew were dead again. I had torn their bodies apart. I had beaten Death.

A sense of hopelessness permeated the stale air of the cabin as wails ebbed and flowed overhead. Bodies thumped to the deck boards. Blood spilled in rivulets between the slats. The scent of it filled the cabin, sweet-smelling to my nose.

My own blood ran in thick streams down my arms. My hands tingled where they dangled above me, and I tested the hook again. It didn't budge.

Time passed at an agonizing pace. My vision wavered from blood loss, and I slipped out of consciousness more than once before another explosion would startle me awake. The dull heartbeat thudding in my ears continued to lose strength with every moment that stretched uncomfortably long.

My head drooped forward.

Water lapped at my ankles, but it was several dizzying moments before I understood what was happening. Panic shot like lightning through my veins, clearing my head as I looked down. Ocean water swirled into the room through a crack in the outside wall.

"Seaglass!" I screamed, yanking hard on the metal chain. The edge of the cuffs bit into my raw skin, but I gritted my teeth against the blossoming pain and pulled harder, dropping my weight to the floor in hope of popping the hook free from its beam. "*Seaglass!*"

The crack expanded up the wall. If the hull was compromised, I'd easily become one of those ghosts Evhen was so scared of—the ones who drowned at sea, to sail endlessly on haunted vessels.

There were many ways I had imagined my death—freezing on a mountain, bleeding out beneath the moon, marching through the depths to meet Death on the other side of the Dunes of Forever. Never once had I considered drowning.

Then I smelled the fire.

Thirty-Five

There was blood under my fingernails. And for once in my life, it wasn't my own. It was Icana's.

Icy wind whisked my tears into the storm. I hadn't yet found the courage to wipe away the last memory of her. There was no one I could take my anger out on either, because all the assassins—even the ones who had answered her call—had dissipated when they had learned her fate. The whisper had raced like wildfire through the ship before we had even boarded, and even the dark shadows who had pledged themselves to Haret had vanished without a trace. Civil war brewed over Geirvar.

I doubted anyone in this seas-damned country was still loyal to House Snake. She'd come home with us. I'd send her out to the Endless Seas alongside my parents. For now, all I could do was hold on to her memory and my anger and finish what I had started all those months ago.

And the only thing I had left of Icana were her twin blades and her blood beneath my nails. Her twin blades felt *right* in my hands when I twirled them. As if all those years of training had prepared me to be worthy of them one day. Today was that day.

Sheets of rain pelted sideways as we dropped anchor beside a ship with pale blue sails. A familiar sigil embellished the fabric—one that made my heart stutter in my chest. A memory surged alongside the anger burning my skin—a death sentence disguised as a dance—Kalei in a dress that shimmered like the night sky. Threats whispered. A confession made in panic. Alekey's blood. Every moment—from the time I saw Kalei at the top of the stairs to the time Alekey's scream rent the night—had been laced with gasping breaths. As though the man responsible had stolen all the air from my lungs. I froze again.

"Ev?" Aunt Caz's voice sliced through the rain.

I shook my head at the distraction and set my jaw. Teeth gritted together in painful scrapes. Rain hissed against my skin as I flipped the hilts of Icana's blades into my palms. I couldn't afford to be distracted by King Ovono's presence, not this time. He would get the same fate as the rest of his glittering kingdom.

"I'm ready," I said, my voice hoarse.

Cannons boomed around us in succession. There was no turning back now.

Planks of wood thudded between our ship and Chief Mikala's, just as his crew scrambled into formation and answered with cannons of their own. Fog parted in swirling tendrils, like fingers drifting across the surface of a stream, but wind howled over the ships, and rain cascaded down from the green-black sky, making it impossible to see. I swiped a sleeve across my face. It didn't help.

"I'll be right beside you," Aunt Caz said in a reassuring tone, though her face was grim when I glanced sideways at her. A slender eyebrow arched when she caught me staring.

"I should have trusted you," I said. Guilt ripped through me at the way her eyes softened. If I hadn't expected the worst, if I hadn't suspected my aunt of treason, Icana might still be alive.

"I should have been honest with you about Wystan," she murmured.

"We're here, too, Captain," Akev said on Aunt Caz's other side. Beyond him, Eiramis stared ahead, jaw tight. Rain blurred both their features until I looked back at Chief Mikala's ship.

And the man himself, rising out of the fog like a creature of vengeance. Blood stained the massive sword in his hand, and my stomach plummeted as I wondered who it belonged to.

Hopefully not Kalei.

Half of Captain Beynet's army—proper soldiers with proper weapons—had already crossed to the chief's ship, engaging with the crew as cannons fired. The other ships in the Wystanian armada were sending their crews over in rowboats. A cry I never thought I would hear in my life rose up from the sea—a Wystanian war cry, punctuated by the metallic ring of swords being unsheathed.

The chief's glare locked on me as I put a foot on the plank spanning our ships.

I had trained with Icana in every weather condition and across every variable terrain. Walking the short distance with two swords and wind tugging at my clothes should have been easy, but it felt like time slowed to a standstill. The waves churned beneath me, promising to bash me against one hull or the other if I fell. Rain and ice slicked the wood beneath my feet, and the wind grabbed at my cloak, pulling me backwards while my feet continued to move forwards. It was like they moved of their own accord, my body knowing that I had to cross this board, and my mind refusing to catch up.

I should have been scared, should have been petrified by the elements doing their seas-damned best to kill me before the chief had a chance, but I wasn't. I hardly felt anything, aside from the sting of ice pellets against my cheek and, finally, the solid wood of a blood-drenched deck beneath my feet when I hopped down from the plank. The space in my chest where my heart had been was vacant, echoing with a thud that repeated in the form of thunder in the clouds overhead. There were no emotions left, only the searing white-hot pain of rage.

Feet thumped onto the deck behind me, and I didn't have to look to know everyone had made it across.

The chief stalked towards me through the fray of clashing swords, shoving aside anyone who got in his way. Sometimes with his muscular arms, sometimes with his massive sword through a stomach, a neck, a head. Bodies heaped in his wake, but it wasn't his path of destruction that gave me pause.

It was the bodies slumped against the railing, the ones that showed signs of dying by something more horrific than a simple sword through the gut. These bodies had sections of flesh that *peeled* back from their limbs, revealing gaps where bones should have been. Some of them had torsos ripped open. Others, sprawled on their stomachs, showed jagged lines of torn skin from neck to waist. As if their spines had *crawled* out of them.

My stomach dropped. Kalei.

"Fuck," Aunt Caz whispered, her voice barely audible above the crashing thunder and pounding rain. "What did she do?"

I couldn't answer. Whatever she had done, it had significantly depleted the chief's numbers. With Wystan's help, the scales had tipped in our favour.

A seedling of emotion blossomed in my hollow chest. I smothered it with cold rage before it had a chance to grow into something more. Until the chief was dead—until Kalei and Alekey were safe—there was no room for hope.

Cannons continued to shred through the railings and splinter the masts, rocking the ship with each answering boom.

Even without assessing the damage, I knew this ship would never leave this cove again.

The chief snarled when he had finally cut a clear path towards me, and the only thing that separated us was the blood running in streams across the deck.

"Come to die again?" he asked, and my blood boiled in response.

His was the only blood I wanted beneath my nails, and I would make sure I spilled all of it to secure my crown.

"Here to kill you," I growled. The weight of Icana's blades in my hands was a comfort.

"Have you forgotten?" he called with a harsh chuckle. "I'm immortal. You can't kill me."

My lip twitched. Kalei had given her lifeblood to him. Maybe all I had to do was bleed him dry. Either way, I would finally have my revenge. But Icana's blades were shorter than the horrendous thing in his hand, and I wasn't fast enough to get in close before he could swing that at my head.

Indecision gripped my bones. My reckless nature told me to charge, to attack, before he had a chance to engage—to do something that would likely end in shambles like every other plan I've ever made. Instinct told me to hold my ground, to think of a way to test the limits of his immortality while the rest of the Wystanian armada battled to victory.

I tilted my head towards Aunt Caz to get her attention. "How do I defeat someone who is immortal?" I whispered, feeling the familiar talons of panic tapping against the base of my skull.

"If he bleeds, he can be killed," Akev answered.

Daring to break eye contact with the chief, I glanced sideways at him. "You're positive?"

His eyes twinkled, though it could have just been the lightning flashing across the sky. "I didn't only study politics at university, Captain," he said. "Myth and folklore was an elective last year."

Misery flooded through me. If I believed him, I would be putting my faith in nothing more than stories. *Again*. Great seas, I needed something solid. Something tangible. Something to prove that an immortal man could *actually* die.

I didn't immediately dismiss Akev's notion, but it did make me squirm in discomfort. I nibbled on a finger.

"Fire," Aunt Caz whispered in my ear. "Burn the ship. Let's see him try to come back from the ashes."

My hands stilled against my mouth. The idea sparked, and a grin spread, and that damned emotion dared to prick against my chest like it was waiting for nourishment.

"At once?" I asked, and the three of them nodded.

I looked to my other side, where Icana should have been, and felt a pang of grief slide between my ribs. The journey home was going to be a long one without her quips.

I glanced down the line once more to Eiramis. His eyes were hollow, blank. Just days ago I had seen him and Icana at the helm, bickering about something mundane, and his eyes had been so bright, his smile so wide. She was a challenge to him, and he hadn't given up. He noticed where she should have been beside us, and that stark reminder made me curl my lip as I faced the chief again.

He looked between the four of us, immediately recognizing Aunt Caz as a worthy opponent. Or at least someone who would give him a proper fight. Next to me, she adjusted the grip on her sword, and flicked her braid out of her face.

Lightning speared across the sky in fractured lines. In the following darkness, patches of fog rising and falling with the motions of the ship, the chief lunged.

Akev and Eiramis darted to the side to circle him, and Aunt Caz jumped forward, slipping under his rising arms.

The sword came down in a flashing arc towards my head. It met my twin blades in a bone-jarring clash, and I gritted my teeth against the pain that screamed along my ribs. Shoving him back, I raised my blades in front of my face, feeling blood ooze through the bandages.

Aunt Caz swiped at his exposed ribs, but instead of tucking in his arms to protect his sides, the chief jerked his elbow back into Aunt Caz's nose. She slipped on the wet boards, a dazed look on her face before he turned on her. The sword angled up, aimed at her stomach. A warning snagged in my throat as Aunt Caz twisted sideways. The blade skimmed along her ribs, slicing through the fabric of her tight-fitting tunic, but when she looked down, there was no blood on her exposed skin. She jabbed quickly with her daggers, in and out of the chief's shoulder with rapid thrusts.

Blood coated their sharp edges. The rain washed it away almost immediately, but there was no denying the two punctures on his shoulder. They didn't heal over as we watched. They pulsed with blood, running in streams down his chest, but he only bared his teeth at me.

He could bleed. He could *die*.

Aunt Caz lunged at him again, so he swung to deflect her, and Eiramis's whip cracked through the storm. The end wrapped around his wrist, pulling him aside as Aunt Caz slipped a blade under his other arm. Inhaling sharply, the chief smashed his fist into the side of Aunt Caz's head, and she crumpled to the deck. He yanked on the whip, tearing it out of Eiramis's grip, and tugged the knife from where Aunt Caz had lodged it beneath his arm. Blood spilled from his side as he raised his arm and the dagger, poised above Aunt Caz's prone body.

A figure slid across the deck, emerging from the fog like a wraith with dark hair and darker eyes. He collided with Aunt Caz, a sword that was much too heavy for him in his cuffed hands tilted upwards. The dagger sparked along the edge of the blade and skittered to the ground. Looking supremely satisfied with himself, *Alekey* lurched to his feet, fumbling to kick the dagger aside while keeping his sword pointed at the chief.

"Hey, Ev," he said cheerfully, and my stomach flopped. Or was it my heart? I wasn't sure anymore. Either way, it was a relief to see Alekey alive, though not unharmed.

Dark bruises mottled his face, standing out starkly against his pale cheeks and sunken eyes. His lip was swollen when he smiled crookedly at me, and I wanted nothing more than to wrap my arms around his neck and never let go.

Except the chief was already moving again, his sword cutting through the rain to slam into Alekey's.

My brother gave up a step, eyes widening as the chief swung again with vicious, precise slices from left and right.

Akev darted forward to protect Alekey's left side, both of them parrying even as the chief forced them backwards.

"Eiramis!" I called, lifting one of my blades in the air to get his attention. The chief's back was exposed, and if I could get my blade to Eiramis, the helmsman could land the final blow. I knew if I tried to skirt around the trio, the chief would just turn his attention on me, and do whatever it took to cut me down.

As it was, he kept forcing Alekey and Akev to retreat, and they were backing up into me, trapping me in a corner against the railing and quarterdeck.

Eiramis nodded, understanding what I intended. It was a difficult angle to throw something as large as one of Icana's twin blades, but I cleared my head, focusing on her lessons. Where to place my fingers. How to flick my wrist. Except it was raining, and the blade was heavy, and my throwing arm was injured.

I drew back to release when a figure loomed in my periphery.

He caught my wrist before I could throw, and pinched the fragile bones. The blade smacked against the deck with a dull thud. He immediately kicked it away.

We both watched it skitter to a halt against the staircase. I whipped my head around to glare at him and his exceptionally bright green eyes that looked like broken emeralds.

With a warning grumble deep in my throat, I swung at his midsection with my other blade, ignoring the pain that rippled down to my fingertips.

He jumped back, releasing my arm, and gave me an appraising look as I slashed at him again.

"Nice to meet you, Princess," he quipped, clearly amused by the scowl that twisted my features. "Apologies for that. I am sworn to protect my captain."

"It's *Your Majesty*," I corrected with a hiss, thrusting my remaining blade towards his chest.

He caught the flat edge of my blade against a metal guard on his arm. When he twisted his wrist, the hilt sprang out of my grasp, and tumbled directly into his open palm. Aimed at my ribs. I froze, my back hitting the railing. The ocean frothed below.

"Well, this is an odd turn of events," he said with a grin, revealing two missing teeth in the back of his mouth. "You're without a blade, and I've gained a blade. What next?"

"You fall on it," I suggested dryly.

He tossed his head back and laughed. Rain ran down his cheeks like tears of mirth. "You have the same sharp tongue as your brother," he said, eyes sparkling. They looked like mosaics on the sea floor, gems in wavering hues. "When he finds the courage."

A flutter of fear beat in my chest. He knew my brother? Did that mean he knew Kalei as well?

Alekey grunted a few paces away from me, bumping into the wall of the quarterdeck.

Akev crashed beside him, slipping as the chief's sword came down hard against his leg. Blood splattered hot across the deck as the chief yanked his blade free of my advisor's flesh. Akev cried out, hand pressed against his leg, and Alekey shifted in front of him with the sword raised between them.

My heart thundered, a frantic beat in my ears that drowned out the sound of the storm.

We were trapped. We were going to die.

A calmness washed over me as the wind whispered against my ears. This had always been my fate, in one way or another. Perishing at sea. Dying on an adventure. Wrapped in the spray of the ocean. If I couldn't claim my crown with blood, then at least I could inherit the salt of the sea instead.

Blood and water. Iron and salt. That was what we had gone through to get here. And maybe a crown wasn't my future. Maybe the loss of Vodaeard and the loss of myself didn't have to be etched into the gold rods Haret had stolen from me. They could melt it and mould it into something else. Something less painful. Something that wasn't stained with the blood in our veins and the salt of our tears.

The Endless Seas were rising to meet me.

If I had closed my eyes to accept my fate, I wouldn't have noticed Aunt Caz rising to her feet behind the chief. I wouldn't have witnessed the shock on his face as she thrust one of her many blades through his back. I wouldn't have seen the tip protrude from the centre of his chest, dripping with blood.

I was glad I hadn't fully accepted my fate in that moment, because it was extremely satisfying to watch his mouth flap open and shut and fill with blood. Alekey and I both slipped away from the wall, but instead of falling to his knees as I expected, the chief grumbled something garbled and turned to face Aunt Caz.

"I told you," he said around the blood dribbling out the side of his mouth, "you can't kill me."

The blade sticking out of his heart seemed to be proof enough.

"Fuck," Aunt Caz said, disgust pinching her face.

Chief Mikala sliced his blade upwards, apparently unhindered by the other one stuck in his chest. Aunt Caz leaned back, not quite fast enough, and I heard her sharp gasp.

Before I could see how the chief had injured her, Alekey closed the distance between them, and shoved his sword into the man's chest. The tip exploded out of his back with a spray of blood, and the force of it was enough to drive him to his knees.

Still, he chuckled, blood speckling his lips.

I scrambled across the deck and retrieved one of my fallen blades. The man with the jewel-toned eyes still had my other one, but he merely stood to the side, watching. He didn't move to stop me as I laid the sharp edge against the chief's throat.

The man still tried to raise his sword. I kicked it out of his grip.

"Fire," Aunt Caz choked behind me. "Just to be sure."

"Wait," I gasped, the adrenaline leeching out of my body all at once. We had done it. The immortal tyrant was on his knees, condemned, and my brother was alive next to me to witness this retribution. But there was the matter of my heart.

What remained of it, at least.

I leaned towards the chief. "Where is she? Where is Kalei?"

Thirty-Six

My body sagged against the chains. Frigid water sloshed around my knees, pulling me down and stealing my strength. I couldn't see it in the darkness, but felt it seeping into my clothes and bones, turning my skin to ice. It was rising too fast, and I was trapped.

Smoke wove through the air from cracks in the floorboards above. It scratched my throat, but every cough jostled my frozen bones until I ached from the effort of holding on and staying alive. I wanted to believe they hadn't forgotten about me, but I was so cold and so tired.

Silence wrapped around me. It wasn't like the silence of the crypts or Death's dark shores. This was a heavy silence. A quiet so deep it pressed on my ears, filled me with lung-choking anxiety, blood pumping in my veins. Sluggish. Subdued. The quiet of loneliness. Of believing I was the only person left in the world.

The silence stretched. So long that it started to bother me. I raised my head, peering through the dark, straining to hear past the rush of waves filling the room. There were no more cannons filling the air with booms. The wails of the dying had faded.

Was it over?

"Help." My voice was barely a whisper, cracked and choked. The water rose a little higher. *"Please."* Another cough wracked my body. The force of it jarred my shoulders, and one bone popped right out of its socket. All the weight of the water pulled me down on the chains, and I screamed. Pain glittered behind my eyes. The ship rocked, wood groaning and splintering, and water rushed into the room.

Heat coursed through my veins, the pain sharp and bright in my shoulder. It was enough for me to raise my head and scream.

When my screams were spent and my energy flagged, I collapsed against the chains and let the darkness wash over me. I had finally defeated Death, pushed him back into his realm, but he was going to claim me all the same.

Only this time, it wasn't a monster at my heels—just the cold oblivion of a watery grave.

Something fell against the door. When it happened again, followed by a sound like scrabbling fingernails, I lifted my head. The room spun around me, darkness swirling in my vision, water gleaming like oil around my body. Jagged pain ran up and down my spine like knives.

Another thump. Deliberate. Determined. A spark of something warm and alive kindled in my chest, then a fresh wave of darkness crashed over me and my fractured vision went black.

Hands on my face pulled me out of the darkness. When I opened my eyes, blazing red hair haloed by lantern light filled my vision. Eyebrows drawn tight over golden irises. Concern etched into every line, and a mouth I've wanted to kiss since it first tormented me.

"Kal," that mouth was saying, urgently. It pulled me out of the watery depths of despair, and reality came crashing over me all at once, fear causing my heart to race. I struggled again, a scream building in my throat.

A familiar figure surged around Evhen's frame, mosaic eyes glittering. Seaglass winked at me and wrapped his arms around me to support my weight as Evhen reached up to unhook the chain from the beam.

I cried out as my arms dropped from over my head, but then Evhen was there again, her warm body holding me up on one side while Seaglass lifted me on the other.

Crowns of Blood and Salt

The ship was rapidly taking on water. Icy waves frothed against the walls as the ship heaved under the pressure.

I tried to focus on anything other than the pain in my shoulder as they carried me through the belly of my father's sinking ship, but as feeling slowly returned to my limbs, the pain intensified. Tears streamed down my cheeks. I wanted to scream and curse my way through it, the way Evhen would, but all I could do was cry. When we reached the deck, the tears froze on my cheeks and eyelashes.

"Kal, don't look," Evhen whispered in my ear as we crossed the deck, but the smoke and fog parted on an icy breeze like the breath of a great beast, and I saw anyway.

My father, looking like a piece of artwork tied to the mainmast with two broadswords bursting out of his chest at different angles. His head hung forward against his chest, sweat and blood plastering his hair to his face. He still drew breath, ragged and broken.

He had been a monster haunting my dreams every night since he stole my life, and now he truly looked the part. An image flashed in my mind, a poison-soaked memory from a night filled with dancing and screaming. The image had been an illusion, a waking nightmare—my father, clutching his wounds, pleading with me, *How could you let them kill me?*

My body went limp, and neither Evhen nor Seaglass could hold me up as I slumped to the wet deck boards. My knees scraped the wood, but I didn't feel the splinters. I didn't feel anything anymore. Not hold nor cold. Not power nor weakness. Not horror nor relief. Not even the pain in my shoulder.

My father lifted his head to gaze at me through the haze of smoke. *Minnow*. His mouth formed the word, but I couldn't hear him. Blood spilled down his chin, staining his shirt. Once—so long ago it felt like a lifetime—he had come home from a voyage across the sea, wounded and bleeding. The figurehead was still scarred from the damage Evhen had done to his ship that day.

I had healed him then.

I couldn't heal him now, even if I wanted to. He didn't deserve it. He didn't deserve the eternal life that ran through his veins.

He should have died that day. And I didn't have the energy to care that he was going to die today.

Evhen was saying something, trying to pull me to my feet. I ignored her, her words like rushing water in my ears, and pushed myself up. I hobbled to the mainmast, to my father, who looked so much like a stranger. He tipped his head back.

"You wanted to be immortal. You wanted a legacy. Instead, your bloodline ends here," I said, my voice distant and detached. The words came without me thinking about them. There was no more energy to be spent on him, on final thoughts. Only the spark of anger and grim satisfaction that it was ending here and now. "I renounce the name Maristela. I renounce Marama. I renounce *you*."

Rage flared in his dark eyes, and then I walked away from him.

Forever.

THIRTY-SEVEN

Seaglass helped Kalei cross the planks between her father's sinking ship and the *Midnight Saint*. He had surrendered too quickly for my liking, but he was also the only one who knew where Kalei was being kept. So I had told him I wouldn't run him through if he helped me find her.

When Kalei was safely across, I turned to find Aunt Caz, who concealed half her face while she spoke in whispers to the captain of the Wystanian army.

The commander looked up as I approached. "We've secured the ship," he said. "Anyone alive is now a prisoner aboard the *Wylliott*."

I nodded, though I barely heard him. Pain drilled into my temples, radiating from my core. "That one, too," I said, pointing at Seaglass.

The other man stood in the middle of the *Midnight Saint*, gazing up at the fluttering flag on the mainmast. The mountain and the ocean. I wondered what he saw when he looked at it.

A second chance, or another prison.

"There's something I have to do first," I added, gaze sliding across the deck like a torrent.

Aunt Caz followed my gaze and nodded. She gestured for the commander to follow her to the other ship, and I turned to face the mainmast and the man pinned there like a butterfly on display.

The agony this man had wreaked on my life in the past four months finally came crashing down like a tidal wave, sweeping me out to the dark depths of the ocean.

A kind of tidal wave I knew I couldn't survive on my own. But I wasn't on my own anymore.

Halting in front of the chief, I steadied my breathing. He had been a monster haunting my dreams every night since he killed my parents. He was still that same monster. Only bloodier.

Rage flared through my veins, hot and quick like a spark. I didn't have the energy for final words, only enough strength to lift my blade and place it against the hollow of his throat.

Dark eyes locked with mine as I leaned forward, slowly pushing the tip through his neck, until it dug into the wood of the mast behind him. Panic flashed in those depths, and then I walked away..

The walk back across the plank between our ships was easier this time, and I felt a tether snap in my chest, releasing me from the vengeance I had spent months chasing.

Aunt Caz had lowered her hand by the time I returned. A jagged line split her face from the bottom of her right cheek to the edge of her left temple, directly through her eye. The socket itself was already empty, a hollow black hole in her face, muscles pinched as she fought to control the bleeding with multiple cloths.

"Fuck," I muttered at the sight.

"Yeah," she said, and wrapped an arm around my shoulder. I leaned into her strength, her warmth.

Alekey snuggled against her other side, and I laced my fingers through his.

A splash caught my attention, and I glanced up. Eirmais and Akev finally crossed over, the plank lost to the roiling ocean below. The anchor clanked out of the crashing waves.

I found a spot against the railing as the fire they'd set caught against the mast. I wouldn't believe the man was dead until the fire consumed him. Aunt Caz let a medic lead her below deck, but Alekey joined us, leaning his head on my shoulder. I ruffled a curl, throat seizing with that dreadful emotion—hope.

It was over.

CROWNS OF BLOOD AND SALT

Heat fanned my face as the chief's ship crackled. Flames licked up the mast, setting the night on fire through the fog and mist. For a while, it was quiet except for the pop of burning wood across from us.

Then came the screams.

The muscles in my stomach clenched as the sound rent the night. Everyone still on the deck paused to listen, until soon enough, only the crack of wooden beams reached our ears. Flames danced into the sky, smoke billowing higher as more pieces collapsed. The waves frothed with a red glow. Ash fell like snow over the wintery seas.

The ten-day journey back home was busy. I didn't have time to be left alone with my thoughts, between funerals for the two sailors who died under my command, and the dozens of others who died under Haret's. We sent them all out to sea, as was the custom for anyone who died on the water or far from home.

All except Icana. I couldn't bring myself to set her adrift yet, so her body remained below deck, shrouded and covered with her twin blades. They had served me well, but I didn't need them anymore.

The rest of my time was given to making preparations and writing letters—we had a proper coronation to plan upon our arrival back in Vodaeard, and I needed to send invitations to neighbouring dignitaries, kings, queens, and leaders who could ally with Vodaeard and strengthen us.

So much had been broken during the chief's war that I was afraid we'd lost all ties with other kingdoms on the continent. As queen, I needed to make reparations. I needed to reassure the world that Vodaeard was strong again, and would not seek out war with anyone under my rule.

The commander of the Wystanian ship, Captain Beynet, invited me onboard the *Wylliott* on the seventh day of sailing. I'd spent enough time in stuffy quarters with Akev and Breva discussing my duties as queen that the change in scenery was welcome, though the topic of conversation weighed like a rock in my stomach.

Alekey accompanied me. The colour was slowly returning to his cheeks, and he didn't look so gaunt anymore, but there were hollows under his eyes. A distracted look in his gaze. He wasn't entirely here, his mind trapped elsewhere. Tortured aboard a sunken ship.

I grabbed his hand and squeezed. He met my gaze, offered a tired smile, and squeezed back as we crossed the deck of the *Wylliott*.

I'd learned that every ship in the Wystanian armada started with *Wy*. It was a funny little thing to me. In Vodaeard, we gave our ships creative names. *Grey Bard* had been mine, a name I had stressed over for months after my parents had gifted me the small vessel for a birthday a few years ago. It seemed appropriate. Vodaeard was grey, and the ocean always seemed to sing to me, to beckon me onto its waves with a melody that begged me to sail forever. Like a bard in a tavern singing of great exploits. That's what I wanted to have on that ship, and I had let it sink.

The reminder made me falter. I'd had so many failures in the past few months, but now was the time for success. Now, I could grow.

The *Wylliott* was a gorgeous, three-masted vessel, with cream colour sails that snapped in the strong wind. The Wystanian arrow cut through the air from each mast. It was the kind of ship I had once been envious of, envisioning myself on its deck, at its helm, sailing into the horizon.

The deck glimmered under our feet as we followed the escort to the captain's quarters. The boards had been wiped clean of battle. The crew's uniforms gleamed, freshly laundered, gold buttons catching the morning sun's rays. I felt almost dirty next to them, in my plain outfit of grey and black, but I held my head high. There was a reason their army held renown throughout the continent. I wouldn't let the matter of fresh uniforms make me feel little now.

Now I had my sights set on Vodaeard. On home. On my crown.

A stained glass window set into the captain's cabin door cast a rainbow on the floor as we entered. It fractured over our feet, and then I was looking across a vast room at Captain Beynet and Aunt Caz.

He sat behind an ornate desk inlaid with pearl and opal, orderly papers gathered across its surface. An inkpot waited next to his elbow. A lantern swayed above the desk, casting a warm glow into the sunlit room.

Next to him, Aunt Caz stood at attention, bent ever so slightly as the older man continued their conversation in quiet murmurs. A black patch covered her injured eye. The other, an amber colour like Alekey's, flicked up to me.

Thank you for coming, Queen Evhen," Captain Beynet said, nodding at our escort.

The man in uniform left with a short bow, and the captain gestured to the seats in front of his desk. Tall, plushly cushioned chairs that looked more like thrones than visitor seats. "Please sit

"I don't know if I can be considered queen anymore," I told him as I sat on the edge of my chair. Alekey sank back into his seat next to me, looking casual, while anxiety wound through my body like coils of lightning. "I don't know if my coronation on the sea was exactly…legitimate."

It felt silly to say out loud. I'd said the words. I'd done the rites. I'd worn the crown. The ship might have recognized me as their queen, but would other nations? That's why I needed to invite them to a proper coronation on Vodaeard soil—to secure my rule.

Captain Beynet waved a dismissive hand. "Legitimate or not, you are going to be queen, are you not?" He glanced between me and Alekey, as if searching for a different answer. Everyone knew I had been planning on abdicating, since I was too scared to take on the responsibility of a kingdom.

Alekey was the popular choice to take over after our parents. He would give the kingdom the heirs it needed.

My brother looked at me now, a question written in the crease of his forehead as his eyebrows drew together. Even he knew I didn't want the crown. Or at least, he knew I hadn't wanted it. Now, he seemed to see the change in my face as I angled towards him.

"Alekey," I said, fighting the sudden urge to cry. I hadn't expected this decision to bring me so many conflicting emotions, but now I had to lay them bare. I took a deep breath. "I've decided to keep it. Father's crown. I want to be the queen of Vodaeard."

His smile was so sudden and cheerful, it filled the whole room with light brighter than the sun's glow through the bay of windows behind Beynet. My heart lurched at the sight. When had he last smiled like that? It seemed so long ago, I couldn't picture it.

"Yes!" he exclaimed, jumping to his feet to embrace me. He smelled warm, like morning sun on the beach.

I laughed into his shoulder. "You're not upset?"

He rolled his eyes. "Evhen, I never wanted you to give up the crown for me."

My mouth fell into a frown, and I gently pushed him back. "But the people wanted you. I thought you'd like the attention."

"Oh, I would have loved it," he preened. "I'm adorable. But I never expected it. I wouldn't have chased you down if I wasn't named king on my eighteenth birthday. If you handed it to me, then, sure, I would have accepted it. But it's your call, Ev. I was always rooting for you."

Tears pricked my eyes. I swiped the back of my sleeve roughly across my face and turned back to Captain Beynet.

"Well, that's settled," I said, surprised by the confidence in my voice. For so long, the voices of others doubting me had been louder than my own wants. Now, those voices faded to nagging whispers. I would always worry that I wasn't good enough, worthy enough, but I had the right people helping me. I didn't have to worry about traitors and snakes anymore.

"Good," the captain said, pushing a heavy stack of parchment towards me. Treaty of Borders ran across the top of the first page, and my stomach clenched.

""Your aunt has made quite the case for you," the captain continued, and I glanced up at Aunt Caz in confusion. "When we land in Vodaeard, I'm going to request an audience for you with our queen."

"Why?" I asked, brows furrowing. I didn't have anything to say to the queen of Wystan.

"The *Treaty of Borders* is a centuries-old document," Captain Beynet said. "I think it's time for a rewrite."

Aunt Caz met my gaze again. With the eye patch, she looked more fearsome than ever. "We'll help you go through it, make changes, write new sections. It'll give Vodaeard more freedom. It'll give you more power."

My mouth was dry. No one had touched this document in hundreds of years. No one had the courage to challenge it.

Maybe no one in my family line had been as stubborn as me.

I finally swallowed, and nodded. "All right." Fire grew in my chest, warm and bright and hopeful. "Let's change the world."

THIRTY-EIGHT

Ten Weeks Later

Evhen turned eighteen today.

The kingdom had spent weeks preparing. Flowers were brought in from the north—nothing bright grew here—and the air in the castle was perfumed with the variety of multicoloured blossoms draped along every banister. Summer air breezed through the open windows in my bedchamber, thin curtains fluttering. Early yellow sunlight streamed across the floor.

It was the first clear day of the season. It was coronation day.

I rolled over in bed, stretched, and enjoyed the sunlight landing on my face. These quiet moments were my favourite, when the world was caught between sleeping and waking, when I could savour the fact that I had survived another night.

The days were getting easier. I was getting stronger. My nights were no longer plagued with nightmares of death and decay, rot and ruin. I had survived, and I was starting to heal from it

So, I spent my mornings being grateful. Comforted by the knowledge that I was where I belonged with the person I loved most. She slept next to me, guard down, red hair splayed across the pillow like the sun's rays. The morning light turned her skin gold.

Her eyelids fluttered open. Dark lashes dusted her cheekbones, and eyes like sun-kissed waves met mine. For the first time in months, the tension and worry did not immediately return to her body upon waking. A soft smile touched her lips.

"Morning," she said sleepily. She dragged an arm across her eyes.

The sleeve of her cream-coloured nightgown slipped off her shoulder, revealing the flower-shaped scar I had given her months ago—I had sent a crossbow bolt through her shoulder into the undead man behind her. I had never hurt someone like that before. My powers had only been used for healing, for bringing the dead back to life, but she hadn't hated me for the action. It had saved her life.

And she had saved mine in more ways than I could count.

"Morning," I whispered, running a finger over the scar. Evhen shivered, gooseflesh erupting across her skin. I grinned at the little bumps, chasing them with my finger along her arm.

"I love these," I told her, easing some more to the surface along her collarbone.

She grabbed my hand, pressing a kiss to my knuckles. "And I love these," she said, pecking each scar.

There were so many along my fingers and the backs of my hands. Each time I had used my new power, the bones had left new wounds, new scars. I didn't want to count them. Tried not to look at them. Each one was a painful reminder.

Evhen had once told me she needed the reminders, but I could have done without them dotting my skin like new constellations.

Instead of telling her that, again, I smiled at her. She shifted onto her side so we were facing each other, nothing but pillows and promises between us. I traced her lips with my eyes.

"Happy birthday," I whispered.

Flowers spilled out of the throne room to line a path through the castle, from the residence wing all the way down the grand staircase, towards the doors flung open wide for the ceremony. A red carpet rolled down the aisle, lined on both sides with hundreds of chairs, all draped with cream and crimson blossoms. Banners bearing the

Vodaeardean mountain hung from the vaulted ceiling. The gold chandelier had recently been polished. It gleamed with the brightness of a dozen suns.

Two thrones sat atop the dais. They were the same height, gilded in gold along the armrests, thick cushions lining the seats. The symbol of Vodaeard—the mountain surging out of the ocean—was engraved into the backs, surrounded by a circle of dark metal mimicking the sun's rays.

A single crown rested on the chair to the left. It was the same one Evhen had worn, however briefly, on the journey to Geirvar.

Now, her birthright waited for her again.

I stood at the front, Alekey beside me, and Talen beside him. Evhen's first mate hadn't been happy to see me upon our return to Vodaeard, but his hardened shell was cracking. Slowly. It might take years for him to forgive me, to stop blaming me for what happened, but I wasn't going to rush him. I still held some anger for the prince next to me, and it would take some time to completely forgive him. But we were healing.

Vodaeard was healing.

Behind us sat four chairs. Akev and Eirmais occupied the first two. The councillor and helmsman were both resplendent in gold and red outfits. Beside Eirmais was an empty chair, and my heart twanged at the sight. A sign over the front read, *Reserved in memory of Icana Vipden*. She was buried in the castle's crypt next to Evhen's parents. I hadn't found the courage to go visit their graves yet..

Next to the empty chair was Seaglass. Evhen had pardoned him after a few weeks, and I was glad he had chosen to stay. I liked him. When he caught me looking, he winked, eyes shining like gems beneath the sea. The cheer never left his face.

The rest of the room was filled with people. Many of them were from other nations, kings and queens and dignitaries who had come to show their support of Vodaeard's new monarch. They wore their own colours, a rainbow of fabrics filling the grey seaside kingdom with brightness. Several of them looked at me with suspicion or curiosity, but I kept my eyes on the doors at the end of the hall.

They could whisper all they wanted. I had survived, and I wasn't going anywhere.

Evhen appeared in the doorway to a heralding of trumpets. At sea, she had worn red, flames curling around the hem like she was the sun itself. Now, a gold dress cascaded from her frame, catching the light and casting it around the room like she was covered in a thousand tiny gems.

My breath hitched, the same way it had that night in the ballroom in Xesta. When I had seen her in gold across the room, like a beacon in the dark guiding me towards her light, and I had finally understood what it meant to love someone.

Her red curls had been tamed into an elegant braid, showing off her proud jaw and prouder eyes. Those eyes landed on me like beams of sunlight over the heads of hundreds, and she smiled. She kept her gaze on me as she made her way to the dais. The tail of her gown left sparkles on the carpet in her wake.

When she reached the front, she turned to me. Warm hands clasped mine. Her father's signet ring bumped against my knuckle.

"I love you, Kalei," she said in front of the entire kingdom and its allies. "All of you."

"All of you," I echoed.

This time, there was no hesitation.

I grabbed her face, pulled her close, and kissed her for the first time. The salt of the sea burst across my tongue, and I knew in my bones that I was home.

ICANA

Exclusive Hardcover Chapter

I stared at the lifeless body of my father.

Part of me wanted to kick him, to disrespect him as he disrespected me in life. Part of me wanted to vomit, thrown suddenly back to that night over six years ago when he slaughtered my grandfather and ascended the throne and looked at me with the expectation that I would do the same to him, eventually. And another, smaller part of me, a part I had locked away long before that red day in this very throne room, wanted to cry.

Instead, I lurched up from the throne as soon as the room cleared and lifted my chin in spite of the scrutinizing glares from the elite guard around me. They were suspicious of my sudden return, as though six years on the other side of the world had somehow changed my mind.

As though I wanted to be here, surrounded by snakes and swords.

I had left for a reason. Tradition and time couldn't change the fact that I never wanted to be in this position. My life in Vodaeard had been good. Safe. I didn't have to worry about being assassinated or attacked simply because I had been born in the land of monsters. Children who killed their parents to keep the throne within the family. It had belonged to us for three hundred years, and I had been the first Vipden to break that tradition by leaving

The ugly thing behind me had still pulled me back like a tether that couldn't be cut, no matter the length of distance or length of time that had separated me from it.

The guards watched me warily. Beneath their gleaming helmets, blue and green eyes bored into me like the baleful gazes of the gods.

The gods had never looked kindly down on me, and now the guards did the same. News would spread. The heir to House Snake had returned, and she was not welcome. The other Houses would send their best assassins, and I needed the guards in this room to honour their pledges to House Snake. To me.

I did not want to die in the land of my fathers.

"Well?" I snapped at them, growing more annoyed under their silent stares. It took a lot more to make me uncomfortable, and a lot less to make me angry, and everyone in this room knew my true nature. They knew their silence would only piss me off.

"We have already pledged ourselves to House Snake," one of them answered. They sounded almost annoyed by my attitude, as though it was disrespectful to question their loyalty now.

I scoffed and stepped over the body of my father to descend the dais stairs. The room was starting to smell like piss and shit and blood.

"You pledged yourselves to a dead man," I said, pointing at the corpse beside the throne. "You have a living queen now. How many of you can say you are loyal to her?"

"Can she say she's loyal to her country?" someone asked near the far end of the room. The voice was familiar, nagging at the back of my mind, loosening a memory stained in blood.

I frowned down at the line of guards. "Take off your helmets," I ordered. "Let me see your faces."

The elite guard moved in perfect unison. They were trained to work as a nebulous unit, and their movements were fluid as they removed their helmets. My gaze roved over them, recognizing a few. I had trained with them when I was younger. Three of them I had chosen to be my own elite guard, before I ran away. I met their stares now, hoping to see the familiar spark of loyalty they had once offered me.

In those three only, it was faint, hidden behind a glimmer of uncertainty like dark storm clouds. The political climate in Geirvar had been fragile when I left, and now I had all but thrown the country into civil war.

Loyalties could turn as quickly as dawn broke over the land.

"She is loyal to herself," I said, scanning the room for their reactions. As expected, many of them were displeased with such a response. "And she doesn't need weak-minded children in her elite guard. If you can't accept me as your queen, then take your loyalty elsewhere, or die next to the man you pledged your lives to."

The elite guards were chosen specifically by each monarch, and changed just as often as the monarchs did. I didn't trust anyone my father had picked to be my guard, especially not now. Most of the country saw me as a coward for leaving. If my guards didn't like the fact I had returned, they wouldn't try to stop anyone from taking my life. And there were only three people in this room I trusted.

I stared at them, long and hard, daring them to move. If they didn't leave of their own volition, I'd cut them down and turn the throne room into a red lake.

Someone finally moved, setting their helmet down on the ground. They left without a backwards glance. Five more followed in kind, helmets on the ground and eyes on the door.

My heart hammered against my ribs, anger flashing through my veins like liquid fire. There were no traitors in Geirvar, only cowards, but this felt very much like a betrayal. Their old monarch was dead, and they still maintained their loyalty to him. To a corpse. As if he deserved it more than I did—a living, breathing, angry monarch.

Only four out of ten elites remained. Three of them I recognized, chosen to help me destroy their families before I left six years ago. One of them was new, not someone I had trained with, or someone I had seen before I left. Too young to have been completely swayed by my father.

They looked at me expectantly. Like I had some great declaration to share with the country, with the world. *There is a new monarch in the land of assassins, and the world will bow to her.*

Instead, I jutted my chin towards the open doors of the throne room. "Kill them all."

The guards came back less than five minutes later. Blood dripped from their weapons like ruby gems. I didn't need to ask to know the six others were dead, probably felled between here and the palace doors.

I did, however, get more information than I expected when they returned. Jini, a girl originally from House Whip, wiped a red smear from her face as she approached me where I stood at the foot of the dais, staring numbly at the throne with its blood-tipped spears sticking out the back.

"Those foreigners spilled blood inside the city perimeter," she told me. Her green eyes were dark, shaded like a forest floor.

I rolled my eyes towards the domed ceiling. The light coming through the thin windows was already starting to turn orange with dusk. A storm was approaching.

"How many dead?" I asked, chest tightening. Who had attacked whom? I shouldn't have been surprised that neither Haret nor Chief Mikala would leave without shedding more blood, but they were playing with fire where I was concerned. It would only spread, and even though I knew my hold on the throne was tenuous at best, the Houses of Geirvar wouldn't allow foreigner blood to be spilled without profiting from it. I had to do something about it.

Jini shrugged. "It's hard to tell who fights for whom. They all look the same to me."

I bit my lip. "I'll ride out," I said finally. "Send the redbirds." A call from the crown—any assassins loyal to me would be asked to join the fight. I hoped it would be enough.

Jini disappeared with a nod, and I forced myself to look at my father one last time before I left the throne room.

It was well past nightfall when we finally returned to the palace, battered and bruised after a hard ride into the barren fields north of the city.

I hadn't intended to go after Haret and Cazendra—I still didn't trust the woman—but the timing was perfect.

Most of them had fallen to our arrows, and it had been easy enough to snatch Evhen from the fray amid the chaos. A good number of assassins had answered the redbirds, but that didn't lessen the panic crawling up my throat at every turn. It was only a matter of time before it all came crashing down.

Civil war in Geirvar was inevitable. I couldn't stop it if I wanted to. But for now, I let Evhen get some much-needed sleep, and I went somewhere I hadn't been in over six years.

The training yards and barracks stretched around the palace in a half-circle, bumping up against the perimeter walls and guard towers. Night blanketed the stone courtyard in swaths of navy and pitch. A few braziers burned in intervals along the surrounding wall. I couldn't see them, but I knew archers waited in the pools of darkness between the circles of light, eyes trained on the city beyond the bridge.

This had been my life for sixteen years. Knowing where the attacks would come from, and being prepared for them. Honing my skills with the blade and whip, poison and fire, fist and spear. I hadn't just been training to kill my father one day—I was going to be the best assassin Geirvar had to offer. Fearsome and fearless. A wraith. A shadow. A *snake*.

If I had stayed, I would have been terrifying. So I left and burned Geirvar like a bridge behind me. I could almost hear the fire crackling and the screams that followed me to the docks that day. The night of my sixteenth birthday had been ablaze with a country in flames and a legacy turning to ash behind me.

Now, familiar stars speckled the sky like the eyes of the gods. They had never looked kindly on me, and I didn't expect them to start now. A sudden blast of cold wind whipped through the courtyard, as if in response to my private thoughts, and I huddled deeper into my fur cloak, scowling. This land was harsh, but I was harsher, and I would not let it destroy me.

I slipped across the bridge, blending into the night, and cut left along the edge of the river. Ice crusted the surface, pale in the dappled starlight. Tension hung in the air above the city like a bated breath, waiting for something. I just wasn't sure if it was waiting for me to fall down or rise up.

The city was quiet. The country was divided. There was blood in the streets. I had responded when it was first spilled, but that wasn't enough. There was more to do, and precious little time to do it.

The graveyard came into sight around the next bend in the river, and I heard my breath catch. Massive gates barred the entrance, iron wrought in a scrolling design that belonged to none of the Houses and all of them at the same time. It was the only thing that united all the Houses together, a place where the dead were all the same. Noble family or lesser family or anywhere in between—they were all the same in death. Whether a corpse had been buried or burned, the remains were interred here.

If it were up to me—and I supposed it was now—I'd burn my father's body and scatter the ashes in the Eyrland Sea. There was no reason to hold a funeral for him here. Those loyal to him might try to stop me, but hopefully I'd be long gone by the time they realized his ashes were gone as well.

Pushing thoughts of my father out of mind, I gritted my teeth and scaled the slippery gates. Cold iron seeped through my leather gloves. I fell onto the other side with a suppressed groan, biting my lip as the pain made my eyes water. I hadn't brought my cane with me, opting for stealth over comfort, and I briefly regretted the choice. As much as I hated the thing, it definitely helped ease the pain in my side. Now that agony flared up again, sharply screeching along my ribs. Hissing, I pressed a hand to the injury, hobbling away from the gates.

The path wound in a spiral towards the centre of the cemetery, stone markers growing older and older the closer they were placed towards the middle. There, they sat in crumbling piles atop ancient graves, their epitaphs barely legible. There were centuries of Vipdens buried here, including my grandfather, but I barely made it past the gates before I found the graves I was looking for.

Two plots, two markers, two droplets of water slipping out of the corners of my eyes. They were only a few years old—the grass grew in coarse clumps over the outlines of shallow graves.

Atlys Lancy (born Fira) of House Spear, aged eighteen.

Artemys Lancy of House Spear, aged sixteen.

As far as anyone knew, the siblings weren't related by blood. They had both been adopted by House Spear when they were younger, and they had both shared my bed several times in the week leading up to their deaths.

An emotion I didn't recognize crashed over me like a wave of frigid water, and I sank to my knees in the spongy grass at the edge of their graves. Apologies blubbered up inside of me, but I swallowed them down. *I'm sorry* wouldn't placate the dead.

I was there when they had both died, when my father had them murdered, and I'd seen the light go from their eyes. I hadn't cried then. Crying was a weakness that had long been driven out of me by chains or whips or flames.

I let myself cry now.

PLAYLIST

Villains Aren't Born (They're Made) - PEGGY
Everybody Wants to Rule The World - Lorde
LET THE WORLD BURN - Chris Grey
Castle - Halsey
Castles Crumbling (feat. Hayley Williams) (Taylor's Version) - Taylor Swift
Afterlife - Hailee Steinfeld
ivy - Taylor Swift
I am not a woman, I'm a god - Halsey
Lover. Fighter - SVRCINA
The Other Side - Ruelle
you should see me in a crown - Billie Eilish
All the King's Horses - Karmina

Listen on Spotify:

ACKNOWLEDGEMENTS

It is a wild concept, coming to the end of a project and writing the acknowledgements. It requires thinking back, to those who helped me along the way, and I constantly struggle with reflection. I'm also worried I'll forget someone important, so this is a general thank you to everyone involved in making this series come to life. And specifically to:

Zara and Inimitable Books, who made all of this possible. Thank you for letting Kalei and Evhen exist outside of my head.

Jessi and Sam, my favourite writers, who have been there from the very beginning. I'm constantly inspired by you two, and I'm so grateful for all our retreats at the cottage.

Wyatt, my best friend, who gave me the idea of killing an immortal with fire. The image of the flaming ship and creaking wood and falling ash is all yours.

Brad, my new dream, who was there with me when the doubts became too loud. Who encouraged me and supported me and shared this story with his family.

My family, who are always asking me when I'm going to publish something. Someday.

Last time, I thanked V. E. Schwab, who doesn't know me.

This time, I want to thank another author who doesn't know me—Adrienne Young. Her work speaks to my soul. The *Midnight Saint* is for you.

Lastly, you, the reader. Who picked up the first book, and waited for the second. Who fell in love with my Rapunzel retelling, and stuck with me when it became so much more. Who will hopefully be there when the next retelling gets told.

ABOUT THE AUTHOR

Kay Adams is a fantasy author living in Toronto, Ontario surrounded by a massive TBR pile and an equally massive teapot collection. Her books feature fairytale retellings with dark plots, queer girls, star magic, and religious angst.

When she isn't writing or forgetting about the tea she made, Kay enjoys watching ghost videos, watching Jeopardy with her boyfriend, and watching her boyfriend play video games while she dreams up new worlds and new stories.

Follow Kay on Instagram & Threads @KayWritesYA.

LAFORI

COSTUN

AZRIA

OXIMEEN

SIREN  LAGOON

MARAMA